Praise for #1 *New York Times* bestselling author Robyn Carr

"This novel of sisters and secrets has a pleasant setting, a leisurely pace, and a sweet story line for Krista that will please fans of Carr's Virgin River series. Themes of responsibility, forgiveness, and the agony and ecstasy of female relatives will appeal to readers of Debbie Macomber and Susan Wiggs."

—*Booklist* on *The Summer That Made Us*

"The summer flies by as old wounds are healed, new alliances are formed, and lives are changed forever... With strong relationship dynamics, juicy secrets, and a heartwarming ending, it's a blissful beach read."

—*Kirkus Reviews* on *The Summer That Made Us*

"Carr addresses serious problems...realistically and sympathetically while seamlessly weaving them into the fabric of her engrossing story."

—*Booklist*, starred review, on *Any Day Now*

"A satisfying reinvention story that handles painful issues with a light and uplifting touch."

—*Kirkus Reviews* on *The Life She Wants*

"Insightfully realized central figures, a strong supporting cast, family issues, and uncommon emotional complexity make this uplifting story a heart-grabber that won't let readers go until the very end.... A rewarding (happy) story that will appeal across the board and might require a hanky or two."

—*Library Journal*, starred review, on *What We Find*

"Robyn Carr has done it again... *What We Find* is complex, inspirational, and well-written. A romance that truly inspires readers as life hits them the hardest."

—*San Francisco Review Journal* on *What We Find*

"Carr's new novel demonstrates that classic women's fiction, illuminating the power of women's friendships, is still alive and well."

—*Booklist* on *Four Friends*

ROBYN CARR

A Summer in Sonoma

mira

mira

Recycling programs
for this product may
not exist in your area.

ISBN-13: 978-0-7783-3126-1

A Summer in Sonoma

For questions and comments about the quality of this book, please contact us at
CustomerService@Harlequin.com.

BookClubbish.com

Printed in U.S.A.

A Summer in Sonoma

1

Cassie and Ken walked out of the bar together at seven-thirty. In the rapidly descending darkness of a perfect June night, he pulled her into his arms and covered her mouth in a powerful kiss. Wow, she thought. It was a good kiss—consuming and deep. His hands were running up and down her back. Then one slipped around her side, reaching for a breast, and she withdrew. She pushed him away, laughed nervously and said, "Hold on, pardner. Getting a little ahead of yourself, aren't you?"

"Sorry," he said. "I've been looking at you, wondering, you know..."

"Well, wonder no more, big fella—rest assured I am definitely a girl. Now, don't we have plans? Live music in the park?"

"That's right," he said, laughing. Then, again, "Sorry."

As he walked her to his car, she said, "Girls don't get mad at guys for having romantic ideas. But you do have brakes, I assume?"

"Absolutely, Cassie."

"Good. You were moving a little fast for me."

The car was parked at the far end of the lot and she thought, Ahh, he's car proud. He'd rather walk across the lot than risk a dent or scratch from neighboring cars. He opened the door to the passenger side and she slipped in. She immediately pulled on her seat belt while he got in the driver's side.

He started the car, but didn't put it in gear. Instead, he reached over to her side and began to gently caress her upper arm. He leaned toward her across the console, his eyelids becoming heavy, his mouth slightly open. It was like kiss-on-demand, but at least he was moving more slowly, giving her time, waiting for her to respond. She met his lips for a sweet, short kiss. He moved over her mouth with precision, but when she pulled away from his mouth, laughing nervously again, he grabbed her upper arms in his strong grip. "Cassie," he said in a breath. "What do you say we rethink the music? Maybe skip it?"

"I don't think so. I was looking forward to it," she said, her heart rate speeding up a little. She started to smell an ill wind.

"Come on," he begged. "Think about it. You won't be sorry…"

She did a quick memory check. She'd been out for happy hour with friends from work when she met him. They'd talked for a long time. She was an emergency room nurse, he was a paramedic—they'd never met before but she did a lot of business with the fire department and had come to think of them as the good guys. He had been polite, attentive, interested. He was a nice-looking guy with a sense of humor. She'd taken his cell phone number and agreed to meet him again, this time for a cup of coffee. That's how you play safe dating. He'd been a gentleman, walking her to her car after coffee and saying goodbye with a brief, platonic hug. Then she'd given him *her* cell phone number. So, after a few getting-to-know-you conversations, she'd accepted a date for live music in the park. She still hadn't let him pick her up; they'd agreed to meet at a bar because finding each other in a park full of people could be difficult.

His behavior now took her by surprise. She'd have to back him down quick. She'd been attracted to him, but no way was she ready to take this to the next level.

"I don't have to think about it," she said, her palms pressed firmly against his chest. "I was looking forward to some music. It's a beautiful night. And what you apparently have in mind is not on the agenda in the parking lot of the—"

Her words were cut off as he slipped a big hand around the back of her head and pulled her, roughly, onto his mouth. She pushed at him, making unintelligible sounds beneath his lips, but he was actually *climbing* across the console while silencing her with his mouth. For a guy about six feet tall, this was unimaginable, but he seemed to do it with ease. In seconds, he was straddling her hips, towering over her so fast she hardly knew what was happening.

"Hey!" she said when he released her lips. "Hey, what are you *doing*?"

She was thinking quickly. There were a few cars around his, but he had parked away from the crowd and his windows were darkly tinted. Her next thought was, How is this possible? This is a nice guy! This is a paramedic! My best friend's husband is a paramedic; I know a lot of their friends! They're salt of the earth—angels!

But he was pressing her back against the seat, devouring her mouth, breathing real hard and fast through his nose. He popped her seat belt off and although she pushed and her protests were lost as whimpers beneath his mouth, she was focused on the logistics of his attack. He couldn't possibly plan to rape her in the front bucket seat of an SUV? She was wearing shorts; freeing her from her clothes would not be simple!

Then her seat began to recline—he had his hand on the button. He was slowly laying her down. She was beginning to understand his plan. If he got her flat, he could pull down her shorts. If he raped her and let her loose, if he didn't leave bruises or marks, he'd claim she wasn't forced. She'd run her share of rape kits in the E.R., heard her share of he-said-she-said stories while a skeptical detective took notes. Well, by God, she was at least going to force him to leave bruises! She began to kick and push and wiggle, throwing her head and body wildly back and forth, side to side.

"Stop it," he said. "Stop it now. Come on. We know what we want!"

"Get *off* me, you son of a bitch!"

"Aw, Cassie," he laughed, as if she'd uttered some kind of endearment. "Baby, come on—I'm totally into you!"

"You're *crazy!* Let me go! Get off me! *Now!*"

"Come on, come on, settle down…"

"No!" she screamed. Just scream, she told herself. Bite, kick, scream, yell, hit, gouge, anything. She pushed at him with one hand, searching for the door handle with the other. Then, failing to find it, she pounded on the window, hoping to break it, screeching and turning her head away from his mouth so she could get volume. She tried head butting him, but he held her shoulders down and lifted his head back, and he *laughed*. She was moving around so violently, the car was actually bouncing. He tried to grab her wrist but she socked him in the eye. He grunted in pain and growled, but he didn't hit back. She continued banging on the window and yelling. She knew one thing—he couldn't get her out of this parking lot without moving to his side of the car, over that console,

and by God she was going to fling herself out of the car before he could take her anywhere.

Suddenly there was a sharp rapping on her window. "Hey!" someone with a deep male voice yelled. "Hey!"

"Oh, God," she cried, suddenly overcome with relief and hope. *"Help!"* she screamed. *"Hel—!"* And then Ken put his hand over her mouth.

Ken lowered the window an inch. "Hey, go away, pal. We're busy!" And he powered the window back up. Cassie bit his hand as hard as she could and he jumped so abruptly, he hit his head on the ceiling of the car.

Cassie heard the man with the deep voice try to open the locked door. Then the window's glass suddenly cracked and, like a spiderweb, spread into a million cracks. But it was tempered glass and didn't break, merely crystallized, leaving a dent in the glass where it had been hit. A sharp object she vaguely recognized as a key popped through the compromised glass and started boring a hole into it, releasing diamondlike pebbles of glass that fell into the car. Ken decided to return to the driver's seat. "What the hell are you doing, man?" he screamed at the intruder.

A huge hand attached to a huge arm entered through the hole in the window and reached down to flip the lock. The door opened instantly and Cassie stumbled out. She was gasping as she looked into a face far more frightening than Ken's. This was a giant wearing a tight white T-shirt covered by a black leather vest adorned with chains. On the arm that had freed her was a tattoo of a naked lady. He had a lot of facial hair—long, thick sideburns and a handlebar moustache that framed his mouth. His hair was pulled back into a ponytail. With his hands on her elbows to help her stand upright, he asked, "You hurt?" His voice was very menacing; he frowned blackly. Cassie was five-three and this guy had a foot on her, at least.

"No," she said, gasping. "Yes. I mean, no. He…" She couldn't finish.

He pulled her away from the SUV and turned her around so that he stood between her and the car. "You need the police? Or the hospital?" he asked as he pulled a cell phone out of his pants pocket.

"No," she said, shaking her head. "You were in time." Then she hiccupped and choked; a fat tear ran down her cheek. "Oh, God!"

"Can I call someone for you?" he asked, his voice miraculously softer.

Suddenly the SUV was in gear, and Ken—the polite, salt-of-the-earth paramedic—took off. The passenger door slowly drifted closed as the car banked and turned, leaving some skid marks behind.

"My purse…" she whimpered.

Suddenly the SUV skidded to a stop just before exiting the parking lot. Through the broken passenger door window flew an object, crashing to the ground. Then the car sped away. "Your purse," the big guy said. "Stay here." He walked across the parking lot, squatted to return scattered items from her purse back into it, then brought it back to her. "Here you go," he said, holding it out.

Cassie looked up at the guy who had saved her. A biker dude. He looked scruffy and scary, like he could be a Hells Angel or something. But Ken, so clean-cut, turned out to be the dangerous one.

"God," she said. "I never saw that coming. If you hadn't…"

"You okay? Because I can call the police. I got the plate number."

"I wasn't hurt—just scared to death. I swear, that shouldn't have happened."

"It looked pretty bad there for a minute."

"For a minute, it *was* pretty bad. I think maybe he was going to—" She stopped. She couldn't say it.

"Hey, now. You sure you're okay?" the guy asked again.

Cassie fished around in her purse for her keys, her hands shaking. "Yeah," she said with a sniff. "I'll be fine. I think."

"You want me to follow you home or something? Make sure you don't have any trouble?"

She let a huff of laughter escape through her tears. Imagine having a guy like *this* follow her, know where she lived? Suddenly the world didn't make any sense. "I won't go straight home. I'll go to my girlfriend's. She has a protective German shepherd and a six-foot-two-inch husband."

"You sure you don't want to just check in with the police?" he asked, his brows furrowing. "Talk to them about it?"

"She also has three kids," Cassie said.

The big man laughed, a deep and rumbling sound. "Well, I guess that oughta hold anyone back."

Another laugh puffed out of Cassie, but then she instantly plummeted into tears. Loud tears. Her purse dropped from her hands and she leaned against him, wailing.

"Whoa, kiddo," he said. "I think maybe I should buy you a cup of coffee, get you a little straightened out before you drive..."

"I'm not... I wasn't... I haven't been drinking or anything," she finally choked out.

"I didn't mean to sober you up," he said with a laugh. He bent down and picked up the purse and then, with a big arm draped around her shoulders, he gently, protectively, led her back toward the bar.

Looking up at him, she asked, "What if he comes back?"

"He's not coming back," the man said. "You're okay for now. Come on, let's have a cup of coffee. Calm down a little. Then you go on to your girlfriend's. Huh?"

By the time he got all that out, they were nearly at the door to the bar. She wiped at her cheeks, her eyes. "I really don't know what to do," she said.

"I know," he answered. "Coffee, that's what we do."

In just a few minutes she was sitting in a corner booth, staring into a cup of black coffee, across from one big, mean-looking biker. And he had a cup of coffee, too.

Cassie could hardly lift her head; she was exhausted, frightened, wrung out, relieved. But as she slowly realized what she really was, she looked up in some surprise, right into the amazing blue eyes of her rescuer. "God, I'm so *embarrassed,*" she said in a breath.

"You shouldn't be embarrassed," he said. "You didn't attack him. He should be embarrassed, but he's probably not. Bet he's scared, though."

"Of you?"

"Not necessarily. You know, it's not too late to call the police. My little brother's a cop, actually. He's not working tonight, but we could still call him. He'd be good for some advice, at least." Then he laughed. "Of all us boys, he was about the worst one. Figures he'd turn into a cop. And a real hard-case cop, too. Not a lot of gray area with him. Listen, how well do you know that guy?"

"Apparently not well enough," she said, shaking her head. "We met at happy hour, then had a coffee date and talked on the phone quite a bit. He works with people I know. I guess."

"You guess?"

"Well, he said he was a paramedic and my best friend's husband is a paramedic. I know a lot of their friends. I thought we had mutual friends. Jeez. What if he was just lying?"

"License plates don't lie."

"How did you know to help me?"

He smiled. "You're kidding, right? I *heard* you. The car was rocking. Two people in the front seat? I figured if it was consensual, you'd both be in the backseat." He shrugged. "It was worth checking out."

"What did you use to break that window?"

He lifted a hand. He stared at his own knuckles for a second. They were bruised and swelling.

"Holy cow," she said. "Are *you* okay?"

"Yeah. It'll be fine." Then he grinned. "Maybe he'll try to sue me or something, huh? I'd love that. So, I'm Walt. Walt Arneson."

"Cassie," she said. Then she shook her head. "You must think I'm pretty stupid."

"Doesn't sound like it," he answered.

"I thought I was being careful. I didn't run him through a private investigator or anything, but I met with him a couple of times, talked to him a lot, and I didn't think he was that type of guy. I agreed to go out with him, you know. And I let him kiss me, too."

"It's okay, Cassie. That doesn't sound foolish. Sometimes you just can't tell…"

"If you can't tell, then what are you supposed to do?" she asked, more of herself than him. "I've dated some real jack-asses, but never one like that."

"As I understand it, most assaults come from someone you know," he said. "At least, that's what I've heard."

"Assault," she said, trying out the word. "I guess that's what that was."

"Oh, yeah, that's what that was." He cleared his throat. "Um, he know where you live or anything?"

"Well… I never gave him an address, but he knows my last name, where I work and the general vicinity in which I live…"

Walt reached inside a breast pocket in his vest and pulled out a business card. He passed it to her and she read it. His name was on a card for Riders, Inc., a motorcycle dealership. *Sales and Maintenance,* it said. "In case you need a witness or some backup of some kind. Don't hesitate. Really. I wouldn't mind another crack at him."

"You work on motorcycles?"

"Yep. And other things. Bikes are my specialty."

"How many motorcycle mechanics have business cards?" she asked.

"Probably more than you think. Motorcycles—big business. People are very fussy about their machines."

"And you fix 'em, huh?"

"I've been fooling around with bikes for about…gee, I guess sixteen years or more. Since I was just a kid." He frowned as he watched her lift her coffee cup to her lips. "Looks like you might've hurt yourself there."

She put the cup down and looked at the back of her hand. One of her knuckles was bluish and puffy. She smiled sheepishly. "I socked him in the face. I think I got his eye."

"Good for you." He smiled.

"Listen, if it's all the same to you, I think I'd like to get out of here now."

"Sure," he said, reaching for his back pocket and pulling out his wallet.

"No, let me get the coffee," she said, her hand in her purse. "It's the least I can do…"

"Taken care of," he said, cutting her off. "I'll just get you to your car—"

"Um, please don't take offense, but I think I'd almost feel safer alone."

"I get that," he said. "But, hey, I know the owner here. Want me to ask one of the managers or bartenders to walk you out? Just to make you more comfortable?"

"No. Really. But thanks for everything." She scooted out of the booth.

"Cassie," he said, picking up his card from the table and pointing it at her. "In case you change your mind about the police. Or just in case he gives you some trouble and you need a little help, or want a witness to back you up. Huh?"

"Yeah," she said. "Sorry, I wasn't thinking. I just forgot."

"Not a problem. Be careful now."

She gave him a wan smile and walked out of the bar. She was barely outside when the darkness and the silence just freaked her out. She turned around, went right back to his booth and said, "Um, sorry, could you please take me out to my car? It got really... It just got so quiet out there."

"Sure. Be glad to. You have a cell phone?"

"I do," she said, nodding.

"Okay, you'll be fine." He slid out of the booth and cupped his hand under her elbow, escorting her out in a very chival-rous manner. "You're just going to lock the car doors, get your cell phone handy, watch the rearview mirror. But I guaran-tee you, he's going to leave you alone. I mean, come on—he left you with *me*." And then he chuckled. "And remember, Cassie, I know the plate number."

"You didn't write it down or anything..."

"XKY936, teal-blue Tahoe," he said. "I think it might be good to go see a friend, talk it out, be around people where you feel safe. But really, your bad date—he's going to pretend none of that ever happened. Just the same, if he calls you or drops by, no excuses. Call the police first. Then call me—I'll tell them everything."

"That's very nice of you."

"You'd do the same thing," he said. They arrived at her car and she used the remote to unlock it. He held the door for her. "You're still a little upset, so drive carefully."

"Yes," she said. "Thank you."

Cassie drove straight to Julie's house. She and Jules had been best friends since seventh grade. But while Julie married at nineteen and started her family, Cassie was still single at twenty-nine. Julie and Billy had been together since their junior year in high school. They were like a Lifetime movie—the star quarterback and the head cheerleader. The perfect couple. They were scrapping a little these days, but they'd get it together, as usual. After all, they had three kids and a dog—a lot to bicker about.

What Cassie would give to have a guy like Billy in her life. She didn't have a crush on him; he'd become like a brother because Julie was like her sister. But still...

She could hear the chaos in the house when she rang the bell. It was only eight-thirty; Julie would be right in the midst of trying to round up the kids and get them to bed. Julie opened the door with a mother-shout over her shoulder to *Get in that tub!* Then she looked at Cassie. "What are you doing here?" she asked. "Didn't you have a big date?"

"Can I come in?"

"Of course! You didn't get stood up, did you?"

"No. Very bad attempt at a date," Cassie said, stepping into the foyer. The place was suffering that end-of-a-day wreck, as was Julie. Her blond hair had gone limp and was flopping in her eyes, she was braless in a T-shirt, shorts, her bare feet dirty, her face with no makeup. And behind her, chasing each other through the family room and kitchen, were a naked three- and four-year-old with a barking German shepherd in pursuit.

When the kids saw her, they yelled, "Cassie!" and ran to

her. She stood in the entranceway with one nude child hanging on each leg.

But Julie just stared at Cassie. "What happened?" she asked.

Cassie said, "I'm going to help myself to a glass of wine, if you still have some. Then I'll tell you all about it." She shrugged and her eyes welled up. "I don't feel like going home right now." She sniffed back the tears and said, "Go. There are naked children running wild all over the house." Cassie bent down and kissed the top of each little head.

"The bottle you left a week ago is still in the fridge," she said, running a hand through her lank hair. "You don't look so good."

"I'll be fine." The kids broke free and ran off, followed by their mother. Cassie threw her purse onto a chair and headed for the kitchen. Then she turned back and flipped the dead bolt on the front door.

In the kitchen she found a wineglass and poured herself some cold white from the refrigerator; she'd gotten in the habit of bringing a big jug of wine over when she came. Julie and Billy were on a tight budget and didn't splurge on extras—even the kind that could give you a shot of relaxation at the end of a long day, with a husband working two jobs and a wife managing three kids almost entirely alone.

Cassie went into the family room and sat down on the sofa, kicking off her shoes and putting her feet up on the coffee table. Within what seemed like seconds, Jeffy came into the room. He was nine. He went right to the couch and sat so close to Cassie, he was almost on top of her.

"Wanna see what I'm doing?" he asked, balancing a small laptop computer on his lap. Cassie remembered—this was an old laptop handed down by Julie's brother.

"You bet. Whatcha got here?"

"I'm making skyscrapers. See? You can get between them with ships and catwalks."

"You're a genius," she said. "Where'd you get your brains? You get them from me? Nah, I'm just the auntie. Jeff, this is so cool." She ruffled his dark hair, kissed his temple. "You have your bath?"

"Not till after them," he said. "Look, I can make 'em fly." He maneuvered some keys, clicking away, and sure enough the small airships moved between tall buildings.

"Can I try that?" Cassie asked.

He showed her how and they entertained themselves for about twenty minutes before Julie reappeared. Now she was water splashed and even more wilted. Billy was at his second job. He was a paramedic for the fire department and, on off days, worked in a builder's shop cutting wood for cabinets and everything from marble to granite for countertops. Firefighters worked twenty-four-hour shifts, during which they didn't get much sleep. He'd get home at eight in the morning, grab a nap, go to the shop for a few hours, then go back to the fire department for another twenty-four the next morning. After three twenty-four-hour shifts in six days, Billy would get four days off in a row from F.D. and those were the best days—he only worked one job, at the shop. The best thing about his second job was he could make his own hours, as long as he got the work done. And he put in a lot of hours; money was real tight. Usually Julie would be coming to the end of her rope after days of managing on her own, as she clearly was at the moment.

Julie pulled the small computer out of Jeff's hands. "Can you get your bath before you do any more virtual building or flying?"

"Yeah, okay."

"Can you pick up your dirty clothes and throw them in the hamper?"

"Yeah, okay."

Then they disappeared, leaving Cassie alone.

When Cassie and Julie spotted each other the first day of seventh grade, it was an instant bond. Tall, thin, blond Julie and short, round, dark-haired Cassie—they were an odd-looking pair. A couple of years later Cassie's stepdad was transferred from California to Des Moines and Cassie couldn't bear the thought of leaving her friends, her school. Plus, Cassie's mom had married Frank when Cassie was eight and they'd proceeded to have two babies and had a third on the way. Cassie couldn't put it into words at the time, but she didn't really feel like a part of their family. It had gone from Cassie and Francine alone to Frank and Francine and the kids, and Cassie as babysitter and guest.

Some begging and negotiating evolved into Cassie moving into Julie's house, right into her crowded little bedroom, sharing a regular-size double bed. Their parents didn't think it would last long; they assumed they'd start to fight like sisters or Cassie would miss her mom and the little half sibs too much and want to move back. Neither happened; Cassie and Julie were best friends and roommates all through high school.

Cassie got her first job at fifteen, paying her way so she wouldn't have to rely on help from her mom and stepdad or put a strain on Julie's folks when she needed essentials like underwear or school supplies. She supported herself but for room and board. At graduation Julie's mom handed her a check; she'd saved every penny of support Cassie's stepdad had sent, from the piddling fifty dollars to the rare two or three hundred. "If you decide to use this for college, you can stay here rent free as long as you're in school. If you do something else with this, we'll work out a reasonable rent for you."

It was an unexpected opportunity for Cassie; her mom and stepdad didn't have a cent to spare. Birthday and Christmas presents had always come in the form of plane tickets to visit the family. So she went to college, studied nursing and got her R.N. degree, working while she went to school to support herself.

Julie went to college, too, but didn't make it through a whole year. She got pregnant, dropped out and married Billy, the love of her life. When Jules and Billy got their first little apartment, Cassie stayed on at Julie's parents' house, finished college and landed her first job in emergency room nursing.

And then Cassie's mother died. That left Frank with three kids to support on his own. The plane tickets stopped coming; they were replaced with gift cards from Starbucks or Borders.

When Cassie was twenty-five, she managed to buy her little house, not coincidentally real close to Julie and Billy's. And she got Steve, her Weimaraner.

She briefly considered going back to the house to pick up Steve and ask Jules if she could sleep on the couch tonight, but quickly decided she'd brave going home, after a glass of wine and a little decompression time. She'd never leave Steve alone all night—he was such a baby. Right now she wished she'd taught him to bark and snarl menacingly, just in case she ever needed him to be protective. But he was so sweet just the way he was.

It was a long time before Julie finished with the kids, getting everyone settled, though it was obvious she'd hurried through bedtime rituals. Instead of picking up the house, she passed Cassie and went immediately to the kitchen, pouring herself an apple juice in a wineglass. She brought the bottle of chardonnay to Cassie, offering to top off her glass. Then she plopped herself on the other end of the couch, with her legs tucked under her, facing Cassie.

"Tell me what happened," Julie said. "You're actually a little pale."

"You won't believe it. I don't believe it. He attacked me—right in the car, right in the parking lot of the bar where I met him for our date." Julie gasped and covered her open mouth with a hand. "It was bizarre. Otherworldly. It took me by such surprise, for a minute I couldn't even move, couldn't even push or yell." She went through the details, right up to the breaking of the window and the cup of coffee with Walt, her friendly neighborhood thug.

"He climbed *over* the console?" Julie asked.

"Yeah. That threw me, but I realized later, there was an awful lot of room in that front seat. He had both bucket seats back as far as they'd go. And where he parked—real far away from most of the cars—he must have done that deliberately before we met for the evening." She shook her head with a short, unamused laugh. "I remember thinking he was worried about dents and scratches. But no—he planned it. He was prepared to take matters into his own hands if I insisted on going to the concert."

"God! You must have been terrified! How did that biker guy know you were in trouble?"

"He said he heard me, that the car was rocking. I was fighting so hard, it made the car wobble." She showed Julie her knuckles. "I don't know if I got this from banging on the window or punching him in the face."

"Holy shit, Cassie. You think about calling the police?"

"I thought about it, yeah. Thing is, I've run rape kits on victims for detectives, and even when they're banged up, torn apart and hysterical, the police can hardly make a case. What am I going to say? A guy I accepted a date with—who I let kiss me in the parking lot and again in the car—held me down while he kissed me? He never hit me, never got to my clothes, never unbuttoned his pants… The fact that we both knew what he was going to do will be completely irrelevant."

"But you've got that guy—"

"Yeah, Walt. He called it assault. It *was* an assault, but it only got as far as an attempt." She shrugged. "Although it still scared me half to death."

They heard the sound of the garage door opening and Julie threw an unmistakable look of disgust over her shoulder toward the door. Billy came in, wearing his jeans and T-shirt covered with sawdust, putting his tool belt on the washer in the laundry room, which connected the garage to the kitchen. He looked pretty wiped.

"You're early," Julie said.

"I finished up. I could've found a little more to do, but I thought maybe you could use some help."

She laughed. "And what the hell kind of help were you going to give me after the kids are already in bed?"

"Jesus, I don't know, Jules—want me to paint the house or sand the floors?"

Cassie put her fingers against her temples and rubbed. "God. Do you two have to do this right now?"

"You're a witness, Cass. You can see all I did was walk in the goddamn door!"

"After nine at night, to *help!*" Julie said.

"Okay, I'm going home to Steve," Cassie said, starting to get up.

"No," Julie said, grabbing her hand. "No, you're absolutely right. We'll stop. Besides, you need to tell Billy what happened."

"Why?" she said wearily, sinking into her place on the couch.

"Because the guy said he was a paramedic, Cassie," Julie said.

"Who said he was a paramedic?" Billy asked. He pulled a beer out of the refrigerator and brought it into the family room. He sat down on the coffee table and faced Cassie. "Something wrong?"

Cassie went through the story again. Billy leaned forward, his elbows on his knees, holding his beer with both hands, and several times he just looked at the floor. He ignored his beer till the end of the story. Then he took a long drink out of the can.

"The only thing I'd really like to know," Cassie added, "and there's no way to find out, not even by going to the police, is if he's attacked other women. I don't know if I drew the wild card or if he's a chronically dangerous guy."

"Maybe you can't find that out, but we can check if he's a paramedic," Billy said, getting to his feet. "If he's even with the fire department. I'll tell you what, if he's a firefighter and he's doing this to women, he's going to be sorry."

"I have a feeling if you make him sorry, I could pay the price."

"But, Cass, I gotta know. We have some bad apples sometimes, but I never heard anything like that before."

"It's not like you introduced us," she said. "It has nothing to do with you."

"I feel like it has everything to do with me. I don't love everyone in the department, but it kills me to think one of our boys would do something like that to a woman. Kills me. I'm going to find out right away."

Billy insisted on following Cassie home—the whole two miles—and coming inside with her to be sure everything was secure. While Billy busied himself doing the man thing of checking windows, locks, et cetera, Cassie was on her knees loving on Steve, kissing and being kissed. It's not as though she'd been gone long; she'd had the day off and had only left him a few hours ago for a date that should have worked out, should've been late and fun. It was just after ten-thirty and Steve had been fine, curled up on the couch on his special blanket with several of his babies—small stuffed toys that he carried around with him like a cat carries kittens.

When Billy was getting ready to leave he asked, "How are you feeling, Cass?"

"A little edgy, but mostly disappointed. Very disappointed."

"Are you scared?"

"I admit, I'm a little shook up, but the whole incident was over in five minutes or less. And I have good locks, a phone with a backup cell phone and we know Steve's a killer. Really, I'm so disappointed with the way things turn out most of the time. You and Jules—I know you've been fighting lately, but you just don't know how rotten it is to be looking, waiting, hoping to find the right person…"

"Lotta people love you, Cassie."

She smiled. "Thanks," she said. Not exactly the kind of love she was hoping for, but nice.

He shook his head and looked away. "I don't know what the hell's going on with Jules," he said. "I can't do anything right. I have no idea what's eating her."

Cassie had some ideas. Three kids, tight budget, hard work, absent husband. But it wasn't her place to get into their squabbles. They'd work them out, as always. "Maybe you should ask her" was all she said.

"You think I don't ask? I shoulda just gone to the frickin' bar tonight, had my one beer of the day there. Never mind— I don't mean to unload on you tonight. Listen, I'm home if you need me. If you have any problems, call me. I can get here in two minutes."

"How much sleep have you had?" she asked.

"I got in eight," he said.

"Eight hours after twenty-four on the job? If I have any trouble, I'll call the police," she said.

"Fine, do that. Then your next call is to me." And then he

grabbed her shoulders gently and put a brotherly kiss on her forehead. Steve looked up at him, wagged his cropped tail wildly and whined. "I am *not* kissing you!" Billy said to the dog.

"Aw. He needs a kiss," Cassie said. "He knows his mommy's upset about something and he needs a little reassurance. It wouldn't kill you."

"No. I don't kiss dogs or boys or boy dogs. You try to trick me into this all the time."

"Steve doesn't ask for much," Cassie said. "He has no male role model except you. He adores you, can't you see that? How can you be so ridiculous about it? Just a little peck on the head—that's all it will take to make him happy. I mean, come on, it's *Steve!* He's like a son to you! Or at least a nephew!"

Billy, hands in his pockets, bent at the waist and kissed the gray top of Steve's bony head. And Steve, contented, sat for him and put up a paw to shake.

"You kiss boy dogs," Cassie said with a laugh.

"Jerk. Lock me out. Call me if you need anything. Anything at all."

And he was gone. Cassie looked at Steve and said, "Good job. Humble him every chance you get."

Cassie changed into summer sweats and searched for something on TV. Steve curled up beside her to watch an old movie. He had the bunny, the frog and the octopus curled up with him. The movie wasn't sad—it was a comedy—but within fifteen minutes, tears began to run down her cheeks.

She had a job she loved, great friends who'd been close for many years, two families—Julie's and Frank and three half sibs. She was independent, completely self-supporting...and lonely. So very lonely at times.

At the end of the day, it was always like this—Cassie and Steve on the couch, just the two of them. She'd had very few relationships over the years, all of them excruciatingly short and, in retrospect, none of which held any potential for permanence. Some had ended by mutual consent, but the majority had seen her dumped, her heart shattered, her expectations destroyed. She didn't like to think of herself as one of those pathetic single women who was always looking for a man, but there was no way around it. Every time she met a new guy, she got hopeful. Her thoughts always went to the same place—please, let him turn out to be *the one,* a good guy who wants to have a wife and children, who loves me and treats me like I'm the best thing that ever happened to him. But she hadn't even come close. She'd never even lived with anyone.

Tonight had been worse than heartache—it had been terrifying. She kept going over it in her mind, wondering if she should've known. He'd been a little on the eager side, but that had been kind of fun when it had seemed innocent. There was no way she could've known he'd turn out to be what he turned out to be. There was a chance that without the rescue he might've backed off when she proved too much trouble, but in her gut she felt there was an equal chance he could've turned into a rapist.

Is this what it's come to? she asked herself. Is it not enough to be let down, disappointed, that I have to be scared to death and real damn close to being a victim? Is that what looking for the right man gets you? It's utter madness—and it has to stop. I have to quit looking for the right guy. I just can't take it anymore. The heartbreak is just too much.

Single women of twenty-nine never admit to anyone, not even their priests, that what they fear most is being alone *forever,* dying alone someday. Since she was about twenty-five, her greatest fear was that she'd *never* find a partner. Cassie wasn't independent by conscious choice, it was by default—she had no real family. She knew women her age who'd had a couple or even a few false starts before they found the one, the for-ever guy, but Cassie's longest relationship had lasted maybe four months. Four terrible months. She didn't know anyone like her-self—with no living parents, no close relationships with siblings, no one. All she wanted was someone permanent who loved her, wanted children with her, a family man. She even wanted the bickering that went with all the regular adjustments—bick-ering that ended with making up and great sex. She hated it when someone said, "But you're still so young. There's *plenty* of time!" Plenty? She would be thirty in six months and she had yet to meet someone who lasted six months with her. Or, "He'll show up when you least expect it…" And then they'd tell a story of meeting their own lifetime mate, but they were never more than thirty with a bad track record. If there was anything harder than facing the terrifying truth, it was hav-ing that fear not taken seriously. "You're beautiful and smart—you'll find the right guy." Well, it wasn't happening.

Her mind was jumbled with numbers. If I'm thirty when I meet him, give it a year to see if we're in sync, a year-long en-gagement, and then if I don't get pregnant easily, am I thirty-five before that first baby's coming? And always: What if he doesn't come along until I'm thirty-five? What if he never shows up? Really—never! I can get together with girlfriends and say, yeah, it would be great to find the right man, but, hey! If I don't, I have a lot more fun than you girls. After all, I've had sex with a couple dozen men…

"Steve," she said in a tearful whisper. "I've had sex with a couple dozen men." She rubbed his floppy ears. "Do you still respect me?"

She had sex the first time at seventeen. She had been soooo in love. She'd had sex the last time five months ago. In thir-teen years of sexual activity, it didn't take long to get to a cou-ple dozen, or the vicinity; she couldn't actually count them without writing them down, an act that repelled her. Even so, she didn't feel promiscuous. She felt, frankly, completely lost.

Steve turned his beautiful black eyes up to her and made a sound. Then he licked her arm. He would never leave her.

But he would, she reminded herself, and Steve was her only real family. Big dogs didn't last long. The life span of a Weimaraner was twelve to fourteen years and Steve was five. What would she do without anyone special, without her mom, with a life so solitary? She had her girlfriends—Julie, Marty and Beth—but everyone else had parents, brothers, sisters, spouses.

The tears came harder. She missed her mom so much sometimes; they had been best friends. Even though she hadn't gone to live with her when she'd moved away, they'd still talked all the time—two or three times a week for an hour at a time. And she'd been with her mom for the months preceding her death, caring for her, loving her into the next world.

Since she'd been just a kid, she'd been on her own. And all she'd ever wanted was to have that kind of connection happily married women had—the loving commitment her mom had had too briefly with Frank, that Jules had with Billy, Marty had with Joe. A good, strong, solid guy to lean on who'd share the responsibility and joy. Was that so much to hope for? Why was that asking so damn much? Didn't everyone have a soul mate *somewhere*?

There were times she thought life just wasn't worth living without some kind of deep love and intimacy. The thought of growing into an old woman without ever having that kind of reliable connection was unimaginable. Another ten years of looking for the right partner, being let down again and again, was simply more than she could bear to think about.

2

Even though Julie and Cassie were best friends, they belonged to a foursome of girlfriends who'd hung tight since junior high. Marty and Beth were their two other close girlfriends. They'd all been cheerleaders together in school and had been tight ever since. Beth was the only one who wasn't socially available that often; she was a brand-new doctor and her schedule was horrible.

The rest of them had remained relative neighbors since high school graduation, getting together regularly. They also had larger gatherings including still more friends from the past. The tradition started when Julie and Billy, as newlyweds, threw a small party, and it grew from there. Some years after high school Billy introduced Marty to one of his firefighter pals and they ended up getting married. Now the friends' parties—potlucks held four or five times a year—included some firemen and their wives or girlfriends, plus whatever old high school chums were around.

The Fourth of July party this year was at Marty and Joe's house, in their rec room. It was a big room, complete with bar, pool table, a pinball machine, state-of-the-art stereo equipment, plenty of seating and standing room. They lived in a mansion by Julie's standards, and she looked around the rec room jealously. They had lots of toys—quads, a boat, Jet Skis, an RV. Joe made a little more money than Billy, since he was a few years senior at F.D., but their lifestyle was probably even more affordable because they hadn't married right out of high school, had only one child and Marty worked full-time. True, she was a hairdresser—not a high-ticket career field—but she had a full roster of regular clients and Julie certainly couldn't afford her cuts and colors.

Julie had managed a part-time job after Jeffy was born, while Billy worked and finished college before getting a job with the fire department. They went through years of tough schedules, school loans and scrimping by. With Billy barely on the F.D. payroll, which was modest to start, they had a lot of debt to clear. But then Clint came along and, a year later, Stephie. It ate up the toy money pretty quick. Hell, it ate up the *food* money.

Joe was an established firefighter who had his own house when he met Marty. They didn't get married right away; by the time they did, they were able to sell Joe's house and buy a bigger one. Their little boy was now three and while Joe complained he wanted more kids, Marty said that was it for her. It seemed to Julie that when other people didn't plan on kids, they didn't have them. Julie and Billy didn't plan on them and had them, anyway.

It felt as though everyone had come a long way in twelve years, except Julie and Billy—voted couple of the year in high school. They had a decent little home they couldn't afford, drove somewhat reliable cars with tons of miles on them, had a house full of kids, big bills and no extras. No grown-up toys, no vacations. Also, no nice dinners out, weekend escapes for just the two of them, and they avoided hiring sitters—sitters were very expensive. If Julie's mom or Cassie couldn't watch the kids, they just didn't go out. Julie cut out coupons constantly, haunted the sales and even thrift shops, paid the minimum balance, put a sheet over the couch to keep the worn fabric from showing. When she was crowned homecoming queen, this was not how she envisioned her life. She'd had her fifteen minutes of fame when she was seventeen.

Tonight, to add to her overwhelming feeling that she was in a steady decline, another one of the old cheerleaders had shown up—Chelsea. She made an appearance every year or two, just to establish she'd hung on to her tight body, perky tits and effervescent smile. In fact, quite a few of her physical traits had greatly improved since high school. Julie suspected Chelsea's breasts were even perkier—high, full, prominent and aimed right at the eyeballs of men. Chelsea had been cute as a button before, and she was better put together every year, while Julie felt she was sliding too fast into old age. But, if you'd asked her at seventeen which way she'd like to go— blossoming in her late twenties or having it all at seventeen— Julie would still have taken seventeen. Stupidly.

So she watched Chelsea from across the rec room, doing what she did best—flirting with Billy. It was amazing how long your nemesis could follow you without ever losing interest in your man. Julie had threatened Billy with unspeakably painful things if he ever touched Chelsea, if he even accidentally brushed up against her. Thus, Billy's arms were crossed protectively over his wide, hard chest, laughing at absolutely everything Chelsea said. Now and then she'd put a hand on his forearm and gaze up at him, chatting away, making him grin like a fool.

"Some things never change," Cassie said, climbing up on the bar stool beside Julie.

They watched together as Joe joined Billy, passing him a

beer. Then he leaned down a little and asked Chelsea some-thing: *Can I get you a drink?* She just shook her head and laughed, drawing Joe into the conversation. Then a third man joined them. Hmm. Chelsea had three good-looking men cornered, holding them captive with her cleavage. Yet again she put her hand on Billy's forearm.

"If he laughs at her once more, I'm going to throw a dart at him," Julie said. "Then I'll chop him up in little pieces."

Cassie sipped her wine. "Maybe you should have a drink. Loosen up a little."

"I'm the designated driver. And I'm going to designate him right out of here in about ten minutes." Then she said to Cassie, "I'm just not fun anymore, am I?"

"Well, you're not a lot of laughs right now. But there have been fun times…"

"Did I ever flirt like that?" Julie asked.

"I've known you to have a flirt or two, but usually with your own guy," Cassie said. Then she glanced at Chelsea and said, "How does she make never getting married look so good and I just make it look so…fat?"

"Cassie, you're not fat. You're…"

Cassie gave her a second and then put a hand on her arm and said, "Don't. When you have to search for the right word for longer than three seconds, you're just going to come up with a synonym. And I'll hate you."

"We used to do some really fun things. We stole a port-a-potty and put it in the football coach's front yard. That was fun. Wasn't it fun?"

"I think it spilled and violated us…"

"We laughed till we peed," Julie pointed out.

"Yeah. We were idiots." Cassie sipped her drink. "We went on that all-girl camping trip once," Cassie said. "But there was a leak and it didn't stay all-girl too long. I lost my virginity for the third time that weekend." She sipped some more. "Maybe we should do that again. An all-girl camping trip. And this time, keep it to ourselves."

"Can't. If Billy ever finds out I'm willing to camp, my life is over. Sleeping on the ground is about the only vacation we can afford." She sighed. "I'm not fun anymore," Julie said. "I'm a drudge." Billy came up behind her and put a hand on her shoulder. Julie turned and looked up at him. "Did you touch her?"

"No, Jules. I've gotten really attached to my balls. But if she's going to keep rubbing those tits on my arm, I'm going to need a lot more to drink."

"Funny," she said. "How much longer do we have to stay?"

"Joe has some fireworks," he said.

"There could be fireworks right in this room if I have to watch Chelsea gaze at you like a lovesick puppy for one more second..."

"Everyone else is having fun watching her flag her butt and preen. What's wrong with you?" he asked with a grin.

"I admit, it's been entertaining as hell, but I was thinking maybe there's a *Law and Order* rerun on TV. It's a tough choice, but I might have to go with the rerun."

"Isn't this just a rerun?" Cassie asked, laughing.

Although it wasn't late—eleven or so—Julie and Billy said their goodbyes and left the party. They drove by Julie's mom's house, scooped up three sleeping kids and went home. While Julie made sure everyone was tucked in for the night, Billy turned on the TV. She washed her face and brushed her teeth and crawled into bed. Before she could fall asleep, he was shedding his clothes, leaving them in a pile on the floor and getting in beside her. She could feel him naked and primed against her thigh.

"Oh, Jesus," she muttered.

"What? You wanted to come home early. You didn't turn on a rerun..."

"Billy..."

"Tell you what—just for fun, let's not fight. Let's just do it. That always puts you in a better mood."

"Did Chelsea get you all spooled up?" she asked him.

"Chelsea?" he asked, laughing. "How many years are you going to ask me that, Jules? I don't want Chelsea."

"I can't... Come on..."

"Why? You on the rag or something? Cramps?"

"Late," she said.

He rose up on an elbow and looked down at her. "It's not that late..."

"*I'm* late," she said. "My period's late."

Shock was etched into his handsome features. Then dawning. "Oh, so that's what's got a bug up your ass lately. We're caught again? We can't be."

"If we are, I'm going to kill myself. Then you."

He grinned at her. "We could use another girl to even things out."

"What we could use is a vasectomy!"

"Yeah. I guess. After this one..."

"Billy!"

"What?"

"We can't have another baby!"

"Well, you act like this is my fault!"

"It wasn't the UPS guy!"

He grinned into her eyes and brushed a little hair away from her brow. "I bet I know when it was," he said, his voice thick and husky. "We had dinner with your folks and you liked me. I didn't fuck up all night, which is a miracle, huh? Then after the kids were in bed, you liked me a *lot*. Kind of took me by surprise, but I think I stepped up to the plate pretty good there." He gave her a kiss on the nose, on the lips, on the chin. "I did such a good job, maybe you popped about ten eggs and one of 'em slipped right by that IUD…"

Her eyes welled with tears. "We can't afford another baby. We can't afford the ones we have."

"We get by okay. It won't be a struggle forever."

"It will if you keep knocking me up!"

He chuckled. "You're so damned knock-upable. I just can't help myself. And it's not like I planned it. I'm just so *potent*."

"See, you think you're so manly right now. They'll swim through anything—through condoms, IUDs, diaphragms… And you're goddamn *proud* of yourself!"

"Nah, that's not it," he said. "But I have to admit—I love you pregnant…"

"You're just an idiot! I can't pay the bills! Don't you *get* that?"

"Except the part where you're in a bad mood all the time and throw up. But you're probably not crazy about that part, either."

"Did you look around Marty and Joe's tonight? The big house, the nice furniture, all the stuff they have? You know why? They didn't get married when they were twelve, they have only one child and she works, that's why! While we're eating casserole made out of tuna or, on a big night, wings and thighs!"

"Yeah, it's really tight, but I don't think we should give any children away…"

"I'm not finding this funny at all! We'll never get out of debt!"

"Listen, you can't make assumptions about people, about their lives. Who knows what's going on in their private lives? For all we know, Marty and Joe have fifty-thousand-dollar credit-card bills and a second, third and fourth mortgage. And besides, I wouldn't trade one of our kids for a pinball machine or pool table." Then he rolled his eyes upward. "Well, I'd probably trade Clint for a boat and an RV…"

"We haven't planned one single baby," she whimpered.

"Apparently we don't have to."

"Really, I'm very upset about this," she said, pursing her lips, trying for control.

"Okay, I'm not going to let you get me all stirred up, because you're…well, you know what you are," he said. "We try our best to keep from getting pregnant, but we've had a surprise or two and we take what we get. Not because we wanted another one right now, but because it's on the way, it's ours and we *can*."

"Well, don't get all hooked on the idea. This would be an IUD pregnancy and there's no telling…"

"You take the home-test thing?" he asked.

She shook her head.

"Ah. You already threw up."

She nodded pathetically. "You know, it might not make it…"

He leaned over her more closely, slipping his big hands under her short nightie. "Jules, this is you and me—the baby factory. It'll make it. And we might not have a boat, but we've been so goddamn lucky. Look at those kids, huh? They're *smart!* Healthy. And damn good-looking."

"Clint's hyperactive. I can't keep up with him. I'm at the end of my rope…"

"He'll settle down. Jeffy was kind of like that. Listen, I could get a few more hours a week…"

"You're never here as it is."

"I'll work as hard as I have to, baby. I'll do whatever it takes. And I swear, I'll get that vasectomy before this one even gets here."

"If one swims through that, I'll kill you in your sleep!"

He laughed and put his hands over her breasts. He jostled her a little, rubbing against her thigh. "One good thing— you don't have to worry about getting pregnant for a while."

"That's not exactly an incentive," she told him, sniffing back a tear.

"You can eat like a pig. Everything you want," he said.

"I get postpartum depression," she said.

"No, you don't. You get early pregnancy depression, but when you have a new baby in your arms, you're alive like no other time. Just how late is this period?"

"A couple of weeks. But you know me…"

"So far you've been late exactly three times. But why didn't you do the test right away?"

"It costs seven dollars! And besides, I don't want to know for sure," she said softly.

"After dinner with your folks," he said dreamily. "I loved that—that was wonderful. I wish that would happen more often."

"I wish you'd turn me off, not on."

He grinned. "Well, that explains why you've been such a bear. Jesus, there was no making you happy. Except, what's up with the wine? You've had wine."

She shook her head. "Apple juice in a wineglass with Cassie, that's all," she said. Then she started to cry and he held her close. "Billy…" she cried. "Billy, I don't want this to happen… not now. If we were on our feet…"

"Yeah, it's okay, baby. You're just feeling the pressure—I understand that. But we'll be all right. In the end, things always work out for us. Listen to me—I want you to listen to me now. We have something special. We've had it since we were kids, and it's never been about money. We're not going to be broke forever, honey. But we're going to have something special forever. I love you, Jules. Since I was just a boy, I've always loved you—only you."

"This is the talk you give me when I'm upset about being pregnant…"

"Which is just about every time you're pregnant," he laughed. "I'm not a real religious guy, but these kids—they have to be meant to be. They just keep sneaking up on us. And they come out perfect."

"You're a Mormon, aren't you? All along, keeping it from me…"

He covered her mouth in a kiss. "I must be," he said. "Makes me so happy, watching you round out, get big and moody. Please, Jules. Don't be unhappy right now, because it's going to work out. Somehow, it always works out."

"Oh, Billy," she said, putting her hand against his cheek. "I just don't know if I can do it again…"

"You'll start to feel better pretty soon. It's just the first couple of months that are hard on you, then you feel good. And you stop being so *mean*."

She sniffed. "I think I've been a little cranky lately."

He laughed. "Well, no shit, honey," he said. "Now love on me. It doesn't cost anything…"

Cassie had trouble sleeping soundly through the night for a few nights, and then it got worse before it got better. Billy told her he checked high and low, talked to a lot of people about the guy. There was a real Ken Baxter, but he was out in northwest Sacramento and he was fifty. Billy had looked as far as Folsom, a pretty long drive from the Sacramento bar where Cassie and Ken had met, and he hadn't turned up another one. It gave Cassie the cold willies to think he had lied about everything; he made up a name, profession, tricked her into trusting him, all for the purpose of overpowering her.

"The way I see it," Billy said, "the guy played off you and what you said and insinuated himself into your comfort zone. Have a couple of glasses of wine, tell him you're a nurse and several of your friends are firefighters and paramedics, and bingo—he's practically family. If he'd met an aerobics teacher, he'd have made himself the owner of a fitness center."

"Scary," she said. "I wonder how much success he's had with that modus operandi."

That's when she called the police and asked to speak to a detective, preferably a woman who handled rapes.

"Have you been raped, ma'am?"

"No, but I had a close call, and one of the detectives might be interested in what information I have…"

"You can come in and make a report."

"Can I just talk to someone?" she asked impatiently. Then she was connected to voice mail; the voice was male, and she left her name, cell phone number and said the very same thing—setup, close call, barely escaped, she had information. She didn't get a call back. After a few days, she gave up on that. She hadn't found the police real receptive; she wasn't about to beg. She had absolutely no charge to file.

"Here's how I see it," Billy said. "They're busy, you're okay and, under the circumstances, that guy isn't going to show his face around that bar or that part of town again. Since he doesn't know whether you actually talked to the police, gave a description of him and the car and all that, and since he left you with some big bruiser who broke a car window with his fist, he's probably going to make himself real invisible." Then he shook his head and laughed. "With his *fist*. Holy shit, huh? I bet he's just glad the guy didn't kill him."

"Yeah, maybe…"

Her phone didn't ring, no one bothered her—the police apparently weren't interested in close calls—and she began to relax about that. I dodged a bullet, she said to herself. And I'm not going to be in that position again. Then she did settle down; she and Steve curled up and slept soundly.

All Cassie was left with was a need to get beyond it. Not

just the assault, but the position she'd allowed herself to drift into, needing a partner so bad her judgment was impaired. She needed to clear her head. So she wasn't going to date for a while. If anyone offered a fix-up, she'd politely decline. If she ever went to another happy hour—and definitely not at *that* bar—she'd buy her own drinks or leave. For the rest of the summer, at least, she'd enjoy walking Steve along the river, reading and watching movies and tending her little backyard vegetable garden, which produced tomatoes and lettuce, carrots and enough zucchini to sink a battleship. Julie lived for Cassie's summer produce. She would work—she loved her work; it defined her. And she would think. Something was wrong with the way she'd been handling this part of her life.

So maybe her first choice was to be a wife and mother, but her second option was definitely all right—a career that felt completely right, a decent income, friends she trusted who felt like family even if they really weren't and pastimes that relaxed and soothed her. She thought about getting a puppy in a year or two—a backup Weimaraner. She'd probably never get a dog as great as Steve, but she wasn't going to have Steve forever. She shouldn't be without a pet; there was no point in setting herself up to be so alone she could hear her nerves fray.

For now, she would swear off men. At least, she would give up on the notion that there was a special one out there, just waiting for her to find him.

After a couple of weeks, once she felt a little more secure, she went to that motorcycle dealership on her way home from work one day. It turned out to be a Harley Davidson franchise. There were shiny new bikes parked out front on either side of a sidewalk, twinkling in the summer sun. She walked into the pristine showroom. Behind the counter was a guy in a blue shirt, camel-colored sports coat and pink tie, looking for all the world like a used-car salesman. He grinned that car-salesman grin and said, "How can I help you?"

She stared down at the business card in her hand and said, "Um, I wonder if a man named Walt Arneson might be here?"

"Walt? Let me ask in the back." And he turned and left her to browse among the bikes. She found herself running a hand along the chrome of a particularly big one.

"Classic Road King—touring bike," a deep voice said behind her.

She turned and there he was. A great big guy in a T-shirt and denim vest, jeans and boots with chains around the heels. And, of course, all that hair and the naked lady on his arm. And a cast on his right hand, almost up to his elbow.

"Oh, God," she said, her eyes fixed on the hand.

"It's nothing," he said. "Just a little crack." Then he grinned. "It was worth it."

"I'm so sorry," she said.

"Don't be. I wouldn't have it any other way. Seriously. Besides, it comes off in a couple of weeks—it's really nothing."

"Oh, brother," she said, shaking her head. "So. How are you? Besides, um…"

"Good. But how about you?"

"Fine. I'm doing fine. I thought I'd drop by to say thank-you. It occurred to me that after all that went on, I didn't even thank you." She laughed. "I thought about buying you a fruit basket or something, but what do you buy a biker?"

"I don't have the first idea," he said. "How about a cup of coffee? You didn't finish the last one."

"You have time for that?"

"I could sneak away. There's a bookstore across the parking lot. They have a coffee shop. Good coffee."

"You like your coffee."

"I do."

"Only if you let me buy," she said.

"Why not?" He shrugged. "Been a while since a lady bought me a cup of coffee."

He spoke to the salesman for just a second, then walked with her across a wide parking lot to a big bookstore. He let her buy them two coffees while he waited, then instead of sitting down at a small table in the coffee shop, he led her into the store. He seemed to know exactly where he was going. Tucked away in a corner were a couple of plush leather chairs with a small table separating them—a reading or study corner.

"Nice," she said.

He cut right to the chase. "Everything going all right with you now?" he asked, sipping his coffee.

"Yeah, I'm getting by. I'll admit, I was a little tense for a while, but I'm better now. Very grateful you stepped in. I'm very lucky nothing worse happened."

"I take that to mean you haven't heard from him or seen him?"

She shook her head. "Thank God. I guess you were right— he's going to pretend nothing happened. Everything he told me was just a line, a lie."

Walt frowned. "Somehow that wouldn't really surprise me. You know that for sure?"

"Yeah. My friend, the paramedic, checked to see if he was with the fire department and he didn't turn up."

"You really ought to tell the police," Walt said, sitting forward in his chair.

"Well, funny you should say that. I called. I left a message on a detective's voice mail saying it was a close call, I was rescued in time, but I was clearly set up and they might want to know about the situation, the guy. They never called back."

Walt just frowned.

"At this point, I just want to forget about it. I guess it's going to have to be someone else who goes up against him. Or maybe he learned his lesson." She grinned. "You might've put the fear of God in him."

"I hope so. The dirtbag."

"I was putty in his hands—I probably fed him all the information he needed to make up his lines, make his move."

"You mind if I ask, how'd you do that?" Walt said.

"Well, I told him I was a nurse," she said, sipping her coffee. "Emergency room. We do a lot of business with police and paramedics. I don't remember exactly, but I might've told him that before he said he was a paramedic."

"Ah, so that's how that went down," he said. "Makes perfect sense. So, you're an emergency room nurse? That sounds exciting. What made you decide to be a nurse?"

"At first, nursing seemed practical. I had to make a living. I wasn't very far into it when I discovered I really loved E.R. nursing. I found out I like to be where the action is. I'm not very patient." She sipped her coffee. "What makes a person decide to be a biker?"

He grinned at her and she noticed that in the midst of that scruffy face was a very warm, inviting smile. "In my case, a scooter," he said. "I was pretty little. Then a bigger bike, and bigger..."

"You look like a pretty hard-core biker..." She stopped herself and bit her lower lip.

"I do, huh?" he said patiently. "Well, I am, I guess. I'm not a Hells Angel or anything like that."

"Do you belong to a—"

"A bike club?" he asked, leaning back in his chair. "Haven't had time for anything like that in a while. I might go on a group ride now and then, but mostly I'm on my own. I kind of like just taking off—that's the beauty of the bike. When I was a lot younger, I took eighteen months to tour the U.S., with just a bedroll and backpack. I met a lot of riders out on the road. Sometimes we'd hook up and ride together, camp together, for a week or so, then I'd move on. I learned a lot about the machine that way. About the people who are drawn to the machine."

"Eighteen months?" she asked, astonished.

"Yep. It was awesome. There's a lot to check out in this country. You can see a lot more of it from a bike. You like to read?"

"Uh-huh. Girl stuff."

"Well, there's this book—not girl stuff, but it's good—*Zen and the Art of Motorcycle Maintenance*. It tries to explain the feelings bikers have toward their bikes, their freedom, the power of the open road, the whole experience."

She laughed at him. "I know golfers who think it's a spiritual experience to get the ball in the hole, but it's still just a little white ball you hit around with a club."

"Ever been on a bike?" he asked, lifting an eyebrow.

"I hate them. The worst casualties in the E.R. are bikers."

"Yeah," he admitted. "Anyone on a bike who isn't fully conscious, totally safe and has an accident, I don't sympathize with as much as I should. But bikers who get hurt because they're more vulnerable than the vehicle—that's a calculated risk. We understand that. Being on a bike is so great, that's why people take that risk. I mean, there's no metal around us, no air bags. It's not a tank. You have to be sharp, you have to be good. You should have a good machine." He smiled at her. "If you're riding, you better have a good driver." He sipped his coffee. "Ever been on a bike?" he asked again.

She shook her head, her mouth open a little.

"Who knows? Maybe I'll get you on one someday."

"I...ah...doubt it."

"Never say never."

★ ★ ★

It was pretty unusual for Walt to take a coffee break that lasted an hour and a half. It was unheard of for him to take that kind of time away from the store with a pretty woman. They'd had such a nice time, talking about his rides, her nursing. Walt didn't have hobbies outside of bikes and rides—his hours were long and he enjoyed his work so much he never considered cutting back—but they discovered they both liked to read. Walt was drawn to the guy stuff; she went for the girl stuff. Before leaving the bookstore, they did a little browsing—first in his section, then hers. They left with a couple of books apiece—Walt bought her a copy of *Zen and the Art of Motorcycle Maintenance*. They both admitted they'd had a nice time when they said goodbye. He told her any time she'd like to get together for a coffee or whatever, she should give him a call at the store. He'd love to hear from her again. She didn't offer her phone number and, knowing what she'd been through, he didn't dare ask.

After she left, he called his brother Kevin, the youngest in the family. The cop. "You working this afternoon, bud?" he asked.

"Yep. Going in around two. Why?"

"Okay, here's the thing. I had a little incident that I never mentioned…"

"Aw, Christ, you got cops after you for something?"

"No! Could you listen for once? Here's what happened. I was leaving this bar a couple of weeks ago and there was a woman in trouble at the far end of the parking lot. She was yelling for help from the inside of a car that was rocking off the shocks. I could make out two people in the front passenger seat and she was putting up a fight, so I checked it out. I knocked on the window and the guy slid it down an inch and told me to go away, but I could see he had the seat reclined and his hand over her mouth. So I broke the window and got her out."

"You *broke* the window?" Kevin asked. "Is that how you hurt the hand?"

"Yeah… I don't think we need to tell Mom about that, huh?"

"He coming after you for that? For breaking the window?"

"Oh, I wish. Nah, he ran for his life. The woman—nice woman, by the way—was out on her first real date with him. She'd met him for coffee, talked on the phone and she was meeting him at the bar rather than letting him come to her house. You know, trying to be careful, I guess. She was real shook up, so I got her a cup of coffee. I gave her my business card in case she needs me to back up her story. The guy was assaulting her. He was going to rape her, Kevin."

"You sure about that?"

"Nah, maybe he just wanted to hold her down and kiss her a little while she was screaming her brains out and kicking hard enough to rock a big old Tahoe. You're right—he probably just wanted to talk about Greek philosophers and she was just so fucking uncooperative—"

"Okay, okay. What's this got to do with me?"

"I saw her today. She dropped by to say thanks. She's holding up okay. She hasn't heard a word from him or anything. She's getting past it real good."

"Yeah?"

"But I think we should know who he is."

"We? Got a puppy in your pocket, brother?"

"You and me, big shot. I got the license plate number, make and model. See, she's an emergency room nurse and he told her he was a paramedic. It makes sense she should figure him for part of the family, you know? But a friend of hers who really is a paramedic checked and couldn't locate him. Maybe he's just some sick jerk who knows what lines to use to get women to feel safe."

"Oh, I get it. You'd like to have a discussion with him about that?"

"Oh, no, that's not what this is about. I'd like to know who he is, though. For safety reasons. And you—as a cop—might want to check and see if he has a problem in this area. Maybe you look him up and it isn't the first time, huh? Maybe you'll want me to officially report what I saw? Because I saw something real bad. Or maybe you'll want to talk with the woman I helped out, see if she can corroborate that he's just a lying slimeball who…" Walt took a breath. "I know you're not supposed to tell me about his record. But you could check."

"Why didn't your girl call the police that night?"

"Well, that night, she was all shook up and just said no, forget it. But today, when we had coffee, she explained. She did call the police and left a message that she'd had a real close call and had information they might like to have, but no one called her back. See, because she tried telling the police and they ignored her, I decided it's time to get involved, call you."

"Probably because there's no crime, except maybe you breaking the guy's window…"

"We wouldn't have wanted to wait until there was a crime," Walt said a little hotly. Then, more calmly, he added, "She's done a lot of rape exams for police in the emergency room and it turns out that even when the victim is all beat up and hurt real bad, it's still hard to pin it on the guy. This situation never got there. She had a real bad feeling about what he was going to do, but he never even popped a button. I told her about you. I offered to call you at home, man. Get your opinion."

"Doesn't sound like there was that much to it, when you get down to it."

"It was an *assault*," Walt said. "I gotta wonder if it's ever happened to some woman who wasn't lucky enough to have a big, ugly guy leaving the bar just when she was screaming and rocking the car. I just gotta wonder."

Kevin was silent a moment. "I can check that. If so, your girl might come in handy. I can't tell you that, you know. By the book, you know."

"But you can tell me a name. Would you get in trouble for telling me a name?"

"I could, yeah."

"Okay, then it'll be in the vault. No one will ever know you gave me a name. I could find this stuff out some other way, but—"

"Then why not do that, Walt? Find it out some other way?"

"Because, Kevin—if he's attacked women before, it's not me who should know about it. It's the police. Right?"

Kevin sighed. "Right. Yeah."

"But if I want to keep my eyes open for this guy, be ready in case he gives her more trouble—ready to call you, of course—a name would help. I give you this story, you give me a name. That's all."

"And you swear to me, you never approach this guy? Never touch him?"

"Absolutely, I swear. No approaching, no touching."

"All right, give me the data."

Walt smiled into the phone. "So, I'm a confidential informant. A C.I. Cool."

Walt recited the plate, make and model.

"You get a good look at him, Walt?"

"Oh, yeah. I saw him in the bar, saw him leave with her. I can identify him. Six feet, brown and brown, chiseled chin… His hair is long enough to comb. You know what I'm saying? Not a butch military cut, and not over the collar. Styled."

"Okay, good. I think we don't tell the woman," Kevin

said. "I might ask you for her name and phone number later, all right?"

"I don't have that offhand. I don't even know her last name. I know her first name and that she's an emergency room nurse, so you could probably find her easy. I don't know that I'll ever see her again," Walt said. "But I gave her my card, my office and home numbers in case she needs me for anything, and she's nice. You can tell in one minute she's kind. That she only wants to help people. And this asshole was going to hurt her. That's not something you just let go."

Kevin laughed into the phone. "Really, who would take you for a Good Samaritan."

"That's the thing. People never know who they're dealing with, do they? This woman? She'd never go out with someone who looks like me, but the guy she thought was safe as a kitten, he turned out to be the bad guy."

The fourth member of the tight group of girlfriends, and the least often available, was Dr. Beth Halsley. Beth started in premed at USC and stayed there for medical school, becoming a women's doctor. She had always been one of those students who didn't have to work for grades and excelled effortlessly on tests—until med school, at least. She had a nerdy brain inside a model's body.

She had been more beautiful than any of the other high school girls, but not as popular—people thought of her as stuck-up. She wasn't. She always had a lot on her mind and she was easily bored. True, she was a cheerleader like Julie, Cassie and Marty, but she was also a scholar, debater, gymnast, chess champion and president of the science club. She had almost never gone out on a date; it wasn't long before boys avoided her like the plague. She was just too intimidating. And she'd never learned those wily, flirty games.

But the girls—Cassie, Julie and Marty—though nothing like her, loved her, understood her, envied her in so many ways. Beth was the one to unequivocally make good and when she graduated from premed and medical school in L.A., they were there, cheering the loudest of all. And now that she was newly transplanted back in the Sacramento Valley in a small women's clinic, they were bringing their privates to her for their exams and other medical needs.

Beth called Julie in the morning. "Hey, don't faint, but I can get out of the clinic for a couple of hours today. I got in touch with Cassie and Marty and they're free for lunch. Noon at Ernesto's. How about you?"

"Hmm. Lotta mommy stuff going on today, but I'll see what I can do," Julie said.

"Well, try," Beth said. "I miss the heck out of you. I haven't seen you in a couple of months!"

Julie couldn't bear the thought of missing lunch with the girls. But she couldn't *afford* it. And the morning had been stressful. Right after a bout of morning sickness, Julie spent a couple of hours going over the bills, trying to decide which one to pay, which one to let slide. She'd barely recovered from her early-morning nausea when the dog, Tess, threw up right on her shoes. *In* her shoes. Armed with paper towels she usually tried to ration, she began mopping. As she was on her hands and knees scooping and wiping, Tess licked her face, knocking her back on her butt, disgusted, with an *"Ewwww."* She had to hose out her shoes on the back patio, which made her cry. If she'd had two nickels to rub together, she would have thrown the damn shoes in the trash.

When she had the kids all loaded in the car to take Jeffy to a Parks and Rec summer program, the engine wouldn't start. It wouldn't even turn over. She got her mom to drive over, give her a jump and, thank God, that did it. On to Jeffy's program to drop him off, then to the auto supply to buy a new battery. She had to try three credit cards for one to be approved. It was looking like both those bills she was sitting on would have to slide. Then she dropped Clint and Stephie off at their grandma's for a couple of hours so Julie could join her friends for lunch. She had already decided she would make an excuse, say she had already eaten, but wanted to meet them for at least a glass of iced tea. When she got back to the car, reaching into her purse for her keys, she noticed that her mom had tucked a twenty into her purse.

And she cried. Again.

"It's just pregnancy," she muttered to herself, wiping at her eyes. But it was also the anxiety of having no money, worrying about the shame of having the electricity shut off, having her mom always slip a twenty into her purse because she was so pitifully broke.

Julie had just one older brother—Brad. Brad went to college, met a girl and got engaged, married fourteen months later after he was settled in a nice, cushy CPA job. Then and only then he went to work on an MBA to make his job even cushier. After that he and his wife decided to start their family and, like many of their friends, they seemed to have a choice about that. When they used birth control they didn't have children and they never had a slip; when they went off birth control, they reproduced. At thirty-two, Brad and his wife, Lisa, had a three-year-old boy, a one-year-old girl and a vasectomy.

Such was not the case with Julie and Billy. She'd been a few months pregnant already when they married at barely nineteen. Billy worked part-time and went to school part-time, earning his degree at twenty-four, when Jeffy was four years old. If they'd had it their way, Jeffy would be at least ten before they had another baby; they were still so young, completely strapped with school loans, credit-card bills and low-paying jobs. They were compulsive about protection, except one night when they didn't use a condom and spermicide because they were so worked up, in a fever, wild. One time, just one time, and it hadn't even been during a vulnerable time of the month. Hello, Clint! Clint arrived when Jeffy was barely in kindergarten, the first year Billy was with the fire department. The next year, Stephie—the result of a diaphragm that Beth said probably wasn't a good fit.

Billy knew the value of an education and had pursued it while waiting for an opening in the fire department. He'd wanted to be a fireman since he was six; it was a childhood dream. It was also a good job with good benefits and a pension, but when you have three kids, lots of bills, a stay-at-home wife, the early years can be tight. If he had any real fascination with any other field, there were probably endless opportunities for a man with a degree, but in his job he had adventure and saved lives, and that meant more to him than anything.

Although Julie's parents were both generous and patient, Julie felt she'd let them down by marrying so young, having three children before she was thirty. She could sense they were frustrated with Julie and Billy's chronic trouble of keeping up with expenses. It was taking them a damn long time to get on their feet. Her parents slipped her money they didn't have to give Brad, picked up the tab for things like Jeffy's soccer or Parks and Rec programs, and Julie never told Billy about any of it. Any fancy toys the kids had, like the laptop or video games, came from Grandma and Grandpa or maybe Uncle Brad. The thought of telling her mother she was pregnant again chilled her. She would say, What about that vasectomy you'd planned on? What about it, indeed? Billy was supposed to take care of that and had simply put it off, a little nervous about having his testicles sliced into, as if oblivious to the complications of piling child upon child on a modest income. She had the IUD; they should have been safe for the time it took him to come to terms with it. But she was pregnant again, anyway.

Julie complained to Cassie about money, about stretching things so far month after month, but she could tell Cassie didn't take it all that seriously. After all, they somehow always managed and Cassie would die to have her problems. To Cassie, who was getting by but alone, a tight budget seemed like less of a problem than not having a partner, a family. And Julie just couldn't tell Marty, who seemed to have it made.

But Julie went to lunch even though she could've put that twenty in the gas tank, because sometimes she just needed to be with her friends. She was the last one to arrive and the girls greeted her as though they hadn't seen her in a year, though she'd seen Cassie and Marty recently.

"Wine?" Cassie asked as Julie sat down.

"No, thanks," Julie said. "Carpool." Of course, there was no carpool. "Beth? You're not having a glass of wine?"

"On call," she said, smiling. "Again. But I'm covered for lunch."

"Is that how you keep your figure? Being on call?" Julie asked.

And then all four of them ordered salads, even Julie.

"I weigh the same, but they're working me to death," Beth said. "I'm delivering all the middle-of-the-night babies. The joys of being the new guy."

"Speaking of new guys…any in your life?" Cassie asked, because this was Cassie's main interest. And one of the only things that perplexed her was how a woman as accomplished and beautiful as Beth remained completely unattached. True, Beth was hard to please, a perfectionist. But still, with that in mind, she figured Beth would have landed the perfect man by now.

"You're kidding, right?" she said, sipping her tea. "I went out with an anal, boring internist a couple of times, but I'd rather have been reading a good novel. He almost put me to sleep."

"I guess he's not getting an encore," Marty said.

"Absolutely not. Honestly, I work, then I go home and sleep until the phone rings..."

"How are you liking the new clinic?" Cassie asked.

"I'm going to like it a lot better when I'm not the new guy anymore, but it's a great little shop. Good staff. A lot of fresh-faced young pregnant girls as well as some older pregnant women—one of our docs has a real nice fertility practice." Then to Cassie she said, "How about you? Any new guys?"

Cassie and Julie exchanged quick glances. Cassie hadn't mentioned her incident to the others and, really, she just didn't want to go through all that again, even in the telling. "I've sworn off men," she said. "I draw only jerks and assholes."

Beth just laughed. "The right one will probably turn up when you least expect him."

"So everyone says. I don't think I care that much about the man, but it's going to be damn hard to have children without one."

"You don't need a man to have a baby, Cassie," Beth said.

"Gee, I know I didn't get the best grades in school, but according to my biology teacher, that's one of the things you absolutely *do* need," Julie said.

"What you need is sperm," Beth said. And with a dismissive wave of her hand, she said, "Easy."

"Holy smokes," Julie said.

"Good idea," Marty said. "Marriage is *way* overrated."

Julie's gaze shot from Beth to Marty, but Cassie was focused on Beth. "Would you do something like that? Have a baby without a husband?"

"I'm not in the market for a baby," Beth said. "I have a feeling I'll be better at delivering them than having them. But really, half the female doctors I know are married to doctors. They're both under pressure, working long hours, and they do fine. It kind of looks like a good nanny is more valuable than a good husband."

"What do you mean, marriage is way overrated?" Julie asked Marty. And then she reached for Cassie's glass of wine, but before taking a gulp, she slid it back.

With precision timing, the salads arrived, along with a basket of warm, fresh bread.

Julie wasn't done with Marty. "What do you mean?" she asked. "I thought you and Joe invented marriage! You're not having trouble or anything, are you?"

Marty tore off a piece of bread and with a shrug said, "We're fine. I guess. But I ask myself—is this it? Forever? This guy who lives like a slob and doesn't want to do any of the things he liked to do before we were married? He used to take me out, you know. Movies, dinner, nice things. Now it's sports or boating or camping. On his days off, he doesn't bother to shower till he has to go back to work. I come home from work and it looks like some homeless guy broke into the house and tore the place up. And once he slipped the ring on, that was it for romance. Now foreplay at our house is, 'You awake?'"

Julie actually sprayed a mouthful of iced tea as she burst into laughter. When she came under control, fanning her face, grinning, she said, "I can answer that question. Is this all there is? Yeah—this is it, girlfriend. And I signed up."

"See, there's a reason some women decide to just have the family on their own," Beth said, lifting a forkful of lettuce to her mouth.

But Julie was more fascinated by Marty than Beth. "Marty,

I've never heard you talk like this. I thought you were crazy about Joe."

"Sure," she said, chewing a mouthful of salad. "I am. Joe's a great guy, a good father, a dependable man in his own way—and God knows the women he's carried down the ladder out of a burning building are in love with him forever—but around home he's a bum. He's got sweats and gym shorts he hides so they won't get washed until they're so ripe they could walk to the laundry room. His whole closet stinks." *They have two closets,* Julie thought jealously. "He spit shines the boat, but he can't shave the bristle off his chin before he rolls over onto me. The yard has to be perfect, which by the way is sweaty, smelly work, and that vagrant-esque odor sticks to him—at the dinner table and when we go to bed at night. And believe me, he is limited to the yard, garage and the sporting equipment in his ability to clean things."

"I've *never* seen Joe looking like a vagrant," Cassie said.

"You would if you were married to him. He cleans up for company," Marty said. "Really, what he gives F.D. is perfect. If we're having people over, he's all spiffed up. But when it comes to his wife, his marriage—he takes it totally for granted. He doesn't even *try*."

"Marty, you should tell him," Julie said.

"You think I haven't told him? I've begged him!" Marty insisted. "He doesn't care. He thinks it's funny. He tells me to *relax*. Don't you get sick of Billy sometimes?" Marty asked Julie.

"Uh, yeah. But not for the same reasons…"

"Well, what reasons?"

He's too fertile. I'm too fertile with him. He's *too* romantic, like we're still in high school, doing it in the backseat of a car, like two kids who can't help it, can't stop it from happening. He's disgustingly optimistic, like the world we live in doesn't even exist—the world of too many bills, too little pay. She'd give anything if Billy worked only for F.D. and actually had days off to help around the house, help with the kids. But she said, "Well, some of the same reasons, but…"

"But?"

She shrugged. "That stuff doesn't get to me so much." Because I have *real* problems, she thought, feeling angry and envious. A house that's too small with a mortgage too big, cars that are too old, out of control bills… "Okay, some of that stuff gets to me. But, Marty, it looks like you and Joe have a pretty good life."

"Because we have a *boat?*" she asked. "Jules, I didn't want a *boat*. And I'd rather die than spend another week in that RV! I'd give anything for a vacation somewhere cool, just me and Joe. Like Hawaii or the Bahamas or something. I'd like to watch a movie that doesn't involve fifty-seven people getting shot or out-of-control farts. I'd like to go out to dinner. Or to Las Vegas—to spend the night in a classy hotel, have a day at the spa, then lie by the pool—but Joe says, 'Why go to Vegas to get a tan when we have a boat?' Could it be because it's up to me to shop, prepare food, fix everyone's meals and then clean up everything when we bring the boat in? That's not fun—it's just more work!" Marty lifted some of her salad to her mouth, chewed and said, "You're lucky. Billy still treats you as if he'd like you to marry him."

Hmm, Julie thought. Why don't I feel so lucky? Could it be because you can't live on just love?

3

Julie stopped off in the ladies' room after lunch before leaving the restaurant. Right before she scrolled off some toilet paper, she prayed, Oh, God, let there be *blood!* But alas, it was what she knew it would be. She flushed and exited the stall. She met eyes in the mirror with Chelsea.

"Well," Chelsea said, beaming. "We just keep crossing paths."

They gave each other little cheek presses. "What are you doing here?" Julie asked.

"Lunch after a sales meeting," she said. "Our dealership is just a few blocks away."

"That's right—you're selling cars now," Julie said.

"Well," Chelsea said, laughing indulgently, "Hummers. And I'm a sales manager. My dealership won a couple of awards recently."

Julie noticed that Chelsea wore a very attractive suit and her shoes were to die for. Julie no longer knew anything about brands—she'd been picking up her duds at Target when she had money to spare—but she knew they were *tres* expensive. Julie wore a sundress and sandals, each about three years old, the same thing she might wear for a trip to the grocery store. She felt as if she'd been thrown together out of a thrift shop. "Aren't they kind of hard to sell these days? Hummers?"

"Nah," Chelsea said, shaking her head dismissively. "Even in a down economy, we move a lot of them. People just love them. They think of it as a symbol of affluence—the bigger the better."

"With gas prices so high?" Julie asked, noting all the little extras about Chelsea—manicured nails, shaped and waxed brows, highlighted curls, rich-looking makeup that appeared almost professional.

"I don't think our sales have even dropped. What are you doing here today?"

"Lunch with the girls," she said with a shrug. "It isn't very often we can drag Beth out."

"Oh. Sure. You're looking very smart today," Chelsea said. "Cool and comfortable and pretty."

Julie immediately felt as if Chelsea was throwing her a bone. She said, "Thanks, that's nice of you to say. I just grabbed this at Costco." Then she thought, Why did I have to say that? Chelsea's purse was worth Julie's weekly household allowance. "Why did you leave that company you worked for before? Insurance, wasn't it?"

"Health care," she said, lifting a brow. "It was quite a while ago, actually. I'm just following the money, Jules. Health care is good, but there are a lot of business degrees in there humping for management. This is better."

"Wasn't it a hard transition? They don't seem to have much in common…"

"On the surface, maybe. In the end, business is business.

When I thought I needed a change, I started working weekends at the dealership, and when I'd made enough money to see the potential, I quit Health South and went full-time. Do you have any idea what the commission is on a Hummer? But what I'm really interested in is upper management, eventually a dealership."

"A Hummer dealership? At twenty-nine?"

"It's not going to happen next week," Chelsea said with a laugh. "Listen, one of these times when you girls get together for lunch, give me a call, huh?"

"Sure," Julie said, thinking, Never gonna happen. "Today was pretty last-minute. I don't think it was even planned till ten this morning…"

"I'm flexible," she said. "I have to run. The owner is waiting."

"Sure, go ahead," Julie said, busying herself at the sink. "Take it easy." She washed her hands while the door closed behind Chelsea. All that kiss-kiss-call-me bullshit, she thought. They'd stopped fighting like cats in a sack the year after graduation, but little else had changed. Chelsea had been a cheerleader, too. She'd managed to stay friendly with Marty, but Chelsea had dated Billy during one of his rare and brief breakups with Julie, which had lost her any chance of being friends with Julie. Because of that, Cassie wrote her off. Beth had never cared about all that drama. And to this day Chelsea's eyes lit up when she saw Billy. It made Julie furious.

But there was no question that Chelsea had made good. She, like Billy, had a degree in education. If it weren't for the fact that Chelsea had gone to college full-time while Billy picked up night classes whenever he could, Julie would suspect her of following him into that major. Billy had gravitated toward industrial arts while Chelsea was elementary education. Neither of them had ever worked as teachers.

Like her or not, what Chelsea said got Julie thinking. Why wasn't Billy doing something like that? Finding a field he could work in part-time, looking for a better opportunity, instead of cutting wood and countertops for extra money? Why wasn't Billy following the money?

When she left the restaurant, she saw Beth and Cassie standing by Beth's car, talking, probably saying goodbye. She gave them a wave and got in her car. She slipped the key in and thought, If it doesn't start, I'll sue those people at the auto supply. But it started. She glanced at the odometer—a hundred and four thousand miles and change.

After lunch with the girls, Cassie cornered Beth at her car for a minute. "Are you serious about that? Having a baby without a husband?"

"If I wanted a baby and didn't have a husband on the agenda, I would do it," Beth said. "I don't know why everything you want out of life has to be put on hold because the right man hasn't turned up."

"Huh. That never occurred to me," Cassie said. "But, Beth, you had a real serious guy back in med school. Couple of years—you lived together…"

"Believe me, I'd rather have a child without a husband than go through something like that again. That ended so badly. A lot of hard feelings. Makes me pretty suspicious of relationships…"

"Yeah, that was horrible," Cassie said. "Well, I know people do it all the time—have children even though they're single. But it seems like they're always celebrities or millionaires, not ordinary people. Not working women."

Beth smiled. "Those celebrities—they probably work harder than you and I."

"Maybe I should think about that. I want a family, but I always thought…"

"Listen, Cassie, you and I might be coming at the subject from different perspectives. I'm not sure I'm even interested in having a husband. I'm so rigid, so set in my ways. So completely selfish. A problem like Marty has with Joe might seem small, but it would seriously make me want to kill him. But with you—isn't it really a husband you want most? Even more than a baby?"

"When you get right down to it," she admitted. "But come on—I'm almost thirty. And I'm so sick of going out with losers. I never even considered alternatives."

"You have to think out of the box," Beth said. "So…you think Marty and Joe are all right? Is that just wifey bitching?"

"I have no idea. Really, I thought they were fine."

"They don't seem too fine. And what about Jules? Something's going on with her. She acts like everything is okay, but something's wrong there."

"Yeah, they're going through some stuff. Money's tight—Billy's working two jobs to make ends meet and is hardly ever home. Julie's tired—the kids are wearing her out. But this is Jules and Billy. They argue, but they get it together. It's not like Marty and Joe—it's not about a boat."

Beth laughed. "See the problem with marriage? People get all upside down about a boat?"

"Sounds like there's more to it than that. No compromise. That would get anyone upside down."

"See?" Beth said. "I'm not a good candidate for marriage. I'm the one who wouldn't be able to compromise—I like things the way I like things."

And I'd do anything, Cassie thought. Really, *anything*. But that opportunity hadn't even presented itself. "So, you don't think it would be crazy?" she asked. "To have a baby?"

"Nah, I don't think it's crazy," she answered easily. "Actually, I think it's intelligent. What's crazy is marrying the wrong person because you want a family. If I wanted a child but didn't have a partner, I'd definitely consider it. But that's a far-fetched thought for me..."

"How much time do you think you have? I mean, how much time do *we* have?"

"Six or seven years, realistically. Longer under the right circumstances. We're getting women through healthy pregnancies older and older. Right now I'm too consumed to even think about things like partners, babies, and that's the truth. I don't know what I'd do with a boyfriend if I had one. Run out on him every time the phone rang, probably. Listen, I don't have any advice—I think that one very bad boyfriend might be it for my love life. I've always been too busy. I can't pay attention to a man for long, which is probably the real reason that last one ended so badly. My mind wanders. I'm always thinking about other things. I'm self-centered. And if I found a guy like me? We'd be like strangers in the same house—totally preoccupied with our own agendas. I might be better off never running into a guy I could tolerate. That's why I can't have a child without a nanny—I'm probably not capable of being completely responsible for a child."

"Aw, that can't be true..."

"It can be. Look at my parents. They were just brilliant nutcases—a couple of smart people who didn't care about much outside of their work. Other than my education, they didn't have a clue what was happening in my life. You could talk to either one of them for fifteen straight minutes and they might not hear a word. It's a DNA thing—it's in me, too. That's why everyone thinks I'm weird."

Cassie smiled at her. "Well, I don't. I think you're amazing. And your patients love you."

"I'm so lucky that way," she said appreciatively. "I think I accidentally became a good doctor. It's a miracle. And believe me, I don't take it for granted. I love my work so much." She smiled wistfully. "Honestly, I live for it. It's all that matters."

Cassie had always envied Beth's brains and success, even though what she really wanted was what Julie had. Beth had always seemed so sure of everything she aimed for in life. When they were younger she'd never been the least bit insecure about not being popular, not having a boyfriend. Even major setbacks—and Beth had been through some heavy stuff—barely seemed to slow her down. She marched on, following her instincts, doing what she was born to do.

Beth's parents were oddballs—a couple of middle-class eggheads. Her mother was a librarian at the college and her father was a professor—helminthology. The study of worms. Beth grew up in a messy house cluttered with papers, bulging bookshelves and microscopes, dishes stacked in the sink, beds unmade, dirty clothes piled high, her parents completely distracted by their intellectual obsessions. They never had a lot of money to throw around, nor did they pay much attention to their daughter, but they had real high educational standards and had raised themselves a young genius who proved she could be the best of both of them. Beth had been in gifted programs since she was six.

But Julie... Julie had Billy, who had adored her for thirteen years. He still looked at her as if she was the only woman alive. They might have to pinch their pennies most of the time, but their relationship was solid, unshakable. Jules might not be able to count on being able to pay the bills, but she could always count on Billy loving her, being there for her. And if they ran into a big problem, they never failed to tackle it together.

Given a choice, Cassie would take the kids, money troubles and true love, which she figured must make her a *fool*. A rational look at the world around her indicated an M.D. was more practical and reliable than a Mr. and Mrs.

Driving home from lunch, she found herself passing that motorcycle dealership. She let herself go three more blocks before making a U-turn and going back. She went into the showroom and faced the same grinning salesman. "Hi," she said. "I wonder if Walt Arneson is working today?"

"One second." He smiled. He went down the counter to a phone, dialed, spoke into it briefly and said, "Miss?" He held the receiver toward her.

"Hello?" she said into the phone. "Walt?"

"Hi," he said. "How are you?"

"Good. I was on my way home and passed the dealership and thought…maybe you'd like me to buy you a cup of coffee?"

"Are you in a big hurry?"

"Well…no, I guess not. Why?"

"I'm at another store, but if you want to wait a few minutes—like, twenty—I'll be right there."

"Oh, listen. I don't want you to go to any—"

"Cassie, I love having coffee with you. It's not any trouble, believe me."

"Are you sure?"

"You made my day. Go to the bookstore, get us a couple of coffees, settle into our spot if it's free and I'll see you in twenty."

"Okay, if you're sure."

"I'm sure. Walk slowly." And he hung up.

This is loony, she found herself thinking. What in the world do I hope to gain by a dumb-ass move like this? "You called him at another store?" she asked the salesman.

"Sure. That's where he was. He's on the move a lot."

"Oh. Well, thanks." Then she headed for the bookstore, slowly. She browsed a little before buying the coffees, settling into the corner that had become theirs.

Thirty minutes later, she knew what she hoped to gain. She was laughing with him as she told him about lunch with her girlfriends, about Marty complaining about her husband, about Beth suggesting it was perfectly logical to have a baby without one. She told him all about Steve and her plans to get a puppy in a couple of years to keep him company. He told her about the ride he took up to Tahoe over the weekend—just a quick one, a few hours in the morning. When he described the views, the lake, the mountains in full summer green, she began to get a sense for why he found this enjoyable. It was odd that this grease monkey had such an appreciation for the outdoors.

"Seems like if you're so fond of nature, you'd hunt or fish or camp."

"I camp," he said, sipping his coffee. "Sort of. If I have time for a weekend ride, I take a bedroll and backpack, find a nice piece of beach under the stars or a soft pad of grass on a hilltop and...camp. I don't think I'm patient enough to fish and I could never shoot anything."

"How about golf?" she asked teasingly.

"You're kidding me, right?" He laughed hard at that. Imagine this guy in his boots and chains and naked lady swinging around a golf club with the Polo-clad crowd.

They learned a little more about each other. Neither of them had ever been married; they both came from families of four children, though hers were half sibs. His family was local, hers was in Des Moines. And they'd both worked at their current jobs for more than five years.

At one point he asked her if she was still feeling nervous about her incident and she told him she was slowly getting past that, but she'd decided to be a lot more cautious. She didn't want to find herself in that position ever again. "I'm all done dating," she said. "At least for a good long time. I think I've been through enough."

"Understandable."

"That really shouldn't have happened. I usually have much better instincts than that."

"It doesn't seem like you did anything wrong, Cassie. He's a freak, that's all."

After an hour or so of coffee, they browsed together, helping each other pick out books. In the parking lot he said, "You know, I like these coffee dates. It's a real nice break in the day."

"I enjoyed it, too."

"I know it's only been twice, but I'm already looking forward to the next one."

"Even if you have to drive across town?"

"Even if," he said. Then he pulled a short stack of business cards out of his pocket, sifted through them and handed her one. All it said was his name and a phone number. "If you call that cell number when you feel like coffee, I won't keep you waiting so long. I don't give it out that often—I get too many calls from bikers with mechanical problems when I do. They like me to walk them through home repairs. But I'd like you to have it."

"Gee," she said. "You have that kind of schedule, that a person can just interrupt you in the middle of work and it's okay?"

"I put in a lot of hours. No one minds when I take a little personal time. You call—I'll come," he said.

"You know… I haven't offered you my phone number, and there's a reason—"

He put a big hand gently on her forearm. "Oh, I'd love to have your number, Cassie. But I know it's important you be in charge right now. You call me anytime. I'll be there."

"Thanks. That's nice. That you understand."

"Hey. I was there, remember?"

Billy's part-time job in addition to the fire department was in construction. He could've made it his full-time job and maybe make more money than he currently did at F.D., but it didn't have the same potential for growth. It offered good money for flexible hours that he could fit around his F.D. schedule. The contractor let him work a few hours here and there while he was doing his twenty-four-hour shifts with the department and full days on his off time. He could get in at least twelve full days a month, usually more like sixteen. Cutting wood and stone for countertops was often tedious, but he did it perfectly and it paid well.

And it was damn hard work. Both his jobs were physically demanding. Although he was a paramedic, he didn't drive the rescue rig every day—he was a firefighter first. So about every other workday, he worked the rescue rig and other times he was on the engine. Then he'd cut wood and rock—exhausting, dirty work. He had about enough time to eat, sleep and go back to one job or another. But he and Jules needed the money. He hadn't called in sick to either job since the day he started. He didn't average a day off a week. If he could just stay with F.D. eight to ten years and promote himself on time, the money and overtime would get real good. Right now he was keeping his finger in the dam.

Today he had come home from his twenty-four-hour shift at F.D. and gone to bed for a few hours, despite the noise in the house. He knew Jules was going to lunch with her girl-friends, which was a good thing—it could put her in a decent mood. A little break from the kids, some girl talk, maybe she could get in some serious complaining about Billy and un-load it. So he woke himself up after about four hours of sleep and went straight to his mother-in-law's to pick up Clint and Stephie before their nap time. They'd already had lunch, so they were ready to settle in when he got them home.

Ordinarily, he'd take advantage of the quiet and try to catch a nap; he hadn't had much sleep and was planning to go back to the shop after dinner and hopefully work till midnight. But instead, he went after some marital points; he cleaned the kitchen, picked up dog-doo, trimmed the hedges and put the ladder up against the house to see if he could fix the drooping gutter that was breaking away because *someone* hadn't cleaned it out in the late fall and it had been too burdened with leaves and twigs to stay attached. That someone was him.

He put his toolbox on the slanted roof to his right and was going after the gutter with a screwdriver, leaning a little to the left, when the toolbox began to slide. He dropped the screwdriver in the gutter and grabbed for the toolbox, which he shoved back up on the roof. But the sudden action caused the ladder to sway and teeter and he couldn't get the toolbox stable. He grabbed the gutter for ballast, but it was a poor choice—the gutter was already weak and breaking away from the eave. His feet pushed the ladder away and it fell to his right. Billy hung on to the gutter but not for long. It gave under his weight and tore away, but at least his descent was slower. After dropping a few feet, he let go so he wouldn't tear the whole damn thing off, and fell the rest of the way. It wasn't all that far.

The ladder crashed to the ground with a loud clatter and he hit the ground right after it. He landed on his feet first, then fell back on his ass. He let himself roll back on the grass and lay there for a second, thinking, First, that was so stupid, and second, what I do *not* need right now is an injury. He didn't move, assessing his hips and spine. He let his eyes briefly close and thought, There is no one better with a ladder than me; that was idiotic.

"Billy!" He heard Julie yell from inside the house. He could hear the tempo change as she yelled while running from the kitchen to the back patio doors. "Billy! Billy! Oh, God, Billy!"

He lay there, a very slight smile on his lips, thinking this was probably mean, keeping his eyes closed. She knelt beside him, lifted his head in her arms and said, "Billy! Are you dead?"

He opened his eyes. "You should never do that. Move a person like that. I could've had a spinal injury."

"Are you all right?"

"Do you love me?" he asked.

"What *happened?*" she asked, her eyes wide and fearful.

"I fell off the ladder. I was lying here wondering if anything was hurt. I didn't know you were home. Do you love me?"

"You're an asshole," she said, dropping his head with a thump.

There was a sound, a sliding sound. Billy grabbed her and rolled to the left, putting himself on top of her, covering her to protect her. The toolbox clattered to the ground about six feet away, a couple of tools bouncing out. When the crashing subsided, he lifted his head. "That's two stupid things in one day," he said. "I think I'm too tired to be doing this stuff."

"Let me up," she said.

"No. First you have to tell me if you love me."

"No, I hate you! You took ten years off my life!"

He pressed his lips against hers. She didn't respond, so he lifted his head and grinned into her eyes. "I cleaned the kitchen," he said. "I put Clint and Stephie down for a nap. I picked up dog shit and trimmed the hedges."

"And fell off the ladder."

"That's right. And I'm not getting back on it today. Did you have a nice lunch?"

"Uh-huh."

"Did you get to dump on the girls about your little condition? About your bad, bad husband?"

"I haven't said a word to anyone. And don't you, either."

"Okay. Then can you help me into the bedroom?"

"You're hurt?"

"I'm horny. You could lie naked beside me for a little while, then after I've put you in a good mood, I can have a little nap."

"Is that all you ever think about?"

"When I'm on top of you like this, that's all I think about. I'll be very, very sweet to you. Very careful. Well, not too careful."

"This is the root of all our problems," she said. "Right now all I want to do is clobber you, and you still get to me."

He grinned handsomely. "If that's the biggest problem you have, Jules, you have it pretty good."

"I'm not so sure about that," she said.

"You feeling okay, baby?" he asked sweetly, gently brushing her blond hair over her ear. "You're not feeling sick or crampy or anything, are you?"

She shook her head.

"I worry a little bit about that IUD, in there with the baby." His brow furrowed. "If you don't think it's okay…"

"I still want to clobber you," she said, shaking her head.

He just smiled. "I know." He got off her and pulled her to her feet. "Come on. Let's take advantage of nap time."

A little while later, feeling calmer and more affectionate, Julie said, "I ran into Chelsea in the ladies' room at the restaurant today."

"Yeah?" he responded with a yawn. "You didn't hurt her, did you?"

"I talked to her for a while. Did you know she left that insurance company to sell Hummers? And that she's a sales manager now?"

"So she said," he replied, bored or sleepy.

"So... I don't like Chelsea, but what she did makes sense. Before making a change, she worked for that dealership on weekends for a while until she could see the potential, then she quit her old job. Good idea, huh?"

"Hummers," he snorted, rubbing his head back and forth on the pillow tiredly. "No one wants a Hummer right now..."

"Chelsea says they're selling as well as ever. People like them. It makes them feel rich."

"Not for long," he said, his eyes still closed.

"But that's not the point, the point is it's very smart to find a business opportunity and work at it part-time to see if there's any real possibility there, and then make a move. There's absolutely no future in cutting countertops—it's just part-time work and the pay is good, but never gets better. Right now you have all your eggs in one basket, but you're so smart. You have a degree. You could check around, see if there's a place to go where you can really put your education to use, be successful..."

"Hmm," he said. And then she heard him softly snore. She leaned over and put a gentle kiss on his cheek. "What if you fell off a ladder at work?" she whispered. "What would we do?" She was answered by a light snore.

When she had looked out the kitchen window and seen the ladder on the ground and Billy beside it, motionless, eyes closed, her very first thought was, Oh, no! Not my Billy! No! No! Soon after that came relief. Then what quickly followed was that old fear. Firefighting, paramedic work, cutting granite—none of this was low risk. If something happened to him, their strapped lifestyle would become catastrophic. Julie and

the kids and no income, and after the insurance and small frac-
tion of pension ran out...she would lose the house. Her mother
would be forced to look after the kids so she could work, just
to keep her from sinking out of sight. And what work could
she do? She'd done a little waitressing and secretarial work
after Jeffy while Billy was working and going to school, before the next two kids—and neither job had paid a damn.

And now there would be *four* children?

Billy didn't have accidents like that; he was too sharp. His
reflexes were good; he was strong. But he was also tired from
working all the time. How tired would he be with a new baby
crying to be fed every two hours for weeks? How could he be
so blissfully happy about another baby when it put the future
of the entire family at risk?

She heard Stephie wake up with a cry and a cough and
it changed her entire thought process. Oh, no, please don't
get sick! she thought. She went instantly to the bedroom the
two younger kids shared and scooped her up, took her to the
kitchen and quickly dosed her with decongestant and Tylenol, praying off a fever or cold. Then she spent the rest of the
afternoon and early evening tending to food, picking up Jeffy
and taking him to soccer practice—she had to stop off with
three kids in tow to pick up Gatorade for the team because
it was her turn—throwing together meals, tending a crying,
miserable, sick kid, cleaning up vomit, tossing in laundry,
picking up toys and clothes. When Billy finally roused from
his nap at about six, at least a couple hours later than usual,
which magnified how tired he'd been, she was sitting in the
kids' bathroom with Stephie on her lap, the bathroom filled
with steam to loosen up her congestion.

"What's going on?" he asked sleepily.

"Stephie's got something. She threw up three times, couldn't
keep supper down and she's hacking like the croup."

"Fever?" he asked, running a hand along the back of his neck, trying to get his bearings.

"I'm keeping it down with Tylenol. But she's sick."

He reached for Stephie and she went to him, whimpering, "Daddy," like a sick little pumpkin. "Clint?" he asked.

"So far, so good."

"Okay, take a break. I'll do steam room duty," he said.

She left him sitting on the closed toilet seat, holding his daughter against him, knowing he hadn't had enough rest and would still try to get in some hours at the shop no matter how late he started. He had to be at the fire department first thing in the morning for his twenty-four-hour shift. She couldn't let him do night duty with the kids—it would be on her so he could be rested and safe. But she was so *tired*. Early pregnancy made her want to sleep around the clock, but she couldn't.

And she thought, I can't go on like this. I just can't.

After lunch with the girls, Marty did a little shopping before going home. Joe was with three-year-old Jason; there was no reason to hurry. She tried on clothes, found a couple of nice things on sale and bought them, though she'd have nowhere to wear them. All she really needed in her wardrobe these days were clothes for work and clothes for the lake. But she fell in love with a pair of crepey pants that were snug around the hips and butt, flowing at the hem. Then there was this low-cut top that showed off her cleavage and fit so nice—the perfect ensemble to go out for an evening, maybe dinner, maybe dancing. And she couldn't resist a fitted dress with a slit up the side that showed off her figure; it was lavender and really drew attention to the light brown of her soft, shoulder-length curls.

Joe didn't like to dance. For evenings out he liked to get together with the gang from F.D., usually at a sports bar. Vacations were taking the RV up to Tahoe, pulling the boat along with it. Weekends were spent either at the lake or watching sports on TV—at a bar or someone's house or, most often, at home on his own big screen. They never did the things she'd like to do anymore. He chose all their recreation.

So she bought shoes, too. High-heeled sandals with ankle straps. Very sexy. Marty was small and trim; she could get away with those three-inch heels, and she was agile in them. They'd look great twirling around a dance floor. Sometimes she bought these things while in the fantasy that life could be fun again. There was a time that dressing up like this got Joe all excited, especially the shoes… He'd see her legs in those heels and go crazy. That was before they were married.

When she got home Jason and Joe were in front of the TV playing a video game, sitting cross-legged on the floor like a couple of kids. Joe thought these games were a perfect way to help Jason develop hand-eye coordination, but Marty secretly believed Joe just wanted to play them, himself.

She dropped her packages on the dining room chair and surveyed the kitchen. It looked as if they'd been grazing all day, not bothering to pick up a single dish, rinse out a glass, wipe bread crumbs off the counter. Around them in the family room were more plates, empty chip bags, cellophane from snack cakes, used and balled-up paper towels as opposed to napkins. Joe had gone through the newspaper there, as well, leaving the couch cushions all askew, some on the floor, and the newspaper strewn around on the coffee table and floor, along with his coffee cup and toast plate from breakfast. She had left everything immaculate, having cleaned while he slept in.

And of course Joe was wearing only those navy-blue, rotting gym shorts—his summer day-off uniform—under which he was naked. He had a hairy body, a heavy, scratchy growth of stubble. It would never occur to him to clean up a little, look presentable for her on his day off, though she'd asked him to a thousand times.

"Hey, babe," he greeted at the sound of her entry, but he didn't turn around. He was very busy stacking and collapsing colorful blocks on the screen, pretending to compete with his three-year-old son while he helped little Jason develop some competence with the game. "You get the mail?"

"Joe, look at this kitchen! It's a mess."

"Yeah, I'll get it later."

No, he wouldn't. He didn't clean. At least, not inside the house. He didn't even clean the *inside* of the RV. Now, the boat or yard or garage, he kept them perfect. This mess would be left for her.

"Joe, can I talk to you a minute?"

"Yeah, sure. Sit tight." Then after a full minute passed, he shouted, "Whoa! You see that, buddy? You got me! Wanna go one more time?" And he started a new game.

"Joe!"

"What?"

"I want to *talk* to you!"

"Aw, Jesus," he said, irritated. He put down his remote game stick and got to his feet. He looked like a monkey, all that black hair covering his legs, chest, belly, his shadowy face, his hair goofy from not being combed. He gave his gym shorts a tug but they slipped right back down, low on his hips. The elastic was giving out and half the time she could see his butt crack; she did *not* consider it a precious sight. Of course, she'd brought home new gym shorts to at least have decent clean ones on that naked body. They sat on his closet shelf, rejected. "What?" he said, hands on his hips.

"The house is a wreck."

"Yeah, I've been busy outside and in the garage. Plus, it's

my day off. Me and the little guy have been hanging out. But I got the yard work caught up."

"It wouldn't take you ten minutes to clean up after yourself in here. With another ten minutes you could shower, shave and look decent."

"It's my day *off!* I just want to relax and be comfortable!"

"If I hung around a messy house looking like you look, you'd leave me in a second!"

"I don't know about that," he said, a slight sneer to his lips. "Maybe you'd be a little easier to get along with if you loosened up. Jesus, it's just a couple of plates and glasses! How big a deal is that? Didn't you just say it would take ten minutes…?"

"We both work," she said. "I'm getting really tired of coming home to a mess all the time."

"You work today, Marty?" he asked sarcastically.

"You know I didn't work today, but I put in my forty hours every week, and I do everything around the house, too. And the only time I see you looking clean and decent is when we have company or you're on your way to work!"

"Look, I didn't get home till eight this morning and we had a busy night. I just want to be comfortable," he said again. "Why don't you lighten up a little bit, huh?"

"No," she said, tears coming to her eyes as she shook her head. "No, I'm not lightening up. I'm sick of this. I don't ask much of you—just pick up after yourself and shower." She shook her head in total frustration. "I'm leaving for a little while. I'm going to get out of here and cool off. I'll be back, I'll bring dinner, and if you heard me at all, clean up this goddamn mess and shower and *shave!*" She grabbed her purse and headed back out the door.

Marty really wanted to have a good hard cry, but she didn't want anyone to see her like that, so she sucked it back where it stuck in her throat like a rock. She drove around for about

twenty minutes, seething, hurting. He wasn't like this before she married him! They dated for a year, were engaged
for a year, and during that time he always asked her what she
wanted to do. Even then, she'd tried to give him balanced
time by getting together with his friends for sports and boating things; she happened to like sports and outdoor activities
when it didn't take up a hundred percent of their recreational
time. She didn't even mind if he seemed a little bored at a
nice dinner out or fell asleep during a chick flick. Back then,
during the premarriage days, she spent as much time at his
house as her apartment, and his relaxation mode might involve
sweats or jeans, but he was never this smelly, naked monkey
in falling-down shorts with his crack peeking out.

Of course, he hadn't been tidy back then, either. His bathroom was usually carpeted in hair; he left things lying around
and didn't keep the kitchen spotless. But if she offered to help
him clean up, he did his part. He'd let her tell him what to
do—strip the bed and throw the sheets and towels in the
washer, run the vacuum, take out trash, scrub out the shower.
Well, he was all done participating now. And back then, if
he wanted to make love, he went to a little trouble. He was
squeaky clean, smelled nice, was shaved and sweet. He knew
how to get her in the mood, worked up and excited. He didn't
bother with that anymore, either. And now he complained if it
took her too long to climax. *Come on, Marty, come on. What's
the matter? I can't last all night!*

She just couldn't seem to find anyone to talk to about it.
Julie had that kissy-face thing going on with Billy after so
many years and, even when she was at her most discontented,
it was apparent she still thought she had the best husband in
the world. Which maybe she did. Cassie seemed to think if
a woman had a warm body in her bed there was nothing to
complain about. Beth had much more important things to

concentrate on than Marty's marital gripes; she hadn't been involved with anyone for almost five years now and was more focused on her medical career than relationships.

Marty ended up at a small Italian restaurant not far from home. There was a quiet little bar and they weren't too busy on late weekday afternoons. It was just after four o'clock. She decided to have a glass of wine, order some takeout while she sipped it and see if she could cool down.

She sat at the far side of the bar in a dark corner, sipping her wine, staring at a menu, though not reading it.

She'd been prepared for things to change after marriage; she knew he wasn't the neat freak she was. She'd given the relationship two years before marrying him, just to be sure she knew him, knew his habits, his values. She hadn't expected him to go into such a complete decline; she never thought he'd relax all his standards, dump all the household responsibility on her. In the past, he had occasional kick-back days of not shaving, but now it was whenever he wasn't working. He let himself get so disgusting. What kind of a guy refuses to shower and shave when his woman asks him to?

And the thing she really never saw coming—that she'd stop loving him.

It was hard to love an insensitive slob. Of course, not many people saw him that way. He was a real man's man—a scruffy, masculine Italian with some old-world views, like the woman is there to bear the children and take care of the house and kids while the man does the mechanical stuff, the physical stuff, the yard and all that. The men at F.D. thought he was a kick; in a way they sympathized with her, telling her she was a saint for putting up with him. They didn't know the half— he wouldn't dare go to work stinky, with his face unshaved and his thick, black hair greasy and sticking up in spikes everywhere—so all they were really aware of was his inability to pick up dishes, wash and dry. He was a hell of an Italian cook—his spaghetti and sausage and lasagna were legendary in the department—but they joked at F.D. that while they loved his food, he *destroyed* the kitchen. She would always say, Welcome to my world.

At work, he went the extra mile in other ways—ways the guys could appreciate. He kept the equipment spotless and organized; he was powerfully strong and the first one up the ladder, to the rescue.

The sexy man she'd fallen in love with was gone, replaced by this Neanderthal who couldn't care less about her feelings. He'd been so great when he was trying to get her into bed, then trying to get her to stay in bed, then trying to get her to the altar—because he was an Italian Catholic and needed a wife to take care of his household, to have his kids. When they were engaged, they talked about having two or three kids, but she quit after Jason. She just didn't have the energy to work, keep the house civilized and take care of a bunch of kids, Joe being one of them.

She didn't think she loved him anymore…and she was beginning to wonder how she could stay with him…

"Marty!"

She lifted her head to see Ryan Chambers grinning at her. He picked up his beer and wandered over to her. Oh, God, she thought. This is the last thing I need right now.

"How you doing, baby?"

"Fine, Ryan. How are you?"

"Great. You meeting someone? Having dinner here?"

"No, I'm just going to pick up some takeout. I've had a long day, so I thought I'd have a glass of wine. How about you?"

"I thought about a pizza, but I don't know. I'll just have a beer, then decide."

"How's Jill?"

"Jill?" he laughed. "Marty, Jill and I are over..."

"Oh, I'm sorry," she said. "I didn't know."

"Yeah, that's okay—you're not expected to keep up with the love life of an old boyfriend. It happened about a year ago."

"A year, huh? So, who is it now?"

"No one, as a matter of fact," he said, sitting on the stool next to hers. "I thought I could use a breather."

"*You're* not dating anyone?" she asked, stunned. He usually dated several women at a time.

"Oh, I've been out a couple of times, but it didn't amount to much. I'm getting a little old for all that playing around— kind of tired of the whole bachelor scene. I think I finally worked through it. I'm looking for something different now. Something a little more stable. Reliable."

"Really?" she said, leaning on her hand, not believing him for a second.

He looked into his beer and shook his head with a little silent laughter. "Really. I might finally be growing up." He lifted his eyes. "At thirty-one, I don't think it's premature. Do you?"

"Hardly. Still, it's the last thing I expected to hear out of you."

"I deserved that. Did I ever apologize for that? Because if I didn't, I should..."

"Don't bother," she said. "Long ago and far away."

"How's the family?" he asked.

She immediately looked away before she said, "Great. They're great."

When she looked back at him, he said, "Oh, yeah, sounds great. What's the matter? Having some trouble?"

"Nah," she said, "it's nothing. Definitely nothing I feel like talking about."

"Okay, let's change the subject. Who have you seen lately?" he asked, and she knew he meant from their old gang.

So she told him about who was at the party she and Joe had hosted and lunch that day with the girls, but all the while she was thinking about their past. Ryan was her first love. He was a couple of years older, the big jock at school. Good-looking, flirtatious, funny, smart. He was also unpredictable, had a short attention span and a roving eye. She fell for him at fifteen and they were on and off for about five years with long breaks while he stole other virginities. He'd always come creeping back after four or six or eight months—sorry, re-pentant, seductive—and she couldn't resist him. They'd have another few months of bliss, then he'd do it again—get side-tracked by another girl. By the time she was about twenty, maybe twenty-one, she had finally had enough and wouldn't let him back. But of course, she never really got over him.

Funny, Ryan and Joe didn't have any of the same flaws. Joe was incredibly married; he didn't even flirt. In the looks de-partment, they were pretty equal, though completely differ-ent. Ryan had a dimpled smile and twinkling eyes that could just make a girl wet herself. Joe was a damn fine-looking man when he was cleaned up, but Ryan took impeccable and fashionable to the next level; he could be a model. Joe had an incredible, strong, toned body—pecs, biceps, a narrow waist and six-pack such that when he wore that F.D. T-shirt pulled tight across his chest and shoulders, women went weak in the knees. Ryan was so adorable and good-natured; of course, he could look you in the eye, smile that heart-splitting smile and lie through his beautiful, straight, white teeth. Joe had darker good looks, almost black eyes, a shorter fuse, but he was the most honest man she knew.

They talked for about forty-five minutes before Marty or-dered a couple of medium pizzas to go and Ryan ordered a second beer. Then he opened his wallet and pulled out one of his business cards. He was with the local cable company, having started at the bottom right after college. He was already a director—good income, a shirt-and-tie position. He slid his card across the bar. "That's my office and cell number," he said. "It's okay to call me if you want to talk. I get the feeling you have things on your mind. Worries."

"Listen," she said, "running into you is one thing, calling you is another. I'm married."

"I know that," he said. "And I'm a good friend. Kidding aside, Marty. We might have had our romantic troubles, but one thing about us—we were always good friends. We could count on each other when things weren't going great."

"Yeah, but…" Her words trailed off because there was no way to politely put it—she had always been tempted by him, even when it was insane. If there was anything she had wished for even more than being able to reach Joe, straighten him out so they could be in love again, it was that Ryan hadn't been such a damn playboy. And right now, feeling so unloved and vulnerable, this was not a good idea.

He put his hand over hers. "Marty, you mean a lot to me. You always have, you know that. You'll never know how often I wished I'd met you when I was a little more mature and not such a kid, a jerk. We wouldn't have kept getting back together if we hadn't had something pretty special. Maybe I can make it up to you now by being a friend. If you ever want to talk…"

"I don't think that would be smart," she said, but she slid the card off the bar and into her purse. "But thanks for the gesture. And good luck in finding whatever it is you've been looking for."

Her pizzas came soon after that exchange. She paid her bill, and when she was slipping off her stool, he pulled on her hand, brought her close and kissed her cheek. A jolt of desire passed through her. Oh, God, she wanted to feel loved again.

"If I don't talk to you again for a while, it was really great seeing you," he said. "You look fantastic, by the way. I don't know how you do it. The rest of us get older and you get younger."

Liar, she wanted to say. He was a knockout in high school and he was at least four knockouts now. "Thanks," she said. "Take care."

She left him there and drove home. It wasn't yet six o'clock when she pulled into the garage. She'd been gone more than an hour and a half, but her cell phone had never tweeted in her purse. The house was caught in the late-afternoon summer shadows. She soon realized the reason there were no lights on inside was because Joe and Jason were sprawled on the couch, asleep. Joe was on his back—not showered, shaved or dressed in human clothes—and Jason was lying on his chest.

She flipped on the kitchen light. Not one single thing had been moved. She put the pizzas on the breakfast bar, dropped her purse on the dining room chair with her purchases and began cleaning up. The dishwasher she'd run before leaving for lunch was full of clean dishes that Joe hadn't bothered to put away. She put everything away and began reloading, wiping counters, tossing garbage, frustrated tears falling on her hands.

Beth wasn't on call. She had an appointment in San Francisco with Dr. Jerod Paterson, a very well-known and highly respected oncologist. She hadn't been on call two weeks ago, either, when her girlfriends had gone to the party at Marty and Joe's. She'd been recovering from a breast lumpectomy. And it was malignant.

It wasn't the first malignancy—that had come at the age of twenty-five in her right breast, and a lumpectomy wouldn't

do the trick because there were three masses that seemed to
appear overnight, along with some lymph node involvement.
So first she had three substantial lumpectomies and finally a
radical mastectomy. That was when Mark left her. Well, he
was nice enough to wait for her to get through her radiation and chemo and get on her feet before he left. She would
never be entirely sure if it was the cancer, the sickness, the
fear or maybe the mangled body that listed to the left. It's not
as though she had big breasts to start with—they were just
little things.

Now she was starting on the remaining breast.

She already knew a lot about Dr. Paterson, having researched him thoroughly and chosen him carefully. He was
in his late forties, married, with two teenagers, and seemed to
have a pleasant smile in his bio photo and a reputation in oncology that put him in such high demand it was hard to get an
appointment. But not for a physician like Beth—all she had to
do was call, explain who she was and she got in immediately.

When she entered his office for the very first time, she was
reminded how little pictures could convey. He stood from behind his desk to a full six feet, had thick dark blond hair and,
when he smiled, one dimple under his left eye. He stretched
out a hand. "Dr. Halsley, it's a pleasure to meet you. Please,
have a seat." And then he waited for her to be seated before
he sat back down.

"Dr. Paterson," she said with a nod.

He folded his hands on top of what surely must be her
opened chart. "I guess we come from the same undergrad
program—premed at USC. That gives us a lot in common.
Sacramento is your home?"

"It's where I grew up," she said.

"If you don't object, I'd like to know a little more about
you before we get into the reason for your visit."

The reason is cancer, and it just won't stop, she thought. "Like?" she replied.

"Siblings? Partner? Living parents?"

"Only child, and yes, my parents are still living and appear to be perfectly healthy. I have one grandparent left on each side, and only one early death—at fifty-five from heart failure. My maternal grandmother is a survivor of breast cancer—over twenty years. She's eighty-eight."

They chatted for a little while, maybe fifteen minutes, during which time he asked if she had a husband or partner and she said, "He left with the last breast."

He wanted to know about her hobbies, what she did for fun, that sort of thing. She laughed at him. "I've been certified in OB-Gyn for one year. You think I have hobbies?"

"Your first malignant onset was very early," he said, not looking at the chart. "But, despite the fact you're still quite young, this is another primary manifestation. The cancer doesn't appear to be spreading. Still, because of your age and history, I'd recommend aggressive treatment. Unfortunately the MRI results show some suspicious sites in the breast. Tell me how you feel about this: we can start with a round of radiotherapy, some chemo, and then reappraise and determine if more surgery is the best course."

She shrugged and shook her head. "It really doesn't matter. I'm not desperate to hang on to the breast. It's not that much of a breast…"

"You haven't considered any reconstruction after your last surgery?"

"No. It seems pointless."

He lifted one brow. "Do you have a good support system, Dr. Halsley?"

"You can call me Beth if you like," she said. "Yes, sure. I work in a women's health clinic—they're very sensitive. I

have friends and family. But I'm trying to look at this medically, not emotionally."

"I understand, but try to remember—it's an emotional disease."

"That's why I'm trying to look at it medically."

He smiled. "Doctors. Pragmatists, almost to the last bone.
Are you going to be a terrible patient?"

"Probably," she said. "I'm pretty pissed off about this."

"You should be. I would be. If you're comfortable with it,
I'd like to have a look. Feel like putting on a gown for me?"

"Sure," she said, standing. "Where would you like me?"

"Exam room two will be fine. I'll see you in ten minutes."

A few minutes later she was sitting on the exam table, her
left arm over her head while the doctor palpated the breast.
She looked away while he studied her. "Do you have hobbies?" she heard herself ask.

"I have a sailboat," he said.

"That would explain the tan…"

He straightened and waited for her to turn her head and
make eye contact. "I originally bought it for the family."

"A wife and two kids… I read your bio."

"Ah, old bio. No wife. We divorced three years ago. I still
have two kids, however. Two girls—fifteen and seventeen.
Honestly, I can't believe I still have hair."

She smiled, but briefly. "Am I going to have hair after this?"

He frowned. "I don't think so, Beth."

"It's going to be hard to keep this a little secret, isn't it?"

"Is that your plan?"

She sighed deeply. "Dr. Paterson, if you had any idea what it
was like going through a radical and chemo at twenty-five—
so young, the high drama, the fear all around me, eventually
the pity and terrified abandonment—you'd understand. I've
barely made the five-year mark…" *Mark.* Maybe he was right

to leave; maybe she wouldn't survive this. "Not only do I feel like I can't do it again, I'm not sure my parents can take it. They're not young—they were almost forty when I was born, though both are still healthy and working. My friends will be more devastated than I am. It's not just stubbornness, I assure you. It was almost harder dealing with my friends and family than the disease."

He pulled the gown over her shoulder to cover her and took her hand, holding it briefly. "I can imagine. And please—I'm Jerod."

"Well, Jerod, this is a disaster. And if I don't somehow hold it together, I'm going to go berserk."

"Beth, I want you to remember a couple of things. The most important thing is that there doesn't seem to be any cancer anywhere but in the breast. Lightning has struck twice, but only twice—and in the same general place. I'm very optimistic. I think I can get you through this. Give me a chance. And don't go it alone."

"I'm not going it alone, Jerod. I'm going with you. I'm sure you'll be very supportive."

4

Cassie wasn't sure where she'd made her mistakes with men, always betting on the wrong ones. One look at her closest friends—Billy, for example—didn't reveal her to have rotten taste or not recognize a good man when she saw one. Whatever it was, she was determined to change the pattern, maybe think more like Beth, a woman who didn't have expectations at all. Cassie was twenty-nine. She had time to pick up her threads at thirty, thirty-one. Reevaluate. Maybe there were only so many Billys in the world and she'd have to go the route Beth was considering—reconcile to living as a single woman, possibly have her family that way.

But she was lonesome. Beth was busy, Marty was annoyed with her husband, Julie was completely stressed out and distracted by a couple of sick kids. There was one person, however, who had been very nice to her, and proved easy to both talk to and listen to. And as far as she could tell, he had no secret agenda—he was just pleasant and helpful. After all, she didn't

look like his type any more than he was hers. For him, she envisioned a bleached blonde with tattoos, wearing leather pants.

She surprised herself by staring for a long time at that business card with just the cell phone number on it. A person
would have to be desperate to actually call a guy like this to
suggest meeting for anything more than coffee. The truth
was, Cassie *was* a little desperate. Not for Mr. Right but for
someone to fill up an hour or two. This might be exactly the
person to call during her moratorium on dating, since she'd
never go out with a man like Walt.

But he'd been so congenial to have coffee with, his brother
was a police officer and, not least of all, he'd rescued her from
a bad guy and offered to help back her up if she had further
problems or needed a witness. Despite his hard, scary looks,
he'd turned out to be one of the most docile and polite men
she'd been around in a long time. She couldn't deny she enjoyed his company. There was something about Walt that was
more than just sincere; he had an almost nurturing quality.
The word *guileless* came to mind. And *genuine*.

Still, she would pick a crowded place with a well-lit parking lot.

She called the cell phone number and left a message. "Hi.
This is Cassie. I got off work at three and I have to be back
on duty at seven in the morning, so it's going to be an early
night for me, but I would sort of like to have a glass of wine
and a salad or something. If you're interested, give me a call.
Here's my cell phone number."

She immediately felt ridiculous. Why was she calling this biker
in grave need of a decent haircut and a shave? She had nothing
in common with him. Men who had that crisp and polished
look appealed to her—khakis with starched creases, even their
casual shirts professionally laundered. Walt wasn't very well put
together—a tightly fitted T-shirt, denim or leather vest, jeans and
that ponytail. So retro. He looked road worn. Then she thought,

Well, that's *perfect*. There was no way she'd find herself falling for someone like him, hoping he could turn into more than a friend. She was perfectly safe from another disappointment.

A half hour later her cell phone rang and she actually felt a lift, a grin spread across her face. She wasn't sure if it was because she'd left way too many messages in her day and far too few of them had been returned or if it was because she actually liked Walt.

But there it was, on the window of her cell—*Walt Arneson*. Oops, that would mean Cassie *Rasmussen* would be showing up on his; he now knew more than she intended him to know. She hadn't given him her last name before.

"Hey," she answered.

"Cassie?"

"Yeah, hi, Walt. How are you?"

"Good, thanks. So, you feel like an early dinner?"

"I do. How about you? But I don't know your hours—are you off work yet?"

"Don't worry about that, it's no problem," he said. "You have a place in mind? Something convenient to you? I'm all over the valley, so it makes no difference."

"I'm thinking...something casual. There's a Claim Jumper's on Harding, not far off I-80. They have big meals and good salads, so we could both get what we want."

He laughed into the phone. "Yeah, I guess it's pretty obvious—I don't mind a big meal. I know the place. What time?"

"Six?"

"Great. I'll meet you there."

And he hung up. No goodbye, no *I'm glad you called*—just hung up. Well, she thought, this wasn't a date. Just someone to talk to, keep her from being completely alone for an hour.

She got there at ten to six. When she asked for a booth in the bar and told the hostess she was expecting a big guy with a ponytail who looked like a biker, the young girl asked, "Is that him?" pointing to a table.

"Well, I'll be..." she muttered, amazed.

When he saw her coming, he stood. "Hey," he said, smiling.

"Are you starving, Walt?" she asked with a laugh. "You're here early."

"I'm always hungry, but that's not why I got here early. I didn't want to be late and the traffic overcooperated."

She slid in across from him. She noticed, not for the first time, right in that hairy face which longed for a shave, that too-long hair pulled back in a messy ponytail, he had the bluest eyes. They somehow seemed even bluer tonight.

"Tell me about your day," he said.

"Two motorcycle accidents," she reported.

"Oh, jeez. Not bad ones, I hope," he said.

"Actually, not too bad," she said, a little embarrassed at baiting him like that. "One was a teenager, some scrapes. And a highway patrolman versus car—messed up his knee and cracked his pelvis, but he'll be fine."

"Phew, that's a relief. Always hate to hear about those. Otherwise, your day was pretty good?"

"Always busy, which is one thing I like about E.R.—the time flies. Hard work, but interesting and fast. You?"

He grinned. "Absolutely nothing new about what I do. I did get out for a great ride through the foothills last weekend. What else? Besides work, what have you been doing with yourself?"

"Not so much. If I'm off work, I walk with Steve in the morning, and if I work, I take him out in the afternoon. I keep my little garden going. And I already told you a few days ago, I got together with my girlfriends from high school for lunch. The four of us have stayed close."

"Yeah, but you didn't really tell me about them." He grinned.

"We were cheerleaders together. I was lots thinner then…"

"Cassie," he said, laughing and shaking his head. "You look perfect."

"That's nice," she said. "Well, one's a hairdresser, one's a stay-at-home mom with three kids—both of them are married to firemen. And get this—one's a doctor. It's because of the doctor we can't all get together that often. Her schedule is tight. But I see my best friend Julie all the time."

"That would be the one with the three kids…"

"You remembered."

He lifted his eyebrows. "I might remember that night almost as well as you do," he said. "You still okay on that score?"

"Yes, thanks. And the hand?" she asked. "You still have the cast."

He lifted the hand with the cast. "They have to get an X-ray before taking off the cast. Every time I see the doc, another X-ray. It's just a little crack, really. Maybe next week."

The waitress came to their table. He ordered a Coke, she ordered a glass of pinot noir and they decided to take a few minutes to decide on dinner.

"Nothing to drink for you?" she asked. "No beer or anything?"

"I've had enough," he said.

"Really? You get an early start or something?"

"No," he said. "I mean, in earlier days. When I was much younger, I hit it pretty hard—got myself in some trouble, disappointed my family. My parents. I was just a kid, but it was time to hang up the mug. No fanfare, no big pronouncements, no meetings. I just decided enough was enough."

"Oh," she said.

"Alcohol and motorcycles are a bad combination. And my job depends on me being at my best when I'm on the bike."

"Then what were you doing at the bar that night? If you don't drink?" she asked.

"I usually look for the bikes. I run into customers, talk awhile, hand out cards, invite them to the store to look around, bring in their mechanical problems, that kind of stuff. Plus I like bikers. A lot of them are cops, by the way. I just want to be friendly," he said, shrugging. "Except that night you were having some trouble—I wasn't feeling friendly. I'd have gladly decked that guy, but my first concern was if you were all right."

"You did a very good job with that." She laughed. "You look like the kind of guy a person should duck away from. I mean, you have all the warning signs—the tattoo, the biker clothes, your size alone…"

"That's gotten me into trouble a time or two," he said. "I look like a fighter. I don't mind looking strong—it can come in handy. But I'll do anything I can not to fight, honest. Fighting just complicates things."

"But if you had to?" she asked just as their drinks arrived.

"I could probably hold my own," he said with a self-effacing shrug.

"Ya think?" she asked with a laugh. "Let's decide what we're eating, then you can tell me about this place where you work."

She already knew Walt grew up in Roseville, the second of four boys. But over dinner she learned he was thirty-two, had only completed high school and by the time he was twenty-two had been arrested three times and had two DUIs, not to mention a variety of trouble he caused or got caught up in for which there were no permanent records. A self-described idiot and badass. At that time he was mad at everyone, everyone was mad at him, so he took off on his bike. He wasn't going to put up with anyone's crap anymore. He took his hiatus on the road, that cross-country ride.

"I went through a transformation, don't ask me how. I'm

probably too thickheaded to have been looking for something like that, but I'd lie on the ground, look up at a dark sky full of stars and it would come to me—I'm a speck. In the grand scheme of things, I make almost no difference in the world. On the road, in the mountains, valleys, beaches, I kept thinking, This is such a huge, amazing, beautiful place and I'm just a meaningless dot. Nothing. So should I be a speck, a dot, whose single contribution is making people like my mom and dad embarrassed and miserable? Or should I try to do something better than that? Nothing profound, heroic or amazing, but how about just not humiliating my family."

She reached across the table and put a couple of fingers lightly on the tattoo. "This come before, or after?"

"One of my little pretransformation sprees," he said, grinning. "Serves as a very good reminder. Besides, I've gotten kind of attached to her."

"You could dress her," Cassie suggested.

"It just wouldn't be the same."

When he got back to California after his sabbatical, looking for something productive, he got a job in a small bike shop, and it was a good fit. After his experience on the road, keeping his bike running and learning from other groups of bikers, he knew a lot about the machine, about the people who gravitated to those machines. It was a perfect match for him; he could converse about every model, fix them, sell them, give advice. Much to the shop owner's consternation, he did a lot of things for customers at no charge—referrals to other stores, a mechanical tweak, inexpensive part thrown in. He was just acting the way bikers out on the road acted toward one another, but the result was a growing clientele. Bikers trusted Walt.

"Since then that little shop has grown into a chain, a franchise, but the philosophy is the same—we cater to bikers' needs. They think of the store as a clubhouse—they like to hang out a lot, talking to other bikers, so we stock up on trade magazines, give 'em free coffee, set up plenty of comfortable chairs. We've started organizing group rides on weekends—no charge, of course— and people sign up. Works great," he said. "Since I've been doing this for more than eight years now, I know just about everything about the business. There are four stores in four corners of the valley. Great little business. Because I love bikes, it's kind of like getting paid for your hobby. The best day I have is when some- one comes in with a bike I can fix, and I know it's fixed perfectly and at least what I did won't give 'em any more trouble. I know that doesn't sound like such a big deal, but it sure feels good."

He talked about his brothers—his eldest brother was an accountant, the one just younger was still in school, study- ing entomology. "Bugs. Guess he's gonna be an Orkin man," he laughed. "And you already know about Kevin, the cop."

Dishes were taken away, coffee arrived. Walt had a huge slice of chocolate cake that she automatically dipped her fork into and sampled, as though they'd been friends for years. Then she glanced at her watch and said, "God, it's eight-thirty! I have an early shift!" She lifted her hand toward the wait- ress for the check, but when she brought it, Walt snatched it.

"Come on," Cassie said. "I invited you!"

"Let me," he said. "Please. I haven't enjoyed myself this much in a long time."

"Aw, Walt… I didn't mean to let you grab the check! At least let's split it." She thought, He's a bike mechanic, a grease monkey who spends a lot of time visiting with his custom- ers—he must be totally broke.

"Come on, you're going to have to let me do this. I want to."

"Well, if you're sure, but…" She didn't finish. She was thinking, but this isn't a date. You can't get the idea we're ever going to date! How do you tell someone as nice as this, whose company you've enjoyed so much that two and a half hours have disappeared like seconds, that you're not even slightly attracted to him?

When they walked into the parking lot, he left her at her car and said, "Would it be all right if I called you sometime?"

"Um, sure, but...well, I don't want to mislead you. Friendship is about the only thing that interests me right now. You understand. After...you know," she said. What she couldn't say was, *Friendship is the only thing that interests me with someone like you.*

But he smiled and said, "That's fine. A person can always use a friend."

Cassie was barely home when her cell phone rang. She grabbed it, hoping it was Julie or maybe Marty. But it was Walt. Don't answer it, she told herself. Don't encourage him. "Hello?" she said.

"So, how about Sunday? A nice ride through Sonoma County? It's supposed to be a beautiful weekend. I know a great breakfast place. The biggest biscuits you've ever seen."

She laughed. "By 'sometime' I really didn't think you meant in a half hour."

"How about it, Cassie? See if you like the wind in your face and the sun on your back."

"You understand, I'm not up for dating."

"It's a bike ride, Cassie. It'll be fun. And I know you feel okay about being around me. I'm completely safe. You can call Kevin at Rancho P.D. if you want to, but I warn you, he might not give me a recommendation. I think he's still holding a grudge from when he was about fourteen. But come on, take a chance on me. Maybe I don't look like one, but I'm a good guy."

Oh, he was a good man, of that she had no doubt. "All right," she laughed. "Why not?"

"Great. And…much as I'd love to see you in a pair of shorts, you should wear long pants. Jeans. Maybe boots, if you have 'em."

"Fine. What time?"

"Seven. You gonna let me pick you up?"

Oh, God, she thought, what am I *doing?* "Sure. Let me tell you how to get here."

Cassie was up and dressed on Sunday morning well before seven, oddly excited about Walt coming for her. She'd had to lie on her back on the bed to get her jeans zipped; she'd put on a few pounds again. But she didn't worry about that with Walt; she wasn't trying to impress him. That was a refreshing change. She heard the rumbling motor of his bike as he pulled into the neighborhood. At the stroke of seven he rang her bell and she answered her door with a big smile, stepping back a couple of feet to present herself in jeans and boots. "Okay?" she asked.

"Better than okay," he said. "You look fantastic. But you might want to tie up your hair. It could get all tangled in the wind." He balanced the collar of a leather jacket on a finger. "This might come in handy in the shaded back roads and hills," he said.

Steve came forward, a green stuffed frog filling his mouth, wagging his tail and looking up at Walt.

"Well, hello," he said, leaning down to give him a scratch under the chin. "I've heard about you…" Then to Cassie, "Will he be all right if you're out awhile?"

"He'll be fine. He's a mature man now." She plucked the jacket off his finger and, out of habit, examined the label. "Walt, where did you get this? It's a Vince!"

"We started selling a few items at the store. Biker clothes, you know."

"I've lusted after this jacket at Neiman Marcus," she said. "It goes for over seven hundred dollars."

"That right? Well, we don't like to let the prices get too high, but it's no secret—bikers like to spend on their machines and accessories. I brought some chaps, too, if you're interested."

She noticed he was wearing heavy denim jeans and boots, the usual chains around the heels. "You think I need chaps?" she asked.

"I think we're going to be completely safe, but if you're concerned about anything, you might as well suit up."

"The chaps came from the store, too?" she asked. To his nod, she said, "And they don't mind you borrowing this stuff for a weekend ride?"

"Not a problem," he said. "I give a lot to the store. It's okay."

"Well, then…" she said, shrugging into the coveted jacket. She pulled her long, straight black hair into a ponytail and tied it in a knot, then kissed Steve on the head and told him to have a nice day. Once outside, she let Walt help her into the chaps. He fixed her up with a rider's helmet and got her situated on the back of the bike.

He revved it up and, over his shoulder, said, "You're going to have to hang on around my waist." He grinned at her. "That's the best part for me."

She put her arms around him and he took off, slowly through her little neighborhood, and soon they were zooming west along the freeway heading toward San Francisco. At first, being the emergency room nurse who hated the way bikers would take stupid chances passing between cars and on the shoulders of freeways, she was focused on his driving, but she soon realized he was cautious and courteous. He'd signal before passing and raise a hand to thank the driver if they let him in; often she could hear a toot of acknowledgment. Comfortable in no time, she concentrated on the scenery. He turned north and left the

city behind, then west again through the rolling hills toward
Sonoma County. The green hillsides were dotted with grazing cattle, acres of rice fields and farms. He was off the freeway
and on back roads in no time; they passed through small towns
she'd never seen before and finally entered the little town of
Petaluma. He pulled up in front of a shabby-looking café outside of which stood a line of people; apparently this place had
a reputation. They waited at the end of the line, which moved
quickly, and when they got inside the door, a waitress beamed
at Walt, all smiles. "Hey, Walt. How you doing?"

"Good, Shirl. Two for breakfast."

"You got it," she said, leading the way to a very small table
in an extremely crowded, very busy restaurant. "Coffee?"
Shirl asked.

Cassie nodded, taking a menu. There was something nice
about being with someone who was known in a place like
this. She'd been out with more polished guys who seemed to
be known in fancier places, but they were never as friendly,
as accessible, as Walt. In a place like this, where the meal was
cheap and the people seemed ordinary, Walt's notoriety was
special, more authentic. She found herself thinking, I'm not
the only person who likes him. Right here, deep in the center of this big thug, is a just plain old nice guy.

"You must come here all the time," she said.

"If I'm heading west, this is the best place to start the day.
If I'm heading east, there's a place in Folsom I like to stop."

"Do you do this every weekend?" she asked.

He smiled. "When I can. Some people golf, some jog. I
like to eat and ride. How do you like it so far?"

"Well, I've always liked to eat," she said. "And I think I
don't hate the riding part. Yet."

"It's just going to get better," he said. "Mind if I order for us? You like just about everything? Because I know what's good."

"Go for it," she invited. "Guess I won't be having salad for breakfast. Thank God."

"You're going to love this," he said.

Less than fifteen minutes later their small table was over-powered by large helpings of food—eggs, sausages, home fries, pancakes, biscuits and gravy. "Oh, my God," she said, over-whelmed.

"Just enjoy some samples," he said. "Even I can't eat every-thing they put out."

"Where are we going? Napa Valley?" she asked.

"There's a lot more to Sonoma County than Napa. I like the outskirts—we'll get into the hills so you can catch a view, then pass through the valley. That okay?"

"Sounds great. Listen, I never even asked you how long we'll be out riding today," she said. "I told Julie I'd stop by later if I was back in enough time. Just a standing thing on Sundays when Billy and I are both off work."

"However long you want," he said with a shrug. "Want to give me a time to have you back?"

"No worries, it's very informal. She knows I have plans for the day. I'm kind of like…family." And then she became very conscious of two things. She was *like* family, but not ex-actly the real thing. And…he might wonder why she didn't ask him along.

"You just say when," he said. He began serving her a plate out of the massive platters on the table. "Give yourself a lit-tle extra time. Even though you're just riding and the bike's doing all the work, it can be tiring. And dirty. Don't cut it too close—make time for a little rest and a shower. You'll want it, believe me."

"I hope I didn't just spoil your plans…" she said.

"Not at all," he said, putting some biscuits and gravy on her plate. "This is your first ride. We're going at your pace. Try some of this. It's awesome."

She cut through the biscuit with a fork, scooped up some white gravy and lifted it to her mouth where it melted. "Mmm," she said. "You are very good with food."

"I read a helluva menu, huh?" he said with a laugh.

A different waitress appeared at their table. "How's everything, Walt?"

"Great as usual, Sue, thanks," he said. And before breakfast was over, a couple of other waitresses swung by just to say hello. A diner and his wife said hello on their way out and Walt introduced them to Cassie.

"Do you know everyone?" she asked as they were leaving.

"Just the regulars. Nice folks." He handed her the rider's helmet and watched while she tied up her hair again. "That's just amazing, how you do that," he said. "I should have you show me how." She laughed at him. Imagine them sharing ponytail secrets. "I thought I'd take you up into the hills and I know a couple of off-road trails with good views. You think you're up to that?"

"Is it scary?"

"I don't think so, but if you get nervous, all you have to do is give me a sign—pat my arm or something—and we won't go any farther. How are you with heights?"

She shrugged. "I don't know. I've never done heights on two wheels before."

"Fair enough. You just let me know."

They mounted the Harley and headed out of town, winding through the hills that surrounded Napa Valley. Cassie hung on as they wove up and down the roads, past farms and ranches built into hillsides and nestled into valleys. The rolling landscape was lush and she could see cattle grazing, now and then sheep or llamas. Below them the occasional tractor trundled along but mainly there were houses on a few acres, separated by their land, their horses wandering in pastures, here and there a vineyard, maybe the occasional winery or resort or spa. Everything back here away from the freeway was so peaceful and pristine, so quiet, not the crowded California she was accustomed to. A couple of times he pulled off to the side of the road and asked her how she was doing and she answered, "Fine." In all honesty, she was loving it. The higher they went, the fewer the farms and ranches and the cooler the air. She was grateful for the jacket, the beautiful leather garment she would never buy because of the cost. She hoped she wasn't sweating in it.

Walt stopped every twenty minutes or so, giving her a chance to appreciate the views. They didn't talk; they just gazed. Then with her okay, he started back up. The road was paved, but mostly one lane, and wound around hills that got steeper, the valleys getting deeper. They passed a total of four pickup trucks; the area was deserted but for the locals. Before long they passed points from which she could see the entire valley, and beyond it a mist that suggested the Pacific.

There was still a lot of steep road left when Walt pulled over. There were a few trees, some soft grass and big boulders. Not far away a bull, snorting behind a barbed-wire fence. They were so high, she wondered how the bull had gotten there. She also wondered if that fence could hold him. Walt got off the bike and took off his helmet; he smoothed a hand over his messed up hair but it didn't help much. He grinned at her and asked, "How you doing?"

She pulled off her helmet and, smiling, said, "I have bugs in my teeth, my whole body is vibrating, I'm freezing and I think I have bedsores on my butt."

"Wanna start down?" he asked with a laugh.

"Maybe in a while. How'd you find this road?"

"I just go exploring," he said. "This is one of my favorites."

"You think he'll stay back there?" she asked, indicating the bull.

"The fence is charged. He isn't getting through."

"How'd he get up here?"

"I guess he walked," Walt said. "What do you think so far?"

She tilted her head. "I'm kind of impressed with myself. I didn't think there was a chance in hell I'd actually like this."

He laughed deeply, a big rumbling sound that made the bull lift his head and snort.

"Don't get excited—I'm not exactly a convert, but it wasn't bad. The scenery is wonderful."

"Better than from the inside of a car?" he asked.

"Well, maybe. But the point is, a car would never find this place. We're too programmed to stick to state-approved roads."

He just smiled at her.

"Can we take a break? My butt really is vibrating."

"Absolutely. Feel like some coffee?"

She looked around. "I don't see a Starbucks anywhere."

He reached into one of his saddlebags and withdrew a thermos and two plastic mugs. He poured two steaming coffees and handed her one. Then he settled himself on the grass in full view of the bull. Cassie sat down beside him, a little more cautiously. "You're sure about him?" she asked, nodding her head in the bull's direction.

"Relatively," Walt answered. "I've done this at least twenty times without him charging."

They sat for a long while enjoying the view, sipping hot coffee while the bull occasionally glared at them. Long minutes passed before Walt said, "Mind if I ask you something kind of personal?"

"Shoot," she said, taking another sip.

"Why aren't you married with three kids?"

She turned to look at him. "What makes you think I want to be?" she asked.

"Sorry," he said. "I was just wondering."

"Why would you ask?" she returned.

He shrugged. "You're so easy to be with. Nice. Funny and sweet. And if you don't mind me saying so, you're awful pretty. Seems like there'd be no break in your action for a bike ride."

She tipped her head down and laughed. "Walt, I have a real bad dating history. Mostly jerks and creeps. And that last one could've been real dangerous if you hadn't accidentally been there. I have rotten luck with men."

"Whoa, Cassie," he said. "That's unbelievable. You should have a long line of men just waiting for you to give 'em a chance. Good men. I sure can't figure that out."

"Thanks, that's sweet. I'm not sure why, either. I've thought a lot about that lately. Maybe it's me. Maybe I have a problem with wanting the right guy too much... You know what I mean. I have friends who married real young, friends who just aren't interested in marriage at all. But I don't have any friends who have been like me—always looking for Mr. Right and coming up with nothing but Mr. Wrong. I think sometimes I know in my gut that he's Mr. Wrong and, out of sheer blind hope, I shut off my brain and ignore the truth." She looked at him and her eyes twinkled. "Don't know why I'd do that," she said, shaking her head. "It's a perfectly good brain."

"It is," he agreed. "I could tell pretty *quick*."

"So, I'm through with all that. No more looking. I'm re-signed."

"Resigned?" he echoed.

She took a breath. "I guess if it happens along, fine. But the next one is going to have to hit me over the head with a club and drag me away—I won't be looking, hoping, wanting that so much. That last little mishap of mine really got my attention. Whew. That was scary. I think on some level I must have known he was a phony. There was just something about him that didn't add up. I didn't know him well enough, but he looked good on paper, as we girls like to say."

"On paper?" Walt asked, frowning.

She sighed. "He said he worked for the fire department and I've come to trust the fire department. He was polite, decent-looking, had a good-paying job, filled the basic criteria. I've always skimmed the surface. Maybe I moved too fast because it was so important to have…" She didn't finish; it was embarrassing how much she'd always wanted a man in her life, a family of her own. "So, that part of my life is over. I've been going about this all wrong. It's time to focus on my life, my independent life. After all, it's not a bad life."

"I like that idea. But what convinced you to take a chance on me? On a motorcycle, yet?" he asked.

"You're different," she said, putting a hand on his forearm, right on the naked lady. "You've turned into a pretty good friend. You helped me out of a tight spot, your brother's P.D. and I know you understand why I'm not interested in more than friendship."

"Just out of curiosity, what've you been looking for? In a guy."

"I don't know," she said. "Somebody permanent. Reliable. Trustworthy." Then she grinned and added. "Good-looking, decent future, wants kids, adores me…" But in the back of her mind a little voice taunted, *Male and breathing…*

"Very reasonable," he said, smiling.

"I always had a rule about men—and I ignored it over and over again. If he's nice to you but mean to the waiter, he's not a nice person."

"Huh?" he asked, his brow furrowed.

"There are lots of people who can be nice when they want to be, when they're after something. But at some point their true colors come out—when they're getting a haircut, ordering a meal, having the car washed. When they snip and pick and criticize and...well, you know." Uh-oh, she suddenly thought—Walt is nice to the waiter, nice to everyone. But no...she liked Walt, but not in that way.

"Yeah. I know," he said.

"So, I ignored the rule. I'd see a sign and blow right through it, hoping a relationship would work. It usually didn't take long for the guy to treat me just as bad—no returned calls, I became invisible...and my heart would be in pieces, over and over. I'm all done doing that. First, I'm not dating, period. Second, if I ever dip into the market again, I'm going to be very careful and pay better attention."

"You ought to," he said. "You should have the best, that's all."

"Right," she agreed. She realized that there was something about Walt; she kept telling him things she didn't tell anyone other than Julie, not even her other girlfriends. "So what's your story?" she asked.

"My story?" he repeated.

"With women? Been serious? Engaged? Have a million broken hearts in your past like me? What?"

He just laughed. "Cassie, I hardly ever date. I stay busy with the bikes, the stores. I mean, in the grand scheme of things what I do isn't much, but it can tie up a lot of hours every day, every week. There have been one or two women I kind of rode with a time or two..."

"When you say you rode with them, is that biker talk for slept with them?"

"Actually, that's biker talk for taking a bike ride together."

"Oh," she said, laughing. "So. You're a virgin?"

"It's not as bleak as that. But there's no one. I guess I'm in the same place as you—nothing turned up and I quit looking. I really love what I do. I'm real happy. It's a pretty simple life, but it works for me."

Oh, she thought, he's good for me. I want to be in exactly that place.

He drank a little coffee and looked out over the hills. Then he turned back to her. "You watching the time?" he asked.

"Nah. I'm fine."

"If you're not in a hurry, there are vineyards in the valley. Tasting rooms and restaurants. You're probably not hungry yet, but you might be later."

"You're going to feed me till I'm big as that bull!"

"Not a chance. And anyway, even if you got big as that bull, you'd still be beautiful." He pulled himself up to his feet. "You ready?"

"Ready," she said, putting her hand in his so he could help her up.

She got back on the bike; they went higher into the hills where the views were even more majestic, stopped a few times, then started a slow and frightening descent. But Cassie wasn't nervous about the altitude or the fact that she was on the back of a bike. She loved hanging on to Walt because he was so solid, so big. It made her feel anchored. He made her feel safe.

They stopped in the valley, visited a couple of vineyards where Cassie tasted some wine and Walt insisted on buying her two bottles. They finally wound up at a nice, quiet, elegant vineyard restaurant that they entered in dusty jeans, all road worn and wind beaten. Walt was greeted as if he was a preferred client. "But I thought you'd given up drinking?" she asked him. "The wine here has alcohol in it, you know."

"I have an occasional drink or glass of wine, maybe a beer," he said. "I didn't mean to mislead you about that—I knocked off for a few years. I don't think I'm in any danger of overdoing it again. I never drink alcohol when I'm riding. If I'm driving my truck, I might have something with a meal and a coffee chaser. I'm a lot more careful now. I was lucky—never had a bad accident. It wasn't just about drinking too much, Cassie. I took a lot of stupid chances back then. But like I said, I took a hint."

"And you've obviously been here before."

"Several times," he said. "I'll get a couple of good bottles for the folks. They like that."

"What do your folks do?" she asked.

"Well, my dad's involved in different businesses now. He started out as a grocer and my mom was a special ed teacher and over time they started buying rental houses, which ended up being a good investment for them. California real estate was out of sight when they started selling. If I bring 'em a couple bottles of good wine, they love it. You keeping track of your schedule?" he asked for at least the fifth time.

"I think I'm a no-show at Julie's," she said. "No big deal. They don't keep tabs on me. I'd rather have dinner here."

"They won't worry?" he asked.

"Nah. Like I said, I'm welcome any time I'm free. And guess what? I'm totally exhausted."

"Told you," he said. "It's not like exercise, but it sure feels like it at the end of the day."

"I guess I can see why you love it. It's very freeing. Exhilarating."

He smiled. "Your cheeks are awful pink."

"Might be the wine," she said.

"Might be the wine and the ride," he said.

"I've noticed something about you," she said. "The first night I saw you, you looked so scary I wasn't sure which one of you guys to run from. Your arms were crossed over your chest, you had this terrifying scowl on your face…"

"I think I've perfected that," he acknowledged with a chuckle.

"But you haven't looked like that since. Your face is… open. Kind. Very sweet. Everyone likes you, feels comfortable around you."

He reached across the table and held her hand. "Cassie, I didn't want any trouble with that guy. It just looked like you needed some help. That was wrong."

"So it was an act?"

He lifted his hand, still in a cast. "No," he said, shaking his head. "I could've been mean. It's not my first choice."

She laughed. "You're at least two people," she said.

"I'm just one guy, Cassie. I just happen to be multipurpose."

After dinner, riding home in the dark was amazing, with the lights of the city welcoming them, drawing them closer. Cassie actually hated it when they left the back roads and got on the freeway, becoming nothing but commuters again as opposed to adventurers. Too soon they were pulling into her neighborhood. She was spent—full on good food, wind-burned, tired to the bone.

Cassie realized she might have stumbled into something fantastic—a best friend of the male persuasion. Like a girl-friend in a great big man suit. Being with him was a little like coming home. He felt like family, like a best buddy. For once she was trusting someone she knew in her gut was absolutely trustworthy. She hadn't looked at his résumé before going off for a day with him on a bike, but she knew he didn't look that good on paper. He wasn't her type, he didn't have a good job, he wasn't great-looking and he hadn't been searching for the right woman.

He walked her to her door and she slipped off the jacket, handing it back to him. "Will you sell this as a used garment now?" she asked.

"Why don't you keep it handy for our next ride?"

"Walt, this is very expensive," she informed him again.

"Looks real good on you, too," he said. "You should really have it, but I think I can get a couple more rides out of it first."

"You're totally nuts," she laughed. "You don't give out things like this on a motorcycle mechanic's salary."

"I might sell you a bike, get a commission," he said. He grinned at her and she found herself thinking she hadn't seen such a warm and wonderful smile in all her looking, all her prowling. When he smiled like that and his blue eyes twinkled, he wasn't that bad-looking. "It'll guilt you into a couple more rides," he said. "I had a good day, Cassie."

"I did, too," she said. "It was fun. I never expected it to be so...nice."

He never took the jacket. He handed her the two bottles of wine and, while her arms were full, he put a big hand on her waist, right on her love handle, pulled her closer, leaned down and gently pressed his lips against hers. She let him do this without once remembering she wasn't interested. The feel of him, smell of him, taste of him was very agreeable and she leaned against him, slowly exhaling as he kissed her. But he didn't take too much of her. Just a brief, delightful kiss, then he pulled back.

"Just friends," she said in a whisper.

"Nothing like a friendly little kiss," he said.

"I can't be friends with you if you're getting ideas..."

"Don't worry about that, Cassie. You're in charge. And we get along pretty well. I'll call." He turned away from her. She still held the jacket and wine as he walked down her drive to his bike. As he drove away, she cuddled the wine and the jacket close to her chest.

5

Walt had always been a man of few words, a big, quiet, mostly serious guy. Cassie seemed to get the conversation rolling off his tongue and he loved that. Time with her was amazing to him; it seemed to fly. After a couple of long coffee dates, dinner and a Sunday ride into Sonoma, he began calling her just to say hello, to catch up on the day. He hadn't done anything like that in longer than he could remember. And it's not as if they were jumping off the phone real fast, either.

He could tell Cassie was enjoying their time together, as well, and also that she had no idea what to make of him, what to do with him. Here was this prim and proper little nurse, probably used to dating doctors or at least golfers, spending time with this big scruffy biker. He was sure he didn't look like any of her other friends; it was probably going to be a long time before she sprung him on them, if ever, afraid they'd think she was crazy. The first time they were book browsing, he suspected she was surprised he could read.

Cassie needed to move real slow for obvious reasons, but that had very little to do with Walt's behavior. He took his time because that was his nature. He knew in ten minutes Cassie was special. She was sweet and funny. And so beautiful, with her pale ivory skin, rosy cheeks, red lips and large brown eyes. And her hair—it was thick and straight and so shiny, flowing down her back almost to her waist. She braided it and wound it around her head for work and tied it in some kind of knot for riding—a knot she could release with one tug and let fall down her back in a silky sheet. He'd been wanting to touch her hair to see if it was as soft as it looked, but he pretty much kept his hands to himself. There had been that one kiss, and he hoped for many more.

It was only because of Cassie and the fact that he was fond of her the second he met her that he asked Kevin to check out that license plate number three weeks ago. Kevin had called the very next day and told him the vehicle was registered to Ralph Perkins.

Naturally, Walt asked, "He a paramedic?"

Kevin answered, "I'm not saying any more than his name, which you said would be in the vault, but I'll look into this a little further."

Walt got two things from that short response. First, it would have been easy to say he wasn't with the fire department, thus removing him from a relatively small group and lumping him with a million other men. After all, Walt had already intimated the guy had played off Cassie's conversation, made up a simple lie to gain her trust, setting her up. And second, there were very few reasons for Kevin to look into something that didn't even happen in his jurisdiction, unless he suspected it just wasn't right. Kevin was a Rancho Cordova cop—Cassie's close call had occurred in Sacramento, Rancho's neighbor. Kevin was a busy patrol officer; he didn't have a lot of extra time for things that weren't important. And he hadn't been all that excited about the story in the first place. Maybe something was up.

So Walt called the fire department and said that a man he worked with had a fire and the firefighters had been just fantastic—one in particular. Walt said he wasn't sure which firehouse had responded that day, but the man he was looking for was named Ralph Perkins and he'd like to thank him. It took only a few seconds. He was told the man worked out of the northwest area.

Since he floated between four stores on a regular basis, Walt looked up a map of firehouses in that area and began taking very brief detours to drive by some of them. It only took a couple of weeks and some luck to spot that teal-blue Tahoe parked outside one of them. At least it was a long way from where Cassie lived. It was the end of July; the weather was hot and humid. Often the firehouse door was standing open. Walt had taken to driving by that firehouse often, sometimes twice in a day. If that teal-blue Tahoe was in the lot, sometimes he'd sit out there a while, across the street, and just watch. Wait.

Walt was very conscious of what he'd promised Kevin; he would not approach or engage the guy. But Walt knew how he looked—big and dangerous. His style alone suggested he had disreputable affiliations, which he did not. It couldn't do any harm for Perkins to think Walt could bring the whole local Hells Angels club to his aid in a second, though even if he could, he wouldn't. At the least, it wouldn't be a bad idea for Ralph Perkins to see he was there. One of these days Perkins would be working on the rig or the fire truck would be leaving the station and he wouldn't miss a great big biker with a cast on his right arm sitting outside. It was a good idea for Perkins to know Walt was on to him, because if he ever went near Cassie again, if he ever threatened her or hurt or scared her, he was going to be so sorry.

That's when Walt figured he was probably sunk. He was hooked on her bad. A guy had to be real careful when something like that happened; it was tempting to try to figure out what the woman wanted most and fit himself into it. It was a huge mistake to do that. When people tried to change to please other people, lots of things went wrong. At the very least, it was hard to guess right—things could be made worse instead of better. At its most destructive, the woman could be attracted to the wrong man, an imposter.

Walt was stubbornly himself. This was who he was; this life worked for him. It brought him a lot of personal satisfaction and he felt good about his work, the quality of his life. He could already tell she liked him. If her feelings were going to grow stronger, they would have to be for the real Walt—big and hairy and dedicated to bikes and the open road.

But he wasn't above working at it a little. The next time he called her, after asking about her day, he said, "How about this weekend, Cassie? We could take off in a different direction this time."

"Oh, Walt, I'm sorry," she said. "I have to work. Hospitals don't shut down on weekends and holidays."

"I admit, I haven't really figured out your schedule yet, except that you're on the day shift."

"It's not easy to keep track of. I work every other weekend and half the holidays. I've been there five years now, so I can actually score a big holiday sometimes—like New Year's Day, which makes it possible to stay up late on New Year's Eve. But that means working Christmas Day. We have to share the load."

"Kind of sucks, I guess," he said.

She laughed at him. "It's not as bad as it could be. Our doctors don't take many days off. E.R. docs don't do rounds, don't have patients admitted they have to watch over, so their schedules are a little more flexible, but on every other service the doctors are checking in by five, six in the morning almost every day, holidays included. Their families complain constantly."

"I hadn't thought about that. So, you have any days off coming up?"

"Sorry. Until next weekend, I have only Wednesday and Thursday."

"How'd you like to go for a ride on Thursday?"

"Aren't you working?"

"Trust me, I put in so much time that if I want a day, no one asks any questions. But, hey, I'm not trying to corner you. Only if you feel like it. I was thinking of driving up Highway 1, north of San Francisco along the coast. Maybe along some beach."

"Really? God, that sounds nice. It's been so hot lately."

"Nice and cool along the ocean. A lot of great fish places to stop and eat."

"I'd love to do that," she said. "But I don't want you in trouble with work."

"I wouldn't worry about that," he laughed. "I'm in charge of my own schedule."

"You are?"

"Everyone there knows I come in whenever I'm needed. If Thursday isn't a special day at the store, I'll be with you. Riding up the coast."

Julie sat on the exam table in her paper gown, swinging her bare feet. It seemed as if she waited forever for Beth to open the door. "Hey," she said brightly. "I didn't know I'd be seeing you today. How are you?"

"Pregnant," Julie said, looking down at her knees for a

moment. She smiled emotionally, fighting tears. "What else is new, huh?"

"Uh-oh. You don't look thrilled."

Instantly the tears ran over. "Beth, this couldn't come at a worse time…"

Beth immediately went into doctor mode. She sat on the little stool and balanced the chart on her knee. "What's the matter, Jules?"

"Another accident. My *fourth* accident. No one gets pregnant as easily as me. I'm a broodmare. I should breed for a living. We've used everything. This time it's an IUD!"

"Are you sure you're pregnant?"

"Oh, I'm sure," she said. "I spent all morning going through the checkbook, looking for an error in my favor. We're completely strapped. Billy works on all his days off. We fight. I throw up every morning. We have a house full of kids, money is nonexistent—we'll never get ahead, we're so far behind already… I was just thinking that when Clint gets in kindergarten next year I could put Stephie in day care and go back to work and maybe we'd have a fighting chance." She sniffed. "Beth, I'm at the end of my rope."

"You do a home pregnancy test?" Beth asked.

"I don't have to. I can tell you exactly how far along I am. I'm the most regular woman in California."

"That isn't always a diagnosis," Beth said, smiling patiently. "I might want a second opinion."

"You want proof? Help yourself. I'm pregnant. Six weeks. And I'm thinking about… What if instead of having a baby, I made Billy have that vasectomy?"

Beth laughed. "That wouldn't really stop you from having the baby, Jules."

"Can we please not call in the nurse?" Julie asked, reclining on the table. Her feet found the stirrups by habit. "Can we do this, just you and me? Because I'm truly screwed up with this one."

"Sure," Beth said. "Special privileges. Now, besides money, what's the problem?"

"What is there besides money?" Julie asked. "You know when we were all at lunch? Well, Billy decided to try to impress me by helping out. He was going to fix the gutter that was breaking off from the eave. He'd only had a few hours of sleep, had been up most of the twenty-four hours before, was too tired to being doing chores like that and he fell off the ladder."

Beth stopped what she was doing and her head snapped up. "He okay?"

"He's fine—luckily he didn't hurt himself. But that really got my attention. What if he got hurt on the job? We'd be so screwed. What if something even worse happened? I wouldn't even be able to keep the house. We're barely hanging on to it now. How would I raise my kids? On welfare?"

"Are you sure things are really that bad, Jules?"

"That bad," she said. "No one knows this—I've been late on a lot of mortgage payments. I've totally missed two. I keep expecting them to come and arrest me or something." Julie put the back of her hand on her forehead. "I try not to bitch about it all the time. Cassie thinks I have the world by the balls with my sweet, good-looking husband and all these kids. Marty just wouldn't get it. She might want a little more attention out of Joe, but if I had her problems, I'd manage, believe me. I'd just hose him down and enjoy my boat."

Beth found the gloves; the speculum was laid out.

"I don't want to be pregnant right now!" Julie blurted.

"Now that I understand," Beth said. "Sooner or later, you should put a stop to this. You have a record."

"Boy, do I."

"Let's get the facts, okay? Slide down for me." Beth did

what she was trained to do. She inserted the speculum, positioned her lamp and had a look at the cervix, which had the nice blue tinge common in early pregnancy. Yup, girlfriend here didn't need the test. She pulled out the hardware and measured the uterus with her hands, fingers inside and pressing down on her lower abdomen with her fingertips. "My, my—you're very good at this. Feels like you have a touch of pregnancy. Let's have a look." She flipped the switch on the ultrasound machine.

In a couple of minutes Beth was able to insert the transvaginal probe for a good view, and there in Julie's womb was a tiny mass, a beating heart and an IUD.

"There you go," she said to Julie. "Alive and pumping. You're something else, you know that?"

"I'm a machine. God," she said, silent tears sliding out of her eyes. "Is it my imagination or does she have that thing in her grip? And is she laughing at me?"

"She?"

"Billy said a girl would even us out. I think it might put me in a straitjacket."

"Billy's not upset about this?"

"I think he's strutting. I want to kill him. He just doesn't take it seriously, because he's not the one juggling the bills. He doesn't know I have to decide every payday which ones I don't pay…"

"Did you talk to him about not having it?"

She shook her head and the tears came harder. "He thinks we should just go with it. But, Beth, he's a fool. I take care of the money because he just doesn't have the time. I tell him how bad it is, but he just keeps saying it won't be a struggle forever. He has a degree, I'm sure he could do something that brings in a better living, but he wants to be a firefighter. It's his life choice, as he calls it. It's noble, and I'm proud of him, I am, but we're starving."

"You're not starving," Beth said.

"We're *starving!* There's nothing left over at the end of the month. We get by on tuna, mac and cheese, peanut butter and jelly and soup made out of scraps. Sometimes I have to scrounge around at my mom's and I feel like a vagrant living out of trash cans. I buy the cheapest of everything. I cut so many corners my life is a circle. I don't know how long I can do this. I feel like I lost my life."

"What life did you lose?" Beth asked.

"Don't ask me that," she said, putting the back of her hand over her eyes. "The answer is shameful. Even to me."

"What life did you lose?" she pushed.

"The one where we were supposed to be in love and happy and having fun and not scared or worried or pinching so god-damn hard we squeak! I'm okay with a little struggle, but every goddamn day is a struggle! The kids were screaming for Mc-Donald's the other day, something they *never* get, and I was counting pennies out of the bottom of my purse! I let them split two Happy Meals three ways and they were all still hungry afterward. It's not supposed to be like that!"

I have so much money even with my debts, Beth thought. Even with med school loans—so much money. A swank town house, great clothes, a sharp car. Problems like these aren't even real to me! In fact, I'd give anything if these were my biggest problems. But she had to rein that in; it was her job to take care of Julie and not the other way around. "Aren't those the kind of stories you tell your kids when they're older? About how you had to manage it? About how tough it was? Billy's not irresponsible with money, is he?"

"Oh, stop it," she said with a sniff. "On our budget, he only gets one beer on a night off, which is a rare thing. That's his big splurge."

"Yeah, he's disgustingly good, isn't he? Sorry about that."

"You have no idea how hard it is..."

Beth smiled. "Well, I owe two hundred thousand dollars for school loans. I have no guy in my life, not even a really bad one."

"Oh, Beth," she said, rising up a bit. "God, I'm sorry. Sometimes I just think of myself! Why don't you seem worried? You're not at the end of your rope."

I'm close to suicidal, Beth thought. But she said, "Well, I'm lucky there—the practice is working me to death, the loan people are patient and I make a decent wage." But, she thought, I have some issues that might get me before I get them. "It's all how you see it. And you're seeing it all to the south right now. There's good stuff in your life—I've been to your house. Billy is a great guy, the kids are pretty cute for kids and they don't seem to have any idea you're broke. You're in good health and you're still as disgustingly pretty as you ever were."

"We had a get-together a couple of weeks ago at Marty and Joe's. Chelsea was there, coming on to Billy. She looks better than all of us put together."

"Chelsea? She's still got her eye on Billy?"

"That's how it looked to me..."

"Well, let's just concentrate on you right now."

Julie was quiet for a second. "I can't have another child, I just can't," she said, so softly she could barely be heard.

"Did you talk to Billy about this?"

"I told you, I—"

"No, did he tell you it was up to you? Because I know you're struggling, but he's struggling, too."

She looked away. "He said everything would be all right. That's what he always says." She propped herself up on her elbows. "Have you ever known a woman to complain because her husband is too happy-go-lucky? I don't understand him. It's not like he lives in some la-la land. He scoops people off the freeway, pulls them out of mangled cars, pumps on their chests to get their hearts going—he lives in a world more real than most of us will ever know. But when it comes to our problems, which are major, he treats them like they're just a minor inconvenience. Beth—if anything happened to Billy and I needed help, I'd have to go to my brother or my parents. And I've gone to them before. Lots."

"I take that to mean he wouldn't consider ending the pregnancy."

"He wouldn't go for that idea, no." And if she could find even a smidgen of hope in her ability to keep the house and food on the table, neither would Julie.

"Well, this might actually come as welcome news to you. Depending on where that IUD is situated, you have a better than average chance of miscarriage. Also depending, this could turn out to be a high-risk pregnancy…" She shrugged. "On the other hand, I've pulled many an IUD out right behind a perfect full-term baby."

"What if you pulled it out now?"

"We *can* take it out. We do that from time to time. Usually a little later, with an ultrasound to guide. But that carries a risk—it could compromise the pregnancy. Sometimes it's a tough call."

"Compromise it later? Or now?"

"Either time, I'm afraid. But we'd take every precaution."

"And if you just pulled it today? Now?" Julie asked, wiping her tears away with the back of her hand.

Beth shrugged. "Maybe nothing. Maybe some spotting and that's all. Maybe a spontaneous miscarriage."

And maybe no pressure to make a decision about keeping it or let-

ting it go? Julie thought for a second, then said, "Do it. Get it over with."

"Jules, if you want it out, we should wait, do it with an ul-trasound, when the fetus is larger."

"There'd still be a risk of losing it, but I'd be further along? No," she said, shaking her head. "This is bad enough. I don't want to make myself accept this and then lose it. I don't want to feel it move and then... Just pull the goddamn little trai-tor IUD out!"

Beth tugged on Julie's hand to help her sit up, then she sat on her stool and looked up at her friend. "All right, listen. It's legally your right to choose termination, but I strongly urge you to get a little quick counseling—it's free. Get Billy on board so it doesn't affect what appears to be a very loving and supportive marriage. Huh?"

"Is it my legal right to have that IUD removed?"

"Julie, think this through..."

"Beth, I have thought it through. I'm afraid of what one more will do to our family and it's a real fear—not just me overreacting. And I definitely can't get used to carrying a baby and then lose it. I don't know how I'd recover from that."

"Then I suggest you make an appointment and take Billy with you, tell him this is urgent and critical and you need his support and—"

"Beth, can you just remove my IUD? Without all this crap?"

Beth pursed her lips for a second. Then she said, "Yes, I can. It may or may not make any difference."

"Explain. Again."

"I can remove the IUD and the pregnancy could be unaf-fected. Or you could have spotting, bleeding and possibly a miscarriage. If you really don't want to be pregnant, it makes better sense to see a doctor who can take care of both the IUD and the pregnancy. But..."

"But if you just take it out right now, I might be saved the trouble," Julie said.

"Jules, don't you want to think about this?"

"I *have*. Take it out. Now."

Beth connected eyes with her for a long moment. Then she said, "It will go in your chart—that I removed the IUD at your request, that I informed you—"

"I know."

"You're sure?"

"I'm absolutely sure."

"Lie down." The gloves went back on, the speculum back in. Beth began to work, talking to Julie's vagina. "You might have some cramping, some spotting. The spotting could last a few days, then stop. Or you could miscarry spontaneously, in which case I'd like to check you, maybe do a follow-up D and C. If you have any heavy bleeding, please let me know immediately—I'm on call tonight. You have my cell number. If I don't answer on the first try, just leave a message and come into the E.R. and I'll see you there. I don't anticipate problems, but you should be aware. No matter which way this goes, I'll have to see you in two weeks." She glanced over Julie's drape. "Sure?"

"Do it."

And while Beth did her work, Julie cried silently, tears sliding out of her eyes and into the hair at her temples.

Cassie was getting pretty flexible with this riding stuff. She packed them some sandwiches and wore a tank top and shorts under her jeans and borrowed leather jacket. They went back to Sonoma, but this time north of San Francisco they got off the road and went along the beach toward Bodega Bay. They found a peaceful spot to park where she disrobed a little bit and produced food and drink. Then Walt surprised her by pulling out a blanket and they sat in the sun on a cool, rocky northern Pacific beach and enjoyed the seascape.

"Tell me what it was like, growing up with three brothers," she said.

"Like a circus," he said, laughing. "We were each born two years apart—I was the second. My mom always worked, so when we were real young, my grandma took care of us. It's amazing she lived as long as she did—she only passed a couple of years ago. But my mom was a teacher, so once we were in school, we were on the same schedule. She taught special ed—did I tell you?"

"You did," she said, chewing on a pastrami sandwich. "And your dad was a grocer. What does that mean, he was a grocer?"

"Well, he bought a little corner grocery store—kind of like the precursor to the 7-Eleven. It was in a crappy neighborhood, but did a great business. Rental houses were his thing, though—great for him, awful for the rest of us."

"Why is that?"

"He'd search for a deal—a repo or falling-down piece of junk—and then we'd live in it while he fixed it up. The second any of us could hold a hammer or paintbrush, we were working on it, too. We lived in one once that had no kitchen appliances at all. My mom kept a refrigerator in the garage. We had a grill in the backyard and a hot plate. There were times he had to turn the water off to plumb—now we're talking about four little boys and a gnarly mom. We boys would pee in the yard and we'd all shower at Grandma's before going to work and school. Mom would rag on Dad to get the water or electric or whatever back on before she killed him." He laughed. "We had a new place every year. I mean an old one every year. Sometimes we could turn 'em in less than a year. I think I remember every one, and there had to be more than twenty. They were awful. When they were fixed up, he'd rent 'em and buy another dilapidated house. At some point my mom was fighting to live in a finished house while he fixed up an empty one, but he wouldn't hear of it. He just couldn't throw away money like that."

"Is he still doing that?"

"Nah, it worked out for him. About twenty years ago or so when we had a real-estate boom, prices doubled or tripled. The other thing—he bought small houses all the time, so the margin was greater and the market better. You know, more people can afford three-hundred-thousand-dollar houses than million-dollar houses. Plus, if you can't sell 'em, rent's cheaper. So when real estate was good, he started selling 'em and bought a few more small grocery stores. Same drill— he'd buy 'em in trouble, get 'em right, sell 'em—but at least we didn't have to live in those! My mom and dad live in a real nice house now—she finally beat him down. Me and my brothers, we give them a lot of grief about never having lived in a finished house, growing up."

"Tell me about your brothers," she said.

"They're all married, have kids. You know about Kevin, the cop. Twenty-eight, wife of one year, pregnant with their first. Joel—the student. He's working on a Ph.D. in bugs so he can be super Orkin. He has two kids and a wife who's a professor already. And Tommy—he's a CPA. He has his own little firm. He handles all the family's stuff along with his other clients. He's thirty-four, been married ten years already—three kids."

"Six grandchildren," she said. "You're the only one not contributing."

"I know," he laughed. "I don't think anyone expects much out of me that way..."

"Aw, they shouldn't write you off so soon."

"That's what I say." He grinned. "Your turn. Tell me about growing up."

"Hmm. Well, it was just me and my mom until I was eight, and then she met Frank, my stepdad. That made her so happy. When I was ten, their first baby came—and I was pretty thrilled to have this little play toy. When I was twelve the next little baby girl came. Then, when I was fourteen and the third one was on the way, Frank got a promotion and transfer to Des Moines." She looked at him and said, "By that time I was pretty reluctant to move, so when Julie's family offered to let me stay with them, my parents agreed to it. I found out later that nobody expected that to work out, but it did. You know, Frank and my mom had this whole new life, new family. I never really felt a part of it."

"Did you miss them?" he asked.

"Sure I did. I visited, spent whole summers there for a couple of years. But then I started getting jobs and my visits were shorter."

"What about your dad? Your biological father?"

"Never knew him," she said with a shrug. "My mom died young—she was only forty-four—a freak brain tumor. She only lasted six months, and I was in Des Moines most of that time, taking care of her. I tried to locate my father then, but I didn't find him. There are all these networks to post your search so the missing parent who might not want to be found can get in touch with you, but he never has. Who knows, maybe he's gone, too? Anyway, I don't care anymore. He was never a part of my life. If he got in touch now, I'd ask him some medical history questions, but I don't have much else to ask. Except…"

He gave her a second and then said, "Except?"

"Well, I'm curious about why he left us."

"You don't know anything about that?"

"My mom said they weren't together long. She got pregnant, he married her but never really lived with her, wasn't around for my birth. The divorce was final before I was six months old. They were both young. It was like a big mistake, an accident he ran from. So far in the past and so irrelevant, it seems ridiculous to wonder anymore."

Walt put his big hand against the hair at her temple and ran it back in a caress. "Are you okay about that now? Does it hurt?"

She shook her head. "What hurts is not having my mom anymore. She went on to a new life with Frank, but we stayed real close. We'd spend hours on the phone, talking about everything. Sometimes I miss her so much."

"I can understand that. In case you didn't get the message, I'm real tight with my mom and dad. They hung in there with me when I was in trouble a lot, when I tested every rule they came up with. Losing either one of them would hurt real hard."

"Our histories plan our futures," she said. "I think some of that explains how I could end up fighting for my life in the front seat of an SUV…"

He frowned. "How?"

"Walt, when you get down to it, I have no family. No real family."

"You have your stepdad and siblings, even if they're halfs."

"It's not the same. I never got close to Frank or the little kids, and now the oldest one has started college—to her I was just an occasional visitor since she was five. When I was a kid, it was me and my mom—I was her life and she was mine. Then it was my mom and Frank and the babies and she was *so* happy. Even I was happy with those babies to take care of. I think the message I got was that a fulfilled life is one where there's a spouse and family. Ever since I separated myself from my mom and the little kids, I've always thought what I wanted from life was exactly what she had—someone who made me that happy and gave me children. It's possible I was trying too hard to make every guy who asked me out into that. I have an image of what I want my life to be, but none of the details. No instructions. My mom—she wasn't hunting. She never went out that I remember. I was never left home alone or with a sitter. She met Frank at the copy machine in her office and the rest is history."

"Things happen like that," he said. "Without much warning."

"Really?" She smiled. "Something like that happen with you?"

"Almost everything. I never planned that eighteen-month ride—I was pissed and took off—and it changed my life. That bike shop, my first job when I got back? It was a little job fixing bikes, but it grew from a little store into a successful store, then four stores... I thought we were doing a good job, but I didn't know it was that good. I never saw that coming. And I've been there from the beginning. If you'd asked me ten years ago if I thought things would work out like this, I wouldn't have believed it." He laughed. "Ten years ago, I thought I might end up in jail or something..."

"You love your work, don't you?" she asked, smiling.

"I do. Things just keep getting better there. And in my personal life, too—I mean, look at you in those shorts, Cassie. How could I ever complain? And we didn't exactly meet through a dating service." He grinned at her.

"You've been real nice to me, Walt," Cassie said. "You've turned into a real good friend."

"Thanks, Cassie. I like hearing that. Wanna put your jeans back on and ride up the coast for a while?"

"I do. I like your silly bike."

"There's a fish house in Bodega Bay—not fancy, but some of the best fresh fish you can imagine."

"Do they all know you there?" she asked, shimmying into her jeans.

"Of course. I've been there a lot."

"Of course," she laughed.

Billy came home from the shop at ten-thirty after eight hours. He was all dusty from the saw, dirty from wood, grainy from marble and granite. The house was dimmed. There was a light left on in the kitchen over the stove and he assumed Julie was in bed, asleep. He was exhausted; he'd worked every day for the past six days, three of them twenty-four-hour shifts. Now he was facing four days off from F.D. in a row, but he'd spend all of them at the shop. He reached into the fridge for a cold cola, after which he'd shower off the grime and pass out.

"Billy?"

He turned toward the living room. "Jules? You still up?"

"Billy…" she said weakly. "I have a problem. I'm losing the baby…"

He rushed to the sofa and found her there, lying down, an ice pack on her lower abdomen. He knelt beside her and brushed the hair back from her brow. "What's going on?" he asked.

"I went to see Beth to confirm what we knew. I asked her to take out the IUD. She told me this could happen. It's happening. I'm bleeding a lot. I have to do something…"

"Did you call her? Ask her what to do?"

She nodded. "I have to go in now. To the hospital. We'll have to call Cassie or my mom to come over for the kids. I wanted to wait for you. I needed you with me."

"Jesus, what if I'd been late!" He jumped up and headed for the phone. "You should've called me! I could've come right away." Into the phone, he said, "Cass? We got a problem. Can you come over for the kids? I have to take Julie to the hospital. She might be miscarrying." A pause. "Yeah, that's what I said. I guess she didn't tell anyone—she was upset. We can't talk about it now. I need you to come. Thanks."

By the time Cassie arrived, Billy had Julie in the passenger seat of the running car. Cassie ran straight to Julie's window. "Miscarriage?" she whispered, an alarmed look on her face. "You didn't say anything about being pregnant."

"I couldn't," Julie said in a voice barely audible.

Billy leaned forward. "We'll talk about it later, Cass," he said. Then before she could move fully away, he had the car in reverse, backing out of the drive. To Julie he said, "How bad is the bleeding?"

"Seems bad," she said. "Scary bad. But I don't know—I've never been through this before."

"What did Beth say?" he asked.

"She said to come in—"

"No. At your appointment. Why'd she take out the IUD?"

"I asked her to."

"Is that what they normally do?"

She was quiet a moment, then she said, "No. But I wanted it out of me. She said it could go either way—it could affect the pregnancy, cause a miscarriage. Or maybe nothing would happen."

"Why didn't you just leave it alone?" he asked.

"Because it was going to be a problem, either way. Same odds—maybe nothing would happen, maybe it would have to come out later with some risks, maybe it would be a high-risk pregnancy. If there were going to be problems, I wanted it over with. Early. Before we got used to the idea. Before the deductible got too high."

He ground his teeth. "You made it pretty clear you weren't going to get used to the idea..."

"Billy...not now..."

"Shouldn't we have talked about it?" he asked. "Made

the decision together? Fuck the deductible, I could get more hours in—"

"We couldn't talk about it!" she snapped. "You wouldn't listen! And when were we going to talk, Billy? You work all the time. You're hardly around. And when you are around and I try to talk to you, you just keep saying everything will be all right! That we have something special that doesn't include money! And that's for goddamn sure!"

"Would you prefer it if I got all freaked out all the time, like you?" he said, his voice rising to match hers. "Someone's gotta stay positive—what the hell are the choices?"

"One choice would be looking hard for a better-paying job! I didn't have these kids alone!"

"The job's going to get better-paying! I get a raise every year! We're up for a new contract and—"

"And that could take two years! Jesus, Billy, we're not *making* it! Don't you get that?"

He drove in silence for a couple of minutes. Then in a voice quiet and controlled he asked, "If you had wanted this baby, what would you have done?"

She started to cry. Through hard tears she asked, "You think I didn't *want* it? You think it's that simple? I'm *afraid* to have it! Do you know what it's like to have my mom stuff a twenty-dollar bill in my purse every time I see her? Having her pay for soccer uniforms and summer programs? To go over to her house and rummage through her refrigerator and cupboards for enough food to get us to another payday? To have to tell the kids no to McDonald's every time they ask?" She looked over at his beautiful profile. "I eat oatmeal for supper, or twenty-cent mac and cheese, to save the meat for you, so you have the strength to work seven days a week. Billy..." she said, putting her hands over her face to cry into them. "Billy, I've missed mortgage payments... I'm afraid of losing the house. There isn't enough... We're in such trouble."

"Okay," he said, reaching a hand over to rub her thigh. "Okay, stop. It's going to be all right..."

"It's not going to be all *right,*" she sobbed, shaking her head, weeping into her hands. "This isn't a recent problem! It's been like this from the beginning! I keep telling you, and you act like I'm just overreacting! There isn't enough money to pay the bills much less pay the bills and buy food! Every month someone goes unpaid so we can eat!" she wailed. Then, more softly, she said, "I gave it up, let it go, and it was the hardest thing I've ever done. And now God's going to punish me by making me bleed to death! And maybe that's not...such a bad thing."

"Jules! Stop it! You're not going to bleed to death, and I'm not going to lose you! You know I can't make it without you! Baby, calm down." He pulled his cell phone off his belt. "What's Beth's number?"

"I don't know. I already called her. I didn't even bring a purse..."

Billy had other resources, given his paramedic job. He called the hospital and had her paged, an emergency. When she came to the phone, he said, "I'm bringing Jules—we're almost there. Listen, she's bleeding real bad, and she's scared to death and panicked. Meet us in E.R. in five minutes. Yeah, yeah, thanks."

He reached across to Julie, put a hand on her shoulder and said, "I need you to calm down," he said sternly. "We're going to make this right. I'm going to make this right—I'll figure something out. I love you, Julie. Now, come on—don't make this worse with hysteria. I need you..."

When he pulled into the E.R. loading zone, he told her to sit tight. He went around to the passenger door, lifted her into his arms and carried her inside. She laid her head against his dusty, gritty chest and wept.

Beth was right inside the door, wearing scrubs. She told him to follow and took Julie straight to an exam room. "She shouldn't be hemorrhaging," she said softly. "Let me have a look before we get all worked up."

Billy laid her gently on the exam table and a nurse was already there, helping Beth to get Julie out of her clothes. Billy stood lamely watching. Over her shoulder Beth said, "Don't you have a car to move or something?"

"Who cares?" he shot back.

"By the time you get that done, I'll know where we are. Go. Do something. Give me ten minutes."

"Don't you let anything happen to her," he said, his voice a mixture of menace and desperation.

"Go," Beth said, helping to get Julie set up for an exam, not looking at him. "Ten minutes."

All the way to the parking lot and back, he fought panic and grief. Why's she doing that—eating mac and cheese and cereal like that? I eat good at the firehouse—I get more meat than I need in a week! I had no idea it was that bad. Why's she taking it all on herself? Why'm I letting her take it all on? Jesus, I'm losing my family. I don't even know what's going on with my own wife. Work… I thought if I just kept working…

When he got back to the exam room, Beth was just emerging, drying her hands on a towel. She had a slight smile on her lips. "It's not as bad as she feared. There can be a lot of blood, but she's not hemorrhaging…"

"She lost the baby?"

"Yes. I'm so sorry, Billy. It just happened—spontaneous— and the bleeding slowed right down. Listen, you understand, there was a chance of that, anyway, no matter what she decided to do…"

Not my wife, he thought. *She has the iron uterus; she'd have carried the baby, but lost her mind.* But he looked at the floor and nodded.

"I'm going to do a D and C, make sure she's all cleaned up and intact. Shouldn't take long. We'll watch her for a little while and then she can go home if you can arrange someone to keep the kids so she can rest tomorrow. There's a little recovery time involved."

"I'll handle it," he said.

She put a hand on his arm. "You okay?"

"Yeah," he said, lifting his head. "Yeah. I'll stay till she's done, till she wakes up, maybe till morning, to take her home. Cassie's at the house."

Hard work was not uncommon for Billy; it had been a way of life since he was a teenager. His father suffered a construction accident when Billy was fourteen, his older brother sixteen. He never recovered; he was laid up for a year, then a jobless cripple for the rest of his life, which was short. There had been some disability insurance for a while, then unemployment and finally county subsistence, but it was a drop in the bucket. The boys went to work immediately, pitching in with what pittance they could contribute, the greatest contribution being that they covered their own expenses. His brother, Dan, went into construction at eighteen; their dad died a couple of years later.

Now Dan, married with kids, lived and worked in San Jose; their widowed mother lived with his family and took care of their kids so Dan and his wife could both work. Maybe part of Billy's problem was that he was used to tightening his belt, used to working two jobs.

But even with all those jobs, all that scrimping, his high school years had been memorable, positive. He got good grades, was able to play some ball and he'd had Julie from an early age. He didn't have a car, but his brother did and Billy had been able to borrow it sometimes. Julie had a car; she'd drive him to work or pick him up when Dan couldn't. They could go out on cheap dates. All they really needed to be happy was the opportunity to get together with friends, go to school events or park and make out. All things considered, it had been sweet. Except for the fact that his mom and dad had it rough, his family life hadn't been as bad as it could've been. Everyone held up.

Maybe that was another part of the problem—they always held up. He figured as long as he stayed upbeat and just kept working, everyone would hang in there, get through. He really didn't expect it to be that tough forever. Dan and his wife had it pretty much under control now; their money problems weren't terrible anymore. Billy figured a few more years with F.D. and finances would straighten out.

Getting on the department was like a dream come true to Billy. It wasn't just a decent job; it was all he'd ever wanted. And the department was a good, solid job with good benefits—that wasn't what was wrong. It was starting out broke, years of working low-paying jobs, going to school, running up debt. Julie's folks helped them get in the house so their income wouldn't be lost to rent, but real estate in California was expensive—it was a very little house, but not a little mortgage. Still, if they could just hang in there a few more years, things should get considerably better. He had absolutely no doubt he'd promote himself at the earliest possible slot. And he had a plan; he intended to retire early enough to take on a second twenty-year career and draw a couple of decent pensions. By the time the kids were college age, things should be manageable, and by the time they were grown, life should be comfortable. Nice.

But this was too much for Julie. She couldn't take it anymore. She was afraid to have their baby, for God's sake—afraid she'd be eating cereal for dinner for the rest of her life. What kind of a man lets his wife go through that?

He sat by her bed while she slept off the anesthesia, reaching out to touch her hand every few minutes. Near dawn, her eyes opened and he jumped up, leaning over the bed. "Hey, baby."

"Billy," she whispered. "Billy, I'm sorry…"

"Shh, all that matters is you'll be all right. It wasn't as bad as you thought. Everything's okay now."

"I didn't do that to hurt you, Billy. I love you, you know that…"

"Don't worry, Jules. I don't hurt that easy, honey. As long as you're okay, everything is okay." But she's not okay, he thought. She has it rougher than I realized. I thought she was bitchy and hard to please; she's been deprived and hungry and terrified. I have to find a way to make this right. He leaned over and kissed her brow. "We'll get through this, honey. As long as we have each other."

"I'm sorry," she said. "I'm sorry. I didn't know what to do…"

"Jules, it's over. We're not going to let it bring us down. I know I don't deserve it, but if you can trust me a little longer, I'll think of something. I swear to God, Jules. I'll make this better. All of it."

"I didn't want to lose it—it was yours, and I love your babies so much."

"It's okay, baby. Sleep off the drugs and I'll take you home."

Her eyes fluttered closed and he sat by the bed again. Sat and tried to keep the tears that ran down his cheeks concealed from the nurses.

6

Cassie entered Julie's darkened bedroom carrying two glasses of wine. Julie had spent all day in bed, had a substantial early dinner that Cassie made herself and brought over, was not on pain meds and…was no longer pregnant. Along with the dinner, she brought a bottle of wine, knowing Julie wouldn't have any on hand. She passed Julie the glass. Julie was propped up on some pillows and the color had come back into her cheeks, a little of the light into her eyes.

"You sure this is okay?" Julie asked Cassie.

"If you're not nauseous from the anesthesia, you're fine. I have a big dinner waiting for Billy and the kids when he gets them home from your mom's. But you and I should talk. Jules, I had no idea what was going on with you. Since when does that happen?"

"I'm sorry. It's not that I didn't trust you, that I didn't think you'd be supportive—I know you'd do anything for me. But I was devastated. Just stricken. In fact, I was thinking of making it go away before telling Billy, but I can't seem to keep things from him." She looked down into the glass, took a sip. Then tears filled her eyes. "I just reached an understanding with women in trouble I've never had before. When you face something like this, you just don't have any good choices. None. The choice I made wasn't good—it was the least terrible." She blinked and a tear spilled over.

"Can you please start at the beginning?" Cassie asked gently.

Julie laughed and rolled her eyes upward. "Let's see… I met Billy when I was fifteen years old, started dating him right before I turned sixteen…"

"Seriously," Cassie said.

"Seriously," Julie insisted. "Look, I know a lot of people have it worse. And believe me, I'd never complain about being married to the best man in the world or about having these kids—they're such awesome kids. But, Cassie, we just can't make ends meet. The only hope is keeping things static, and me going back to work as soon as possible. We can't add another child to the family without adding years to our financial recovery. There aren't just big bills to keep up with, there are *old* bills. Not just loans for Billy's school expenses—we've taken seconds on the house, equity lines, and the charge cards are maxed out." She laughed humorlessly. "You max out, cut up the card, and someone will give you a new one when you clearly have no way to pay the bill! This country is run on madness!"

"So…what happened?" Cassie asked.

"I got caught again," she said with a shrug. "Let's see, I got pregnant with Jeffy because I was taking antibiotics and my pills didn't work. I don't think anyone told me, but I can't remember. I was so young then, so hysterical. We got pretty good at relying on condoms and spermicide, but then there was a slip. We borrowed Joe's boat for an anniversary ride and got all steamed up, carried away and bingo—Clint. I swear to God, it was the only slip in five years, and he nailed me! I had a diaphragm right after Clint and got pregnant immediately. Beth said I must not have had a good fit. I thought I had it made with the IUD, even though my periods were like a train wreck. I made it three years!"

"Phew. Fertile Myrtle. You better hurry up on that vasectomy. Or something."

"I can't wait for him anymore. I'm going to do the tubal thing. I just don't know how to afford it…"

"How's he doing? Billy?" Cassie asked.

Again Julie looked down. "He's sad. He's very, very sad. He can't look me in the eye. I don't think he'll ever forgive me."

"Okay, wait. Let's get real here. That was the path of least resistance, pulling the IUD. This was going to happen, anyway—pulling the IUD just made it happen earlier. You get pregnant in the tube, the IUD keeps the fertilized egg from sticking, that's all it does. You never know what flowed out every month—a regular period or…"

"Or a baby?"

"Or a fertilized ovum. Do you have any idea how many fertilized ova don't stick, anyway, without the presence of an IUD? How many times you manage to fertilize an egg? No one knows, that's how many. Beth was right—you didn't have any control of the outcome. You had no way of knowing if yanking out that IUD would cause a miscarriage or not. It was a risk. But not much more of a risk than having it in there with the baby in the first place, so give yourself a break. It would be different if you went out and had an abortion behind your husband's back…"

"I was thinking about it."

"Thinking about it and doing it are two different things. Julie, you couldn't even keep from him the fact that you were pregnant! You tell him everything." She patted her hand. "He's feeling some loss, just like you are. You both need time to grieve, but you'll get beyond this. Come on."

The doorbell rang and Cassie put down her wine. "I'm on that," she said, rising to leave. She was back in less than a minute with Beth trailing along behind her.

"How are you feeling?" Beth asked, sitting on the bed.

Julie struggled against tears. "Empty."

"Aw, honey. I'm so sorry things haven't been easier…"

"Is it true? I could've lost it later? Like even after feeling it move?"

"We're making lots of progress with the rare IUD baby, keeping everyone safe and intact, but there are still occasional problems. The further the pregnancy goes, the better our chances. But then, every day is a stressful day, hanging on. The important thing is you're fine. Fine, Julie. That's worth being grateful for."

The doorbell rang again. "I'll get that," Cassie said once more.

In less than two minutes Marty came into the room, carrying a glass of orange juice for Beth. She sat on the bed along with everyone else. "Pregnant? And you didn't tell us?" Marty said.

"I was embarrassed," Julie said. "It was another accident. How can anyone believe me that I have this many accidents? I know in your hearts you must think I'm making excuses, that we took a lot of stupid chances…"

"Oh, don't be ridiculous. You can be depressed if you want to, but no paranoia," Marty said. "We know you, Jules. We know you had signed off on reproduction."

"Really, three kids—it'll put you right over the edge."

"Oh, yeah?" Marty laughed. "One more and I might hang myself!"

Beth turned to stare at her. "Is Jason a tough kid?"

"Nah, he's an angel. Joe's a tough kid." Then Marty looked at Julie and asked, "So, what's going on here? I mean, I can understand wanting to cut it off, but is there something else? Something you should be telling us?"

Julie just dropped her chin and shook her head.

"Yes, there are money problems," Cassie said, breaking the silence, giving her up. "Serious money problems— and since Billy and Joe work together, that can't go any further. Are you in this pact of silence?"

"Of *course*," Marty said. "Oh, my God! Did you think you couldn't trust *me?*"

"You know, I don't even care," Julie said. "Billy does nothing but work, and there's no reason he should be embarrassed around his friends. The truth is, we're just about bankrupt. If a car goes right now, we're doomed. It's old loans for college, maxed-out credit cards, a second on the house, a loan consolidation thing—it all piles up. It just keeps getting worse instead of better. There's no end in sight. Another baby sure wasn't going to help us dig out." She took a breath. "I panicked."

"Well, maybe bankruptcy is the answer," Beth said. "Have you talked to anyone about that?"

"That would be so humiliating…"

"But have you?"

"We've been to the bank," Julie said. "They discourage that."

"Of course they do!" Beth laughed. "They wouldn't get their money back! Oh, jeez—girl, you don't even know what you don't know!"

"Beth, I just don't think I could bear the shame of it. We pay our bills, or at least we do everything we can."

Beth just laughed and all eyes were on her. "That's very noble, but there comes a time when your family is more important than all that pride. I worked with a vascular surgeon who filed for bankruptcy, and he sure didn't look ashamed. I think he gave up his leased Ferrari, but he didn't move out of his eight-thousand-square-foot house with the pool! Jules, you have to get some help."

"We've had a couple of loan consolidation deals. We can't get ahead of them. The bills just keep getting bigger."

"That's what I'm saying—some of those bills have probably been paid ten times over with just the interest. There are solutions." Everyone just stared at her. "I read money magazines to relax."

Cassie just shook her head. "Oh, God, only you would read money magazines to unwind." Then to Julie she said, "Until you get this straightened out, we can help."

"Oh," Julie said, shaking her head. "No…"

"I don't mean with money," she said. "I'll commit to two casseroles a week. Big ones. I guarantee leftovers. And everything that's left in the garden."

"I can cover two. Joe will never know," Marty said. "I'll make them up on days he works and I'm home—I'll freeze them."

"Ah, since I don't even know *how* to cook," Beth weighed in, "what in the world can I do?"

"Can you buy lettuce and tomatoes?" Marty asked.

"I can," Beth said with a big smile. "Actually, I'm very good at fruits and vegetables. I'm also good at bread! Well, I'm good at buying it… It won't solve all the problems, but it might get you over the hump."

Julie put her hands over her face and began to cry.

"Aw, now what are you crying about?" Cassie asked, tugging at her hands.

"This is what friends do when someone dies!" she sobbed.

"Or when someone's a little down on their luck," Marty said, grabbing her hand and giving it a squeeze. "Now, come on—you'd do the same. What are you crying about?"

"I don't know," she said through sobs. "I don't know if I'm totally embarrassed, totally touched that you would do that or just helpless. I don't know anything. I don't even know myself anymore…"

"Join the club," Marty said. "I've been feeling that way a lot lately. I walked out on Joe the other day. We had a fight—same fight. I was furious that he couldn't pick up his own mess or take a shower. I drove around and ended up at Martinelli's for takeout and who'd I run into? Ryan Chambers!"

"Oh, no," Cassie said. "What did you do?"

"Just talked to him awhile, waiting for my pizzas. Jules, baby, I wish you could help me with my problems by fixing a couple of casseroles every week. I don't think we're going to make it—me and Joe."

The conversation shifted to Marty and Joe, as happened with them routinely. When one of them became more revealing, others opened up even more. They didn't realize they were like that, but they traded secrets. Marty laid it out—she didn't even want to sleep in the same room with Joe anymore. He'd begun to repulse her. The thought of his whiskers against her breast was unimaginable. She wanted to cut up the gym shorts, sink the boat, put a pipe bomb in the goddamn big screen. She longed for a romantic partner, even if it was only occasional. She'd be happy if he'd shave and shower before coming to bed, even sometimes.

Cassie confessed about the assault, tilting Beth and Marty back on their heels. She admitted to becoming friendly with her rescuer. And she was adamant—she was positively through with dating. Walt was just a diversion, a good friend to pass some time with.

The one person who didn't have anything to share was Beth.

Beth knew that closing herself off was not only a bad idea, it was going to ultimately be impossible. First of all, she'd had to meet with the senior staff at the clinic, let them know she'd begun treatment that would soon not only affect her schedule, it could diminish her energy and ability to put in those long hours. Of course, she was extended all the support her colleagues could offer—it was, after all, a women's clinic. They dealt with these medical issues with patients every day and, unfortunately, had a couple of staff members who had faced similar challenges. Their head nurse was a breast cancer survivor; their senior female physician had undergone a hysterectomy several years ago for a cancerous tumor in her uterus.

The rest of the world she hoped to hold off for a while, at least until and if she began to lose her hair.

She'd always been a private sort, not because she was secretive, but because she had a tendency to be intense, to think about things deeply for a long time before putting her emotions out there to be examined. Some of that was natural, some learned during the minefields of residency when it felt as if everyone was constantly gunning for the young, inexperienced doctor. And, of course, she'd had that history—her last bout with this disease.

She had been in her third year of med school, only twenty-five, and involved in a very comfortable relationship with Mark, a first-year surgical resident. It was serious; he'd chosen his residency to be in the same city with Beth while she finished school. They had moved in together a few months prior to the diagnosis and had casually kicked around the idea of getting engaged as soon as she graduated, got her M.D. It was, in fact, the first serious relationship she'd had.

The news of the malignancy devastated her, threw her into a complete tailspin. She wasn't a totally abnormal girl—she'd cried before—but nothing like the hysteria brought on by facing that battle. Of course, her parents came at once, although, God bless them, they weren't much comfort. She'd never seen her mother more scatterbrained and fretful, her father more helpless than ever. Since they'd never been in the least domestic to start with, they were more trouble than help around the house and with meals. They drove Mark crazy in two days.

Her girlfriends were better, especially Cassie, a born nurse. All three girls were completely domesticated and nurturing; they knew exactly what to do to bring comfort, order and nutrition. And for young women, they had been so wise, coming in turns instead of en masse. But they had such pain, pity and fear in their eyes. They were too quiet and polite, too careful of her feelings, void of the usual relentless laughter when they were together.

She survived the surgery and was managing the chemo fairly well; she didn't have to leave school, though she suffered too much time off. And she held her parents off to keep her medical and personal lives from converging; instead of having them visit to "help" she took a few very quick trips home to let them look at her, see that aside from being a little on the pale and thin side, she was holding up well. But all this time, she could feel Mark shrinking away.

It was so gradual, she hadn't been sure until the end what was coming. Her treatment lasted for six months, and it was hard to pin down what was happening to her relationship— first-year residents are worked so constantly, his absence was not suspect. Mark's time at home was minimal at best.

Within a year of her diagnosis her energy was back. Her MRI looked good, she appeared to be in remission if not cured. There was color in her cheeks again and a soft cap of hair on her bald head when Mark said, "I'm sorry. This is the most terrible thing I've ever done to anyone in my life, but I can't go on. I don't know if the illness took its toll, or if this was going to happen to us, anyway. I swear to God, I don't know."

"What did I do?" she asked. "What *didn't* I do?"

"You can't have done anything wrong, or neglected any-thing. Beth, you've been amazing through all this. Maybe we'd end up in this place, anyway. Maybe it wasn't meant to be. I'm sorry."

It was impossible for her to believe that a surgeon, a man

who not only cut people up for a living but loved his own work, would have trouble looking at that rugged scar. But slowly, through his leaving and talking about his departure, she realized that it probably had everything to do with cancer. He was twenty-eight; he wanted a family, as did she. He didn't want to be a widower at thirty or thirty-two, starting over. He didn't want to be a husband whose wife wouldn't be a good candidate for pregnancy or motherhood. Beth had no crystal ball, but if they'd already been married, she thought he might have stuck with her. No telling on that.

It destroyed her. In fact, his leaving was harder on her in many ways than the disease and treatment.

She thought she had survived both.

"Don't think of this as a continuation of the disease," Dr. Paterson had said. "Frankly, it's not as rare as you might think. What's rare is breast cancer at twenty-five. But this is exactly why we follow so closely, observe so diligently, in the chance this is a vulnerability. We're going to treat this a little more aggressively than the last time, and your odds are as good as anyone's with early detection and reliable treatment. You're not doomed, Beth. You're not."

She liked him. She didn't necessarily believe him, but she liked him. She ran her vitamin regimen by him and he approved. One week after her first appointment with him, she had begun radiation. A couple of weeks later, the start of chemo. She began the long, difficult, lonely climb back to freedom. She'd had two months of chemo and radiation. She was physically weakening; she could feel it.

Billy brought an accordion file folder home from the firehouse and began to gather up all the bills, check registers, receipts and related paperwork. "What are you doing?" Julie asked him.

"I'm taking this mess off your hands." He shoved the last of the stack into the folder and turned to her. "It's a disaster, and it's got you completely stressed out. It's too much to ask of anyone."

"You can't do that!" she said in a panic. "You can't take all my papers! I won't know what's going on!"

"I'm not going to keep anything from you, Jules. I just want it out of your hair. It's worrying you too much. It's like leaving you with the yard work and car maintenance along with everything else, expecting you to shoulder this alone. Besides, you've been asking me to get involved for years, but I spend too much time at work."

"I've been doing the best I can, Billy," she said, getting teary.

He dropped the folder on the bed and put his arms around her. "I'm not taking this stuff because you're not doing a good job, baby. I want you to let go of it. As soon as I get it figured out a little bit, we'll come up with a budget you can live with and I'll just put aside what you need to get you and the kids through the week. I can't have you eating cereal so I—"

"I should never have said that," she said, leaning against his chest and sniveling. "It was just an emotional outburst, that's all. I can keep juggling. I'm good at it by now. I have a system…"

He stroked her back. Her system included so much anger and desolation it was wiping her out. It had caused her to take a chance on losing that baby, and no matter what was happening in their lives, Julie came alive with happiness when they were having a baby. Once she got used to the idea, that is. "I'm probably going to be asking about your system before I start bill paying, but all I want right now is to see where we are, then maybe I can take on some of the stress."

"How are you going to manage this? With two jobs?"

"I'll see what I can do at the firehouse. We have some downtime. A lot of the guys do their bill paying and stuff while they're there. We've got one guy studying all the time, trying to finish up his degree. A couple are working on the captain's test. It's okay. I'll gnaw away at it a little bit every day."

"It's impossible," she whimpered. "How are you going to concentrate on work if you have this on your mind?"

"Same way I concentrate on work with you and the kids on my mind. I think about you guys every second. Half the time we have a sick kid or some disaster going on. I'll do just fine." He lifted her chin and smiled into her eyes. "How are you feeling?"

She shrugged. "Physically, I'm fine. Emotionally... I have a lot of regrets."

"Let's not waste too much energy on that, huh? It's over. We have to move on."

"But I look at you, and it doesn't feel over. You don't look at me the same way. You don't sleep with me like you used to..."

"You're out of commission for six weeks," he said. "At least four to go."

"You're usually begging after two..."

"Not this time," he said, looking briefly away. "I don't want to mess anything up."

"You don't curl around me. You don't kiss me and ask me if I love you all the time. I think you're still mad."

"No, honey, I'm not mad about anything. Shoot me for being such a guy, but curling around you when you're untouchable isn't real easy. I've had a lot on my mind lately..."

"About me. About the baby. About what I did—"

"Jules," he said, stopping her. "About what I can do to change things. I talked to Chelsea. I—"

She pulled away from him. "You talked to Chelsea?"

"Stop. I asked her about car sales. I've been looking around for something better than cutting wood for cupboards and countertops on my days off. She offered me a job..."

"I bet she did."

Billy grinned. "Selling Hummers. Don't worry, I won't be working for Chelsea. I don't care what she says, I don't believe they're selling that well. I think she's full of shit. But the commission on just about any new car is pretty good. Problem is, I just don't think I can be without a paycheck long enough to find out. And there aren't any days left." He kissed her nose. "Let me get the lay of the land here, huh? Then we'll talk."

"Billy… I hope you don't get mad—I mean madder—but I told Beth. She asked if we ever considered bankruptcy." She shrugged helplessly. "I guess it can make some things just go away…"

He frowned. "I know what bankruptcy does," he said. "I'd like to pay what we owe. After all, we owe it."

"But, Billy…"

"We'll get to that later. First, I want to see where we are. Can you let me do that? They're not just your bills, Jules. They're mine, too. In fact, I should have done a better job with this since the beginning."

"Are you ever going to forgive me?" she asked him. "For not making the decision with you? I mean really forgive me?"

He pulled her against him and held her close. In her ear, he whispered, "Jules, none of this should have gone the way it went. I don't blame you for anything—I swear to God. I blame myself, that's the truth. If I'd taken better care of you, you wouldn't have been so afraid…"

"Billy, I—"

"Shh. I guess we both need a little time to deal with it, to get things straightened out."

"Don't let it be too long, Billy. This is very hard for me, too. And I've never had to go through anything without you before."

"Well, that's the problem, baby. I thought if I just kept working, everything would be okay. Instead, I was gone too much. I let you go through everything alone. We have to fix that."

★ ★ ★

Cassie had set a nice table in her small dining room and primped as though this was a decision-making date, when it fact it was almost the first time in her dating history that there was no decision to make, and that felt so damn good. She loved Walt like a buddy, a big brother, probably the most decent, easy-to-be-around guy she knew next to Billy. A buddy who was allowed to steal that little kiss—she couldn't resist. As it happened, it was always a good kiss. As long as it went no further than that, Cassie wasn't worried.

Tonight, she was just returning a few favors. Walt had picked up every tab they'd had since they met and there was no way he was letting her pay for anything, so she asked if she could cook him dinner. She'd asked during one of their many phone conversations, which were just as companionable as those talks they had when they were together. And they were together quite a lot for a couple of buddies—a casual dinner about once a week, about four rides on the motorcycle so far, the occasional coffee date when she was on her way home from work.

She hadn't seen him in more than a week; she'd explained about Julie's miscarriage and the need for Cassie to help out. The last time they talked he said he really hoped Julie got on her feet soon; he was missing their time together. Well, so was she. That's when she suggested dinner. She killed two birds with one stone—made a casserole for Julie at the same time.

She'd said seven and the doorbell rang at exactly three minutes till. When she opened the door, she was slightly taken aback. His appearance was altered. He wore khakis, a cotton shirt and he wore boots, but these were shiny brown leather dress boots, no chains. Of course, he still had the ponytail and naked lady, but there was no stubble on his face and his hair wasn't all messed up by a helmet. "Well, Walt," she said, smiling, "if you weren't about six-five, I'd hardly know you."

"I'm only six-three," he said, presenting her a bouquet of flowers with one hand and a bottle of wine with the other.

"Only," she laughed. "Come in. Let me put these in water right away."

"Something smells real good," he said, stepping inside.

"Lasagna," she told him. "What do you make for a great big guy who likes his food? I'm not good with steaks on the grill—I destroy them. I guess I don't have enough testosterone or something. I was kind of torn between a turkey and lasagna." She stood at the sink, unwrapping the flowers, and threw a look over her shoulder. "Lots of garlic bread. A little salad to keep you healthy."

"Sounds perfect," he said. "Should I have brought a vase?"

"Of course not," she said, laughing. "I have the perfect vase." But while she opened the paper wrap, she was immediately struck by how unique this arrangement was. It wasn't something you picked up at the grocery store on the way to someone's house. These were exotic flowers, calla lilies, birds-of-paradise, orchids, lavender roses—not a typical batch. He must have gotten them from an actual florist. He surprised her all the time.

She laid the flowers on the drain board and opened a drawer, handing him a corkscrew. "I'll have a glass of that wine if you'll open it. And I have Coke and your coffee ready…"

"I drove the truck tonight," he said. "I'll have a glass of that with you, and then I'd love a coffee after dinner. I think this bulk on a full meal will absorb a glass of wine. Or two."

She lifted an eyebrow. "I'm not a bad influence, am I?"

"You might be a good influence," he said. "Nah, kidding. I try to take my folks out to a nice dinner every weekend and I usually drive instead of ride. I sometimes have a drink with them. The bike really demands a lot—I can't afford to take

even a minuscule chance. My reputation depends on it. I have
to be more than a hundred percent."

He popped the cork on the bottle, poured two glasses while
she snipped the ends of the stems and put them in water. He
swirled, whiffed, took a sip and sighed. "I did good here,
Cassie. Taste. Didn't I do good?"

She put the vase of flowers on the table and took a glass
from him, sipping. She tilted her head appreciatively. "You
did very well," she confirmed with a smile. "Now, tell me
about your week. About your jobs."

"You might fall asleep," he said.

"Try me."

So while they had a glass of red wine and a small plate of
bruschetta, he told her about a sticky carburetor problem on a
1988 Harley Road King. He'd had to work on it a long time,
but felt comfortable enough with the outcome to guarantee
the work for a year; if it went down within two, though, he'd
make it right. He told her about this guy who'd been coming
in, drooling over a refurbished Harley, who'd finally taken
the plunge and made the buy. One of the girls in the office
got engaged and they all went out for lunch. Then his oldest brother's kid had a birthday, so there was a family thing.

"How about your week?" he asked. "Not carburetors or
sales, I bet."

"Almost the same drill," she answered. "A compound femur
fracture this morning—that was the big event. That's when the
big thighbone is broken and sticking out through the flesh…"

"Eww…"

"Yeah, it's bad. And the usual number of car accidents, me-
chanicals—that's when someone just falls—critical illnesses,
one hot appy, complicated labor—"

"Appy?" he asked.

"Emergency appendectomy. And one gunshot wound. Plus overdoses, assaults, mostly domestic—"

"Domestic?" he asked.

"Family disturbance. A lot of variation on that, but usually the husband is beating up the wife."

He shook his head. "That's terrible."

"It's *so* terrible. You ever run into that with your biker pals?" she asked.

"Run into it how?"

"I don't know." She shrugged. "Ever hear about those kinds of troubles with biker couples? Because I read a little bit about the biker gangs and some are known for treating their women like objects they own. It can get real—"

"Cassie, I've never been in a gang. Even when I was younger and ran wild with a bunch of bikers, it wasn't a gang. And we were too stupid and ugly to have women."

"I didn't mean—"

"Sure you did. You still want to make sure I didn't have some poor abused young girl on the back of my bike who had *Property of Walt* tattooed on her biceps." He grinned at her. "You want to know if my dad knocked my mom around?"

"No, I—"

"My dad never raised a hand to my mom. There's an old shotgun in the house. I bet she'd have taken it to him if he had. She had her hands full in special ed and she raised four boys. Holy hell would erupt when we weren't polite and decent around the opposite sex. You want my opinion, my brother Kevin was the worst. I guess the girls thought he was cute, but personally I think he's ugly as a stump and a pain in the ass besides. Man, he used to have a different girl every week and couldn't've cared less if they were calling, crying their little hearts out. My mother wanted to kill him. And I never abused a girl, a woman. Though I probably treated some like crap because I was stupid and had no idea what I was doing."

"You're a dichotomy, Walt."

"How?" he asked, eyebrows raised.

"You look the kind of guy who could tear the flesh off running antelopes, but you're so gentle-natured and sweet."

"Looks," he scoffed. "You have to do better than that, Cassie. You look like I shouldn't be having dinner with you. You should've been snapped up years ago."

"Friends," she reminded him.

"Of course," he said. Then he smiled. He liked where this friendship was going. He wasn't leaving tonight without another sample of that delicious mouth.

"Let me see if dinner's ready," she said, rising.

They spent two hours over lasagna, salad and bread. Walt had another glass of wine and between them they finished his bottle. They had coffee and dessert, then washed up the dishes together. While she was rinsing and he was drying, he said, "Summer's almost over. It's already getting chilly on the northern coast in Sonoma County. I have an idea, if you're up to it. How about a weekend ride?"

"A weekend?" she asked, getting a nervous look on her face. "Like, a whole weekend?"

He laughed at her. "That's what I'm talking about. We can do it the way I usually do it, or we can do it the candy-ass way."

"Explain," she said, lifting the plates into the cupboard.

"Well, the way I do it, I take the bike along the coast, find a nice piece of beach and put down a sleeping bag. I build myself a little fire. I usually pack some food that's not fancy, but I hardly ever miss a chance to eat out. We could stop and eat before we stake out beachfront. Or we could do it so you're comfortable—stay the night at a motel, take advantage of beds and showers." He shrugged. "It's up to you. I won't make fun of you if you need a roof over your head. But pretty soon the weather's going to turn and we're going to want to use our rides to check out the fall leaves. And we'll have to dress warm."

"Motel?" she asked, lifting a brow.

"However many rooms you want, Cassie. I'm not trying to set you up for anything." Then he grinned.

"Just how cold and uncomfortable is it right out there on the beach?"

"It's great. The fire is nice and cozy, you hear the waves all night long, the ground isn't too hard. After the middle of August, it gets pretty cool at night. I can pull a little trailer behind so we have a cooler, extra blankets, that kind of thing…"

"A trailer?" she asked. But what she thought was, how am I going to explain this to Julie?

"Just a little one behind the bike, so we have everything we need."

"Do you just not shower the whole weekend?" she asked.

He laughed at her. "It's camping, Cassie. Think you can make it twenty-four hours? We could take off on Saturday morning, get home Sunday afternoon. This may be beyond your limit—I usually don't even change clothes. I do stop for breakfast, though. That's a good time to clean up, a little emergency maintenance."

"Wow," she said. "I didn't think I'd ever try something like that…"

"It's fun, Cassie. It's a little rugged and it gets cool on the ocean, but the sunset is awesome—the whole experience is. Remember, I did that for over a year once. I hated to see it end. But really, a couple of motel rooms—I'm good with that. Your call."

"Gee, I wonder if I'm up to it…"

"I'm real flexible. If you change your mind in the middle of the night and need a bed, I don't mind."

"Really? It wouldn't be like dragging along an old lady? Waiting for me to wimp out?"

"I can handle it. Why don't you give it a try? Just for kicks. If you hate it, you won't ever do it again."

"Well… I guess I could brave it. Gee. A whole weekend on the bike…"

"You might like it. You've liked it so far."

It was eleven when he left, and again at the door, he put a big gentle hand on her waist, making it feel small when, in fact, it was not. He pulled her near, and moved over her mouth sensually, lovingly, briefly. Gentle but there was certainly a hidden power there. She wondered if this was a bad idea, letting him have these parting kisses, but truthfully, it was almost her favorite part. When he pulled back, he smiled. "I like this friendship, Cassie."

"Don't get any ideas," she warned.

"Of course not," he said. "Don't you, either."

After he had gone, she went to the trash and dug out the bottle of wine they'd shared. She rinsed it and planned to root some ivy in it because she liked the label. Then she got on the Internet and traced it to the Napa Valley vineyard where it came from. And she learned that it sold for ninety-five bucks.

He was a fool for her, she thought. Maybe she should cool this friendship before she hurt him and left him totally broke.

Then she realized it was the first time she could remember being concerned that she might do the hurting. That made her smile. It was nice not being the desperate one for once.

She'd have to reappraise the whole thing after spending two days on a bike and sleeping on the sand.

Marty stared at Ryan Chambers's business card at least twice a day. Usually six times. She'd started having wild fantasies that maybe he'd changed, grown up like he said, and that she'd made the wrong choice, marrying Joe. In the midst of her anger with her husband, who happened to show up out of the blue but her old boyfriend? She began to see herself twirling around in those high, strappy heels, dancing. Dining with candles. Being seduced and nuzzled and cuddled and…all of it. The way it had once been with Ryan, when things were going well. The way it had been with Joe before they married.

She and Joe did nothing but argue, and always about the same things—he didn't help her at all, didn't compromise, didn't put forth any effort to make himself appealing. His idea of a compliment was a slap on the ass. The more she bitched, the shorter his fuse got. He had that good old Italian temperament; he didn't fly off the handle right away, but after enough pecking, she could drive him into a yell, a sulk. And God, did she peck! She felt she had two choices—to just accept him the way he was, clean up after him for life, endure his slovenly ways, or keep after him and hope eventually he could meet her halfway. Well, there was a third choice… She could give up and end the relationship. Divorce.

She started asking herself a lethal question—would it be against the rules to check Ryan out a little bit? Find out if he was being straight with her? It wouldn't take long; he'd give himself away in no time. She remembered too well the way his eyes would drift to another woman in the room and get that light that said volumes, that had *new conquest* burning brightly in them. She didn't ask her girlfriends about this; she knew the answer. It would be wrong.

But she called him, anyway. She had an hour break between clients at the beauty shop and went out back, behind the building where she'd be alone. "Hi," she said. "It's Marty."

"I know who it is," he said with a laugh. "What's going on?"

"I just thought I'd… Well, I thought maybe you could talk, that's all."

"I can, but for two minutes. I'm on my way into a meeting. Hey, I have an idea—meet me back at Martinelli's. We'll have a drink. Talk."

"No," she said. "No, I can't do that..."

"Why not? What's the difference between a conversation on the phone and one in person? It's a public place, Marty."

"No," she repeated. "I can't do that..."

"The husband watching you that *close?* You worried about something? Hey, he isn't mean to you, is he?"

"He's not watching me," she said. "In fact, he's on shift. But I— Let's just say I know better."

"Well, whatever you say, Marty. Want me to call you back after the meeting?"

"No," she said. "That's okay. It was just a—" She didn't finish. It was just an attack of the past, a moment of temporary insanity, a sick and lunatic desire to feel happy for a moment. And it was completely nuts because Ryan wasn't the answer. He'd never been the answer, not even long before Joe. "Just thought you might have a minute, but go on—go to your meeting. I'll check in with you again sometime." And she hung up.

Two hours later, while she was in the middle of a perm, her cell phone vibrated on her hip and she felt her cheeks grow hot. But she ignored it. When she was done with her client, she listened to the message. *Hey, Marty, tell you what—I'm going to swing by Martinelli's for a beer at about five-thirty. I get the idea you'd like to talk, maybe lean on a friend or something. I can tell in your voice you're not really all together right now. Don't worry about it, baby. If you're there, you're there—I'm not going to get you in trouble. But if you can't make it, I get it. Call anytime.*

And then she thought, I'm hopeless! He calls me *baby* and I get all sloppy inside. She was with Ryan for as long as she'd been with Joe, except Ryan had been a perpetual cheater.

But he was so young then, just a kid.

Joe was thirty-four. He was mature, knew what he wanted, was ready to make a commitment to one woman. But his transformation from boyfriend and fiancé to husband had been a complete shock. And so immediate! From the minute the honeymoon was complete—a hiking and camping trip to Yosemite!—he was all done focusing any attention on what would make her happy. Oh, he was conscientious enough during her pregnancy, which came immediately following the wedding, but it was all downhill from there. She just couldn't *reach* him!

Ryan, on the other hand, was a master seducer. When they had been together, he was completely tuned in to her, made sure she had everything she needed—from good dates to plenty of compliments. He had made her feel so cherished, so special, so beautiful and sexy. And she'd respond by making sure he was happy, in every imaginable way. Then inevitably his attention began to shift, of course. Then he'd cheat and they'd fight and break up.

At the moment she was having a real hard time figuring out which was worse. A hairy, scratchy guy in bed with her who just rolled over on her and expected favors, but would never, ever look at another woman, or a guy who had this little problem with being faithful but, when he was, made her feel like a queen.

"This is totally insane," she muttered to herself while she sat at the bar in Martinelli's. Her mother took care of Jason when she worked and she had called, told her she'd be a little late. "What in the world do I think I'm going to figure out by doing this?" There was absolutely no question—Joe would not take something like this lightly. He was more possessive than the average man and he thoroughly disapproved of cheating, and not just women. Men stepping out on their wives earned his scorn, as well.

She'd told Joe all about Ryan when they were dating—how in love she'd been, how hurt and destroyed by his behavior. And Joe had been completely sympathetic. He'd had one or two serious girlfriends before meeting her, and he could relate to the heartache that went along with the experience of it not working out.

She tried to summon up the emotions from the early days with Joe, the feeling that she'd never been so lucky. Here was a guy unafraid of commitment, a serious guy, a one-woman man. And he was so proud of her! Even now, even though he didn't do anything to make himself appealing to her, he seemed to show her off to his friends. She always tried to look her best for everything—even football at the sports bar—and he'd say something a little crude but not unflattering. "Look at that ass. You wonder why I'm tired?" Or, "Who has the best-looking woman in the city? No contest!"

What am I doing? she asked herself for the millionth time.

"Hey, Marty," Ryan said, bouncing into the bar, grinning. "I wondered if you'd take a chance."

"I shouldn't be here…"

"Then why are you here?" he asked.

Her eyes welled with tears. "I don't know. Because I'm nuts. Because I've been unhappy lately and I just—" She looked down into her glass of wine.

He put an arm around her shoulders and pulled her against him. "Easy, baby. You're having a hard time right now, that's all." Then to the bartender he said, "Miller Draft."

"I don't know why I called you," she said. "I don't know why I'm here. You can't help me with this…"

"Never know," he said. "You're pretty important to me,

Marty. You have been since I was just a kid. If there's any way I can be there for you, I'd sure like the chance."

"But I'm married! I shouldn't even be talking to you, much less meeting you for a drink!"

"Lighten up, sweetheart. It's just conversation! Now, tell me what's wrong..."

When it came down to it, she couldn't. She was unable to be as honest with Ryan as she'd been with the girls; she protected Joe in the clinches. She just couldn't sell him out. So she said they failed to communicate, they had trouble supporting each other, so much drivel. And she asked him a lot of questions about his relationships. He claimed to have had one serious girlfriend in the past three years that he thought would go the distance, but in the end it just didn't work out. That would be Jill. And no, he hadn't cheated on her—it was the other way around. She found someone else. "Just what I deserved, I guess," he said with a short laugh. "But I've been a little reluctant to get back on the train since her. I guess I finally know how bad it feels."

"I wish I could feel sorry for you," Marty said.

"I don't expect sympathy," he said. "But damn, all along, you were the one, Marty. Otherwise, why would I keep coming back, huh? Because me and you together, that was perfect. I was the idiot who screwed it up, over and over again. I'd give anything to have another chance, knowing what I know now."

"Now, it's too late..."

"Is it? Because you're not happy."

"But I'm going to find a way to work this out," she said. "He's a good man. He loves me. We have a son together."

Ryan's arm was around her shoulders, his hand covering her hand. "Well, if it turns out it can't work out, you've got my number."

She looked at his eyes. He seemed to be sincere, but she'd

been fooled by that in the past. "I have to go. My mom's got Jason…"

He pulled some bills out of his pocket and laid them on the bar, paying for her wine and his beer. "I'll walk you out."

"Maybe you shouldn't…"

He laughed. "You think he's got a detective on you? Relax, Marty. I'll walk you out."

And then, at her car, he pulled her against him and covered her mouth in a consuming kiss that took her back in time, sending her reeling into a bliss so forbidden and welcome, she trembled. God, he tasted so good, smelled so good. He ran his hands up and down her ribs, getting close to her breasts but not touching. When he finally released her lips, the fear of having been seen was so far away, it never occurred to her.

"Call me, Marty," he whispered, threading his fingers through her hair. "We can figure this out, make this work."

"Make what work?" she asked breathlessly.

"Maybe we can get each other over the rough spot. I'm alone, you're not real happy. And we're friends. Very, very good friends…"

"You're talking about—"

"Shhh," he said, cutting her off. "I don't want to complicate your life. I just want to be there for you. I can't stand to see you unhappy, that's all. I'll never stop loving you, you know that." And before she could respond, he was on her lips again, parting them with his, kissing her deeply. Branding her, turning her into the kind of woman she never thought she'd be. When he let her go, she almost collapsed. "Call me when you're free." Then he opened the door for her.

7

Beth had had the lump removed in June. At least it hadn't been three, like the last time. And this time there hadn't been any spread to the lymph nodes, so there were things about this catastrophe that weren't so bad. But when the radiologist had refused to show her the MRI scan, she smelled a rat. So she kept her appointment with Dr. Paterson as scheduled in August.

"How are you feeling?" he asked.

"Worn out, but it could be stress."

"The radiation getting to you?"

"A little burn. All things considered, not too bad."

He took a breath. "You're a gynecologist—you know about these things. It's not routine for women with malignant breast bumps to have a second primary occurrence. In fact, it's rare. Metastasis—spreading of the disease—we run into that, too often. This is different. Every once in a while we see what appears to be vulnerable breast tissue. It's no indication the cancer is rampant around the rest of the body. It presents early—it repeats itself. The suspect spots on your MRI have almost disappeared with radiation, but it's my opinion they'll return. I think, Beth, you'll have a problem with this as long as you allow it to be a factor. My recommendation would be radical mastectomy. My further recommendation would be reconstruction. There's no reason a woman your age should have to live without breasts. The reconstruction can be excellent. Please, consider that along with the mastectomy."

She thought she'd prepared herself for that. After all, she didn't want to increase her risk in any way and wasn't thinking of trying anything heroic to save one breast. What were boobs compared to life? Ridiculous even to think about! Besides, she was down to one, anyway. If the cancer had been ovarian, she'd have everything yanked as fast as possible, despite the fact she had once thought children would be in her future. Yet it stunned her for a second, left her frozen. And the most amazing vision came to mind—Mark on top of her, running his soft, surgeon's hands over her breasts when he made love to her. Two small but sensitive mounds. She remembered she would often orgasm when he was inside her, his wonderful mouth on her nipple. So long ago…

She became aware that her mouth hung open and closed it.

"I'm sorry," he said. "It's very aggressive, but it could save a world of trouble down the road."

"I understand," she said softly. "Certainly, we'll just get it done."

"Listen," he said, coming around his desk and sitting on it, rather close to her. "You haven't given me any details, but I think a relationship problem with your last episode could be factoring into your uncanny acceptance of something so…"

"Radical?" she inserted for him.

"I'm sorry. I don't mean to pry. I only mean to help."

"Then don't pry," she said, standing. "I'd prefer to have the surgery in Sacramento or Davis, closer to home. If I remember, it's a tough recovery. Can you recommend a surgeon?"

"There's an excellent surgeon at your hospital," he said. "And I have the names of some outstanding plastic surgeons all around the Bay Area, L.A., Davis…"

"One thing at a time," she said. "How soon can you get me in?"

"I can make a phone call today. How about Roger Whitcomb in Sacramento? In a week? How's your schedule?"

"I can clear it. Remember, I work with women's doctors. They're a little soft on this malady—they'll give me whatever I need. Have your office manager call my cell with the details." She turned to leave.

"Beth," he said, causing her to turn back. "Really, I'm sorry. But I'd hate to take any chances. My objective is to get you past this. It doesn't have to be a lifetime problem. Your life is in here," he said, putting a hand directly on his sternum.

"Yeah," she said, and thought, For a guy who specializes in breast cancer, he doesn't know enough about what breasts can do. "Yeah, sure."

Billy was on twenty-four-hour shift three times in a week, and went to the shop as often as he could muster the energy. Everywhere he went the bulging accordion folder went with him. He pored over months of statements from the mortgage company, credit-card companies, insurance company and utilities companies. He had his calculator out all the time, figuring. There was a year's worth of pay stubs from the fire department and the shop.

Guys would pass by the table where he was working and ask, "What's up, man?"

He replied, "Bills. Julie's been taking care of them and I'm trying to figure out her system before she has us living on the street." He felt bad about the lie. It was a guy thing. He just

had too much pride to admit the root of all their problems
had come from the reality that he couldn't support his family.

The fact was, looking at the numbers, he couldn't figure
out how she'd managed. He thought he better ask her about
that "system" of hers, because when he looked at the due dates
on the bills and the income, it seemed impossible. No wonder she was completely out of her mind—it just didn't work.
If that wasn't bad enough, there were late fees all over the
place—bills she just couldn't pay on time.

It was the right thing to do, getting this off her plate. But it
didn't help his mood. When he took on the finances, he took
on her worry. It left him quiet and depressed. She kept asking him if everything was all right and he told her his brain
was reeling with numbers. He wanted to tell her he finally
understood why she wanted to smack him for being so goddamn happy all the time. The truth was, he felt the urge to
break down in a bone-deep cry.

The captain of their unit, Eric Sorenson, kept passing by
him at the firehouse, glancing at his paperwork, asking him
how he was doing. Eric was a good guy, a real happy man with
a strong, serious side. He was well respected even though he
wasn't exactly like the rest of them. He was religious—Mormon
fellow—maybe a little straightlaced. He didn't seem uptight and
had an awesome sense of humor, though it never verged into
the off-color like the rest of the crew. He rarely joined them
for a beer, and if he did, he had a cola. But as leaders went, he
was sharp and loyal; he really went to the wall for his men.

After a couple of weeks of keeping his polite distance, he
pulled out a chair opposite Billy and said, "You got something
serious going on there, bud. Any way I can help with that?"

Billy cracked a smile. "You could give me a raise."

Eric just nodded at the stack of paperwork. It was common

for the guys to bring their bills to work, use the computer to pay online. "Household expenses?" he asked.

"You're a genius," Billy said, keeping his smile in place. "I always said that…"

"You been at it a long time now. Must not be making much sense if you're still adding and subtracting."

"Well," Billy said. "To tell you the truth, Captain, I just took it over from Jules. She had that miscarriage, you know. She's been all stressed out about the bills, so I took it on—and it's a wreck. I want to figure it out before I take it back to her and ask her a lot of questions about how she did things." He took a breath. "I shouldn't have let her worry about this so long…"

"Yeah, I had almost the same thing happen," Eric said. "I sure get that."

"You did?" Billy asked.

"Oh, sure." Then he grinned. "Five kids."

"Well, I knew that, but…"

"But you thought it was only tough for you, coming on the department with a growing family in place?" He smiled. "Think you could use a hand there?" he asked, nodding at the paperwork.

"Ah, that's real nice, but…" He gathered up his papers and pulled them toward him, protectively. No way he wanted his captain to know how deep he was in, how much he owed, how desperate it was.

"But you're worried about me seeing the bills?" He laughed pleasantly. "Five kids," he repeated. "I had three when I started at F.D. You think I don't know about this?" Then he leaned close. "You think I can't keep quiet about your personal business?"

"It's not that, it's just—"

"It's that," Eric said. "Plus, you're afraid if I get a look at it, I'll fire you or put you on light duty till you dig out of your

mess and are stress-free on the job? Gimme a break, huh? I
actually know something about this. It's a shot in the dark,
but I might be able to help. I'm good with big families, big
bills." Then he sat back and put up his hands, palms toward
Billy. "Hey, no pressure. I understand if you want to soldier
on. I felt that way myself. I thought I'd offer..."

"You felt that way?"

"Let's see—I was behind in a half dozen mortgage payments, the lights were flickering and I was holding the car
together with duct tape and bailing wire. Um, it was one car,
not two," he laughed. Then he sobered and said, "Plus, my
wife was in tears half the time. That's the part that almost put
me in the nuthouse."

"What did you do?"

He chuckled. "Well, we were on our knees a lot—prayer
is very big at our house. We tried to make it on faith. I figured if I was humble and earnest enough, I'd find a few grand
lying on the sidewalk. Stranger things have happened, right?
Then my bishop said, 'Eric, I'm sure God will be more than
happy to steer, if you'll pedal.' He told me I needed professional help, and I'd better not waste a lot of time. So I went to
one of those free credit counselors, got a little advice. Then I
checked in with a guy from my church who does taxes part-
time, a CPA, just to see if he thought the advice was any good.
I wasn't too big on trust back then."

Almost lying across the paperwork to keep it secret, Billy
asked, "What kind of advice?"

"It's pretty individual, but in my case, we had to renegotiate some loans, put together a payment schedule that fit the
paycheck instead of trying to stretch the paycheck over their
schedule, and I had to start paying the family first. My greatest asset had to be protected before I could move on. Then I
had to face a long-term plan that, in the beginning, looked

to me like there was no end in sight. And I had to take some aggressive action—everything plastic that got near me or my wife had to be cut up."

Billy sat back and put the end of the pen against his lips. "Too bad you couldn't come up with some new ideas, Captain. I already tried all that. There's no way I can get another debt consolidation note and I'd love to cut up the plastic, believe me, but sometimes that's all there is."

"Oh, you just don't know how creative these credit counselors can get," he laughed. "Come on, bring your stuff to my office." He stood. "First, how about a wager? Ten bucks says I was in worse shape than you."

Billy just sat there, reluctant to share this disaster with anyone. "You? Making a bet?"

"Nah. I figure it's a sure thing." He turned and walked to his office.

Still, Billy sat. This was the only thing he'd really feared when he bundled up the bills and carried them out of the house—that someone would see. Judge him harder than he'd already judged himself. He felt a huff of laughter escape as he asked himself how that was possible. He felt as if he'd driven Jules to risk miscarriage because she was just so goddamn scared.

His palms actually sweating, he shoved everything in the folder and followed his boss. He stood in front of his desk, the folder tucked protectively under his arm, and looked down at his captain. "You're gonna be sorry."

"I love a challenge," he said.

Billy pulled a yellow pad out of his file folder and presented it with no small amount of trepidation. "This should sum it up," he said. "I got a family of five living on a net income of right around fifty-five hundred a month, working two jobs. The mortgage alone, without the second and equity line, is fifteen hundred."

Eric put on his reading glasses and began to scan. Mortgage, second mortgage, equity line of credit, old college loans—two of them—utilities, insurance, two Visas and a Master-Card, then a long list of miscellaneous expenses ranging from Jeffy's soccer and baseball fees to doctor's co-pays. "These all the minimums?" the captain asked.

"Yup."

"No car payments—good for you!"

"Right. And absolutely no ability to finance a car..."

"Okay, fish me out a couple of credit-card statements, one of each. Any month will do—it doesn't have to be the most recent."

Billy sat down, the file on his lap, and produced three statements, handing them over. Billy expected the captain to gasp and grab his chest, but he just took a quick glance at each and scribbled something on the yellow pad.

"How about a mortgage statement?" he said. "And maybe that second and equity line..."

Again he complied, again the quick scribbles. Then Eric did some fast calculating and looked up. "Well, holy smokes, we might be at a tie here," he said with a short laugh. "Except I had you beat. At least I put food, clothing and tithing on my list. It made the bottom line look a whole lot worse."

"Yeah, that's the problem. Looks to me like it's all eaten up before we even get to food and clothing, or gas for the cars. Tithing?" he asked.

"I give ten percent to the church. It's real important to me. I'm LDS, but you know that. I ran into more trouble with the college loans, though, because I got married the minute I got off my mission. The mission was another debt. I thought I had mine paid for, but by the end of it I'd run out of money."

"Mission?"

"Oh, yeah, that mission is important to a young Mormon guy. And some girls go on missions, too. It was worth it. I learned more about my faith, my family and myself on that mission than I learned about Guam, which is where I went. I'll never regret it, never. Set me back though..."

"I guess that means you went to college after you were married?"

"Part-time—took me years to finish. That was worth it, too. Listen, you didn't get into this mess alone, you have to understand that."

"Captain, Julie scrimps on everything. It's harder to pry a nickel out of her fingers than—"

"I didn't mean the wife, Bill. They're killing you with these interest rates, for one thing." He flipped through his Rolodex until he came to a name. He wrote it down on a piece of paper along with a phone number. "When I said renegotiate loans, I didn't mean you take out another one to cover the existing ones. I meant, you have to call these lenders from the banks to the credit-card companies and get yourself fixed up with some more reasonable terms. They can make adjustments..."

"I have called a couple of them. They—"

He was shaking his head. "I know, that usually doesn't work so well for the individual debtor. They're gonna go after the maximum they can squeeze out of you. Everyone wants to be first on your pay roster." He handed him the paper. "This guy—he's a licensed and bonded credit counselor. When he calls, they listen. They know you're down to the bottom of the barrel when you meet with him. He's the last barrier between your bills and giving up. I know him. I never used him, but I go to church with him and I've sent people his way before."

"F.D. people?" Billy asked.

"More often young men from the church, struggling with the same stuff as you and me. You know, just starting out, kids coming fast, big bills..." Eric paused a second. "Listen, I've known you quite a while now. I know you don't take expensive vacations and Julie isn't carrying a Gucci purse. I know you're not irresponsible, Bill. This happens to people like us who start out broke, do the best we can…"

Billy looked down at the name Eric had written down. Without lifting his eyes, he said, "Julie—the miscarriage." Then he looked up. "When she found out that one was coming, she asked me if I was a secret Mormon. That would've been number four."

Eric laughed. "Secret Mormon. Yeah, we like our kids…"

"Five, huh?"

"I'd have five more if I could. But I'm not the one pushing them out, so my vote counts a little less than half. Billy, I'm awful sorry about the baby. My condolences," he said, folding his hands on top of the yellow pad and bills. "Your marriage and family is the most important thing. It's worth way more than the credit-card balances. More than the mortgage, for that matter. And these bills are getting in the way of that. That bank has you strapped with PMI—four hundred a month you shouldn't have to pay."

"They won't take it off. I got a ninety percent debt to equity on that house."

"They can take it off," he said. "Plus, they can fix the rate for you so it's not adjustable. Oh, they don't love doing that, they'd rather have your last dime, but if you file bankruptcy, they're not getting anything. The mortgage company won't even get a repo—your house is protected under the law. And these credit cards? Eighteen to twenty-two percent. Robbery. If you had a lower rate, these payments, small though they are, would at least chisel away at the balance. Call John. I'll give you personal time to sit down with him. You might want to take your wife with you."

"You think there's anything he can do with this mess?"

"Oh, yes. He's handled way worse, believe me."

"Actually, it's hard to believe that," he laughed, shaking his head. "So what does this guy charge?"

"I don't know. He'll go over fees with you—they'll be reasonable. And he'll collect the greater portion of it after you've had some results with the other stuff here." He handed back the yellow pad, the statements resting on top.

"He doesn't get screwed that way? Waiting for his payment?" Billy asked, taking his albatross back.

"I don't know that he does that for everyone. But if I send him a friend, he'll do everything he can to keep costs down. This will take some time, Bill. But I don't think you'll feel any more strapped while you're solving the problem than you do while you're living with it every day. And at least there will be a light at the end of the tunnel. Good luck with this."

"I have a college degree," Billy said, standing. "I should be smarter than this. I should've figured out how to manage this myself. I should know all these things you're telling me, and how to make it work."

He just laughed. "My guy—the credit counselor—he got out the Monopoly money to teach me. Based on that alone, I think you owe me ten."

"Get in line," Billy said, smiling lamely.

Cassie wasn't the least worried about safety going on the road with Walt for the weekend. She was a little concerned about her comfort; she thought her butt might go numb for life. And she kind of dreaded admitting to spending a whole weekend with Walt. Still, she did the smart thing. When she asked Julie if she'd babysit Steve Saturday and most of Sunday, she told her exactly what her plans were.

"Are you getting serious about this guy?" Julie asked right away, lifting a brow.

"No," Cassie laughed. "Really, he's a big, friendly lug, sweet as a kitten, nice as anyone I've ever met—and it turns out I like the riding. We go amazing places, see some awesome views. You can tell by one look at him that he knows the best places to eat all over the state. We're just a couple of people with no one in the picture and a shared interest. I'll have my cell phone with me, but who knows where it'll work—we get off the roads or up in the hills. I'm leaving you his name, where he works, that stuff, just so you'll know."

"Just a shared interest, huh?"

"That's it, girlfriend. He's a huge, hairy, tattooed guy who turns a wrench on motorcycles for a job. Really, not boyfriend material. I like him, though," she said with a shrug. "It's kind of amazing how much we find to talk about, for complete opposites."

"Where are you going to stay?"

"We're going to try camping on the beach, but he promises if I get uncomfortable or anything, he'll find a motel—my own room, of course."

"You sure it's safe? Going off with him?"

"Oh, it's safe. I'm telling you, he's my bodyguard."

"Are we going to meet him?"

"Jules, he'll be out of the picture before you know it. It's kind of nice to have someone to do things with sometimes, that's all."

Just a pal to do things with, and amazing how much she looked forward to it.

They left early on Saturday and drove all the back roads into Sonoma, where they'd spent so much of their riding time over the summer. He headed for the beach around Bodega Bay, then north for a couple of hours until they stopped and had a fantastic lunch at a truck stop Walt liked to frequent. They took a detour from the coast to drive through the Armstrong Redwoods, then back to the coast, past some marinas where they could watch the fishing boats come in. At sunset they stopped at a fish shack where they could watch the sunset while they ate a delicious fresh catch. Then on to a piece of beach protected by huge boulders that Walt thought would be the perfect spot to spend the night.

Cassie brought marshmallows, Hershey bars and graham crackers—it made Walt beam with pleasure. Once they were done riding for the night, Cassie opened a bottle of merlot and had a couple of glasses; Walt had a few sips of hers after building the fire. It wasn't a fancy fire made from driftwood—he'd packed several Duraflames in the small trailer. It was a nice, high, hot fire. Then Cassie made s'mores—she put her chocolate bars carefully on the graham cracker, toasted her marshmallow and pressed them together to melt the chocolate. Walt ate a chunk of chocolate, threw a handful of marshmallows in his mouth, wolfed down some graham crackers and took a slug of Cassie's wine. "You'd make a terrible Girl Scout," she told him.

Then he put an arm around her while they sat by the fire, pulled her against his big, hard body and licked the sticky marshmallow off her fingers.

"If you'd told me a year ago that I'd be sitting on the beach by a campfire after a day of riding a Harley, I would have said you were nuts. But, Walt, this is beautiful. Why are we all alone out here? Don't people know about this place?"

"We might see some people come around," he said. "That's another reason for the fire. You don't want to be invisible out here—they could ride a dune buggy over you or something."

"But it'll go out eventually," she said.

"I'll keep it going. For one thing, it gets pretty cold on the ocean at night, and that'll wake me up. I usually get up a couple of times to throw on another log."

"You don't worry about anyone giving you trouble out here, all alone?"

"Come on," he laughed. "I guess it's possible, but I kind of look like my gang's just up the road, ready to back me up."

"I guess that's true. You ever carry a gun?"

"Nah. I suppose I could, but remember, I have a record. I'm the kind of guy who gets pulled over a lot—cops really frown on things like concealed weapons in the hands of big, ugly bikers."

"You're not ugly," she said. "In fact, sometimes, when you spruce up a little—like dinner at my house—you're downright handsome."

"Seriously?" He grinned, pulling her closer. "I love hearing you say that."

"And it's not such a bad record," she said. "You were awful young."

"And awful stupid," he said. "I don't even want to undo it, you know? It all adds up to who you are, what you learned."

"I want to be like you," she said.

"Like *me?*" he asked, pulling back to look in her eyes.

"Uh-huh. I'd been feeling real sorry for myself after that incident—the phony paramedic. Not because of him so much, but because it seemed to put a spotlight on my aloneness—my mom and stepdad left me behind, then my mom died, then I absolutely never had a guy who could become the special one… I never looked at what that taught me. I never let it make me stronger, smarter. I just whimpered about it all the time."

"Aw, Cassie, you don't give yourself enough credit, honey," he said, squeezing her shoulders. "Look at what you do every day. Jumping on chests to get hearts started up again, holding cracked skulls together to keep the brains from falling out, catching babies who are coming too fast… Jesus, you're the most amazing woman in the world. You're like a soldier! And then when we get together and just talk, you're soft and sweet and so kind. Just the nicest person. If you didn't tell me about your days at work, I'd never take you for a tough emergency room nurse who could do all those things…"

"I'm good in the E.R.," she said. "It's made my life. I do things I didn't know I could do. I take chances all day long. Risks. I save lives once in a while, or at least help save them. I'd be lost without that job. No," she said. "It's a lot more than a job. It's a way of life. And you know what else? I'm not a typical E.R. nurse, either—I'm not hooked on crisis."

"Hooked on crisis?"

"Adrenaline. A lot of E.R. nurses aren't happy unless they've always got some high drama going on in their personal lives as well as at work—and I'm not like that. I do it during the day, but when I leave, I have an opposite life. I mean, look at Steve. Isn't he the sweetest thing? We have a quiet life, me and Steve."

Walt laughed. "He's a very silly dog," he said. "He's always got some stuffed thing in his mouth. He'd breast-feed 'em if he could."

"He would," she agreed. "I could see you with a big rott-weiler. Or German shepherd. A very manly dog."

"I grew up with a cocker spaniel," he said. "Small and pretty stupid. Then a collie named Sheba—she used to try to herd us all into the kitchen…"

"You always surprise me," she said, turning her head to look up at him.

"Boys on bikes don't have dogs," he said. "Well, I can't have a dog right now. I'm always on a bike or at work. But kids need dogs—it's fundamental. It shows them how to take care of something, forces them to learn patience. Sometimes at the poor animal's expense."

"I've been thinking about something very crazy," she said. "I've been thinking of having a baby without a husband."

He pulled away and looked down into her eyes. "What are you going to do? Take applications?"

"No," she laughed. "Donor. Anonymous."

"You're to that point, Cassie? So sure you're not going to get married someday?"

"There's plenty of time left, but I doubt it," she said. "At least a few more years before the ticking clock gets real, real loud. But if I want a family, I don't have to take chances on scary men to have one. There are ways. And why not? I'm sure if I married, I'd continue to work, anyway—that hospital makes me feel like I'm doing something vital, and that's about the only thing my self-esteem has going for it. I sure don't get a pick-me-up from my figure…"

"You know, you say that a lot… You act like you don't have a nice body. I wish you could see yourself through my eyes for half a second. You're very beautiful, Cassie. I wonder why you don't know it."

"I've gained twenty-five pounds since high school! And I considered myself chubby then. Of course, next to Jules and Beth and Marty—the skinny-assed girls—it was a terrible contrast!"

He kissed her temple. "You gained it in all the right places. I think you're perfect."

"I think you're hard up or blind," she said with a smile.

"I'm not either one," he said. "Wanna roll out the sleeping bags? We can talk all night or sleep, but you've shivered four times in the past few minutes."

"Yeah," she said. "Let's get cozy. You sure you can manage that fire? I'm a little scared about being at the mercy of armed felons and dune buggies."

"I got it," he said, getting their sleeping bags. "You don't have to worry. I've done this a hundred times and never had a bit of trouble." He threw another log on for good measure, sending the flames up.

So they rolled out the bags, shed their boots and jackets and crawled in. Once they were settled side by side, he grabbed her bag and pulled her up against him. Then he put a big, meaty arm under her head and snuggled her close. "Stay warm," he said.

This was more than body heat. His face was awful close to hers. He cradled her head atop his arm and his other arm was draped over her waist on top of the sleeping bag. He gave her just a moment and then slowly pressed his lips toward hers, gently giving her one of his tender, lovely kisses. Then another one. And then, for the first time since they'd met, he kissed more firmly, parting her lips with his and she couldn't help herself—she let her tongue think for itself and do a little exploring, bringing a deep moan of pleasure out of him. His tongue joined the party, and it was strong, hot and fabulous. Her arms escaped the sleeping bag and held him closer against her, kissing him deeply and wonderfully for a long, long moment. Many long moments, in fact.

When she finally escaped his lips, she said, "I don't think we should be doing this. We're supposed to be friends."

He laughed at her, a soft and gentle laugh. "Take it easy. You've kissed guys before without being engaged first," he said.

"I have," she admitted. "I've done more than this without being engaged."

"Then relax," he said. "I'm not going to take advantage of you, you know that. You're completely safe with me."

"You just don't know how nice that feels," she whispered. "I think it might be the first time since I was fourteen I haven't been all worried about everything. All the complications, the expectations, where it was going, all of it."

"You shouldn't have to worry. But I like kissing you."

"You know, my other best friend Marty—she's just about insane that her husband won't shave before getting in bed. You have a lot of hair and whiskers and it doesn't feel so bad."

He grinned against her lips. "I do own a razor," he said. "I'm rationing blades."

She giggled. "You like that three-day growth," she accused.

"That's partly true. It's kind of antisocial, don't you think?"

"It is." Then she kissed him a while longer. And kissed him and kissed him. Mouths open, tongues wild, penetrating, positively erotic kisses that went hard and soft, deep and shallow. "Phew. I haven't made out like this since high school. I had forgotten how great it feels. Tell me if I'm leading you on, Walt," she whispered against his lips. "Because this isn't going one inch further. And if we should stop…"

"Not an inch, huh?"

"For sure not on a beach in the possible presence of dune buggies," she said. "And I'm pretty sure nowhere else. I'm not looking for anything serious, you know that. But I'm also not a mannequin. I like to feel sweet and cozy like anyone else… and I have to admit, you've got kissing down."

"Even with the whiskers?"

"Maybe especially with the whiskers…"

"It's okay, Cassie. If you want to, we can make out all night long. I like it, too."

"You think this is a terrible mistake? I mean, we're just pals. Buddies. We have so much to talk about, to do together. We're not, you know…"

"It's not a mistake," he said, going after her lips some more. "In fact, I think it's a great idea."

Oh, God, Cassie thought. I *like* him! Really, *really* like him. It wasn't just his kissing, which was incredible. It was all of him— his take on life, his tenderness, his simple wisdom, even his stupid, nutty hobby of riding all over the place on a motorcycle. And, of course, making out most of the night didn't exactly help diminish the strength of her emotions. They had kissed a long while, dozed, awakened to kiss more, slept, awakened to fix up the fire, and before going back to sleep, of course there was more cuddling and kissing. Deep and powerful, soft and sweet.

When she awoke in the early morning, dawn just breaking, with a huge urge to pee, he escorted her to an isolated place behind a big rock, turned his back and kept her safe from Peeping Toms and whatever. He cleaned up their campsite, got them ready to roll, but before they got situated back on the bike he lifted her chin, put a very chaste kiss on her lips and said, "Last night was one of the best nights of my life. Thank you."

"Walt," she laughed self-consciously. "If last night was one of your best ever, you're deprived. Seriously deprived."

"No," he said with a smile. "I'm a guy with a glass half-full. I'm optimistic."

"You shouldn't get ideas…"

"Come on, Cassie, even you had ideas." He ran a big hand down her black hair. "We just stuck to kissing. And it was damn good kissing. At least from my perspective."

Oh, God, she was going nuts. Nuts about him. He was sweet and good and gentle and so frickin' polite! She hadn't been out with a man in twelve years who would hold off like that, let her decide, be that much of a gentleman. Never! He was the absolute best!

And it was totally impossible. She'd had many a vision about her life as it would be when it finally shaped up. Her man would be about five-ten to six feet, he'd be well-groomed and polished, he'd make a decent living and have the potential to go as far as possible in his field. A firefighter or paramedic would be just great—solid, clean-cut, doing admirable work… She'd dated a few of them with no results.

Walt was not like any of her friends. He looked like a social outcast, like he said. She couldn't imagine how Beth, Julie and Marty would find him. For that matter, she predicted that Billy would think she was out of her mind. And as far as the good living, he was a wrench. He had no potential at all.

Yet, every minute with him was so good…

Is this what Marty went through with Joe? she asked herself. A lovely, seductive man during the courting period, then the second you gave in, he became an unbearable slob who couldn't care less about your feelings? Walt looked like the kind of guy with so many rough edges that counting on him could be disastrous, totally disappointing.

But her lips were ruby red, her cheeks and chin a little chafed and all that romantic contact put her in a very pleasant frame of mind. She loved riding with him, stopping now and then for views, for food, for conversation. When he finally dropped her off at home and gave her that terrific kiss goodbye, she smiled into his eyes and said she'd had such fun.

She drove over to Julie's to pick up Steve and when Julie asked her how it was, she said, "It was terrific. We had great seafood, he packed Duraflames so we'd have a fire all night, it was peaceful and…and I think maybe I'm a camper, after all."

"Is he nice?" Julie asked.

"Oh, Jules, he's very nice. But unfortunately, he's just not my type."

"Is that windburn on your face?"

Cassie touched her tender cheeks. "Uh-huh. Maybe some sun."

"You look kind of…healthy. Or something."

"Do I?" she asked. "Well, it gets pretty windy and sunny out there, on a bike for two days." And beside the fire, she thought. Kissing and cuddling with a whiskery man all night. A man she was sorry wasn't going to be around much longer.

Billy came home from the fire department in the middle of the afternoon. He went to the kitchen and threw some forms on the counter, then sat down at the table. He could hear Jules in the bedroom with Clint and Stephie—it sounded as if they were just getting up from quiet time or naps or something. There was the sound of small children's laughter and his wife snuggling them, singing little songs, laughing and tickling. Obviously there was some bed jumping going on— that would be Clint. Billy's shoulders shook with laughter. He was a live wire.

The sounds of his wife and children brought a sentimental ache to his throat. She complained about all these crazy surprise pregnancies and he didn't blame her, but she was so good with the kids, the family. It was as if she was born to do this. Even in the hardest of times, she nurtured and cared for them as though they were the only things that mattered in her life. It wasn't as if he had much of an impact; he was hardly around. It was all her, and she was amazing. So strong and beautiful and wise.

He'd just come from a two-hour meeting with the financial counselor and wanted to talk to Julie before going back to work. The guy had declared her a genius—said it looked as though she'd kept the wolf from the door a couple of years longer than should have been possible. It must have been like carrying a hundred-pound boulder on her back every day. She deserved so much better…

"Daddy!" Stephie screamed when she saw him, racing into his arms. "Daddy!"

It almost brought tears to his eyes, the way they loved him. He wasn't sure he deserved this kind of adoration from his kids. What had he done for them lately?

"What are you doing home?" Julie asked, coming from the bedroom with her arms full of kids' dirty clothes.

He gave Stephie a loud smack on the cheek and let her climb down, sending her off with a gentle whack on the butt. She ran into the family room and bounded over the back of the old sofa. Billy put his elbows on his knees, clasped his hands in front of him and, head lowered, he said, "I have to talk to you, Jules."

"Jeez," she said, looking at him in worried confusion. "You get fired or something?"

He straightened. "Get rid of that laundry and come here a minute, baby."

She dumped the clothes in the laundry room and went to him. He pushed a chair out from the table with his foot and she sat, facing him.

"I just met with a debt counselor," he said. "I'm sorry, baby. It looks like we're at the end of the line. It's not good news."

"What?" she asked in a frightened breath.

"What we knew, but just couldn't face. We can't pay the bills. We're probably going to have to file for bankruptcy."

Tears gathered in her eyes in spite of her wish to stay calm. Her tears were more for his situation than hers; she knew how this would make him feel around the guys. "Oh, Billy. Just tell me what he said."

"Well, he said you were incredible, for one thing." He smiled a small smile. "He doesn't know how you managed for so long. The bottom line looked the same when he added and subtracted as it did when I ran the numbers. There isn't enough income to cover everything. And on top of that, even when you did manage to pay a little something on all the bills, there wasn't anything left. Not anything."

She pursed her lips. "Are we going to lose the house?" she asked in a whisper.

"I don't think so," he said. "The two things that can't be touched are the house and the pension, such as it is. Jules, I'm sorry. This is my fault. If I'd done this sooner, maybe—"

"Stop it," she said, reaching for his hand. "I was in charge of bills—I could've gone to some debt counselor. I thought we *had*."

"No, we went to the bank. Twice. And twice they fixed us up with more loans to pay the bills we couldn't afford to pay in the first place."

"When is this going to happen?"

"I don't know," he said, shaking his head. "He said we're not there yet, but it looks like that could happen soon. We have to go back. We have to fill out a little paperwork, meet with him together, and he'll get in touch with all the creditors to see if they want to offer us any kind of compromise. He generally doesn't do that unless it's almost too late. He said usually if he can see a way we can budget, scrimp a little and make it, he can help us set up a payment schedule that will get us out of trouble. But we're way past that. At this point, he either strikes some deals with everyone we owe, or we file. It's that simple."

"And then?"

"We live on cash. We'll be able to keep up with necessities, like food and clothes, the kids' stuff. But it'll take seven years to recover our credit rating."

"Seven years," she repeated. "That's not forever…"

"It's gonna seem like it. Both our cars are ready to fall apart, and there's no way to get a new car loan. It's not going to be easy." He grabbed her hand and held it in both of his. "At least we're done paying bills…"

"What do you mean?"

"He's got everything," he said with a shrug. "He pulled a couple hundred bucks out of his drawer—a hundred for me, a hundred for you. You have to buy food the rest of the week, I have to put twenty-five in the grocery fund at the firehouse and I'll keep gas in the cars, then he'll duke us again until this is resolved. We'll have to give it back, of course—as soon as this gets settled he'll take it out of our bills. Right now what he needs is for us to each fill out this form. Then we go back on Thursday. You have to be real careful on the form, Jules— you can't forget anything."

"What kind of form?"

"Costs. Expenses. You do the household list—everything from food and clothes to incidentals, like snacks and drinks for Jeffy's team. Everything—co-pays for the doctor and pharmacy, field trips, anything. And on your list, don't put down the cheapest you can get by. He says he can't do much with that—you've been getting by so cheap, there's no room to cut anything. You write down your usual expenditures at the regular price. Real food—no cereal for dinner. You don't have to buy filets, but write up a reasonable list. Then if you manage to save money, you'll have a little extra to roll over to the next month. Can you do that in two days?"

"Sure," she said. "It's not going to be easy. I'm not sure I even know everything. I'm always scrounging a couple of bucks here, a couple there—"

"Put McDonald's twice a month on your list," he said. "I'm sick of my kids being told no to everything. It's all they hear—no. When they do get something, it comes from my mom or yours." He ran a hand through his hair. "God, I let you down, Jules. I always told you it was going to be all right. You must have wanted to hit me in the head with a brick!"

Tears began to roll down her cheeks. She hated seeing him like this. It was easier struggling and juggling, being furious with him for his damn optimism, than to look at his eyes right now, filled with regret and shame.

"It's still going to be all right," she said, "because we're in this together. Right?" He didn't say anything and with a hiccup of emotion, she said, "We're still in this together, aren't we, Billy?"

He pulled her hand into his again and kissed the palm. "I

made an appointment for a vasectomy a week from Friday. You have to come with me to the doctor—sign off. I'll get a local. I can drive myself."

"You're not going to drive yourself. God."

He was quiet for a second. Then he said, "If we ever get out of this mess, I swear to God I'll never let anything like this happen to you again, Jules. I let you down. I let the kids down." He wiped at an eye.

"Will you stop this!" she said loudly, standing. "You have to stop it! Now!"

"I'm sorry," he said softly, his beautiful eyebrows furrowed.

"Billy, people do this all the time—our families aren't going to let us starve, for God's sake! Movie stars and professional athletes are filing for bankruptcy every day! It makes headlines and they get through it! Beth said a surgeon she knew filed for bankruptcy and stayed in his mansion of a house, operated every day just like usual!"

"Yeah, I know, but I thought if I could just work a little harder, make it a little longer…"

"Right now I don't care about *anything,* except that you straighten your back and take it like a man!" she said loudly. "If this is how it is, it is. What we have in this family has never been about money!"

He stared at her a long moment and very quietly, very sadly, said, "And that's for goddamn sure."

8

Marty got home from the shop at six, her arms full of groceries and Joe's uniform pants from the dry cleaner, her legs aching after a long day on her feet. She could hear Jason whacking around toys in his room, but all else was quiet. Joe might be lying down in the bedroom. There was a disturbing smell in the house; she wrinkled her nose. Then she put down her groceries and separated them, putting some in the refrigerator, some in the cupboards, leaving out the meat, potatoes and green beans. She flipped on the oven, sniffing again. She'd have to figure out that smell; they didn't have a dog.

She mixed up a meat loaf and put it on a baking sheet. She got the potatoes peeled and boiling, snipped the ends off the beans and put them in the vegetable steamer. Then she started picking up—dishes, toys, clothes, shoes, newspapers, pillows from the sofa. As she was putting things away, she found Joe in the room that passed for his office. The smell was stronger. It couldn't have gotten *this* bad, she thought. "I'm home," she said.

He turned away from the computer and grinned at her. "Hey, babe. First preseason game on tonight!"

"Joe, do you smell like *shit?*"

He sniffed at himself. "Me and Jase—we composted around the trees and flower beds. Fall's here. I washed my hands."

"Joe," she said earnestly, "you have to wash more than your hands. Shower before dinner. We shouldn't have to eat with that smell!"

"It's not that bad," he said, brushing her off. "There's a game starting in less than an hour…" He turned back to the computer.

"It won't take fifteen minutes," she informed him.

"Yeah, sure," he said.

"What are you doing?"

"Fantasy football—it starts in a couple of weeks. I'm boning up. I'm going to kill it this year."

She pursed her lips and left. She went and kissed her boy, gathered up dirty clothes—Joe's off the floor—and threw in a load of laundry. While dinner was finishing up, she ran the vacuum around the family room to suck up crumbs from bread and chips, dusted some of the wood, used glass cleaner to get the fingerprints off the patio doors, kitchen appliances and her bathroom fixtures. Joe was still at the computer. She put plates out on the table, transferred laundry. When dinner was ready, she called Jason and Joe. She was whipping the potatoes when Joe entered the kitchen, came up behind her as she worked, slipped his arms around her waist and nuzzled her neck with his scratchy beard. The smell was *horrible!* She wasn't sure she could eat dinner with him without getting sick. "You look real sexy tonight, babe," he said. "You have a good day?"

"Until I came home," she answered coolly.

"What?" he asked, backing up.

She turned around and faced him. "You haven't heard me the first hundred times, Joe. I don't think you'll hear me the next hundred. But I'll try once more. Your hygiene, Joe. You stink. You smell of compost and sweat. You need a shower before you sit down at the table with me."

He sniffed each armpit. "What are you *talking* about?"

She shook her head in disgust and put the food out while he stood there, staring at her as if she was out of her mind.

When the food was on the table, Joe got himself a TV tray, loaded up his plate and headed for the family room. He sat in front of his big screen. The game wasn't on yet. It was the pregame show, which he could have seen from the table—his place was strategically positioned. She didn't rag on him; he smelled of manure and sour grass clippings. The family room was a good place for him, though not nearly far enough away.

Jason wanted a tray, too, like Dad, but Marty made him stay at the table. She helped him with his meat loaf and beans—the mashed potatoes went fast. She glanced at her watch as the dryer buzzed that there were clothes ready to fold. Seven-twenty. And she thought, I can't do this. I just can't do this anymore. Work all day, clean and cook all night, lie next to a husband whose stench was so bad it was nauseating. It wasn't like coming home to no one; it was like coming home to a bigger problem than she'd have if she was single. The house had an aroma of meat loaf and compost; Joe sat on the couch, engrossed in his football and nothing domestic had been done all day long. He'd gotten off work this morning and Jason had been sent to his Grandma's till noon so Joe could get some sleep. The rest of the day had been dedicated to yard work, foraging for food, entertaining himself and getting all juiced up for football.

I hate my life, she thought. It shouldn't be like this. I don't have to have barrels of fun every day, but I have to live in a tolerably clean environment and share a bed with someone who doesn't smell like manure.

After dinner and dishes, while the dishwasher ran, she bathed

Jason, read him a story and settled him into bed. When she got back to the kitchen, Joe's tray, complete with dirty dishes, sat on the counter, ready for her to clean it up. But the dishwasher was full. She rinsed them, left them in the sink and went to her room.

Since those breathless kisses with her old boyfriend, Marty had been determined to be a better wife. She'd kept up with the house and meals, tried very hard not to complain or nag, though she didn't do so well at that. Today had been long and hard—difficult clients, petty drama among some of the beauticians in the shop, a double booking that had her scrambling with no time for lunch. Her legs ached, her head throbbed, her hands were raw from chemicals. And she'd come home to that disgusting smell.

Here were her options: she could shower off the grime of the day, crawl into bed with one of her romances and a watchable rerun on the bedroom TV, or...or something else.

She showered, fixed her hair, applied her makeup and put on some of those new clothes she'd bought a few weeks ago—the low-slung pants, the tight shirt that showed off her cleavage and the high strappy heels. She sprayed on some perfume.

When she walked into the family room, Joe was nodding off in front of the game. This was so standard. He'd have a big meal, a couple of beers, maybe a couple of bourbons, get all cozy and comfortable in front of the set and by the third quarter he'd be asleep. He wouldn't shower or shave, wouldn't sit at the table with them. She couldn't watch the big TV because whether he was asleep or not, it was his. So this was a preseason game. Fall. Boating would go on hiatus and football would start. There would be a game every Monday, Thursday and Sunday night, and all day on the weekends. Joe was pretty senior at F.D.—he'd bid his schedule to be off for the games so he could either watch them at home wearing the smell du jour or go to the bar. This was going to be her life for the next several months until the Super Bowl—either alone with Jason while

Joe worked or coming home to a mess, a smelly husband and an anger that was rising in her to unpredictable proportions.

She thought about leaving the house and just letting Joe wonder, but she couldn't do that. There had to be a transfer of responsibilities, so she woke him. "Joe," she said, shaking him. "Joe…"

"Huh," he roused. "Huh?"

"Joe, I'm going out for a while. Jason's in bed asleep. You're in charge."

"Huh? Where you going, babe?"

"I'm going out for a glass of wine," she said.

"Oh? With the girls?"

"Yeah," she said. "With the girls."

He stroked her arm a little bit; he smiled through his stubble. "You gonna be home kind of early? Because it's been a while…"

"Sure," she said, showing him a fake smile. "You just shower and shave and I'll see you a little later."

"It's a deal. I'll have it up for you," he said. "I mean, I'll be waiting up for you."

"Sure," she said.

Marty drove around for about a half hour, then she pulled into a strip mall parking lot and called Ryan from her cell phone. "Hi," she said. "Did I wake you?"

"Course not. What's up?"

"I'm out," she said. "I had to get out of the house for a while. Want to meet for a drink?"

"Sure," he said, and she could hear him stifle a yawn. "Tell me where and when."

"How about the Red Lion Inn? I can meet you in the bar…"

"Gimme a little time," he said. "I was just watching the game."

"And you'd leave the game?" she asked, smiling to herself.

"You're damn straight. See you in about a half hour."

That gave her way too much time to think about what she

was doing. She got to the Red Lion quickly, found a place at the end of a long bar in the shadows and asked for a glass of wine. There was no way she could rationalize this into something that was okay. It was dead wrong; she shouldn't be seeing Ryan, even for a drink, even for a talk.

But the right thing to do was even worse. She should tell Joe she was through, that she just couldn't envision her life like this for another fifty years. It was going to get a lot worse before it got better. If she thought another few years would set them right, put them back in touch with each other, she'd gut it out, keep trying. But the opposite was going to happen. He was going to get worse and she was going to get meaner, and older. If this had to be done, she had to do it now, before she was well into her thirties or forties, bitter, angry and exhausted.

This was the one thing she never thought she'd do—step out on her husband. After all the times it had been done to her, knowing the hurt and feelings of helplessness, she was meeting the same man who had cheated on her so many times! It was sheer lunacy.

Before it was too late, she asked herself, Can't I live with most of it? There was a list in her mind that she'd been over many times, and she considered it again. She could give up going out for an evening that was meant for them as a couple and not a sporting event. She didn't mind that Joe wasn't a good dancer; she sure liked to dance, but she could get by without that. She could get used to the RV and there were things about boating that could be fun. It would be okay to never have a reason to dress up again. The domestic stuff... Maybe if he'd just pick up after himself a little bit, a tiny bit, she could handle the rest—all the cooking, cleaning, shopping, laundry. Because there were good things about Joe. For one thing, he loved her completely, would never look at another woman, and they looked at him plenty. He was an involved father, a good provider. She could deal with the stubble, but he had to be clean. Okay, if there was one day a week that he let it all go to hell—wore the worst old shorts or sweats in the house and reeked like an outhouse with B.O.—one day a week, she thought, I could do that. I just need to feel more valuable than the ball game once in a while, just important enough for a shower.

Because this was wrong, so wrong...

And then she saw Ryan walk in and everything inside her seemed to swell. Look at him, she thought, a smile coming to her lips. He was home in front of the same game her husband was watching, yet he walked in wearing a crisp shirt, tailored pants, clean shaven, his light brown hair groomed, that dimpled grin sparkling. He wasn't even married or living with a woman, yet he was put together. Neat and tidy. He saw her, walked right over to her, slipped an arm around her and kissed her temple. "You look so hot," he whispered, sitting down next to her. "What's going on?"

"I needed to get out," she said with a smile and a shrug.

"Trouble at home?"

"Nah. I just didn't have anyone to call—the girls are all tied up," she lied. "And you know what I thought would be really fun? I haven't danced in years. Literally years."

"I could spin you around a little bit. Then you have to tell me what's wrong," he said. "Because I don't want get in the middle of anything complicated. You know?"

"Aw, don't worry about it. Everything's fine."

"You cool with this?" he asked.

"This?"

"Me and you? Just getting together?"

"Sure. Why not?"

"Then grab your wine and let's go downstairs where there's music. How about that?"

"I'd really like that," she said, grinning stupidly.

He held her hand while they went down the spiral stairs to the nightclub, the dance floor, and it was like a date. I'm going to do this one time, she thought. I'm going to dance and laugh and not think about things—and then I'll go home and, by God, I'll handle it.

And that's what she did; she danced with Ryan three, four, five times in a row. Then they went to the bar, he ordered up a beer and excused himself for a few moments. She asked for an ice water while she waited and when he came back a slow song came on and they hit the dance floor again. He pulled her into his arms, held her close, swayed with her, his big soft hands running up and down her back, over her butt and hips, pulling her against him. Tears sparkled in her eyes. It had been too long since she'd felt like this, like a woman and not a mean, demanding bitch.

He kissed her neck as they danced and said, "Marty, do you have any idea what you do to me?"

"Yeah, I have an idea," she said. "But I have a very good memory—anyone does that to you."

"Let's find someplace quieter," he said, ignoring the jibe. "More private. What do you say?"

"I can't, Ryan. I can't go that far, you know that."

"Sure you can, or you wouldn't be here."

She laughed. "Tempting," she said. "But no, thanks."

"What do you have in mind, then?" he asked.

She pulled away a little. "Just a little dancing…"

"But see, now that I have my arms around you, I'm starting to get all those old feelings. And I think you have 'em, too, or you wouldn't have called me…"

Oh, I have them, all right, she thought. I don't want this to ever end.

"Come on. Let's get out of here."

"Your house?" she asked.

"Can't," he said. "A guy from work is staying there for a

couple of weeks. And besides, it's a mess. Come on," he said, and then he took her hand and pulled her along.

He led her into the elevator. "Where are we going?" she asked.

He grabbed her to him, covered her mouth in a searing kiss that took her breath away and said, "Surprise." He pulled her out of the elevator and down the hall to a hotel room, where he slipped a plastic key card into the lock on the door.

"You got a room?" she asked, floored.

"A room with a hot tub," he said, grinning.

When he opened the door to a beautiful, large room with a huge bed, she stood in shocked wonder for a second. To her shame, her first thought was that she'd wanted something like this *forever*. If Joe had done something similar, even once a year since they'd been married, she might've been able to get through the rest. But this attractive, clean-smelling, sexy man was not Joe, and she wasn't supposed to be here. "I just wanted to dance a little," she said quietly.

In two seconds he had her lying down on the bed and was working at getting his hands under her shirt, his mouth all over her. For a moment, she thought about it. Once, she thought. I could do this once, just to see if there's a live woman under all this anger…

He pressed himself on top of her—making sure she knew he was erect and ready—while kissing her, fondling her. It had been years, but she hadn't forgotten an inch of him. "I'm still in love with you, baby," he whispered against her lips.

"No," she said. "No, you're not…"

"I never got over you. And I don't think you ever got over me, either. I think we're meant to be together."

"Maybe," she said breathlessly. But no one knew better than Marty how much it hurt when someone cheated on you. It had happened to her with this guy a dozen times and it was like a knife. She went into her marriage swearing to herself it would never come to that with her; if her husband ever became not enough, she'd at least end one relationship before starting a new one.

"I can't do this, Ryan," she said. "I can't. I won't cheat on my husband…"

"Oh, you will. You're almost there…"

"No," she said and pushed at him, pushed him off. Tears instantly came to her eyes. "I'm sorry," she said. She choked on a sob. "I shouldn't have called you, it was a mistake…"

"What the hell?"

She got up and adjusted her clothing. Tears ran down her cheeks. "I'll make it up to you," she said. "I swear, I'll make this right. But not tonight. I have to clean up the mess at home. Then…"

"What mess? You're going home to clean *house?*"

She laughed and cried at the same time, looking at his stunned face as he struggled to sit up on the bed. "In a way," she said. "Thanks, Ryan. You helped me figure out what I have to do. And when I'm free and clear, I'll call you. I don't think it's going to take that long."

"Aw, Jesus," he said, running a hand down to his crotch, giving the poor unloved thing a sympathetic rub. "You're kidding me, right? You're not serious."

"They won't charge you for the room," she said, grabbing her purse off the chair. "Just tell them you decided to go home and didn't use it."

She got out of the room fast, before she could change her mind. Thinking he might follow her and try to persuade her, she took the stairs instead of waiting for the elevator, and she took them fast. She got across the lobby at a near jog, then to her car before hearing him, seeing him. She started the car and left the parking lot.

Then she cried. Oh, God, she thought. I never thought I'd even *consider* that!

Her tears were dry by the time she got home, replaced with a sense of duty. Purpose. She wasn't going to have that life she almost stepped into—with a husband and child at home and a lover on the side. Oh, she hoped to have a lover—and a glimpse of something promising, maybe—but not until she'd taken care of business.

The house was dark when she let herself in. He'd left on the light over the stove for her. She crept into the bedroom and looked down at him, asleep in their bed. No shower, no shave. Poor Joe, she thought briefly; he could have changed everything by cleaning up for her return. But he didn't want to change anything.

She went into the master bath and gathered up her things— makeup, hair dryer, fluff and buff essentials. She took them all to the bathroom down the hall and went to the guest room, took off her clothes and crawled in the bed. Sleep didn't come easy; she tossed and turned and every once in a while a sob escaped her.

She got up in the morning and showered, getting ready for work. When she came out of the shower, he was standing there, frowning. "When did you get home?" he asked unhappily.

"About eleven-thirty," she said.

"And didn't sleep in our bed?"

"That's right," she said, wrapping the towel around her. "I'm done sleeping in that bed with you. I'm done camping, watching football, going to sports bars, cleaning up after you and getting sick from the smell of your unwashed body. I've had it and I'm through."

"What the fuck are you talking about?" he asked angrily.

"And I'm also done talking about it," she said. "I hoped that if I kept talking, eventually you'd hear me, but it's useless. You're deaf. You're *hopeless*." She turned on the hair dryer, drowning him out, and concentrated on her hair.

★ ★ ★

Julie went with Billy to the doctor, signed the paperwork for the vasectomy and then to the credit counselor. He was a tall, skinny guy with a very sympathetic smile, warm eyes, and she was comfortable with him right away, but she didn't want to be doing this. She had an epiphany—people avoided getting this kind of assistance because the cure felt worse than the disease. Going over every detail of your private financial life was more invasive and embarrassing than putting your feet in the stirrups.

He had a list of his own he used to compare to theirs, to be sure they hadn't omitted anything. "Haircuts?" he asked. "Beauty shop?"

"I cut Billy's hair," she said. "And the kids'. And my own."

"Hmm," he said, checking it off. "What about entertainment? The occasional night out? Pizza? Movie?"

"No," she said. "The only thing we ever do is get together with family or friends. We potluck—everyone chips in. We might pick up a bottle of cheap wine and a twelve-pack of beer—fifteen bucks, tops. I included it in with groceries. It doesn't happen often."

"This is a very low clothing budget," he said.

"I get kids' clothes on sale or sometimes at the thrift shop. I hardly ever buy anything for myself unless it's a pair of shorts or jeans at Costco, and Billy wears a uniform or old jeans to the shop. That's about six days a week, so he's gotten by real cheap."

"Vet?"

"Hardly ever. Tessie is durable, thank God."

"Got the phone and Internet down about as low as you can go. Good that you have that—we're going to talk about that. But the co-pay at the pharmacy and pediatrician is kind of high…"

"I figured on the high side—three kids. One gets something, they all get it. And I figured out a prescription co-pay is sometimes cheaper than over-the-counter stuff."

"Gifts? Birthdays? Anniversaries? Special occasions?"

"We don't do a lot of that," she said. And she felt instant, biting sadness. Her brother and sister-in-law, mom, dad and best friends were given things like cheap stationery when no one wrote letters anymore, bath stuff on sale, a fancy candle, coasters, junk. She and Billy had been exchanging crap the Goodwill might reject for years. She didn't even have an engagement ring. "We've been strapped so long, no one expects too much." But the families and girlfriends hadn't cut back on them. They always received very nice if not lavish presents. And they spoiled the kids a little, knowing their parents wouldn't. Couldn't.

"Okay, Julie, let's go through some of the things you might've lumped into that grocery budget. You have an idea, offhand?"

"Sure. I'll try. The occasional gift, something to take to a family or friends' gatherings—chicken, salad, a bottle of Two Buck Chuck…"

"Two Buck Chuck?"

She smiled. "That's right—Billy told me, you're a Mormon. Charles Shaw wine—two dollars a bottle. It's very good, actually. You don't really have to spend a lot. And maybe some beer—not imported or anything, just cheap stuff. Snacks or Gatorade for Jeffy's school or sports teams. Gifts for the kids to take to birthday parties for friends. Cards. Makeup—very little. Postage. And Billy insisted I figure in McDonald's for the kids twice a month, but we've been getting by fine without that so far. And we don't eat it. It's just Happy Meals for the kids."

"Are these utility bills correct?" he asked.

"Cold in the winter, hot in the summer," she said helplessly.

He put down his pencil. "You've got it cut down to the bone."

"Yeah, but I guess it wasn't enough."

"We don't know that yet," he said. "Now that I know what you can afford to pay on your debts, I can make a proposal to creditors. I always say this—don't get your hopes up. Sometimes they hold out to see if you're really going to do it—file. And sometimes they have policies that prevent them from meeting us halfway. But I can't really approach them until I know for sure what you can commit to."

"What *can* we commit to?"

"Do you mind if I do some figuring and juggling of my own before nailing that down? I mean, if I get close and have maybe one creditor hold out, do I understand you want to try to avoid bankruptcy?"

She scooted forward in her chair and turned her desperate eyes on him. "I want my husband back. He was never afraid or depressed before this." She reached for Billy's hand and held it, but focused on John. "We've been in this deep for a long time, but he was always positive. I want my husband back— I don't care about the money. I'll eat sand for the rest of my life. Do you understand that?"

He smiled kindly. "Of course I do," he said. "I have a family of my own. I know exactly how you feel."

"Yeah, but have you ever been in a mess like this?" she asked.

"Like this? No, we've been lucky that way. I'm afraid our challenges have been other things—not so much this stuff because I do this for a living." He gave a weak smile. "We have a special-needs child. He takes a lot of energy and worries us sometimes, but we somehow manage. So listen, try not to panic. Even in the worst case, you're going to survive this. You're both young and healthy, Billy has a couple of good jobs, you have a solid house in good repair. Those cars—I hope there's a mechanic in the family. That could be your only issue."

"I'm sorry about your son," she said. "I hope you get the help you need. Our blessings have come with the kids—they're perfect. That's why I— Never mind. If we got down to one car, I could drive Billy to and from jobs... And those jobs— I don't know if you noticed, he puts in an awful lot of hours. A lot of days he gets home after I'm asleep and leaves before I wake up. And his work isn't easy—he has to put a lot of muscle in it. He has to be sharp. I'd like him to have more time to rest."

"I'll absolutely keep that in mind. Who knows—I could need a paramedic someday. I want him to be healthy, well fed, well rested..."

"She worries too much," Billy said. "I get good food and sleep in plenty of snatches at the firehouse. I'm fine."

"I'll do what I can to see if we can't get you a little more time with your kids. Would that be all right?" he asked.

Billy held Julie's hand, squeezed it, bounced it on his thigh a couple of times. "That would be all right. You bet. But remember, I'll do whatever I have to do."

Cassie was dressing out to leave the emergency room, thinking about seeing Walt. She had suggested they get together at her house, maybe order a pizza and watch a movie. If they were on the couch in front of the TV, she thought they might get to do some kissing again. It had only been a week since their weekend ride and while she'd worried about it a lot—the fact that it wasn't really going anywhere—she couldn't deny that the thought of kissing him all night long was appealing.

This was a good man, and she kept that in mind. She intended to be very careful with his feelings. She wouldn't let it go any further and…risk hurting him.

"Hey, Cassie," one of the other nurses said, entering the locker room.

"Hey, Jen. Long day, huh?"

"Whew, tough one. So…how's your friend?"

"Which friend?" she asked, pulling off her scrubs top and pitching it in the laundry basket.

"The one who just had surgery—the OB you've known forever?"

Cassie was frozen in place. Standing in her bra and scrub pants, she turned a startled expression toward Jen. "Surgery?"

"Uh-oh," Jen said, turning away.

Cassie went straight for her, grabbed her arm and turned her sharply back.

"*What* surgery?"

"Listen, I guess if you don't know—"

Cassie had an attack of panic and desperation. She shook Jen's arm. "*What* surgery?"

"I'm not exactly sure," she said with a helpless shrug. "Ow."

"Tell me what you do know!" she said, letting go of the arm.

"I took that emergency C-section we had up to O.R. and they were wheeling her out of recovery. Jesus," she said, rubbing her arm.

Cassie went on automatic. She grabbed her scrub top out of the hamper and put it back on, clipped on her badge, closed her locker and went to Admissions, looking like the nurse she was, ID badge and all. "Hi," she said pleasantly. "Where do you have Beth Halsley? Dr. Halsley?"

The woman clicked through her computer register and looked up. "Medical surgical wing—6-A."

"Thanks. Have a good evening." Then she went up to the

floor. She went right behind the nurses' station and flipped through the computerized files. When the team leader came back to the station after some rounds, Cassie smiled at her. "How you doing?" she asked.

"Great, thanks. Can I help you find anything?"

"No, thanks. I sent a patient up for surgery and wanted to check on her before going home, that's all."

"How are things in E.R.?" she asked.

"Nuts, as always," she answered, locating the file. "I'm getting out of here before it gets worse." She read up to the operative report. *Radical mastectomy*. Holy Mother of God! Then she recovered herself. "I should be out of here in just a little while."

"Good plan," she replied. "I won't be out of here till *Letterman*'s over."

Cassie clicked off the page, stunned. Stricken. She was in a total state of disbelief. She had no clue about this—and it couldn't have been a sudden decision. Even in the scariest cases, surgeons didn't whack off a breast overnight. She tried to think if Beth had mentioned anything. But no, it would have stuck in her mind like duct tape. They'd gone almost five years since the cancer.

She had to gather herself up before going into the room. She had to consider that Beth was right now a post-surgical patient, perhaps not in any condition to respond. Perhaps in pain, not to mention grief.

She began to walk down the hall, but before she got to the room she paused, pulled her cell phone out of her pocket and called Walt. His phone was turned off and she was directed to voice mail. He must have his hands plunged deep in a carburetor or something. "Hi, it's me," she said, knowing her voice was stressed. "I'm afraid I have to cancel tonight. I had a problem come up at work. An emergency, with lots of complications. I'll try to call you later and explain if I can get free. Sorry," she finished, hanging up. Then she turned off the phone.

She paused in the hall outside Beth's room—a private room. Hospital staff tended to take good care of their own. She took a few deep breaths, tried to compose herself, then went in on silent feet. There she was, her arm Ace-wrapped close against her, bandages up over her shoulder, an IV tube dangling into the free arm. Oh, God, she thought. This can't be real.

Beth was asleep. And alone. So, Cassie wasn't the only one who had no idea this was happening. Her parents were right here in town; they'd be here with her if they knew. They'd probably be pacing, whimpering and keeping her awake, but they'd be here. Cassie remembered how they were the last time. Just plain not good at this sort of thing—helpless and frightened without the first idea how to be supportive.

Cassie sat in the chair by the bed and, after thinking for just minutes, she realized Beth had kept this a deliberate secret. Yet she was in her own hospital, the very same in which Cassie worked. Even so, the odds were still good in her favor of keeping it to herself; nurses didn't prowl around floors they didn't work, checking out the patients, and it was a huge hospital. And if the surgery had gone well, she'd be discharged in a couple of days. And then what would she say if they wanted to get together? That she was on call—she'd been saying that for a long time.

So Cassie sat. She wanted to call Julie and Marty, but before she did that she would wait for Beth to rouse, tell her something about this. There was no reason Cassie could think of that made sense, but Beth deserved a chance to explain her secrecy.

It was a long time—a couple of hours—and the sun was setting when Cassie heard a moan and cough from the bed and Beth began to stir. Her free hand went to her chest and she grimaced. You could always count on pain to wake a patient. Then without opening her eyes, she found the call button with the same hand and rang for the nurse.

One came very quickly and gave Cassie a nod on her way to the bed. "Evening, Doctor," she said to Beth. "How's the pain?"

"Not so good. Is it time for meds?"

"You're close enough. Just let me get a blood pressure, check your urine output and then I'll get you taken care of. Inhalation therapy is going to start bothering you pretty soon..."

"Swell," she said.

The nurse completed the blood pressure reading, charting it. She glanced at the catheter bag and said, "You're doing very well, Doctor. I'll be right back with that pain medication."

"The faster, the better," she muttered.

When the nurse had cleared the room, Cassie softly said, "Very sneaky."

Beth jerked her head toward Cassie with an unmistakable and very mean frown on her face. Her eyes were narrowed and her mouth held in a tight, unhappy line.

Cassie stood and went to the bed, leaning over. "What's going on? Why did you do this without me?"

Her features momentarily relaxed—caught. Her eyes drifted closed. "I didn't want to go through it again, that's all."

"So you went it alone?"

She took a breath. "I was pretending it was a tooth extraction. I didn't want all the helping. Hoping. Coping. All that fear around me. It's not as bad as it looks..."

"It looks like a mastectomy," Cassie said. "The second one. It's not a tooth extraction."

"They're treating it like another primary cancer. Once the

breast tissue is gone… Listen, the last time was too much. I just couldn't…"

"Beth, you can have it whatever way you want," Cassie said gently, rubbing a knuckle along her soft cheek. "But there's no reason to pretend with me. With any of us."

"Yeah, there is. You're pretty good at this, Cassie, but the others… My parents… Really, if I have to go through that again…"

"Honey, we're not going to leave you for this," she whispered. "That was from hell, what Mark did to you. But the rest of us—we're with you forever. And forever's going to be a long time."

Beth squeezed her eyes and her lips contorted. "We don't know that," she said in a choked whisper. "We don't know anything yet. In fact, we might not know anything for months. Years."

"And you don't want anyone in this with you while you're figuring that out? I don't believe that."

"Cassie," she said on a sob. "Cassie…"

"Okay, Beth, I don't want you to worry about anything," Cassie said tenderly. "I'm the only one who got wind of this. I won't say a word—I'll let you catch your breath. But I'm not leaving you. "

"No, I'll be fine," she said. "I gathered up some groceries before I checked in. The laundry's done, the cat's been fed—"

"You don't have a cat," Cassie laughed, though there was an emotional catch in her voice.

"Oh, that's right. No cat. Wonder what I fed? I'll just lay low—watch some movies, zone out on pain meds. It'll be over before you know it. I'll be back at work in no time…"

"Nice try. I already called my supervisor," she lied. "I have a couple of days off and I'm taking a couple of sick days. When you're discharged, I'll watch movies with you and dose you up. It'll be like old times—you'll do narcs and I'll do Cha-blis. You'll see—I'm a goddamn good nurse. Better than these med-surg losers."

Beth turned her head toward Cassie, eyes open but the expression unreadable. "Don't bother," she said. "Really..."

"It's already done," Cassie said. "I can't let you go through this alone—it would damage me for life."

Beth reached out her free hand, IV inserted and tube fol-lowing, and grabbed Cassie's wrist. "My parents, Cass. Please... don't call them."

Cassie thought for a moment, remembering the last time, calling to mind Beth's parents and their clumsy attempts at caretaking. They barely took care of themselves. In all Beth's growing-up years, her parents were amazing tutors, very in-volved in her education and totally committed to learning, studying, and that was where their nurturing abilities began and ended. They could never have managed more than one child and Beth's cancer threw them into a helpless panic. In no time they had turned Beth and Mark's fashionable little townhome into a hovel filled with clutter and raw emotion.

"Yeah," Cassie said, "I know. They were kind of a load, huh? I'll let you handle them in your own time. But you do understand, they love you like mad?"

"I get that, yes," she answered sleepily. "They're just not good at this."

Cassie smiled. "Fortunately, I am."

The nurse returned with a syringe. "Well, this should help you sleep and feel better," she said, going straight for the IV.

"Oh, baby," Cassie laughed. "That's going right in the vein—you have a good doctor. Beth, I'm going to leave—they're going to keep you as drugged as tolerable all through the night and I'd be wasting good TV hanging out with you. I'll check in on you in the morning."

"Cassie," she said weakly. "Don't tell—"

"I won't call the girls till we've had some time to sort through how you want to manage this. I promise. But me, you're stuck with."

"Okay," she said weakly. "Okay, then." And her eyes drifted closed.

When the nurse had left and the room was bathed in dusk, Cassie stood at Beth's bedside for a long time. I've spent so much envy on her, she thought. And look how her life's going. Why couldn't she have ordinary problems like the rest of us? Like trouble getting a boyfriend or passing chemistry? Or maybe even an un-sympathy-worthy bad MCAT score? But for years everything seemed to go right for Beth, and on top of that she was stunning. Gorgeous. If you didn't know anything about her but her grades, her achievements, her looks, you'd think she just hadn't suffered enough.

Cassie ran a hand over Beth's shiny, thick, wavy brown hair. She remembered with sadness the last time, when the chemo had stolen her glorious hair, but it came back, almost stronger than ever. And unlike with many cancer patients, it hadn't altered its color; it was like before. Rich and full. Beth had carried on—beat it.

But not quite.

Cassie watched her sleeping face for a long time, then finally when it appeared she couldn't get any more insight, she leaned over and kissed her friend's forehead. Then she left the room. She went back to the E.R. locker room where she was alone and ditched the scrubs, putting on her jeans and sweatshirt. She walked a little slowly to her car. Once there, she turned her cell phone back on and listened to a message from Walt. *I hope you're okay, Cassie. I understand emergencies. I'm really sorry I couldn't answer when you called—I was in the middle of something. If you want to, you can call me tonight anytime—I'll answer.*

Well, she couldn't call Julie or Marty; she had promised. So she called Walt. When he said, "Hey, Cassie," she burst into tears.

"Oh, God, Walt," she sniveled pathetically. "I've had the most awful day."

"Oh, honey," he said so sweetly. "What can I do? Anything. Anything that will make you feel a little better."

"I'm just leaving the hospital…"

"You've been there since seven?" he asked.

"Yeah, but… Oh, Walt," she cried.

"Cassie, you okay to drive home?"

"Yeah," she said, sniffing, wiping the tears and snot off her face with the back of her hand. "Yeah, I'll be okay."

"Just go home, honey. Turn off the phone and concentrate on driving. I'll meet you there."

"It's getting so late…"

"Oh, who cares? I'll see you there. Now you be careful, you sound real shook up."

She sniffed. "I've had an awful day."

"Just hang up, Cass. Don't drive and talk—concentrate. I'm on my way."

Cassie had never had anything like this in her life—a man who rushed to her when she was upset. To her complete embarrassment, that was hardly the first phone call she'd made while in tears, but no man in her history had dropped everything and come that fast. Three minutes after she had arrived at home and wept into Steve's long, gray snout, Walt was at the door. He balanced a take-out pizza in one hand and six-pack of beer in the other.

She took one look at him and leaned into his chest, overcome. "Pizza and beer" was all she could say.

"Yeah, I wasn't sure if you'd had anything to eat during

your bad day," he said, trying to hug her while balancing everything. "Let me put this stuff down."

Once he'd set his offerings on the table, he put his arms around her and led her to her little living room, sitting down on the couch with her. Steve immediately jumped up and curled beside Walt, wagging, the frog in his mouth.

"What in the world happened today?" he asked, stroking her back with one hand, petting Steve with the other.

"It's a long story," she said.

"We have plenty of time."

"My friend Beth," she began, and went through the whole story. Before she even got to the part where she accidentally found out Beth was in the hospital again, post-surgical, Walt had drawn her up across his lap and held her as if she were a child. Then she told him the rest.

"Oh, man," he said. "Cassie, I've never heard a story like that in my life."

"She went through so much the last time—Mark leaving her and everything—I guess she was trying to go it alone this time. But why? Did she think anyone else would leave her?"

"She couldn't have thought that…"

"I can't imagine what she was trying to do. I thought we helped before. Maybe we just made it harder."

"Aw, honey, I'm sure you didn't do that…"

"I told her that no matter what, I'm in this with her. I'm going to take some time off, make sure I'm available every day after she's discharged, till she's up and around. I can get her through the surgery and recovery. But what if this is the worst case? What if we're losing her?"

"Try not to think that way, honey. Get some more facts. At least wait till you know more."

She looked up at him. "You came," she said.

He ran a hand over her wound-up braid. "Of course I came. I got the impression you needed me."

"Oh, I needed you so much! I can't call Jules or Marty yet. Beth will come around, but I promised. Until she says it's okay, I have to keep my word."

He wiped a big thumb under her eye. "After you give her a little time, she'll start to make sense out of this and you can call your friends."

"Walt, how did you know what to do?"

"What to do?" he asked. "Well, you just cover the essentials—food, drink, company. Anything else, you call the police. Right?"

"But how did you know that? For me? For a girlfriend problem?"

"Well, this is a little more serious than a girlfriend problem," he said. "And, Cassie, you're pretty important to me."

"You're such a good friend," she said, leaning against his chest.

He sighed and said, "I'm trying to be, Cass. You're special. You know that, don't you?"

She ran a hand along his scruffy face. "I do. It means a lot, believe me."

"Good." He smiled. "That's exactly what I want it to mean."

9

When Beth looked up from her newspaper, she saw Jerod Paterson standing in the doorway of her hospital room. It was an unusual pose for a physician—he was leaning a shoulder into the frame, hands in his pockets, one leg crossed in front of the other, smiling. No charts, accompanying nurse or treatment tray. Just him, grinning.

"Look at you," he said. "Sitting up in the chair, taking in the morning news, all accessories removed." By accessories, he would mean the IV and catheter. "How do you feel?"

"I feel like shit," she said. "How about you?"

"I'm feeling pretty good today, actually. Thank you for asking. What part feels the most like shit?"

"Truthfully, the place where there was once my last surviving breast. But my sore throat is running a close second."

"The intubation," he said, confirming what she already

knew. "You're surrounded by flowers," he observed. "Have you had many visitors?"

"Even though I specifically asked for *no* visitors? You're about the tenth, but then, you're here on official business, I suppose."

"No," he said, coming into the room. "I'm visiting."

"You're a long way from home. Do you drive around the state and check on your post-surgical patients?"

"How do you know I didn't come by helicopter? I was in the neighborhood. I made it a point to be in the neighborhood. You're feeling very feisty, aren't you?"

"Is that what you'd call it? I thought it was more like bitchy."

"What are your plans for aftercare?" he asked.

"My plans were to snuggle in with some movies, but one of my best friends found me out and is going to practically move in. She's a nurse here."

"You probably won't need a nurse," he said. "Can she cook?"

"She's a great cook. But the pain meds and chemo make my mouth taste like tin, so I might not be her best audience."

"You'll be off the pain meds in no time. Now, don't laugh— you're very healthy. Everything looks good, from blood pressure to hemoglobin to white count. I ran into your surgeon and he said the incision looks great."

"Now, that's a matter of opinion…"

Jerod sat on the bed, facing her chair. "They're going to kick you to the curb today. This afternoon. Now, if I was a betting man, I'd wager you drove yourself here, have a car in the physicians' lot…" She smirked at him and he laughed. "That's what I thought. What about your nurse friend?"

"She visits every day while she's working E.R. downstairs but she plans to take care of me after I'm discharged, once I'm home."

"I know you didn't admit to her that you're thinking of driving yourself home because a friend wouldn't allow it. Well, I have a meeting here in about an hour. I'll come back, drive you home, myself."

"No. I want my car," she said.

"I'll bet. Number one, you're on drugs. Number two, driving one-handed isn't recommended. Number three... There isn't a number three. Oh! Against doctor's orders."

"You're not in charge of this part. I need my car at home!"

"I have connections—I can get the entire staff on my side on this one. You won't have any trouble getting your car home when you're better able to drive it. You have the nurse friend..." He looked at his watch. "I'll be done by two. Try to be ready."

"You know, you're very pushy."

"Yeah. And I bet that's what you like best about me. See you soon..." He got up and started walking out of the room.

"Hey!" He turned back to her. "Aren't you getting a little out of your job description here?"

"I'm a full-service doctor."

"But what if I don't particularly want this service? I'll take a cab. I don't want you to see my messy house!"

"Dr. Halsley," he laughed. "I've only known you a short time and I'm convinced your house is in perfect order. I bet you even fold your undies in little squares. Have lunch—I'll be back." Before disappearing, he turned back to her. "Messy house—nice try."

She smiled after him. Of course it wasn't a disheveled house at all. It never was, but in this case it was even more organized. She'd gone through the house from top to bottom to be sure if she didn't make it home, nothing embarrassing or cluttered would be left behind. When you're raised by extremely slovenly parents, you either follow suit or train yourself to become the opposite—fussy and anal.

There were ways out of this, she thought. She could get in touch with Cassie, let her know if she wasn't here right at discharge time, she'd be left to the mercy of an overzealous oncologist. But there was something about him; Beth was curious. Why would he be so accommodating? He was putting the screws to her with his chemo orders and she would shortly be weak and ill and bald. Besides, as a rule, given their schedules, doctors weren't even able to do such favors. It had never occurred to Beth to provide taxi service for a patient.

Then it came to her—he thinks of us as colleagues. Maybe I'm not the first physician he's had for a patient, but I could be the youngest. Perhaps he had an overload of empathy, wondering how his life would be different if he'd been battling this disease since the age of twenty-five, the very disease he'd been treating and had seen the ravages of. There wouldn't be children in his life in that case, she thought. Those teenage daughters who had him tearing his hair out—they might not exist at all, or they would be considerably younger. Chemo or the disease would have greatly delayed if not prevented them.

Children. Beth had wanted them with Mark. After the first episode, before he left her, she knew it would be at least five years before she got the sense she was really free to get on with her life. But at twenty-five, that had given her so much time; she could have achieved some security about her health at thirty, thirty-two—enough confidence to have a baby then. She didn't need a calculator to see it would now be thirty-six, thirty-seven—and even then, after two cancers, there was a huge chance she'd be having children she couldn't raise. Childbearing was moving rapidly out of her reach. She'd have to adjust to that, as well. For a woman whose personal career fulfillment came from bringing babies into the world, this would be a major adjustment. She wanted to be one of *those* women—the regular ones.

Two o'clock came and so did he. She let this happen, but by that time of day, after being up since morning, given recovery from everything—surgery, anesthesia, stress—she'd grown very tired. Then she'd taken advantage of a pain shot for the road. There was none of that feisty, bitchy stuff left in her.

"Good. You're ready to go," he said.

"I don't know why you're doing this," she said. "It's not doctorlike at all."

"I'm a very nice guy," he said, putting the locks on the wheelchair and grabbing her suitcase. "Besides, you're a fellow doctor. We have a strong reputation for both competing with each other and taking excellent care of each other."

Ah, she thought. There it is. The colleague thing. She moved slowly to the chair. "You must be wondering what it would be like to be me—major surgery for cancer so young."

"I do, indeed," he said. "I don't feel I was even born at twenty-nine. I was still in residency."

"You've made a very good name for yourself since then."

"Have I?" he asked, wheeling her out of her room. "I've been lucky."

"I don't even remember your age."

"Forty-nine. Very soon to make the leap into fifty."

"You're holding up well," she said.

He laughed. "Thanks. You're being very nice to me. What's the matter? Has all the fight gone out of you?"

"It's just the surgery," she said. "Basically, I'm not a nice person."

"That's not true at all. We'll get you home where you can rest. Your friend—she'll make sure you can rest, won't she? She's not one of those overbearing nurses?"

"She's an outstanding nurse. I'd give anything to have her

as my nurse. Although it's such a tenuous relationship at times, and I wouldn't want to lose her as a friend. Besides, she's a total E.R. junkie. She's been in E.R. since the beginning."

He chuckled as he pushed her into the elevator. "I like those E.R. girls. They have what we used to call the high-speed wobbles. It's fast, it's concise, there are always incoming crises and they know how to move on to the next one in a blink. But they're usually a little nuts."

"Your business is a lot slower," she said somewhat wearily.

"Unfortunately, it's much slower. But we have some perks they don't have in E.R. When we're patient, smart and lucky, we see people cured. They just patch 'em up and float 'em out in E.R. It takes commitment to work in oncology."

"I'm seeing that…right down to chauffeur service…"

He wheeled her to his car, put her suitcase in the backseat and watched her get in very nimbly, if slowly. But then she leaned her head back against the headrest tiredly. He returned the wheelchair to the E.R. entrance and when he got in beside her, he asked if she was comfortable. Then he said, "Before you start to nod off, tell me where I'm going. Then you can relax."

She gave him an address and he fed it into a GPS system to get directions. She was incredibly glad she hadn't chosen another hospital; nothing sounded as good as getting home quickly, getting into her bed. Then she said, "The pharmacy— I'll need my medication…"

He reached in his jacket pocket and pulled out a small vial of pills. "These?"

"Oh man, you're just too good to be true." When he started to drive, she leaned back and closed her eyes. "You're not flirting with me, are you? I mean, a ride, my pills…"

He laughed at her. "I would, if I thought it would do me

any good. I'm pretty sure you're not in a flirty frame of mind, Beth."

She yawned. "Your sense of timing is way off if you're flirting." She turned her head and looked at him. "I had a pain shot just minutes before you got to my room," she said, slurring just slightly.

"Smart."

"I might not be good company."

"Just let yourself fall asleep. I'm a good driver."

A moment later, she woke herself with a small snore. "God," she muttered, wiping a little drool from the corner of her mouth. But then she was back asleep, completely unaware of the time or space she was in until he gently woke her. She leaned against him, sleepwalking, as he took her into the house and straight to her room. She lay gently, carefully, on her bed, never opening her eyes, and he pulled off her shoes. He propped a pillow under her left arm to give her support on her surgical side. Her lips formed the words *thank you* but she was gone, sleeping the sleep of the drugged post-surgical.

He looked down at her for a moment, just watching her give in to total exhausted, depleted sleep. Then he leaned down and kissed her forehead very lightly.

"I felt that," she said.

And he laughed.

Billy survived his vasectomy, though fretfully. Julie waited patiently outside the small surgical room while he underwent the procedure, then the doctor came out, told her Billy needed to lie down for a while longer before he could be released—just twenty to forty minutes—and she could go in and talk to him if she wanted to. She found him flushed and a little hyper, but victorious. He'd done it. He'd let them cut

A SUMMER IN SONOMA   *225*

right into his sack and stop the babies from coming and coming and coming.

"Jules," he said a little excitedly, "wait till you see what
they took out of me!"

He pulled the Mayo stand closer to the table on which he
lay and lifted the green cloth. There, in the curved emesis
basin, lay two inch-long pieces of what could pass as angel
hair pasta. "Billy," she said somberly. "Did you see what they
took out of me? Three times? Men. Jeez."

He took a couple of sick days—a pure rarity for him—and
tried to keep ice on his testicles and small children off his lap.
Then he went back to work.

The financial counselor was in touch a couple of times,
though he didn't have a lot to report—just that he thought
he might be making some progress. What was unsurprising
to him but flat-ass amazing to Billy, was that the credit-card
companies got right on board and they were negotiating, but
the bank, who'd helped him into this mess, was holding a hard
line. It made no sense; the mortgage holder was the one who
stood to lose the most, since the house would be safe under
bankruptcy law.

He had a lot on his mind—his testicles, for one thing, which
still had the occasional *tug* from the surgery. His finances. His
family. A lot of soul searching that included feelings of inad-
equacy for not figuring this out sooner, and regret that he'd
been so chipper with poor Jules while she was just dying under
the weight of their family's needs. And of course the end result of all that was a baby who could've been their fourth and
was lost. They'd never planned on four; they hadn't actually
planned on three. But they both loved kids, loved the size
of their plentiful family. If they didn't have so many money
problems, four wouldn't throw them at all.

This was too distracting for Billy to take much notice of

other things going on, but it wasn't long before Joe's short fuse and sulk was apparent to him, as it had already become to everyone else. Joe was usually a funny guy. He wasn't exactly even tempered; in fact, he was a little on the scrappy side. But he had a good sense of humor; he was playful and energetic, talkative and always helpful. Not lately.

They had a lot of calls throughout the day, but just before dinner, Billy caught Joe alone out by the rig. Joe was running a rag over headlights and chrome—and he wasn't whistling. Billy leaned up against the truck. "You're not keeping it much of a secret, you're pissed about something."

Joe just kept working. "Yeah? Bug off."

"It's something you don't want to talk about, which usually means you should get it out of your gut before you punch someone."

Joe straightened. "You wanna be first?"

"Whew. That bad, huh? No one ever feels like hitting me!"

"And why's that, pretty boy?"

"Because I'm sweet," he answered with a grin. "Ask Jules."

Joe went back to wiping, shining. "Well, you might find out more about this by asking Jules," he said.

"Well, that can only mean one thing. Marty. But Jules hasn't said anything. Those girls—they never shut up when you want 'em quiet, but if you'd like to know something, they're pretty tight-lipped. You wanna pout and piss everyone off, or you wanna get it off your chest?"

He straightened again. "I don't know what it is," he said, frowning. "She's got a bug up her ass about something."

"You ask her?"

"I don't exactly have to ask her," he said meanly. "All she does is bitch. She doesn't like anything. It's like she wants me to be waiting at the door in my negligee with a glass of wine

in my hand when she gets home, or something like that. I
can't do anything right."

"Been there," Billy laughed.

"Yeah?"

"Oh, yeah. The last time I couldn't do anything right,
Jules was pregnant, for the fourth time. The one we lost—
you know."

Joe ran a hand through his thick, black hair. "Whoa. Think
Marty could be—"

"Well, hell, Joe, how would I know? You're the only one
who'd know that!"

"Yeah, but Jules…she do anything really crazy?"

"Like…?"

"Like move out of the bedroom?"

That one hit Billy hard. It almost made him take a step
back. He thought things had been bad there for a while, but
if Julie had moved out of their bed, out of their bedroom,
he'd have thought it was the end. Through the worst of their
problems—and they hadn't been small—they'd always spent
what sleep time they had together in the same bed, usually
holding each other on and off all night.

"Holy shit, Joe—that's not good," he said glumly.

"Tell me about it." He went back to polishing.

"Moved out of the bedroom?"

"Down the hall. First it was just the makeup and hair dryer,
then it was the stuff in her closet and drawers. It's like she's
gone. I don't know what game this is—"

"Joe," Billy said, putting a hand on his shoulder. "Joe, this
isn't a game. You better figure out what's going on. She's moving away. You don't have that much time."

"How can she do that? We took an oath!"

"Yeah, well, if you think the oath is gonna hold you together, you're dreaming. The oath is about you holding *each*

other together. Listen, can I tell you something? It's private. Not for any other ears."

"It's up to you," he said with a shrug. "I don't talk, you know that."

"But I don't know how much of this the girlfriends even know."

"Well, none of the girlfriends are talking to me right now," he said with a pout and a scuffle of one foot. "Not even the one I married."

"Okay, I don't know if this'll help you or not, but when Jules was hating me, it wasn't just about being pregnant. She was afraid to have another kid, because money's just so damn tight."

"Listen, the first years at F.D., with a family, it's not that easy…"

"Yeah, yeah—that's not half of it. What I wanna tell you is Jules complained about how hard the money situation was for at least two years. Know how I handled it? I tried to cheer her up, get her to think positive. What I should've done is listened to what she was saying, ask her to be more specific, detailed. But I was so damn busy, working all the time, trying to throw money at the problem. And maybe just a little pissed at her for not being grateful for my hard work and great attitude. Joe, she'd been talking the whole time and I'd been telling her to *relax,* everything would be fine. She was *scared* to have our baby. It took getting right up against bankruptcy and having a professional look over the bills to get my attention. He said Jules had to be a genius to keep us from starving for so long."

Joe grabbed Billy's biceps and gave a squeeze, his expression earnest and sympathetic. "God, Billy, I didn't know it was that tough at your place…"

"I didn't tell you that to get sympathy, Joe. We're getting

straightened out. What I'm trying to tell you is my wife was *talking* and I wasn't *listening.* You ever tell Marty to just relax? When she bitches about something—you ever tell her to just cool down and relax? Maybe tell her that her attitude is half the problem?"

"What else you gonna do?" He shrugged.

"That's the way I saw it, too. What's she bitching about? You have any recollection?"

"Name it," he said with frustration. "She hates football, for one thing, and we're just now coming in the season. She wants work done around the house—I *kill* myself around the house! There's no better-looking yard, cars, boat or garage on the street! Everything's perfect! She wants *dates.* What the hell is that? Why would you date someone you're married to? And she hates my shorts! They're comfortable shorts. I don't tell her what to wear—"

"Yeah, but Marty looks damn good, and you don't mind that..."

"It's like she just hates everything about *me,*" he said. "What am I gonna do about that? Plus, instead of staying home like she usually does, she's been going out with the girls."

"What girls?"

"Our girls, I guess."

Julie hadn't been going out. Billy had a sense of cold dread pass through him. He thought maybe his best friend's marriage was on the skids. "Okay, do this," he said. "You ever have a chance to talk to her? I mean, just you two?"

"She says she's all done talking to me, and it feels like she means it," he said.

"Try this," Billy said. "Ask her what you should do to start getting her back. Tell her to make it easy because you're a blockhead and you just don't get it. Ask for one specific thing at a time—real simple. Then do it. It's gotta be easier than this!"

"Aw, Jesus, she's just going to ask something totally ridiculous…"

"Joe! Would you get rid of the comfortable shorts if that was the price of having her back in the bedroom? Would you turn off the football game and meet her at the door in one of her negligees with a glass of wine?"

"I'd probably meet her at the door in a fluorescent jockstrap with my ears on fire. You have any idea how long it's been since I've been laid?"

Billy smiled. He thought he might have just gotten a glimmer of Marty's problem. Joe was a good-hearted guy, but he was long on machismo and short on patience. "You ever have to work at that before you were actually married?"

"Look, you take the vows, you seal the deal. You bring home a good paycheck and do your work around the house, and the begging should end there!"

Billy laughed at him. He put his hands in his pockets. "Man, you don't know anything about women. Joe, you don't stop romancing your wife the day after the wedding. What's she gonna think? She'll think you don't love her, don't want her, don't care…"

"She knows I want her," he said with a pout. "She can't help but know it."

"Yeah, but I bet you used to want her in a way that had you doing anything to make her happy. Oh, man, you better find out what she needs from you. Then you better get ready to turn off the game and get out the fluorescent jockstrap. Whatever it takes, buddy," he said. "I mean, if you want this to work. I dunno…maybe you don't really care that much—"

"I want her back where she belongs."

Where she *belongs*. He had a real property thing going on.

"Take my advice, pal. Let her tame you. Let her domesticate you. Let her tell you what she wants and give it to her. It's a totally whipped life—and it's fucking fantastic."

"Sounds like you're saying the secret to happiness is letting the woman run things," Joe said, surly.

"Joe, she's already running things—she moved out of the bedroom. Aren't you paying attention? Trust me, you give her whatever she needs, she'll not only be your girl again, she'll probably treat you like the king you stupidly think you are."

"I think you're full of shit," Joe said.

"Yeah? Well, I've known Marty a long time—about twenty years now. And usually her problem is not expecting enough, not asking too much. I remember her dating guys who walked all over her before she finally moved on."

"I never did that," Joe said.

"I know—she said you were a prince. You still a prince now, Joe?" Billy asked, lifting his eyebrows. He shook his head. "Hey, I didn't take my own advice a couple of years, and I paid for not listening, believe me. But my wife never moved down the hall. Have it your way. Good luck."

Billy could see that Joe was preoccupied—sulky and quiet— all through dinner. When they were at the firehouse between calls, he was serious and thoughtful, not his usual active and playful self. But maybe he was thinking about things, about what he could do.

Billy sure wished he'd listened to Jules. Maybe he'd have gathered up all those bills sooner, gotten that monkey off her back, accidentally gotten advice quicker. John's words—*Your marriage and family is your greatest asset*—kept ringing in his head. He knew that, he felt that, but it was still hard for him to figure out how you kept that asset safe when all the less important obligations had bigger hammers.

When he got home in the morning, he found Jules in the

kitchen, making a list with her morning coffee. He gave her a kiss and said, "What's up with Marty and Joe? He says she moved out of the bedroom."

"She *did?*" she asked, shocked. "I had no idea it had gotten that bad!"

"He's been loaded for bear all week. I just got that out of him last night. What's up? Tell me—I want to know if the advice I gave him is worth a damn."

"Well, she's had a few complaints lately. Starting with, he won't shower or shave before bed and just rolls over on top of her, like she's a blow-up doll. She says foreplay at her house is, 'You awake?'"

"Oh, man. How does that not surprise me?"

"What advice did you give him?"

"I told him to listen to his wife. Advice I should've taken a long time ago."

When Beth was a week post-op and moving around comfortably, Cassie told her, "It's time. We have to tell the girls."

"Okay, I can do that," she said. "And then I have to go over to my parents' house. I've been putting this off for when I can go to them, when I'm pretty close to a hundred percent. I know they mean well, but I don't want them trying to help me out over here." She took a breath. "I just dread getting sick and weak from chemo and having them trying to prop me up. I sound like a serpent's tooth, don't I?"

"Nah, I understand. I saw them in action growing up. You can handle them any way you like and I'll even run interference for you if I can. But I want you to call the girls…"

She called Julie and Marty at five and five-thirty. By seven they were both at Beth's, sitting in her small living room with her, getting the details.

"If you don't want to talk about this, it's okay, but are you getting a prognosis?"

"According to the doctor, it's good," she said. "It's kind of hard to accept that when you're facing it the second time, but I understand the theory. When breast cancer spreads, the first sites are most often the lymph system, lungs, spine, et cetera. They're treating this as another primary site—a brand-new cancer that we got to early. The surgery was superaggressive, and so is the chemo, but it's what I agreed to do. Kill this bastard before it can kill me. It appears I could be prone to breast cancer, but there's no indication I'm prone to all types of cancer."

"Are you scared?" Marty asked.

"Yeah. But more angry than scared. It would really piss me off to have worked this hard for my M.D., my OB-Gyn certification, only to die in my early thirties before I really get to experience it. If I'd known this was coming, I might've just traveled or something. Played with dolphins, maybe. Done less taxing things that were more soothing and comforting."

"But didn't you always want this?" Jules asked her. "To be a doctor?"

"I guess I did, but I didn't know it for a while. I like a difficult study, a big challenge. I'm such a nerd. When I started med school, I thought I'd end up in research like my dad, but I'm good with people, whereas my parents are more solitary, bookwormish intellectuals. But when I did my OB rotation, it found me. I was hooked right away. I fell in love. It's funny—a woman who loves delivering babies but might never have one. Make that probably—will probably never have one."

"But why couldn't you tell us?"

Beth looked down and shrugged. "It was about me, not you. The last time was so awful, with everyone running to me as if my days were numbered. And then, as if to prove they probably were, Mark left me. It was like being branded, like having the pox or something. For a while after Mark left, I believed I was going to die. You can't get well thinking that way. I wanted to avoid that. I've been trying to treat it like a condition, not a disease, something I have to deal with and then can let go. I guess it's not going to be quite that simple, but still…" She looked up at her best friends. "I just wanted to have a normal life. But that keeps sliding away from me."

"Oh, God, did rushing to you the last time make it worse instead of better?" Julie asked. "I'd hate it if—"

"It's not that, Jules," Beth said. "It's the high drama. I hate drama, you know that. I've never minded being alone, but I sure mind being left. The whole diagnosis and treatment along with Mark's leaving focused so much attention on the severity, rather than the potential to get well. Still, if you girls hadn't come then, what would I have done?" She shook her head. "I had this insane and probably irrational idea that if I didn't advertise it, didn't talk about it till it was almost over, maybe we could all go on living. Have fun. Enjoy life."

"We can still do that," Cassie said. "We can do that and help you through the tough days. But you can't keep us out of the loop anymore, Beth. You have hardly any character flaws, but if you have one, it's holding things inside. I'm afraid that one could come back and bite you in the ass."

"Probably," she agreed. "My oncologist would agree with that. Our first meeting was all about who's in my life. Good people, I told him—all of whom I planned to keep out of this mess."

"Her oncologist calls every day," Cassie told the other girls.

"He's a good guy. Being that we're colleagues, he admitted he's been thinking a lot about what life might've been like for him if he'd gotten cancer at twenty-five. It's reeled him in. He wants to be my friend as well as my doctor. I haven't found anything wrong with that yet. I like him, he makes a good friend. It's okay."

"I think he must adore you," Cassie said.

"As a patient and friend. And," she said, lifting one corner of her mouth in a half smile, "someone named Walt calls Cassie at least three times a day."

"Well, now," Marty said.

"Oh, this *is* getting serious…" Julie said.

"Oh, please, it's just Walt," Cassie said. "He knows I took a little time from work to make sure Beth is taken care of. He knows she's one of my best friends and that I've been a little shook up about this. He's very sweet, actually—he's supportive."

"And why isn't it getting serious?" Jules wanted to know.

"I'm not going to let it get serious," Cassie said. "I'm keeping him as a sweet, supportive friend—that works real well for us. We don't have anything in common. We have completely different tastes. That would wear on a person before long."

"What's that got to do with anything? Different tastes?" Julie asked.

"Well, he has a naked woman tattooed on his arm—not like up on his shoulder but right down here," she said, tapping her forearm. "For all the world to see her tits sticking out every day. I'm just crazy about him as a friend, but if you think I'm getting myself mixed up with some biker…well, just forget it."

When Marty got home after the evening at Beth's, it was almost eleven. They'd clearly overstayed their welcome; when they left, Beth was showing signs of being worn out. But it had been like group therapy—everything came out. Everything. From Beth's anger and fear to shocking revelations about what Jules and Billy had been going through as they tried to hold the marriage and family together through some of the most daunting financial troubles a couple can endure. And there was talk about Cassie's struggle to keep what sounded like one of the most positive male-female relationships of the past ten years in a safe place. There was hysterical laughter that had Beth holding an arm against her incision, and tears here and there.

And, of course, Marty spilled her guts. She was not only tempted by Ryan, she was nurturing a wild fantasy that when it was over with Joe, she'd get in touch with him and maybe they'd pick up their old relationship. Of course that made them all crazy; no one believed Ryan had become a different man, so different from the boy who'd treated her so badly. For that matter, Marty only half believed it herself. The thing that had her so confused and hooked was that she felt better with Ryan in just two hours than she had felt with Joe in such a long, long time. Ryan focused on her, treated her like a woman, not just a household asset.

"Because he wants to get in your pants! It's all he's ever wanted from anyone!"

But, she told them, you can't imagine how great it feels to have someone at least go to the trouble to want to get in your pants! Joe doesn't bother with that anymore; he thinks it's his right. No more sweet talk, no more nice dates, no more helping out, trying to please her. Even in bed, he used to be committed to her orgasm as though it was his responsibility, but now he hated taking the time. He stopped trying and now it was as if it was her fault! She was supposed to just take what she ended up with—an insensitive jerk who thought the lord and master ruled and her happiness wasn't his issue.

That was all distraction, though. Cassie's biker, Julie's money problems, Marty's disintegrating marriage. The real reason for being there at all, and staying so late, was Beth—whose chest was now a flat, scarred wasteland that she had no interest in trying to reconstruct. She showed them. All of them struggled to hold in the gasps and tears; mastectomy scars could be brutal and hers were scary. "Let's get it over with," she had said, pulling up her shirt and unfastening the prosthetic bra. "This is what it is." And then, "It's okay if you cry—I did. But this is what it is."

They didn't dare cry. She was clear about what she needed—to move on, hoping the harsh treatment would get her past the danger and eventually be able to live on without always being afraid. They didn't have any trouble getting the message; she needed strength and acceptance on her side, not pity, not fear, no high drama. So while some of them might've teared up, they held it in and told her, Good! Be rid of the damn things, then, if they're cancer catchers for you! Let's make this pay off; let's trick the fucker! Live to a hundred and five! A lot of great things can happen without boobs!

But when Marty got home, and went into the kitchen of her darkened house, she saw that although she'd moved down the hall, Joe had left a night-light on for her in the kitchen.

Even though she'd have to get Jason to her mom's in the morning and get to the shop by nine, she was a long way from sleep. All alone, the tears finally came. Beth was the one they'd all envied, all secretly wanted to be. How can a woman so young and vital, so beautiful and brilliant, be stricken by a thing like this? A thing that could kill her after punishing her so much? And if the disease didn't beat her down, the treatment was harrowing. It was so wrong!

They'd talked for a long time about how people died young all the time. They were stacked up on U.S. freeways to the tune of almost fifty-thousand a year, in which case no one had time to get their heads wrapped around the passing, the loss. They couldn't clean out their files or straighten the underwear drawers and get rid of any nasty undies with stains; they couldn't decide what their survivors should do with their things. The only thing different about this was time, and Beth said that time, in its own perverse way, was worth something whether you were twenty-nine or ninety-nine. But that had done nothing to soothe Marty. The idea that the one of their clique who'd really made good could be swiped away devastated her.

There hadn't been any alcohol at Beth's. She wasn't drinking with her meds and chemo; she was focused on keeping her body as strong as possible. And if Beth wasn't drinking, none of them were. They had a round of orange juice instead. But, she'd said, if there's ever a wake, I want everyone to get drunk and obnoxious!

Marty got up in the high cupboard and dug out the good bottle of Grand Marnier, tears spilling down her cheeks. Now was as good a time as any to get a little drunk and sloppy. This is what it'll be like when I have major life hurdles to get through—alone in a dimly lit kitchen, figuring it out over a solitary drink. But then, how would that be any different than it had been since she got married? Joe never noticed if she was mad or sad or—

"Just getting in?"

She looked up when she heard his voice. He stood in the entry to the family room, looking across at her. Even sheathed in the darkness, she could see he wore the nasty, smelly gym shorts. He took a couple of steps toward her and revealed his heavy growth of whiskers.

"Yeah," she said, sniffing back a tear. "Go back to bed."

He came toward the kitchen and stood across the island from her. "You crying?" he asked.

She wiped at her tears and took a sip from her glass. "I'm fine. Just go back to bed, Joe. We don't have anything to say to each other right now. It's late. I'm tired."

"Tired and screwed up about something," he said, and not

gently. "Maybe you weren't out with the girls, maybe you got something going on the side, huh?"

"I was at *Beth's*," she said hotly, loudly. "Her cancer's back. She had her second breast removed and now she has nothing, except maybe a shot at living till she's thirty-five. And, yeah, I'm a little screwed up about it. Now just leave me *alone!*"

"Aw, Marty," he said, reaching toward her and then stopping himself before he actually touched her. "Aw, jeez."

Her chin dropped and she just looked into the glass, silent but for the barely audible sobs that shook her shoulders. Then she lifted her glass, took a calming swallow. Why wouldn't he just go?

"Marty, come on, I'd like to do something to help you through this."

"There's nothing you can do, Joe. We hardly even live together anymore."

"Babe, I've been thinking… If you just tell me what you want…"

"You're too late, Joe," she said. "I've been telling you for a long time what I want, and I'm sorry, but now it's just too late. There isn't anything you can do to make up for at least three years of not hearing a word I've said. Go on, get your beauty sleep. I'll be going to bed soon myself and I don't want to talk about it."

"That why you're crying? Beth?"

She laughed humorlessly. "Yes, Joe," she said patiently. What an idiot, that he would even have to ask. That's how unconnected they were. "She's one of my best friends and this is the second time in five years. That's why I'm crying. I can't stand the thought her life might be in danger from this. She's so brilliant, so perfect, so young."

"Yeah," he said, scrubbing a hand over the back of his neck.

"Yeah, that's awful. I'm sorry, Marty. Really sorry." He took a breath. "Listen, Marty, tell me something I can do."

"There's nothing you can do," she said. "Nothing I can do."

"Tell me one thing I can do to make you feel better. Anything."

"Forget it. I'm all done counting on you."

"I've been stupid, I see that. I guess I wasn't taking this seriously, but you have my attention. Tell me something. Please."

"I want you to help around the house," she said tiredly, feeling sucked in by the question, like winning would make a difference.

"Marty, I have been," he said. "Every time you bitched I tried harder. I spent every waking minute on the yard, the cars, the house, the boat and RV, the—"

It pushed her buttons. "Joe, are you brain dead?!" she nearly yelled. "I want you to pick up your own shit! Your dishes and the mess you make in the house all day when you're home! I want you to hang your towel and not leave it in a wet heap on the floor! Put your nasty underwear in the hamper instead of leaving it open-faced on the floor for me to pick up and wash! I want you to help with the dishes and wipe your spit off the bathroom mirror and your hair out of the shower and off the bathroom floor! What in the holy hell is the matter with you?"

The look on his face was priceless. He was in shock. It took him a moment to respond. "You want me to work *inside* the house?"

"Oh, for Christ's sake," she muttered, looking away and taking a sip of her drink.

"*Inside* the house?" he repeated.

She looked at him levelly. "You cannot be this stupid..."

He swallowed, shook his head. "I bet I can be," he said. "Baby, every time you got on your tangent, I went at that yard and garage harder. I thought we had a division—I thought all

married couples did. My mom and dad do—they each have a
territory to take care of. Shit, baby, I planted ten new trees in
the past two years, hoping you'd notice I was trying my best.
I paid the bills, made investments for our future, painted the
house, built the patio cover and brick grill, poured the con-
crete myself, laid brick down the front walk to the street... I
worked like a bull all day, every day."

She shook her head as she looked at the positively earnest
expression on his face. "Joe, how would you like it if I took my
supper dishes, wet towel and dirty clothes out to the boat and
just scattered them around there for you to clean up? Maybe
I could brush my teeth in the front seat of your car and spit
on the windshield."

"But why would you—"

"This house—it's my yard and garage. I leave it perfect
and when I come home it's like some filthy vagrant broke in
and destroyed the place—and is still here, lying on the couch.
Every day, you turn it into a shit hole! You leave your yard and
garage spotless and I don't do *one thing* to upset the immaculate
appearance of it all. But, besides smelling you at the dinner
table and in bed after you spend all day digging in compost,
what's it do to help *me?* What about this don't you get? How
totally stupid are you? Really?"

After a moment of silence, he said, "Whew. I don't think
I got that..."

"See? It's hopeless!"

"Why'd you marry me if I'm such a loser?" he asked. "I've
never been good at housework, you knew that. You even
complained about it, but you still—"

"I married you because you cared! You used to *try!* If I said,
'Joe, bring your dishes to the kitchen and rinse them off,' you
did it. If I said, 'Joe, wipe all your black curlies off the bathroom floor,' you got right on it, because you wanted me to

spend the night and shower in that bathroom! And you never, never tried to seduce me smelling like sweat and compost!"

"Okay, wait a second. Give me something I can do right now to make you happy. Anything. Because I'll do—"

"Joe, you're not listening again! I'm not getting in your bed. I don't care what you fucking do—I'm through begging. I have something else a little upsetting to worry about right now than whether you can finally step up to the plate and be a partner!"

"Partner..." he mumbled. "Partner," he repeated, as if hearing it for the first time. "Okay, I probably deserved that..."

"Yeah," she said, tiredly. She turned her back on him and leaned against the island, swirling her drink.

To her back, he said, "Okay, I'm a blockhead," he said absently. "Marty, I thought I *was* trying. I swear to God, I'd prance around the house with your bra on my head and feathers shoved up my ass if I thought it would make you smile at me one time. Jesus."

She turned around and looked at him.

"You used to smile at me all the time, Marty," he said softly.

"You used to care if I was happy," she said to him.

"Honest to God, I thought there was nothing I could do anymore. I don't know what happened, but all of a sudden I couldn't make you happy no matter what. I thought I was doing my job, doing what a good husband does." He leaned on the island. "I care if you're happy. Jesus, I'd give anything to make you happy again."

"Well, we'll see about that," she said evasively. "Right now you might as well just go to bed, because I have other things on my mind. And guess what, Joe? Whether you and I work things out is *not* one of them. I can't talk about this anymore right now. Can't you see I'm in pain over Beth? God, just leave me *alone!*"

He straightened up and got a look on his face like he was hurt. Cut to the quick. And the thought that came into her mind was, So what? Fuck you for thinking about what you can get from me when I'm wondering how I'm going to deal if one of my best friends since childhood dies. But she didn't say it; she was too angry. Angry with him, with Beth's disease, with the way things sometimes turned out. She just lifted her chin, stared him down and bit on her lower lip to keep it from trembling.

Then he turned and left her and she felt the desolation of having shut him down when, for the first time in her memory, he seemed to actually hear her. But she couldn't deal with that now. Tears rushed to her eyes anew and she wasn't entirely sure why. It could be that she'd given up on her marriage and knew it. It could be about what Beth was going to go through, trying to beat this beast that got to her again. Or maybe it was the fear of possibly being alone forever.

She grabbed the neck of the Grand Marnier bottle and took it to the family room sofa. After kicking off her shoes, she curled up in the corner, her glass resting on one thigh, the whole bottle on the other. And she let herself just cry. Her sniffs were loud, but she kept her sobs as quiet as possible; she didn't want to wake Jason. And she could've grabbed the tissue box from the kitchen counter, but there was something punishingly satisfying about just wiping her nose and face on her good sweater instead, suffering. Through it all, had Beth cried or fallen apart? Not at all! She'd been trying to reassure them that this would be as it would be and they'd all get beyond it somehow. It was devastating that she could be so strong.

Completely unaware of how much time had passed, she felt him beside her before she saw or heard him. He sat down close to her, lifted the glass and bottle from her hands to put them on the coffee table. He said, "Come on, baby." He put an arm around her and pulled her close to him. "Come here, baby. Let me hold you."

Instinctively angry, she slugged him in the chest, hard. But then immediately, her head dropped to his shoulder and her cries came out unrestrained, loud and wrenching, and he only pulled her closer. "God," she said through her tears. "God, God, *God!* It just isn't *fair!*"

"You're damn right about that," he whispered. He kissed her head and stroked her hair while she let it go. Her tears and snot were matting his chest hair, but all she could do was vent. It seemed to her she might never stop; it felt as if she'd been holding in tears like this for a long time. She was vaguely aware of his voice, whispering to her that she was right, it was wrong, this shouldn't be happening. His arm around her was protective; his gentle caresses were comforting.

It was a long while before she lifted her head and looked up at him. She had a bad case of the hiccups and her face was wet and sloppy. "Her chest," she said in a hiccuping gasp, "it's *ravaged!*"

"Aw, Marty," he said, pressing his lips to her forehead.

"It's so mean and painful looking. And she's so brave, you can't imagine how brave. She says this is what it is and we're going to get used to it." She let her head drop and cried a little more. "If I had to go through that, I couldn't be a tenth as brave."

"Oh, I bet you're wrong. You're one of the strongest women I've ever known."

"No," she said, shaking her head. "No, I'm not. I'm scared all the time, you have no idea. I'm scared of what's going to happen to me and Jase. Scared of facing something like Beth's facing, and being alone like she is. You don't know—I'm worried and scared all the time."

He gave her a small smile. "You sure can't tell it," he said.

"You're pretty feisty. Real tough, if you ask me." He gave her hair a stroke. "Listen, she might get through this okay. The worst might be over. She could beat it, you know? Still have a full, long life."

"We were just ready to get married when it happened before. She wore a wig at our wedding, remember? Because she was bald. Mark was going to marry her, but he couldn't take it. He left her."

"I remember that," Joe said. "I didn't even know the guy, but I hated him for that. Weak dick. He oughta be ashamed of himself."

"Now she's in it again, and all she has is us—the girls. What good is that? What can we do?"

"It's better than having that weak dick, that's for damn sure. Marty, listen. You know that I'd never walk out on you for something like that, right? They could carve up every piece of your beautiful body, remove your gorgeous face and sew your vagina shut and I'd be with you for life. You know that, right? That it's not about that with me? I mean, I'm stupid enough to be cocky proud of your good looks, but that's not what's really important. Not what I love. You don't have to ever be scared about something like that."

"Well, that's pretty decent," she said with a huff of teary, disbelieving laughter. "Considering I'm ready to leave you for refusing to shower and shave…" She put a hand against his cheek. She sniffed. "You showered and shaved."

"I didn't think you'd let me hold you if I didn't…"

Her hand dropped to his lap and true to form he muttered a throaty, "Whoa!" But she ignored that. "These are not the crusty, nasty shorts." And then her hand snaked around the elastic waistband and came in contact with the new purchase tags. "They still have the tags on."

"I should probably get those off, huh? Uh, I might've torn

up the closet a little finding 'em, but I set the alarm for early. I'll clean it up, I promise."

"I have hardly any confidence in that…"

"I swear to God!"

She put her hand against his cheek again. "It was nice of you to shave before… Your whiskers are so hard on my skin."

"You never complained when we were engaged…"

"You always shaved before we got married…"

"I did, huh? Jesus, Marty, I'm a dunce. I'm sorry. Your skin's so soft… I'm an idiot."

"I'm still going to my room down the hall."

"Sure. Yeah. Really, I only shaved and showered so I could get near you. I didn't want you crying like that alone. You want me to go to your new room with you and hold you till you're asleep? I know you're so out of your mind with this thing. This thing with Beth."

"No," she said. "Just right here, right now. That's as far as I can go, all right?"

"Okay. As long as you believe me, no matter what comes for you—sickness or health—I don't scare easy."

"I hope we don't have to face that, because seriously…if it takes me moving out of the bedroom to get you to wash up, I'd hate to think how you'd handle something truly serious."

He kissed her forehead and pulled her head back against his chest. "Gimme time, honey. I might not be hopeless."

10

August disappeared. It was still hot in the valley in September; sometimes it seemed hotter than ever. Billy and Jules finally had a meeting scheduled with their credit counselor after weeks of waiting, not knowing if the news would be that they had to file for bankruptcy or if they'd be presented with a recovery program that was even more tight and stressful than what they'd been going through for years. Their tension was prickly in the car on their way to the meeting.

"I really need you to accept whatever's coming, Billy," she said. "If we have to file, we'll get beyond it somehow."

"I don't want to do that, but I will," he said shortly. "I'll do whatever it takes. You know that."

"I want you to like me again."

"That's not part of the problem. I love you. It's just hard to swallow that I couldn't make it work."

"I handled the money—don't you think it's hard to swallow

that *I* couldn't make it work? Be fair. It's a team effort and we did the best we could. I need you. I hate it when you're gone, and now even when you're with me, you're still gone."

He reached over and squeezed her thigh, but his eyes stayed on the road. "I'll work on that. I don't want you to feel that way."

When they walked into John's office—an impersonal cubicle—they took chairs in front of his desk expectantly. Fearfully.

"Hey, you two," he said cheerfully. "Well, we got everyone in the program. You're not in good shape yet, but you're in recoverable shape." He opened their file on his desk and took two identical printouts off the top. "Here's a new payment schedule for you. Let me explain. The college loans have been suspended for two years. You have no idea how many people just default and never repay them, anyway. They're thrilled you want to make them good, and at four percent, they're a bargain. Oh, they reduced the balance for you—firefighting qualifies as government service because they're state loans. They need first responders—firefighters and law enforcement.

"We rolled over your mortgage, second and equity line of credit into a refinance at a fixed rate, no qualifying necessary, thank God. A first and second at eighty percent and fifteen percent, which gives you ninety-five percent debt to equity coverage but eliminates PMI—rates are still good. The bank dropped the loan initiation fee and will split closing costs—you save a total of eight hundred a month. They're sniveling like crazy," he laughed. "They made out like bandits on this deal. There's no default, no repo, they're getting their money at a fair market value and they should be kissing my feet.

"I can't do anything about utilities or insurance, but we have three credit-card companies in the game here. They each reduced their principal, gave us a zero interest rate for six months and a fixed twelve percent after that. Still too high, but we're gonna make that go away. How about you let me see those cards right now, if you don't mind?"

Julie and Billy were just staring wide-eyed at the new payment schedule and only when they heard John say, "Please," did they dig their credit cards out of wallets and hand them over.

"We really have to carve these up," he said, holding six cards from three companies. "You can't do this anymore. It feels like help—it's not help. They'll kill you with the fees, rates, late payment charges. Really, they have to be laid to rest. You stick to your budget, you'll never miss them. I promise."

Julie nodded eagerly and Billy just stared dumbly, still in a trance.

"Good," he said, putting them aside for the moment. "Okay, your expenses were on the low side, and with your income you should be able to run the heater in winter and fix a turkey dinner for the family at Thanksgiving. I increased your budget for household items, from groceries to clothing to miscellaneous expenses. It's a personal thing with me, but I think if you can find a way to take the kids out once in a while, it's good for your frame of mind. Not Disneyland, but how about a kids' pizza joint, or one of those afternoon movies you leave with gum in your hair, or a picnic at the lake? And a husband and wife should have an evening out alone sometimes, and I'm not talking about a family or friends' get-together where there are lots of other people around. Just you two. Dinner. Maybe a movie. Maybe a walk in the park. You don't have to give up the nest egg, but go see a five-o'clock cheap movie and have dinner at the Olive Garden or something. Get alone. Talk. Put your arms around each other. Thirty bucks toward your relationship and perspective can help things more than you realize. Make time for your marriage. You'll never regret it.

"I know I've said this before," he went on, "but your marriage and family is your greatest asset. That isn't just a pie-in-the-sky, goody-two-shoes Mormon thing I'm passing on. Ever think what would happen to these bills and expenses if you split up? The expenses would double and the bills would be divided between you, leaving each of you with debts you could never pay and expenses even more out of your reach. It's not just a spiritual thing, though my commitment and faith are rolled together into one big package. It's practical, fiduciary. No law protects your home from divorce. That's not to mention what happens to the kids. I won't even get into what happens to your spirit when something like money rips you apart. Money's nothing but a tool. So take care of each other—that's my advice.

"Now—"

"Wait!" Julie said, holding the piece of paper. "John, wait a minute! You screwed up here somewhere. This can't be right."

"What?" he said, leaning toward her. He backed right up and picked up his copy of the new payment schedule. "Oh," he laughed. "Sorry." He fished some more papers out of the file and passed them each one more. "Here are your new balances. The mortgage total is about six thousand higher than it was, incorporating closing costs and the equity line, but the payment is lower and the credit cards and student-loan balance reduction is far more than six thousand lower, plus the student loans are on hold for the time being. You'll have to go to the title office to sign papers for the refinance, by the way, but no money is due. Go ahead, look everything over. Take your time. Want my calculator?"

Julie was in shock for a long moment, scanning over one sheet, then another, her mouth hanging open. When she finally looked up, she said, "Maybe I better borrow the calculator. I've never had this much money left over after bills…"

"Julie," John said with a smile. "As far as I could tell, you never had *any* money left over. I don't know how you did it."

"John, how did *you* do this?"

"I took a look at what you needed and divided what was left between the bills. That's the trick, when you put the family first. You *pay* the family first. Then I called each one of the creditors and explained exactly what you could afford to pay them. Now, if you think you can make this work, I have some serious advice."

"What?" she asked, riveted.

"Put twenty percent of that expense money away, at least, because you still have a couple of problems. You have two old cars and I don't think a car payment is going to fit in here too well. Your mortgage won't go up, but your taxes will. And if you pay your bills online, which is free through your bank, you'll save probably fifty bucks a year—a couple of those pizza dates with the kids. If you can manage to stop paying late fees or annual credit-card charges, according to your past twelve months of debt management..." He fished around on his desk for a moment until he located a paper. "Nine hundred and thirty-eight dollars last year alone. That's an extra grand right there."

"Holy shit," she said. "Oh, sorry. I didn't mean to swear."

He smiled. "This budget has the advantage of some better rates, reasonable debt consolidation, a couple of suspensions... You have a fighting chance."

"I tried to do this, you know," Billy said. "I called the credit cards... I went to the bank..."

"I've spent ten years developing a relationship with some of these creditors. Sometimes we have to suggest to our clients they file for bankruptcy, then no one gets paid. If we can't get a level playing field, that's what we do. The client is the important factor. So by now they know that when I call I'm not bluffing."

"But these reduced rates… I feel like I'm cheating them or something."

"They've gotten their money out of you tenfold. You're their favorite debtor. High interest, late fees, escalating balance. Please, don't waste any guilt here. I'm a real stickler for ethics—no one got screwed. Well," he said, "you did. Sort of. I mean, you bought into the programs, but that was because you hadn't studied and practiced this aspect of management. I've been doing this for years. That's why I'm here."

Billy was quiet for a moment. Then he said, "I think we owe you a lot of money."

"It's all on there," he said, pointing with his pen. "I don't hand out services for free, but it's my goal that you think it's the best money you ever spent. And that the product is worth it."

"Oh, God," Jules said, getting a little teary. "Oh, yes!"

"If it works out, maybe you'll recommend me," John said.

Billy connected eyes first with John, then he put an arm around Julie's shoulders, pulling her close. "You happy with this?" he asked in a whisper.

"Oh, yes," she whispered back.

Billy looked back at John. "How long before we're out of the mess?"

John shuffled papers again. "If you can keep those cars running, in four years you should have only ordinary expenses plus a mortgage and hopefully a savings account. I don't know where your salary will be by then, but county employees get pretty good pay as they get seniority. Starting out takes commitment, but—"

"Four years is good."

"Um, Bill, I based this budget on you working your part-time job two days a week as opposed to almost four. You gotta check in with the family, man. It's the most important thing you'll ever do."

Billy stared. He held his lips tight, but his eyes watered. Julie was less controlled. She almost collapsed against him, openly crying. She hadn't seen this light at the end of the tunnel in at least eight years. Billy turned away from John and held her to console her, but he couldn't stop at least one tear from running down his cheek as he did so. It took a few moments for them to compose themselves and finally Billy looked up and wiped at his nose. "I'm, ah, sorry, John. We've been fighting this monster for such a long time—"

"Hey, think nothing of it," John said. "Happens all the time. I appreciate the relief—I felt exactly the same way when I found a potential solution. You realize it's up to you now. You go out and get another loan, another credit card, this whole program falls in the tank. You understand that, right?"

"Sure, absolutely," he said. "You have no idea what kind of gift you gave us, here. This is so incredible."

"Sure I do," he said. "Why do you think I do this? You think it's making me rich? It's making me happy." He grinned very largely. "You just don't know how well I sleep at night— that's what's incredible. Now, what do you say—can we cut up this plastic? Because it's not doing you any good at all."

"Go for it," Billy said.

If riding along the beach in summer was refreshing, riding into the mountains in the fall was miraculous. It was Cassie's favorite time of year to start with, and it seemed the leaves were more stunning this year than ever before. Maybe it was being on the back of a bike rather than in a car that made all the difference. They took a ride every week—on a weekend if she was off, and if she only had a weekday, Walt took that day away from the shop to be with her. The last two weeks in September had given way to October and the hillsides had become stunning, on fire with color.

They drove a little farther north before getting in the hills; most of the color was in the foothills, thankfully. As the elevation increased and temperature lowered, pine, fir and ponderosa took over, which maintained their rich, dark green.

Walt had memorized hundreds of trails over the years and he always had a stopping place in mind that was comfortable, scenic and private. Plus, he had favorite restaurants everywhere. After a couple of hours of enjoying the crisp fall air, he pulled off to a grassy place.

"We're stopping?" she asked, pulling off her helmet.

"Isn't your butt asleep by now? It usually is."

"Since I met you, my butt has gotten even better padded," she told him, dismounting. "This is gorgeous."

"I thought you'd like it. Coffee?"

"Great. Blanket?" she asked.

"Coming up." He first spread the blanket on the cushiony ground, then produced the thermos and cups. He poured for them and said, "By the way, I think your butt's looking real good."

"You're not supposed to be looking at my butt."

"I'm not?" he asked. "Gee, Cassie, you should've told me. I've been looking at your butt for about four months. I'm not sure I can just stop now."

She laughed at him and took her coffee. "We've been riding almost that long, and you come up with someplace new every time. You amaze me."

"I told you. There's lots to see around this world. We'll never run out."

"I guess we'll have to stop pretty soon," she said, leaning back and bracing on her elbows.

"Why?"

"Cold. Rain. You know me—I'm not into roughing it."

"There will be plenty of sunny days, and we'll pick a softer climate. You should be an expert on Sonoma by now—we'll go south when it gets cold. I never stop. I take days off, but never stop."

"You must have ridden through some pretty incredible weather during your eighteen months on the road."

"Oh, yeah. I came real close to a hurricane once, in Louisiana. I got out of there fast. I didn't think I'd ever get dry."

"See," she said, turning toward him, "I don't want to ever do that. Ever."

He laughed at her. "Cassie, by now you should know I'd take much better care of you than that. Here," he said, taking the coffee out of her hands and setting it with his on a flat rock beside the blanket. Then he said, "Come here," and his arms went around her waist. He flipped her deftly onto her back and covered her lips. Her arms immediately went around him and held him, moving under his mouth.

When he kissed her like this, she was lost. His kiss was always careful, tender, but there was power in there she was not only curious about but extremely tempted by. What does it mean, she wondered, when you have a person in your life you can't imagine ever being without, and yet he doesn't fit into your life at all? This was supposed to be something interesting to pass the time—a nice person to enjoy, but not get too involved with.

He lifted his head and looked into her eyes. "You worrying about Beth or something?" he asked.

"No. She's doing very well. I was just wondering…maybe it's not a good idea for us to do all this kissing."

"I thought it was a great idea."

"It might be taking us in a direction I'm just not ready to go. Maybe we should put a halt on the making out."

"I thought you liked it."

"I might be liking it too much," she said.

He laughed at her. "I don't think that's possible. Tell you

what—we can stop after today, how's that? I'd hate to waste this perfect spot." He lowered his lips again and she put a hand on his chest. "What's the matter, Cassie?"

"I told myself I wasn't getting serious about anyone again. For a long while..."

"You feeling serious?" he asked, lifting one brow.

"I don't want to be serious."

"Okay. Take your time." And he lowered his lips again, but the hand pushed back at him and he stopped. She did take note of the fact that it took very little to keep him under control. Men she'd dated who were much smaller, much less muscular and strong, took a lot more convincing. "What's really bothering you? Want to tell me? You know you can tell me anything you want."

"Oh, I don't know. Mixed feelings, I guess."

"Mixed feelings about...?"

"I'm spending a lot of time with you, a lot of time talking to you. You've been wonderful to me. We're getting closer. But..."

"But?"

"When I stopped by your store to thank you, to have coffee, I didn't see this coming. It wasn't something I planned on. In fact, I planned against something like this. I'm feeling a little bit, I don't know, in over my head."

"No, you're not," he said. "You can put the brakes on this anytime and you won't get any trouble from me. You know that. I'd hate it, but I wouldn't give you a hard time. And even while you keep pushing this just-friends idea, you know how much I like you. I think you like me that much, too."

"Well..."

"I'm not moving too fast for you, Cass. We both know that. What are you really worried about? Huh?"

"Well, for one thing, I'm worried about you giving me a seven-hundred-dollar leather jacket on your salary..."

He lifted his eyebrows in mock surprise. "You saw my pay stub?"

She gave him a whack in the arm. "And bringing hundred-dollar bottles of wine to my house when I make do on Two Buck Chuck..."

"Cassie, I've told you before, I haven't had anyone to spend my money on for a long time. Well, Mom and Dad, but that's a little different. I'm not hurting for money. I'm not running up debt to give you one or two nice things—a bottle of good wine, some flowers. I like doing it. You should just say thank-you."

"Thank you, but it worries me..."

"Worries you because you're trying to take care of my finances for me, or worries you because you're afraid it makes you committed to something?"

She pushed him away and sat up; maybe it was time to confront it. "Both," she said.

"Well, rest easy—I can afford it or I wouldn't spend it, and it doesn't lock you into anything."

"It's one thing for you to say that and another thing for me to believe it. I think if I said we should stop getting together so much, you'd be unhappy."

"You're damn right about that—I'd hate it. And it wouldn't make sense because we have a good time together. Listen, you worried that when your friends get a look at me, they're going to say you're out of your mind?"

Her chin dropped and he laughed. She lifted her eyes to his and said, "I don't think that's at all funny."

"You know what—you're a worrier. You're afraid when your friends see me pull up on some big hog with a ponytail and naked-lady tattoo, they're going to have you committed. Cassie, take it easy. I look a little like an outcast, but I'm a nice guy, I don't dribble on my shirt much and people usually take to me after a while. Really."

"I don't think you're funny."

"Yes, you do," he said, grabbing her around the waist and wrestling her to the ground, making her giggle in spite of herself. "You think I'm hilarious. And you hate how much you like me—that's very cool." He gave her a kiss. "I have an idea. I'm taking my folks to dinner tomorrow night, to my mom's favorite restaurant. It's pretty nice—you'll like it. Come with us. I'll pick you up. When you see I have a perfectly normal family, it'll give you a little peace of mind."

"Perfectly normal, huh?"

"Well, I think they're normal. It's normal for a sixty-year-old couple to pull up on a big Harley wearing leather pants, long hair, lots of piercings on their faces and ears with tattoo sleeves to the wrists, right?"

She slugged him in the arm.

"They're just regular, nice folks. I've told them about you and I can tell they think I made you up. They keep asking when they're going to meet you."

"What did you tell them?"

"That I met this gorgeous emergency room nurse who I've been seeing at least once a week for months now…"

"Seeing?"

"Cassie, I know you're trying to keep a leash on this thing between us, but we're seeing each other whether you can admit it or not. The only thing up in the air is whether we keep seeing each other, and I guess you're in the driver's seat there. So, what do you say? It's a nice restaurant—they're nice people."

"I've gained ten pounds since I met you," she said.

"You've gained it in all the right places, too. I have a spot in mind for tonight, on our way home. It's this little place in Paradise that looks like a shack and inside is a world-class Hungarian chef. He'll probably sit at our table through half of dinner, helping himself to your wine. You're going to love it."

She sighed. "Really, I don't know what to do with you..."

"Yes, you do," he said, grinning. And then he went after her lips again and she thought, Oh, what the hell. He felt very good, tasted better. And it was positively remarkable to her that they'd been friends all through summer and were well into fall and he hadn't pushed her to go further.

"Why haven't you tried anything?" she asked him between kisses.

"Because you're not ready. You telling me you're ready?"

"No," she said.

"That's why. When you're ready, I'm ready." And he kissed her a while longer, occasionally sliding his lips to her neck, her ear, her cheek, her eyes.

If he's half as good at the rest of it as he is at kissing, it's scary to even think about!

Cassie walked Steve along the river for about an hour, deep in thought. When Steve was tired and Cassie no more insightful, she called Julie and asked if she could stop by. The family was back from some fun at the park and it was nap time. Julie told her to come right over.

Cassie gave a couple of quick knocks on Julie's door and let herself in. Steve bounded into the house and found Tess curled up on her rug by the back door. Jeffy was on the couch; his feet were on the floor but his body was slumped into a lying-down position and he still wore his soccer shorts and shirt. They must have kicked the ball around for a while at the park. Julie was in the kitchen, puttering. "What's going on?" Cassie said by way of greeting.

"It's quiet time for the little ones and Jeff crashed. Billy wore him down."

Cassie tilted her head and listened. There was the sound of children laughing and what could be toys or balls flying around the room, furniture moving, an occasional squeal or giggle. "Quiet time? Is that what you call it?"

"Well, we couldn't call it nap time anymore. They're bouncing off the walls in there. I've thought about yelling, but what the heck—if they keep it in there and out of my hair for an hour, that's all I need."

"What are you doing?"

Julie put one hand on some apples, the other on a bowl that appeared to have flour and other ingredients in it and said, "I'm going to make Billy an apple pie. I hope I remember how—I haven't done this in a long time."

"Special occasion?"

"Yeah, I'm cooking a real dinner. Want to join us?"

"Thanks, but I have plans. I guess the new budget is working out?"

"It's like a miracle," she said. "I've been shopping cheap for so long, I don't even have to think to keep it in the range. In a couple of weeks I saved enough for Jeffy's birthday party next month. Now I'm working on Christmas. And that isn't including this brand-new thing we have—a savings account. An actual savings account." She sighed deeply. "It's very small, but wonderful. Wouldn't you love to get something better than a red candle from your best friend for Christmas?"

"I don't want anything better than that," she said. "Get on your feet, all the way on your feet, and we'll go to Paris or something."

"How about we drive to the Bay Area for lunch," Julie said. "Or maybe Placerville. And we better take your car." She picked up an apple and started carving away the skin. "So, what are you doing tonight?"

"Well, I'm going out to dinner with Walt. And his parents."

"Really?" Julie asked. "Sounds like this is getting interesting."

Through the family room window, Cassie saw the ladder lean up against the house and Billy climb up. Chores, she thought. Weekend maintenance—something he rarely had time for before he cut back his part-time schedule a little bit. "It surpasses interesting. I've never been up against anything like this before. I'm very confused."

"Why?"

"Okay, here's the deal. I found him to be a very nice guy. Easy to talk to. Interesting—he has lots of fun stories about growing up in his dad's fixer-upper houses with three brothers, about his eighteen-month cross-country on a motorcycle with just a bedroll and small duffel. And not only that, he always asks about what's going on with me and he remembers absolutely everything I tell him so he can say, 'How are things going with your friend Julie and the three kids?' Or, 'How'd Beth's last chemo go?' He's just plain thoughtful."

"This a problem for you?" Julie asked with a raised eyebrow.

"Yeah, it's a problem. What does it mean when you like someone so much, you can't imagine ever having a week or a month you wouldn't get together for dinner or go for one of those bike rides? But at the same time you can't imagine being with him for life?"

"You like that riding, huh?"

"I'm amazed to say, I really do. It's great. I've seen more of this area in the past few months than I've seen in twenty years. I did it as an experiment, you know. I never expected to take to it."

"You've got a guy," Julie said with a grin. "Sounds like you've got yourself a good one this time."

"I don't want him to be my guy," Cassie said. "I've never felt like this before. I've never met a guy I didn't get all excited about, filled with silly expectations and lots of ridiculous hopes and dreams. This is so completely different. I'd like to keep him as just a casual friend, but... Julie, I've been seeing him since last June. And all he's done is kiss me."

"Really? In four months?"

"Uh-huh. I wasn't even sure that was a good idea, but I couldn't resist. I mean, I'm still a girl, right? Everyone can use a little romance here and there. Kissing. Cuddling."

"Good kisser and cuddler, is he?"

"Whoa," Cassie said. "I've considered myself completely in love within twenty-four hours of knowing someone and crushed when it doesn't work out. I'd call a guy ten times before I got the message he wasn't going to call back. I've bought guys little gifts, made out on the second date and jumped into bed on the fourth... This one—I keep trying not to get too close to him, but it's getting bigger than both of us. I don't know what to do." She sighed. "He's just about as good at kissing as talking. And he's very good at talking."

"He hasn't even slipped a hand under your—"

"He said he can tell I'm just not ready, and when I'm ready, so is he," Cassie said. "But really, I just don't think I can go any further with this."

"You don't find him attractive?" Julie asked.

"Not really, no. Well, I mean, he's not one of your classic pretty boys, like Billy. I've described him to you—he's different looking. But he's kind of growing on me. I notice things about him. Like his eyes—he has the most amazing blue eyes. And he thinks everything is funny. He laughs all the time and he has a great big laugh and a really nice smile. I guess if you look at him real closely, imagine him without the hairy face and tattoo, he's probably handsome." She shook her head. "I have to end this before it goes any further..."

"Okay, you're having a mental breakdown or something. Right? He's great, you're crazy about him, he sounds extremely decent, so you better get rid of him… Are you on drugs?"

"Okay, here's my dilemma—help me out here… This is a guy I want in my life, but I'm not sure I want him in my future. Does that make any sense?"

Julie rested the apple and knife on the counter and looked hard into her best friend's eyes. At long last, she said, "No."

"He doesn't have much of a job. He works in a bike shop. He looks like a Hells Angels reject most of the time. He can clean up pretty good, but that beard, ponytail and naked lady aren't going anywhere. He likes that biker look. But I want a normal life! I want a normal future—not a flashy one, but a solid one. I want a family, and it's real hard for me to picture Walt standing outside the nursery window at the hospital, gazing dreamily at the newborns. I can't see him at one of our get-togethers. I bet the guys wouldn't like him so much— he's very sweet, but he looks like a thug." She sighed. "When I think about what the family Christmas picture would look like, I kind of shudder."

Julie just stared at her, her mouth slightly open. "Cassie Rasmussen, I've never heard you talk like this before in your life. You don't think he *looks* right? He's perfect in every way, but he doesn't *look* like your typical guy?"

"That's part of it. He's just not the kind of guy I thought I'd end up with…"

"Is that a little like a guy not getting to know a woman with a fat butt?" Julie asked.

"He thinks I look great. He's probably just lying, but…"

"Did that Dr. George Whatshisname look like what you'd end up with? That skinny, snotty, little nerdy guy with the great big glasses and bald head?"

"Sorta," she said. "He fit a picture of where I thought I was headed. He did belong to a country club…"

"He was an *ass!*" Julie said. "Talk about someone the guys couldn't relate to! He was a braggart and he was rude and treated you like it was your lucky goddamn day he asked you out. I *hated* him."

"Yeah, he didn't turn out so good," Cassie admitted. "At least I didn't sleep with him. Also, if I'm going to let myself get into a relationship, I want it to be with someone who can share the financial load with me, so if there's a family, there's a future. Besides," she said, sitting back, "I'm not sure that's what I'm feeling. I like him, I really like him, but I don't feel madly in love."

"You can't imagine a week without him in it, but you're not in love? You're very confused."

"Tell me about it."

"You don't know what you're talking about."

"I don't?"

"You don't. I think you've been infatuated a million times and haven't had a good, solid, dependable man to love even once. I think you wouldn't know one if he bit you in the ass. And I have a feeling one just did."

"Well, didn't you know you were madly in love with Billy?"

"When I was fifteen? Oh, hell, I was madly in love with love, but a few years later I realized I was just in lust and true love came after that. I can depend on him to always be there for me, to be a partner, a friend, a team player. He makes me laugh, holds me when I cry, is as committed to the kids and our life together as I am. He's a good person—and I don't just love him, I like him and respect him."

I like Walt very much, Cassie thought. I respect him. I could love him if I'd let myself. "Well, I don't know what to do," Cassie said.

"Cassie, you've been bringing around guys for ten years and sooner or later they treat you bad or disappear. You think that's more acceptable than one who treats you like a queen but has a ponytail? Jesus. I think you're all hung up on his image, and you ought to just get over it. What would you be doing right now if he shaved, got a haircut and had a stethoscope hanging around his neck?"

Cassie's eyes got a little round. Walt would sure look sexy with a haircut, wearing a white coat... "I can't really be that shallow, can I?"

"Sounds like it," Julie said.

"Oh, man, this is very embarrassing..."

There was a shout from the backyard. Both women looked at the window to see the ladder moving away from the window, then there was a loud crash as it hit the ground. "Oh, God!" Julie said, dropping the apple and knife. "Not again!"

Julie beat Cassie to the door and ran to Billy, who lay on the ground. She knelt beside him while Cassie shouted, "*Don't...!*" But Julie lifted his head immediately, and by that time Cassie was kneeling on his opposite side.

"I thought I told you, never lift a person's head like that," Billy said. "Hi, Cass."

"Did you fall off the ladder again?"

"Not exactly. I kind of threw it to the ground and laid down, just to see if you had listened to me. I could've had a spinal cord injury, you know."

Julie dropped his head. "Asshole."

He grabbed her and pulled her down on him, then rolled with her until she was underneath. Then he tickled her. And then kissed her.

"I'm going home," Cassie said. "I don't know what's worse—you two fighting or being all gushy kiss-kiss. Why can't you just be normal people sometimes?"

"What's got her so cranky?" he asked.

"She's trying not to fall in love," Julie said.

★ ★ ★

As Cassie got ready for Walt to pick her up for dinner, she realized she'd never even asked where they were going. Walt had a lot of favorite dives, from truck stops to diners, but every now and then he'd walk her into an elegant restaurant, like the one they'd visited at the vineyards on their first ride. They'd entered that one in their dusty jeans and windblown hair, so asking Walt what she should wear probably wouldn't be of much help. Walt was beyond unpredictable.

And then she realized no guy had ever wanted her to meet his parents. Not once. And even though she wasn't sure she wanted this to last, she was suddenly very eager that they think she was well put together. They're just regular, nice folks, Walt had said. His dad was a grocer, his mom a teacher. She chose a pale green pantsuit and wore her hair straight down her back, the way Walt loved it. She forgot about the fact that this potential relationship didn't seem to have the kind of appearance or security she was after; as she put on her makeup, she hoped Walt thought she looked pretty tonight.

When Walt arrived for her at six, he looked just fantastic in tailored pants and a blue silk shirt that brought out the deep color of his eyes; she couldn't find a thing wrong with his looks. He must only own boots, but these were low heeled, black leather, expensive looking. His thick hair was pulled back in the usual ponytail and his sideburns and moustache were neatly trimmed. "I think you've had a little emergency fluff and buff for your mother," she said, running her finger across his moustache. "You look very handsome," she said. "How do your parents feel about the ponytail?"

"I think they've gotten used to it. My mother wants this arm amputated, though," he said, sticking out the naked lady. "Her first words were, 'Very classy, Walt.'"

He said they were going to a small French restaurant on

the river, and once again, Walt was greeted as though a frequent guest. There were fewer than a dozen tables in the
place, plenty of wait staff and a dimly lit ambience that be-
spoke exclusivity. There was good art on the walls, crisp lin-
ens on the tables, fine china, candles. When they walked in,
a handsome couple of about sixty stood from a corner table
and Walt urged Cassie forward.

To say they were not what Cassie expected was an under-
statement. Walt introduced them as Dick and Judy. Dick was
just shy of six feet, bald and striking with expressive brows
and handsome smile. Judy was ravishing. A knockout. Tall
and perfectly proportioned, not too thin, svelte and healthy
with a dazzling smile. She stood at least five-ten in short
heels, had honey-blonde hair in a rich, smooth pageboy cut
that reached her shoulders, perfectly manicured nails, exqui-
site makeup and there was no mistaking a chocolate-brown
Chanel suit with a peach-colored silk blouse under the jacket.
Not to mention a diamond ring that should prevent her from
lifting her hand to shake Cassie's. And that's where Walt had
gotten those wonderful blue eyes, from his mother. The moment they took their seats, Judy said, "Walt tells us you're an
emergency room nurse. I can't wait to hear all about it."

"Ah, Mom, you might not want to hear about Cassie's work
at dinner. She has stories about guts falling out, bones sticking through the skin, brains on the floor, that kind of thing."

Judy's eyes glittered. She said, "Fascinating! How long have
you been doing this?"

Cassie went into kind of a trance. Dick and Judy kept her
talking about herself and she found it impossible to get an ex-
planation for why they were so sophisticated, so richly dressed,
without asking crude questions. They were brought menus
without prices. Walt asked her if she would mind if he selected the wine and Judy complimented her lavishly. Could

Walt's mother be sixty? Because she didn't look it. But if she had a college degree and her oldest son was thirty-four, she was probably that or close. Yet she looked so young and fresh. Stately and mature. Flawless.

Finally, as they were finishing their entrees, Cassie said, "So, Mrs. Arneson, do you ever ride on the back of Walt's bike?"

She laughed. "Not on your life. I can be coerced onto Dick's from time to time, but I don't like those long rides. Really, Cassie, I fought this motorcycle business almost to my last breath, but all four boys have the bug. Walt's the worst, of course. And Dick doesn't have time to putter around or take long cross-country rides. I have my own bike," she said. "Pink. I don't ride it often."

As Judy talked, out of the edge of her ear Cassie heard Dick ask Walt, "You go into the store today, son?"

"Just for a few hours. Everything's in order."

"You hear anything back on that offer?"

"Not yet. We will in plenty of time."

Cassie refocused on Judy. "If you don't mind me saying so, it's hard to imagine you raising four sons."

She answered with a pleased expression. "Are you saying I seem to have gotten through it intact?"

"Four boys is a big load," Cassie said.

"It was my fault," Judy said. "I wanted a girl. I just kept at it, but Kevin tipped me over the edge—I gave up. They were a handful, and I worked full-time till Kevin was twelve. I finally had to quit working full-time and just subbed. I had three teenage boys at home trying to burn the house down and one in college. Someone had to stand guard."

During dinner, Cassie had the fleeting thought that she almost wished they weren't so terrific. She kept looking for reasons not to get any further attached to Walt, and kept coming up empty. Even before Julie accused her of being superficial and worried only about his looks, he had started to become more beautiful every day, inside and out. And it was like he said—it gave her some peace of mind to find he had very nice, normal-looking parents.

When dessert and coffee were finished, Dick said, "Well, I bet you young people have plans for the evening while these old folks are going home to watch TV."

"I think we're just going back to Cassie's house," Walt said. Then he looked at Cassie and said, "But if there's somewhere you'd like to go...?"

"I think this dinner is my limit," she said. "It was wonderful, Walt. Mrs. Arneson, your son is better at finding great places to eat than anyone I've ever met. It's his hobby, I think."

"Sweetheart," she laughed. "Look at him. It takes a lot of fuel to keep him going."

Everyone stood and said their good-nights; the Arnesons kissed her cheeks and carried on about how wonderful it was to finally meet her. She was very quiet as they walked to the truck, which Walt had parked himself despite the fact there was valet service for this tiny, elegant restaurant. When they were under way, he asked, "Did you like my mom and dad?"

She sighed. "Walt, they're wonderful. Although not what I expected."

"No?" he asked, glancing at her, smiling.

"They're very sophisticated. Chic. *Rich.*"

He laughed. "Well, my dad will be the first to admit he's been real lucky. He had that small grocery, a couple of rental houses and a couple of kids—and he was stretched to the limit. But he really went a long way with his investments, then he got in the franchise business. He's done real well for himself. He's a shrewd businessman. When I was a little kid, it was mac and cheese for dinner three nights a week, both parents working, everyone in hand-me-downs except me—I was always too big."

"No one paid the bill tonight," she said. "I never saw a check come to the table."

"It's my mom's favorite restaurant. They have my credit-card imprint. Believe me, the bill's paid. I'll have a receipt by tomorrow morning."

"Your dad's got a lot of money and he lets you buy dinner at a fancy restaurant like that?"

He glanced at her. Frowned. "Cassie, do you think I'm broke?"

"You're a motorcycle mechanic," she said. "I mean, I'm sure you do all right, but—"

"I keep telling you, motorcycles are good business. People spend plenty of money on their bikes. I do just fine."

She thought about that a minute. He was thirty-two and worked long hours, probably a lot of overtime. All he really did was work, take his parents to a fancy meal every week or so and ride his bike. He got stuff from the store, probably parts for his bikes, as well, which he was more than capable of taking care of himself, cost free. For a low-maintenance man like Walt, it probably left a lot to spare.

She realized something. "I've never been to your house." And she sincerely hoped it wasn't a terrible dump in a bad neighborhood, explaining his low expenses and ability to spoil his parents and her so lavishly.

He laughed at her. "It's one of dad's old houses, completely renovated. Small but nice. Would you like to check it out?"

Well, that explained something; surely he got a terrific deal from his dad. Taking them out for a nice dinner, bringing them a couple of bottles of good wine—it was the least he could do.

"I'll have you over. I'd have invited you over before, but I'm always picking you up—and you know I don't cook at all."

When they got to her house, he walked her to the door. He put that big hand on her waist, pulled her close and covered her lips in his wonderful kiss. She loved this part of their routine; she was starting to lose her grip on the lie that this was just friendship. Maybe Julie was right and she was just a shallow snob. What would happen, she wondered, if I just went with gut instinct? If I just followed the feelings? When he let go of her she wobbled a little bit.

"Thank you, Cassie."

"Mmm," she said, her eyes still closed. "No, thank *you*."

"I'll call you."

He walked away and she closed the door. She was halfway to her bedroom when there was a knock at the door. She went back, opened it and he stood there. "I don't want to leave you yet," he said. "Can I stay awhile?"

She lifted her arms to his broad shoulders and her lips to his. And there it was, that power and passion she'd barely had a glimpse of. He swooped down on her and devoured her, taking complete control of her mouth, her tongue. He lifted her to bring her up to his mouth, his arms closing around her. She dug her fingers into his long hair and moved her lips under his. Uh-oh, she thought. Walt seems to be running out of all that patience. And then she laughed against his lips.

"I kiss funny?" he asked hoarsely.

"No," she said, shaking her head. "I was just thinking, this friendship is totally screwed. And I think maybe I'm next..."

"Maybe you are," he whispered. "How do you feel about that?"

"The bedroom is that way," she said, pointing.

11

Walt might look like a bruiser, but he was not. What he was instead was perfect. Gentle but strong, confident, sensitive, *skilled*. He took Cassie to her bedroom and closed the door on poor Steve with an apology. Then he undressed her slowly, but his own clothes disappeared more quickly. His hands on her were very methodical; he'd never touched these places before and he seemed wonderstruck. Thrilled. He ran his hands from her shoulders down to her fingers, then from her neck down to her waist. Over her hips and down her thighs. Between kisses he whispered, "God, oh, God... Cassie, Cassie..."

This was a huge man and Cassie was only five foot three, but she was amazed by the way he could handle her and avoid crushing her, moving her with one big hand around her waist or beneath her butt. He parted her legs with his hands and, while he kissed her, he found her most tender, vulnerable spot with his fingers, gently massaging her there until she was writing and moaning. And then he whispered to her, "Tell me when you're ready for me."

"I think," she said breathlessly, "if you don't do something quick, it's going to be all over…"

And he chuckled low in his throat and, holding himself over her, he found his way and was careful, slow, as if he knew he could be a lot to handle. She gasped when he was inside her and he asked, "Did I hurt you?"

"Oh, not at all." And then she began to move her hips beneath him.

He rocked with her, steady and solid, holding the bulk of his weight off her, and they coupled like that for a while, listening to each other sigh, purr, moan. They softly stroked each other's backs and shoulders and sides. "Take your time," he whispered to her. "I'm waiting for you."

"I don't want it to end," she said against his lips.

And he laughed softly. "It can start again after it ends. It's okay. It's your first ride—we'll go at your pace." And she remembered that's exactly what he had said to her on that first bike ride, so she laughed at him. And shortly after, her laugh caught in her throat and she threw him a climax so tight and hard and hot he shuddered. She cried out, dug her nails into his shoulders. As she was coming down, he deftly took one of her nipples into his mouth and gently sucked as he pumped his hips and throbbed with his own pleasure.

She panted beneath him, but he didn't leave her body. Instead, he stayed where he was and smoothed back her hair, sweetly kissing every part of her face, neck and shoulder. When she had calmed and cooled, he said, "That was unbelievable."

"It certainly was," she whispered. She thought maybe it was the best first time she'd ever experienced in her life.

He gently rolled away from her, but pulled her against him. After a moment he said, "We didn't use anything."

"I was carried away," she said.

"I was surprised," he said.

"Well, I'm on the pill. Have you been—"

"Free and clear," he said. "No danger I'd give you anything. I made a big assumption, honey. I thought, you being a nurse, you'd know exactly where you stand with all that. With birth control, et cetera."

"Et cetera?"

"One of your best friends is a woman's doctor. I assumed you'd be protected and..." His voice trailed off.

"Screened?" she asked, propping up on an elbow, looking down into those incredible blue eyes.

"Jeez, was that rude? Because I'm not worried—I only want to keep you safe."

"Just out of curiosity, when was the last woman?" she asked him.

"Couple of years, I guess. It didn't last very long. Before that, a couple of years again. Like I said, I don't date much. Never have."

"Walt," she said, "I've dated a lot. You're right, though— I've been checked over and I'm also free and clear. But before you get any more involved with me, while there's still time for you to run for cover, you should know—I've been with a lot of men."

"They're not here tonight, are they?" Then he smiled. "I don't care what you've done in the past, Cassie. I'm only interested in what happens between us. And as far as I can tell, what happened between us worked pretty well."

"Don't you want to know how many?"

He stroked the hair at her temple. "I'm not worried that it's a habit you'll have trouble breaking. Just out of curiosity, was it over a hundred?" he asked with a smile. "I don't care, Cassie. You're all I care about right now."

"I keep giving you chances to make a break for it..."

"Nah," he said, grinning. "I'm right where I want to be." He took her hand and gently pulled it, placing it on him. He was hard already. Ready to go. "Want to sleep for a while, or have more playtime?"

"Playtime?" she asked, laughing.

"Seems I can't get enough of you." He put a big hand around the back of her head and pulled her lips down to his. "Mmm. God, you feel so good, taste so good."

And she let herself be drawn to him again, giving and taking, loving.

When Cassie felt the first streaks of sun fall on her face and heard the sound of birds, she rolled over and looked dreamily at the man beside her. This giant looked awfully like a little boy in sleep, so peaceful and harmless. She had never had such a sweet, blissful night.

Figures, she thought. For maybe the first time she had herself a man she was determined not to fall for, and she was a goner. He was an unbelievable man—he had almost everything. Walt was kind, intelligent, strong, confident. He looked pretty goofy by her standards, but she was getting past that real fast. You'd think a man his size would be a little clumsy in bed, or rough. Not so. Walt had a tender but firm touch that made her feel worshiped. And every movement he made was calculated, certain, perfect. The sound of his deep voice was burned into her memory for all time. *Is this okay, like this? Tell me what you like. I'll do whatever makes you feel good.... Oh, Cassie, you're incredible....*

She reached out and gently stroked one of his long sideburns and his eyes came open a tiny bit. A slow smile spread across his lips and he reached out, pulled her close, held her gently.

She thought, Can one live on love? Because if you can, I'm all set here.

"Um, I have something on my mind that might make you uncomfortable…" she said.

"Go ahead," he whispered, kissing her neck, taking a deep breath of her hair.

"We've never talked about anything like this, and I know men and women think differently, but from my perspective after a night like last night, we're not just friends anymore."

He pulled away from her, smiled into her eyes. "That doesn't make me uncomfortable. I can live with that easy." He slipped a hand over her breast, gently kneading, and she looked down at it.

"How do you do what you do and keep your nails so clean and nice?"

He glanced at the hand. "You promise not to laugh at me?"

"I promise."

"When I work on a bike, I use a hand cream so the grease doesn't cling forever, and I get a manicure every week."

She jerked back. "A manicure? *You?*"

"Yeah," he said, grinning. "I have more secrets. Want them all at once, or do you want to discover me slowly?"

"I want them," she said, smiling.

"Well, I'm a very hairy guy," he said.

"I can see that."

"Oh, you haven't seen the half of it. My mother says I was left on her doorstep and I'm a direct descendant of the yeti." She giggled. "I get my back and shoulders waxed. And eyebrows. And when I get a haircut, which is more often than you'd expect, the barber has a little machine that whirs around in my ears and nose…"

"Stop," she said, laughing. "Are you kidding me? Guys don't do those things."

"Some do."

"Did you do that in case you got me in bed? So I wouldn't shriek?"

"No. I've been doing that…just a few years, I guess, but it started when my mother sat me down—after a day in their pool—and said, 'Walt, there are simple things you can do to keep from looking like King Kong.' She wrote down three phone numbers, complete with instructions, and said, 'They're expecting you.'"

"No way!"

"Oh, yeah. I sulked a little, but then I checked it out. And before you ask, I wasn't doing it for a woman." He grinned. "I'd have done it for you, though." He gave her a kiss on the lips. "I love you, Cassie. And you know it."

For a second she was stunned. Stricken. If it wasn't bad enough she was down for the count, so was he. They were sunk now.

"You look upset," he said.

"No," she said, collecting herself. "It's just that…well, I love you, too."

"Isn't that a good thing?"

"God, I don't know. I was trying not to love you…"

He laughed. "I know. I'm not what you expected. You were thinking three-piece suit, nice pension, regular haircut…"

"How did you *know* that?"

"If I were you, that's what I'd be expecting. Sorry. Well, no—I'm not sorry at all. Maybe pretty soon you'll get used to the idea of me and enjoy it. From my point of view, it feels very nice. And unless I'm completely mistaken, it feels nice to you, too."

"Well, yes. It's a wonderful thing. It's just that…well, it

carries some responsibility, that's all. I don't know if you see it that way, but I do."

He lifted his eyebrows. "What kind of responsibility?"

"For starters, I won't be seeing anyone else. Period."

"That's good," he said, smiling. "That could make me cranky."

"Is everything funny to you?" she asked, smiling in spite of herself.

"Damn near." He grinned. "I won't be seeing anyone else, either, not that you were in any danger of that. I haven't been serious with a woman since...well, there were icebergs in hell."

"You said a couple of years ago..."

"That wasn't serious and it wasn't that great, Cassie. I could have skipped it and I wouldn't have missed much."

"Oh, stop. I bet lots of women have been interested in you!"

"Not women who interested me. You said 'for starters.' What else?"

"Nothing we need to worry about now," she said.

"Can I ask you something? When did you think, you know...that you loved me?"

She played with those neatly trimmed sideburns. "I started to realize I needed you in my life pretty quick," she said. "I thought I could mold you into my best friend. Then the deeper feelings started to come—I fought them real hard. You've really screwed up my moratorium on dating. I think I finally caved in completely right before you were taking my blouse off..."

He roared with laughter. "I wondered if we were ever going to get to that part. Boy, you make a guy work real hard for it."

"Not usually," she said with a little self-recrimination.

"Then I guess I'll be flattered. I assume that with me, you had to be sure."

"Oh, I'm sure. You better not screw this up, because I think you're stuck with me. Once I make up my mind..."

"What made up your mind?" he asked.

"Really? You're such a nice person. You're always nice to the waiter."

"I like that. I like that you think that."

"Walt, I feel so good when I'm with you, that's all. Maybe it won't be perfect, I don't know. But if I just listen to my feelings, it feels right. And for you? When did you know?"

"Practically instantly. But you'd had a rough time with men, you said so right away. You had some major trust issues. I had to give you time and patience. And then you had all that friendship stuff on your mind. I didn't want to scare you off. You still have lots of things on your mind."

"Nah," she said.

"Yeah, you do. You haven't asked me any of those practical questions. To see if I look good on paper, as you girls like to put it."

"Like what?" she asked, knowing exactly what.

"Like, am I interested in a committed relationship? Do I want to settle down? Would I like a family? Can I support a family? Am I stable? Those things."

Something occurred to her. "Do you want a family? Children?"

He grinned happily. "I'd like a dozen, but I'd be real happy if I could have one. If I could do half as good as my parents did raising a family, I'd be proud of that. But, if I don't end up with kids, I have a pretty full life. My brothers are hanging plenty of fruit on the family tree."

"You haven't asked me those questions," she pointed out.

"I already know the answers," he said. "You've told me everything I'll ever need to know. You look real good on paper, Cassie."

"Walt, is it true that you haven't had a *serious* woman in your life for literally years? One you were with for a good while? Absolutely true?"

"Maybe never. Makes me look like a loser, huh?"

"Not in any way. But it makes you look like someone who's been real solitary, independent. There was no one to put demands on your time and space. No one else to spend money on before now, and you've been dropping a ton of it, too."

"I'm ready for a little less personal time and space, and more with you. And it feels good to spoil you a little bit."

"Well, I'll try to be patient about your time and space issues, in case you haven't really tested that yet. And you must stop spending such huge amounts of money. You'll be broke in no time, and I don't want that on my conscience."

"Are you worried about money, Cassie?"

She laughed. "Walt, I've always had to worry about money. I told you how I grew up. I've been pretty much alone and self-supporting since I was fifteen. My girlfriend Julie worries about money all the time, too, but if she runs into an emergency, she can call her brother or her mom and dad. I don't have that. Just a stepdad I'm not at all close to who doesn't have much, anyway. I'm real careful with money. Always have been."

He ran a big hand over her silky hair. "I guess that explains why you're so frugal, so careful. You don't have to worry about my money, honey. I have plenty."

She smiled at him. "Well, you always have before, I guess. But I believe the important thing is having work you love. I know you love yours. And I'd really be lost without the E.R. I'm hooked."

"Well, I make a good living. But for you, I'd get a second job if I ever had to," he said. "I doubt it'll ever come to that. I thought nurses made a good salary."

"Well, good enough for me to afford a little house and a car, if I pinch. But there's also lots of overtime to be had at the hospital. I admit, I could work harder."

He looked very concerned. "Cassie, I said I love you. That means I'll do whatever it takes so you'll never have to worry. You understand that, don't you? You trust that?"

"Oh, see how sweet you are? This is the wrong time to have this discussion." She kissed him. "I'm sorry this came up now. We should be thinking about other things, like how nice it is waking up in the morning like this."

"Know what I'd like? I wish it was Sunday morning," he said, pulling her closer. "Because I have to go to work. One of the things you're going to see for yourself when you want more of me is that I work some long hours sometimes." He kissed her and asked, "How long before I can see you again?"

"You mean how long before we can have sex again?"

"I wasn't going to ask that. But I sure liked sleeping next to you."

"Well, I am off today, of course. How would you like to have dinner here tonight? Since I'm off and have time to grocery shop."

"I'd love that..."

"If I buy steaks, can you turn 'em on the grill? I destroy steaks..."

"I'm pretty good with the grill. Big steaks, huh, Cass?"

"Sure," she said. "Big steaks, potatoes, salad. And tomorrow morning I will be up and gone before the sun rises," she said. "But it's okay if we go to bed early, isn't it?"

He grinned. "I can live with that, yeah."

While Marty was at work, she got a voice mail from Joe asking her if she'd like to go out to dinner that evening. It was Monday. He must be brain damaged; no way he would miss *Monday Night Football* to take her out to dinner. Then she realized he probably didn't really mean dinner; he meant some sports bar with a bunch of guys and a platter of wings. Whatever was going on, her schedule was too wild for her to respond. She never even called back.

She was aware he'd been trying to please her, even if it did feel too little, too late. She'd occasionally come home to vacuum tracks and a semiclean kitchen. His underwear was regularly hitting the hamper and the towel was usually hung, but if he started dinner he made a mess and his efforts at straightening—picking up the newspapers, fluffing the couch pillows, taking care of a day's worth of dishes—were clumsy. The last time she looked he hadn't taken care of all the hair that came off in the bathroom or the toothpaste spit on the sink and mirror; since she wasn't sharing a bathroom with him, she hadn't looked in a while. She knew him too well; he wasn't so good at spit-shining a house, but he sure could make an F.D. rig or a boat sparkle.

He was regularly wearing newer, clean sweats or jeans and shaving; he was a little obvious. He wanted her in bed. His libido was a bit on the Mediterranean, hyperactive side...

She walked in at six. Tired, so tired. There were those carpet tracks; he was trying to do the things she could see. And the TV was off. She dropped her purse and by the time she was in the kitchen, he came from the back of the house.

"Hey, babe," he said. "I never heard back. You feel like going out to dinner?"

He was clean and dressed in a nice pair of slacks, a V-neck sweater with a light blue shirt underneath and opened at the neck. It was his four days off; a few weeks ago he'd have been disgusting and stinky. But he looked nice. Crisp. She felt like the disgusting one—sweaty and covered with hair clippings after a long day. She glanced at his chest hair peeking out from his opened shirt collar. He had to shave all the way down his neck. There was a time she found that so masculine and sexy, until she had to start wiping it out of the shower and off the bathroom floor.

"Where's Jason?"

"I took him to your mom's. If you want to go out, we can pick him up on the way home. If you don't want to go out, I can go get us some takeout and pick him up then. It's up to you."

"I'm pretty grungy," she said. "I'd need to shower. Change clothes."

"Whatever you feel like. You want to shower? We can go after you're done."

"Yeah," she said. "But what about football? We going to sit in the bar and watch the game?"

"Anywhere you feel like going, Marty. If you don't have any ideas, we could try that new fish place. And there's always Martinelli's. But no, I wasn't looking to watch the game…"

"Joe, are you all right? You never miss a game!"

"I thought it was more important to take you out to dinner than see a game tonight. Your Mondays at the shop are pretty tough, and I was off. I, ah, tried to clean up a little…"

Reluctantly, she had to give him some credit for remembering about her Mondays, which were brutal. It surprised her; she hadn't thought he ever noticed. "Thanks," she said, heading for her shower. "Give me a half hour. We can go wherever you want."

Marty pinned up her hair and jumped in the shower. She'd quickly rinse off the grunge, fluff her hair, freshen her makeup and pop out in twenty minutes and catch him riveted to the game. Then it might take an hour or two before he decided on a sports bar for pizza or chicken strips as their dinner out. She knew without a doubt that she'd catch him just being himself.

There were a few complications that kept Marty from making a decisive move. She'd been in her own room down the hall for a couple of months and it had given her way too much time to think; she'd had too many nights without the warmth of a loving man in the bed beside her. She'd been angry with Joe for such a long time and now she found herself hanging on to that anger with a vengeance despite his efforts.

And she'd been fantasizing about Ryan...

It had been at least eight years since her last breakup with Ryan. During the years they'd been a couple, though on and off, she was just a girl. As relationships go, that one had been rife with pain and disappointment, but even considering that, she couldn't have asked for a more sensuous, experienced and loving introduction into the ways of men and women. Ryan was a gifted seducer; he knew what to say, how to touch and tempt, and he could certainly deliver. But she'd spent at least as much time crying as she had sighing in contentment.

Now, emotionally estranged from her husband, she found herself obsessed with wondering if, over the past eight years, Ryan had learned. Could he have come to his senses, finally understanding what commitment meant and what the rewards were? Because if she looked back at the time with him and subtracted the ache of betrayal and the tears of sheer loneliness, he would be the perfect partner for her.

She kept asking herself why she didn't just leave Joe, or ask Joe to move out and give her a divorce. It wasn't about finances; there was money in the bank and she'd gladly trade all the toys for the home furnishings. She drew a decent paycheck and she knew she could count on Joe to do right by his son even if he hated her. And it wasn't the promises she'd made that held her in place; as far as she was concerned, he broke those when he started treating her like his maid. The single thing that was holding her was knowing that Joe was trying to put it back together, that he actually loved her. He was trying harder than she was. She thought that before too long she would have an answer; either there was hope she could feel that way about him again, or no hope of getting it back. She was still in flux; when it became crystal clear, she would know.

But there was no doubt in Joe's mind; she knew that. It had been like that since the very first time they met. When Billy introduced them, she saw it in Joe's eyes immediately. After they'd been out a few times, she overheard Joe say to Billy, "I'm going to owe you *forever* for this!" He put every ounce of energy toward winning her, proving his love. He'd been a stupid slob for the past couple of years, at least, but he'd never looked at another woman, never once acted as though life with her was lacking for him in any way even though she complained constantly. She'd become a shrew—at least as hard to live with as he was.

Those two things—indulging fantasies about Ryan's potential that she suspected were ridiculous, and suffering under the pure knowledge of Joe's love and commitment—held her in a limbo she couldn't seem to escape.

She finished her primping in just under twenty minutes, but Joe foiled her plan. He was sitting on the sofa, newspaper opened on the coffee table in front of him, TV off. He looked up and said, "That was fast. You look fantastic." And then he folded up the paper.

"Joe, you're really confusing me. What are you trying to do?"

"Give you some special attention, Marty. Isn't that what you said you needed?"

She just shook her head.

"Where would you like to have dinner?" he asked.

"Surprise me," she said, testing him. And she went to the car.

Twenty minutes later they were seated in a spacious booth in an upscale restaurant. It being a Monday night, it wasn't terribly crowded and the service was prompt. Opposite from them, the dining room bled into a lounge where there was indeed a TV with the game on, but this being a pricey place, it wasn't full of shouting, beer-guzzling men. Rather, it seemed to host several couples seated at high tables. And the TV was not in Joe's view.

They ordered drinks and were given menus. "This doesn't seem like your usual place," Marty said. "I was expecting pizza or wings."

"See anything there you think you'd like?" he asked.

"Lots of things," she said. This was the kind of place she would have chosen and had in fact argued for many times. Now, when she'd rather not be in an elegant place quiet enough to have a conversation in, it was what Joe had chosen.

And conversation was exactly what Joe had planned, she soon learned. When the drinks arrived, Joe said, "Marty, we should probably talk."

She looked up from her menu. "About?"

"About?" he mimicked. "Let's see…you live on the other side of the house and every time you look at me, my bones freeze. That's a good place to start. What's your plan?"

She closed her menu and sighed, searching for an answer, but she was saved by the appearance of a waiter. So they took a moment to order and then Joe lifted his glass of red wine to his lips and looked over the rim at her, waiting. He could look so stern when he wanted to. Scary, if you didn't know him. When you knew him, it was obvious he was decent and kind underneath his gruffness. He was the guy who said he'd never bolt if she got sick, disfigured.

But Ryan? She wasn't sure he could even remain faithful. He could be counted on to be fastidious and smell good, but stick by a woman who was ill? Even she couldn't fantasize that far! "I don't have a plan, Joe," she said. "That's half my problem."

He took a sip, put down his glass and said, "See, I don't get that at all. Is there something more I'm supposed to be doing to get your clothes back in your closet? Because if there is, I don't know what it is."

"You sure it's the clothes in the closet you're after?" she asked.

"I want my marriage back. I want my wife back. Are you planning a divorce? Are you doing it with someone on the side—is that it? Is this going to last another week? A year? You seeing a lawyer or a lover? Come on, Marty. I've been real patient with this—I deserve an answer of some kind."

"I'm not seeing anyone—not a lover or a lawyer. I got out of our bedroom because I just couldn't take it anymore. I guess that's what it took to get your attention, but the sad thing is, now I'm scared to go back. I'm afraid everything goes back to the way it was and I just can't live like that anymore. I can't face that kind of future."

"You can't trust me? That I'll do my best?"

"I need a little more time, Joe. I'm not ready yet."

"Marty. Do you still love me?"

Oh, damn, she thought. What in the world do you do with a question like *that?* But she hesitated long enough that he looked down at the table in front of him, shook his head and under his breath said, "Fuck."

"What's *your* plan, Joe?" she asked, taking a sip of her own wine.

"Well, that depends on a lot of things. I don't plan to keep living in separate bedrooms, that's for sure. In fact, if I'm living with a woman who can't stand the sight of me, I'm not hanging around. How's that for a plan? See, it *was* my plan to do whatever it took to get you back, and to keep doing it to *keep* you back, but if it's not going to make any difference, I don't know why I should stay. You want your house just perfect, which I can't seem to get right, and you're pretty goddamn happy in your own bedroom. That's not my idea of..."

Her mouth dropped open as she listened to him. In all her complications and calculations, she had forgotten a couple of things—like Joe was a proud and pigheaded Italian. He was a real macho man; it wasn't in his makeup to be whipped into shape by a woman. That loving side of him—that was the side that allowed him to make concessions and compromises, but he expected to be rewarded. She finally found her voice and interrupted him. "You'd *leave* me?" she asked, stunned.

"Marty, I think *you* left *me*. You just haven't kicked me out of the house yet, that's all."

"Wait a minute, wait a minute. Joe, I just took a little space, because *I've* felt hurt and unloved. I wasn't planning to—"

"You're planning something, you just haven't cut me in on the deal yet. Are you saying that in the two months you've been holding down the fort in your own wing, you haven't thought about what you wanted to happen next? About a divorce? Because if there was anything in the wind that said you were getting over your tantrum here, I sure didn't hear it."

"Tantrum? Is that what you think happened? I had a tantrum?"

"Okay, okay, you had a point. I was an idiot and didn't know what kind of attention you needed. I realize I needed a kick in the ass. You got through to me. Now I'm asking you...what's next?"

She was quiet for a moment that stretched out. "Is that why you brought me out to dinner?" she finally asked. "To pin me down like this?"

"No," he said, shaking his head. "This was the last thing

I thought would happen. I really thought when I asked that loaded question—do you still love me?—the answer would be on your lips so fast I'd feel like a damn fool. I already felt like an idiot for not knowing how to take care of my own wife, and I've been trying like hell to make that up to you. But something else is going on here and it's not me forgetting to hang up the goddamn towel. Feels like you're done with me. Done with us."

The waiter cheerfully brought salads, made small talk, served them freshly ground pepper, refilled water glasses. When he was finally gone, Marty said, "I wish we didn't have to do this right now..."

Joe held his fork, but he didn't touch the salad. "I don't want to be doing this at all. You have any idea how I feel about you? I'd do anything for you, if I knew how, if I knew what. When I asked you to marry me, you think I was just looking for any warm body?" He shook his head. "I might not have been a whistling idiot every day of our marriage and, I admit, it got to me when you weren't happy, but Jesus, Marty, I never for one second thought I'd made a mistake. In fact, you scared me real good when you moved down the hall, but I still thought we'd get it back. I thought that because I've always been so damned in love with you. And I really thought you were in love with me, underneath all that anger."

She felt the tears come into her eyes. "I thought you barely cared about me at all... I mean, I knew you loved me, but..."

"Listen to yourself," he said. "You knew I loved you, but you didn't think I *cared* about you? When was the last time you let me know how much you cared about me? That you appreciated what I was willing to do for us? It's a damn nice paycheck, Marty. I ever once complain about what you felt like spending? You bitched about the toys, but you never complained when I detailed your car, painted the house, landscaped or laid brick. You're pissed I don't love to dance, but the wallpaper, leaded-glass front doors and hardwood floors didn't do a lot to blow my skirt up—it made *you* happy. Did I give you any trouble about deciding not to have those kids you'd originally said you wanted? Because since Jason, especially since Jason—who I think I do a decent job with—I wanted more kids. Or how about this—you have any trouble looking at the portfolio? It's got two names on it—yours and mine. I started that portfolio a long time before I met you, and it's gotten nice and fat. I've been known to walk into fires for that, Marty, and as far as I was concerned, it was all yours. Aw, fuck it," he said, stabbing a piece of lettuce and bringing it angrily to his mouth.

"Please," she said, a fat tear running down one cheek. "I appreciate what you do..."

"It just wasn't enough, was it? Well, I wanted to make it enough. I tried. I think, in the end, there was nothing I could do to make you happy. To make you love me."

She looked away, and that's when she saw Ryan walk into the lounge with his arm around a woman's shoulders. The woman was Jill. Marty had met her a couple of years ago; they'd just moved in together. There was another couple with them and they found a table, sitting up on high stools around it. They were laughing and having a good time and Ryan couldn't keep his hands off her. He massaged her neck under her full, bouncy hair, kept a hand on her shoulder.

She looked back at Joe, stabbing his salad.

She sucked in a sob. "I have to go," she said very quietly. "I can't stay here. I can't eat."

"Fine," he said, chewing and swallowing. He reached for his wallet and shuffled through the bills, pulling out a generous number, enough to pay for a full dinner they wouldn't eat, plus a tip.

She slipped out of the booth and he followed. He put his hand on the small of her back even though right now he probably hated her. The waiter stopped them. "Is everything all right, sir?"

"With the restaurant? Great. Everything else just sucks tonight." He jerked his head back toward the table. "You're covered for the meal. Sorry to have to leave like this."

While Joe made his amends with the waiter, Marty gravitated toward the lounge. She just couldn't stop herself. She walked right up to Ryan's table. She felt Joe come up behind her and even though he must want to kill her right now, he still put a hand on her shoulder, claiming her. "Hi, Ryan, Jill," she said pleasantly, though there had to be red rims around her eyelids, maybe tear tracks. "Nice to see you. So glad to see you two are back together..."

Jill flashed a look at Ryan, her brows furrowed. "We were apart?" she asked. And Marty noticed a good-size engagement ring on her finger.

"You remember about a year back," Ryan said with an uncomfortable laugh. "We had that little bit of trouble..."

"Little bit of trouble?" Marty asked. "When I ran into you a couple of months ago, you said you two broke up a year ago." She lifted a brow. "Could I have misunderstood that?"

"Apparently you did," he said, scowling.

Jill turned her narrowed eyes toward Ryan and said, "Is that so?" And Ryan squirmed visibly.

"Have you ever met my husband, Joe? Joe, this is Ryan and Jill. Ryan and I went to high school together. God, that was a long time ago." Joe didn't extend his hand, which really wasn't like him at all. She could feel him frowning. "We have to get going. I just wanted to say hi. Nice seeing you both."

Marty knew before she even spoke to Ryan. The second she saw him walk in tonight, she knew everything. There was no guy from work staying with him. He took her call on his cell phone and told Jill something—probably meeting one of the guys for a quick beer. He'd have left his fiancée at home and booked a hotel room with Marty, and he wouldn't have thought twice about it. If they'd started an affair, he would have eventually told her about Jill, and he would've said, 'But you're married!' That's what he was after—what he'd always been after—a lot of women. He just wasn't a one-woman man. Period. And he wouldn't have any trouble convincing Jill that Marty was just some nutcase, that he'd *never* said they'd split up. He was a master manipulator and liar.

When they got to the car Joe started the engine, but didn't drive. Looking straight ahead he asked, "That him?"

"Who?" she asked, turning to look at him.

"The guy. The one who has you all fucked up and living down the hall?"

She shook her head and laughed, though tears were actually smarting in her eyes. "He's just someone I knew in high school."

He yanked the gearshift into drive and she could tell he didn't believe that for a second. And Joe, so tall and strong and masculine, would wonder what a woman could see in a pretty boy like Ryan. And right now, tears streaming down her cheeks, she was asking herself the same question. I'm such a fool, she thought.

Even worse, she had a husband problem she barely understood. She thought it was the messy house, the nasty gym shorts, but that was nothing. They didn't know anything about each other. He couldn't understand what she wanted until she moved out of the bedroom and she had no idea how deep his feelings ran, how far he would go to make her happy. When had they stopped talking? Stopped understanding each other? The other thing between them when they were dating, besides his courting and compromise, was that they *knew* each other. She wasn't sure which one of them entered the marriage with expectations set in stone that were never discussed or negotiated. Possibly it was her. It was at least both of them and not just Joe.

But she cried. All the way home she sniveled, and it was so hard to know if it was because Ryan let her down or because Joe wanted to give her everything and she had closed him out completely. Joe said nothing; he didn't even ask her what was wrong. He didn't try to comfort her. When they got to her mother's house, he said, "Stay here. I'll get Jason." A few minutes later he carried their sleeping son to the car, slipping him into the car seat. When they were home, Joe lifted him out and took him to his bed.

Marty went to her solitary bedroom, lay down in her clothes and sobbed into the pillow. She left Joe to put Jason to bed, something he wouldn't mind doing at all and of which he was completely capable. She wasn't surprised that he just left her alone there, though he knew she was all shook up and crying. He'd finally had enough. He knew he was fighting a losing battle and had given up on her. It was only eight-thirty when they got home, but she cried for a couple of hours. Besides her tears over Beth, she hadn't cried at all since dividing their home into His and Hers.

During this whole time, she would have expected to hear the TV from the family room, the familiar backdrop of sports that seemed to punctuate her life with Joe. The house was eerily quiet for such an early hour. Finally she got off the bed, washed her face and brushed her teeth, put on her robe and left her room. All was dark and still.

Marty walked down the hall to her old bedroom. She entered quietly, softly, and stood beside the bed looking down at him. After a long moment, he pulled the covers back and slid over, and she lay down next to him, her head on his arm, and cried a little bit more.

He ran a hand through her hair, holding her. "Did you fuck him, Marty?" he asked her.

She lifted her head and looked into his eyes. She shook her head and said, "I swear to God, Joe—no."

She heard him let out a sigh of relief. Then he pulled her closer. "You wanna try to make this work? Us? Or do we just admit we can't make each other happy and give it up before it gets even more nasty?"

She put a hand against his cheek and said, "I want us to work on it, Joe. I think we need some help. I don't know why, but we just don't know each other. Didn't we used to know each other?"

"I thought so."

"I'll try if you will," she said with a sniff. "Joe, I think if I lost you now, I'd lose the best person I've ever had in my life. Don't leave me, Joe. Please?"

He kissed her forehead. "I made a promise," he said. "I meant it."

12

Beth told her girlfriends and coworkers that Dr. Paterson was taking very attentive care of her during her chemotherapy because they were colleagues who had become friends. That was as much as she wanted anyone to know. But after a few months they were friends who had become much better friends.

He called almost daily, just checking in, asking about her health first but then quickly moving the conversation on to other things. The ordinary stuff a couple getting acquainted talked about—his practice, his daughters and the mundane, from weather to sitting on the condo association board in his neighborhood. She had likewise been eased into relaxed conversation with him—about the day's work, her girlfriends and their dramas, everything and anything. On the two appointments she'd kept with him in San Francisco, he'd taken her out for a bite to eat afterward and, for what should have been a third appointment, he came to Sacramento and took her out to dinner. He glanced at her lab work over the menu and said, "Good, good and good. Just what I expected."

"You're becoming very obvious," she told him.

"Thank God," he said with a smile. "I thought you were going to string me along forever."

"I'm not going to string you along at all—you've clearly lost your mind. Or you have a demented attraction to sick people."

"Funny, I don't think of you as sick," he said. "I probably should. You're going through an awful lot for a healthy person. It was a dirty trick and the joke was on me. The second I met you, I was attracted and I tried reminding myself it would be unfair to put you in that position. But then I lost my head."

"It's very unprofessional."

"Aw, depends on your perspective. If you weren't a patient, I wouldn't have wasted a minute getting to know you. And I did think about suggesting you see a different doctor, but you wanted me. I doubt another oncologist would change the course of treatment, anyway. I think I'm being terrifically objective. What do you think?"

"How many patients have you pursued? Dated?"

"None," he said. "I was married a long time, for one thing. And the majority of my patients aren't young, beautiful physicians." He grinned. "I've been a gentleman, I think."

"My hair is starting to fall out," she told him.

"It'll come back," he said. "Beth, after what I've seen, you can't scare me off with cancer."

"What if I become dependent on you?" she asked.

"I could probably find a way to deal with that, but to be honest, one of the things that attracted me most was your bullheaded insistence you wouldn't be dependent on anyone. You're going to be fine, you know. Complete the chemo, grow your hair back, get on with your life. There are still a lot of things to enjoy. Maybe I should caution you against being attracted to a fifty-year-old man?"

"What makes you think I am?"

"I'm gaining ground, that's what. The next couple of months could be tougher," he said, growing serious. "You might want to cut your schedule back, even consider a short leave. But after that, we're done and you can concentrate on renewing your strength. Early in the new year, you'll begin to feel like your old self."

"I hope so," she said, taking a long sip of water. "I breezed right through the first couple of months, but I can feel it wearing me down. I haven't been sick, but I've been so depleted. Exhausted."

"I'm sorry about that. The hardest part for me, Beth, is I want to stop all of it and watch you flower. But that would be a mistake. We're going in the right direction, I really believe that. Maybe we should think about a trip in the spring. Something relaxing. A cruise or the Caribbean beaches. What do you think of that idea?"

She just shook her head. "What are you getting yourself into?"

"You wouldn't be thinking I'm getting the bad end of the deal, would you? You'd be wrong. You have a treatable condition, but I don't."

"What's your condition?"

"I'm fifty. When my hair goes, it's not coming back. And other things will follow suit."

"I haven't told anyone, you know. There's no getting around it—what we're doing could be considered dating."

"Could be? You're out of practice—this *is* dating. I don't care who knows." He shrugged. "I've been wondering something—has there been a serious relationship since your fiancé?"

"No. I was reluctant to allow anyone close after that."

He shook his head. "Very curious to me that he could let you go. I wonder what was going through his head..."

"He was young," she said. "I'm sure he was scared. Afraid of committing to someone who'd be chronically ill, unable to have children, that sort of thing."

Jerod seemed to think about that for a moment. "Maybe he thought he was being cautious. That can be very shortsighted in the end. You can end up with what appears to be a perfect specimen and lose her another way. Accidental death, divorce, a lot of variables... Well," he said, shaking his head. "You don't have to protect me from anything. Unless, of course, you're planning to sue me," he added with a smile.

"I was thinking of letting you kiss me good-night. My last good-night kiss came from a very dull, unimaginative internist, and I'm still trying to get over it."

"I'll be happy to help with that."

"And I was thinking—now here's where I'm going nuts—I was thinking of bringing you out of the closet." She smiled at his raised eyebrows. "My girlfriends are having an intimate little party. My friend Cassie, the nurse, is going to finally spring her new guy on the group. She's been dating him quietly for months, keeping a tight lid on the whole thing."

"Why?"

"Well, as she tells it, he's very different from what we're used to. He's some big, burly biker with tattoos. She's planning to toss him out and see if he sinks or swims. I thought it might be kind of shocking and fun to throw you into the mix. 'Yes, that's right, I'm having an illicit affair with my physician.'"

He chuckled. "It's not illicit, it's not an affair and it's not even intimate—yet. Not for a while yet, not until you get some energy back. Your kiss proposition—that even surprises me..."

"You aren't fantasizing about my flat, scarred chest and bald head, are you? It would be like making love to an alien."

He smiled. "I've been fantasizing about your shoulders, the small of your back, your long legs and your butt. Oh, and your neck and lips. Other things, too. Like holding your hand on a beach somewhere. Sailing with you. Laughing—God, I love that you like to laugh, and you're such a smart-ass. Normally I don't enjoy the company of other doctors that much—they can be so dull. But even our phone conversations are entertaining. I've never had any interest in OB until now. You make it sound fascinating. Is that just infatuation, or are you fascinating, Beth?"

She smiled at him. "I'm fascinating," she said quickly. "It's next weekend. Saturday night. Do you have daughter obligations?"

"Everything's negotiable. I'll be here."

"Would you like my guest room? There won't be sex. There won't even be cuddling."

"That's very nice of you. I'll take you out to breakfast in return."

"As far as the evidence shows, we really are just friends," she said.

"Hmm. Good friends. With lots of potential."

It briefly crossed Cassie's mind to ask Walt to trim or dress up for his first appearance with her friends, but she was quick to dismiss the thought. I'm such a dope, she thought. I've been bringing around rude, insensitive jackasses for years, thinking that because they looked the part, they'd fit in. So when Walt asked her what he should wear, she just said, "It's casual." And when he asked if she'd like to go on the bike or in the truck, she said, "Whatever you feel like. If you'd like to take the bike, I'll just drive over with my contributions to dinner a little earlier. Just let me know."

"What are you bringing?" he asked.

"A big salad, bread, a six-pack of good beer and a bottle of wine."

"Can I bring something?"

"Well, it's your party, honey," she said. "You can just show up and be the star."

"I bet they'd like it if I brought something that'll save. We'll take the truck."

For the first time in a very long time, they were meeting at Julie and Billy's for a real dinner—things were going well enough for them to play host. They would provide the meat and dessert and everyone else would pitch in for the rest.

It wasn't just the prospect of meeting Walt that had Julie all keyed up. She was thrilled to feel as though she and Billy were among the living again, actually having people over and contributing more than a loaf of day-old French bread, a few dollars' worth of salad or a six-pack and two-dollar bottle of wine. She was able to spend thirty dollars on meat and made two nice, thick, fattening cheesecakes. It wasn't that much, but it put Julie in a fever of excitement. "We haven't had a good steak in ages," she had whispered to Cassie. "Billy's thrilled!"

Walt picked Cassie up at six and she smiled as she observed he was looking just so much like himself. He had shaved around those sideburns and such, but that could have as much to do with not wanting to chafe her later—he was so wonderfully protective of her. He wore the leather vest complete with some chains, and of course boots and jeans. His short sleeves ensured the naked lady was exposing herself. In the backseat of his extended cab truck was a very large basket in cellophane. "What's that?" Cassie asked.

"I took a run over to one of our favorite restaurants in Sonoma—I think it was our first one. They put together a basket for me. It's real nice. You think they'll like it?"

"Walt, is it full of hundred-dollar bottles of wine?" she asked, frowning.

"No!" he protested. "There's a couple of nice bottles in there, but I was after some good beef and salmon they can freeze." Then he grinned. "If I pass the test, Billy can invite me back and grill it up."

"You're such a suck-up," she laughed. "Well, I just hope you like them. Except for Marty's husband, Joe, they've all been my best friends since I was a kid."

"I like 'em already, honey. They gotta be real decent people to put up with you all these years." And then he grinned at her.

They entered with arms laden—Walt with his basket, Cassie with her dinner offerings. Joe and Marty were already there, helping to put out some snacks. There were quick introductions and Walt insisted Julie get into the basket. She pulled out a big tenderloin and large salmon filet along with four bottles of wine. "Oh, my God," she said.

Walt leaned toward her ear. "I thought it would freeze nice, for the next time you have company over. With any luck, me."

"This is just too much," she said.

"This is my debut. I might've gotten a little showy."

"Ya think?" she said. "Well, I like your style, but you can't keep that up with this crowd. We gather, we eat and drink. You'll go broke in no time."

"Sounds like a plan," he said. "Where are the kids?" he asked, looking around.

"They're at my mom's for an overnight, so I can concentrate on grilling you."

"Cassie said you were grilling steaks," he said with a smile.

"Steaks and you," she said. "You're off to a very nice start."

"That's what I wanted to hear."

The men urged Walt outside where Billy had put a Duraflame in a small patio fire pit. When they were out of earshot, Cassie said to Julie, "Tuck the wine away in a special place. He has a habit of buying really expensive stuff."

Julie picked up a bottle and studied it while Marty picked up another one, reading the label. "Shouldn't I serve it?"

"You can if you want to, or you can save it for a special occasion. He's been bringing hundred-dollar bottles of wine to my house for months. I can't break him of it."

"How can he do that?"

"He hasn't had a serious girlfriend since seventh grade," she said with a shrug. "No one to spend his money on, I guess. It makes him happy. Makes me crazy. You know I have trouble with that kind of spending. I'd be so happy with a cheap little bottle."

"We'll put it on the table," Julie said.

"Walt hardly drinks," Cassie said. "Billy and Joe don't know the difference. Don't waste the good stuff."

But then the front door opened and Beth came in with a man in tow.

"Hi," she said. "I'd like you to meet Jerod Paterson. My doctor. And, I guess, my date."

All their mouths dropped open in surprise, making both Beth and Jerod laugh. After the hellos, Cassie whispered to Julie, "Okay, go ahead and pour some of the good stuff."

As was typical of one of these get-togethers, the women stayed in the kitchen fixing food and gossiping while the men stood around outside, each holding a beer. They were an odd lot—a couple of firefighters, a physician and a biker, spanning twenty years in age. But what they had in common were their women.

Walt and Jerod particularly wanted to know what it was

like growing up with them, something Billy knew only too well. Joe was able to chime in when it came to knowing all of them as adults; he'd been around them about six years and could speak to the bond that had never weakened for a moment. "They're thicker than thieves," he informed Walt and Jerod. "They know things about us we don't know about each other. It's scary sometimes."

But talking about women didn't hold their interest very long; they moved on to Billy and Joe being asked about their jobs. After some firefighting and paramedic stories, they talked about Walt's rides, including the one that lasted more than a year. That held them for a good long while, and finally it was Walt who asked Jerod about his work.

"Very rewarding," Jerod said. "Long hours and worth every second."

"Isn't it a little on the depressing side?" Joe asked.

"Not at all. It's true, there are people I can't help get well, but they're greatly outnumbered by the ones I can. It's good for the heart," he said. "A little like firefighting—I concentrate on the ones we can save."

There was a drawn-out moment of silence before Billy asked, "How's Beth doing? Really?"

Jerod smiled. "As her doctor I'd have to say very well. As her friend I'd say she's got what it takes. She's going to beat this." Then he took a drink from his beer. "I have absolutely no doubt. I'm counting on many years."

In the kitchen, Julie turned wide eyes to Beth and said, "You brought the *doctor?*"

Beth laughed. "I did. He just won't go away quietly. I'm getting a little attached to him. I might keep him."

"Is he very romantic?" Cassie asked.

"He is," she confirmed. "But understand—*I'm* not very

romantic. This chemo is wearing me down. I slept for four hours today so I could make it through dinner. He knows it's going to be a long time before I can even think about what to do with him. It's nice, though, to have someone to talk to. I mean, a man to talk to. And not just any man, but one who understands everything that's happening to me. And isn't one bit scared of it."

"Wow. How are you with the whole body-image thing?"

"Well, there won't be any surprises. When I told him it would be a long time before I'd take my shirt off for him, he reminded me that I already had. He's very safe for me. For a while I wondered if half my attraction to him was for that reason..."

"Are you kidding me?" Marty said. "Look at him—he's gorgeous!"

"He is," Beth said. "So why not? He's smart, handsome, attentive, and if there's one thing I've earned by now, it's to feel safe."

It worked. Four odd couples, strung together by four women who'd been friends since they were girls, laughed and joked through lots of food and good wine, told tales about one another and seemed to connect on many levels. Jerod took Beth home right after the cheesecake, apologizing for not helping with the cleanup. Stamina was not her strong suit these days. Joe and Marty were pushed out the door not long after; they still had a child to pick up from Grandma's house. While Cassie and Julie finished up in the kitchen, Billy and Walt stood in the driveway and talked. Walt reached into the inside pocket of his vest and pulled out a couple of cigars. "What d'ya think?" he asked.

"Oh, my man," Billy said. "You really know how to make a good presentation."

"This probably isn't going to go over that well with the women," Walt said. "But what the hell, huh? Men have to bond, too." He pulled a lighter out of his pocket, snipped the ends of both cigars and handed one over. "Really, a rare thing for me. But special occasions call for stuff like this."

So they talked for a little while about nothing in particular. Billy said something about how nice it was to have Julie so comfortable and happy with the way things were going financially. "Far as I can tell, we have only two potential problems—both sitting right behind you." Walt turned to look at their cars in the driveway. Billy continued. "I'm really good with wood, paint, minor electrical and plumbing problems, but I've always been challenged by engines. And I have to keep those cars running for four years. At least four years."

"Good cars," Walt said. "So what's the problem?"

"Oh, just old age. Over a hundred thousand miles on 'em. They're good and solid, but old. It's hard enough keeping cars that old in tires and stuff. When something like brakes or transmission goes down, I'm pretty lost."

Walt grinned around his cigar. "But I'm not," he said. "Bill, I'm a mechanic. That's my number-one skill. You got a problem with the car, call me. I'm sure I can help."

"Jeez, I blew right by that. You're a mechanic! I guess I thought you just do bikes."

"That's definitely my specialty. But I love engine grease. I hate to brag, but I'm good. And I can get parts at cost."

"Damn, I just like you better all the time," he said. "You know, I've been meaning to say thanks for what you did for Cassie…"

"What I did for her?" Walt asked.

"Yeah, that first time you met her. You got her out of something that could've been real bad. She came over here that night, told me and Julie all about it. She was shook up and it got to me, too. I mean, I think of her as a best friend, a sister. If you hadn't been there…"

"But I was there," Walt said. "It might've been a silly co-incidence, but I was there in plenty of time. She wasn't hurt, just scared."

"Well, I told myself the first thing I was going to do when I met you was thank you for stepping in. And I want you to know, I looked all over Sacramento and the surrounding area for a Ken Baxter, and he definitely wasn't a firefighter…"

"Ken Baxter?" Walt asked.

"That's who Cassie said her date was with. A guy named Ken Baxter who claimed to be a paramedic with F.D. Only one turned up—a fifty-year-old captain out of northwest. Definitely not the guy."

Walt puffed, swallowed, tried to stop himself but then said, "It wasn't Ken Baxter, Billy. I got the make, model and license plate of the car the guy was driving. I managed to find out who he is, and his name isn't Ken Baxter. I never asked Cassie his name—I just got someone to run the plates. His name is Ralph Perkins and I know what firehouse he works out of."

Billy's face had grown dark as Walt spoke. "I know that firehouse, too," he finally said. "Ken Baxter is his captain. I know Perkins. Not well, but I've seen him around. I didn't like him before you even told me this. You do anything with that information?"

Walt looked down. "Kind of," he said. "I drove by there a lot till I was sure he saw me. Then I stared him down for a while. I thought it wouldn't hurt if he knew I knew. Anything more than that would be making trouble with the police. And, Bill, I haven't talked to Cassie about it. She wants to forget it. She's not scared of him anymore, she doesn't have anything on him that would get him arrested and she'd like to move on. Think about that."

"Yeah, but…"

"Think about it," Walt said. "You go talk to him or something, it could come back on Cassie. It could come back on her when I'm not around. We can't have that."

The drive from Julie's to Beth's wasn't far, but Beth was fading fast. Jerod put a hand on her thigh. "You've just about had it," he said.

"It's so annoying," she said. "Where the hell does this fatigue come from? I felt fine until an hour ago."

"Your body's working hard," he said. "Don't fight it. You'll be home soon and can go to sleep." She started nodding off in the passenger seat and he said, "It's okay, honey. Settle back. Close your eyes. I'll wake you when you're home."

He pulled her car into her garage and even the sound of the car door didn't bring her immediately around. He pulled off her seat belt and carefully roused her, though she was very slow to wake. Finally he just pulled her gently out of the car, lifted her into his arms and carried her into the house. "I can walk," she said, wriggling a little bit.

"Be still," he said. "You weigh nothing at all. Pretty soon we'll get some meat on your bones, fatten you up."

She yawned. "I never liked being fat. Now it's starting to sound good."

He took her to the bedroom and sat her on her bed. She flopped back and he chuckled at her. "I should have gotten you out of there sooner—you're completely out of steam." He knelt beside the bed and pulled off her shoes. "I'll help you get into bed. You have a nightgown or something?"

"Just never mind. I'm fine in my clothes."

"Don't be silly—you'll wake up uncomfortable. Where should I look?"

She yawned deeply. "Closet. Hook."

It was simple to find, a long brushed flannel with sleeves. She probably got cold at night, he thought. So thin, alone in the bed. He brought it back to her and helped her get off her sweater and unfasten her bra. The little prosthetic inserts fell out and he scooped them up, keeping them with her clothes. These little babies were expensive. He pulled the gown over her head and she slipped her arms in. Then he put her arms around his neck so she could stand and he got off her pants, sitting her down to remove them the rest of the way. He pulled back the covers for her and she climbed right in, sighing so gratefully. He bent down and put a kiss on her forehead. "Sleep well," he whispered.

He was just about out her bedroom door when she called. "Jerod?"

He went back to the bed. "You need something, honey?"

"No," she said, shaking her head. "Would you like to lie down beside me? I wouldn't mind…"

"I don't want to bother you," he said. "You need your sleep."

"I'll sleep," she said. "It would be okay…"

He brushed her hair back from her face and a few strands came out in his hand. "I'll be right back," he said. "Let me take care of my nighttime rituals."

"Mmm-hmm," she hummed.

He watched her as she gave up, let herself fall into an immediate deep sleep. Then he went to her guest bath, brushed his teeth, put away his clothes and got some pajama bottoms out of his overnight bag. He went back to her room, pulled the covers aside and got in beside her. Putting a hand on her hip, he whispered, "It's just me. I'm right here." She turned toward him with a soft moan and snuggled against him. "Don't wake up startled," he said. "It's just me."

"I know," she said. "That's nice, thank you." She snuggled closer. "There's nothing in it for you. Nothing."

He pulled her into his arms and cradled her against his chest. "Yes, there is," he whispered. He kissed her brow. "More than you realize…"

Marty got Jason into bed, then got into her nightgown and settled herself in bed—in the master bedroom that she shared with her husband. She could hear the soft talking of the TV in the family room, so she turned on the light and picked up her book. It wasn't long before Joe turned off the TV and came to bed. She stared at the pages of her book, unable to read while he got down to his boxers and crawled in beside her. Her clothes hung in her closet again; her beauty essentials shared space in the master bath. But nothing else had happened between them yet. At first he had kissed her good-night and turned his back on her to sleep. Eventually he had kissed her and faced her, but he still didn't touch her. Somewhere in the night he occasionally pulled her closer, as if out of habit, but they hadn't resumed the life of husband and wife. There was still a brick between them—the heavy weight of their short estrangement.

"Did you like him? Walt?" she asked when Joe was in bed.

"Nice enough guy."

"How about the doctor?"

"Sure," he said. "How about that? Beth and her cancer doctor?"

"I have a feeling that might've happened, anyway, even if she hadn't met him under these circumstances. They seem to have a nice chemistry."

"I guess," he said. He leaned toward her and gave her a friendly peck on the lips. As he would have pulled away, she put her hands on his cheeks and held him there. For a second he was just still, frozen, uncertain, and then he began to move over her lips, drinking her in. His hands found her waist and the book slipped off her lap and fell to the floor. Slowly, holding on to him, she sank lower in the bed against the pillows until he was over her. His breath started to come harder, hotter, and he kissed her for a long time before breaking away. "Marty," he said a little breathlessly. He looked into her eyes and his were shining. "What's going on with you?"

"I thought…maybe…you might be in the mood…"

He touched her lips briefly. Softly. "Not until you're sure where you're going," he said, his voice husky. "I'm not going back to that again. I can't live that way every time you're a little pissed off. This is our marriage I'm talking about here. This is the rest of my life as far as I'm concerned."

She sighed. "I feel like I almost made the biggest mistake of my life," she said. "Joe, we stopped trying to understand each other and took each other for granted. Let's keep working on us, huh? Not just me, not just you. Us."

"You sure?"

"I'm sure." She ran a hand along the short hair at his temple. "I love you. I do. I was real mad at you for a while. I'm sorry I didn't know a way to handle that better."

"What about that guy?" he asked. "I know who he is, you know. I'd like the truth about that."

"The truth is, he's the old boyfriend I broke up with years before I met you. The one I told you about before we even got engaged. And I've never been intimate with anyone but you since we met. I swear."

"Where's he come in? There's a little more to it, I think."

"Oh, there is," she said with a sad laugh. "Remember that night I left the house, all pissed off about the mess, and went to Martinelli's? You might not even remember—I spent half of the past two years pissed off about the mess."

"I remember."

"I drove around awhile, and when I finally ended up at Martinelli's to order pizzas to bring home, I was having a glass of wine at the bar, licking my wounds, and I ran into him there. A pure accident. I must have looked like a bunny in the snare—all down in the dumps, pathetic and teary. The son of a bitch actually made a play for me. He said all the things a woman who's upside down and miserable wants to hear—that he'd never gotten over me, we were always so good together, et cetera. I asked about his girlfriend—last I heard he was living with her. He said they'd broken up a year ago and if I ever wanted to get together for any reason, if I needed to talk…"

"You should've been talking to me," he said.

"Our talking hadn't started yet. I was still here in this bedroom back then, but so angry. The only talking we did was to snap at each other and move farther apart. It was all the things you said to me at dinner a couple months later that started to turn things around… I think you said those things before and I didn't hear you, just like you couldn't hear me. But you let me have it at dinner that night. You scared me, you know. You were pretty clear—if you couldn't have a real marriage, one with love, trust and forgiveness…a marriage that focused on working things out instead of living in separate bedrooms, you weren't about to hang around. Whew," she said, getting a little teary. "I wasn't prepared for that. I thought I was calling all the shots."

He brushed the hair back from her brow. "Did you call him, Marty?"

"I did. I asked him to meet me somewhere to dance. I wanted to have fun, feel like I was being courted or something. And of course, he tried to get me to go to bed with him. But I didn't, Joe. I ran for my life—I mean, literally. I bolted. I got out of there as fast as I could and I didn't call him again.

I'm sorry, I shouldn't have even chanced it. It was so stupid. Not only stupid—it could have cost me the most important relationship in my life." She took a breath. "I scared myself pretty good. I know you wouldn't be able to forgive that."

"Aw, Marty," he said, hurt. "I never thought you'd do something like that…"

"Neither did I. I'm pretty embarrassed about it. I didn't think I could be that big a fool! But, Joe, I didn't call him after that."

"But you were tempted. Weren't you tempted?"

She smiled at him. "Did you see him walk into that bar with Jill, who was wearing a very large engagement ring? She could've answered the phone when I called. That would have served me right. That was good for me, to be in the same place at the same time with the two of you— the lying, cheating asshole I got rid of years ago and the loving, committed partner I'm with now. It really put the spotlight on my life, showed me what I had and what I almost risked…" She laughed a little. "I shouldn't have even spoken to him, but I couldn't resist. I wanted her to know he's still just a manipulative, cheating liar, telling an old girlfriend he wasn't with his fiancée anymore."

"When was the last time you slept with him? Tell me the truth so we can move on…"

She lifted her head to place a quick kiss on his lips. "Over eight years ago," she said. "He might've stirred up some old memories when I was feeling down and out, but he didn't stir up anything else, Joe. I'm ashamed of myself for even thinking about him for five minutes."

"You think you know how you feel now? What you want?" he asked her.

"Yes. I want us to talk like we used to, to be considerate of each other's needs, to compromise and make our marriage

better every year instead of angry and confused and unfor-
giving. And I love it when you shave and shower before bed.
You'll get a better lover that way."

He grinned. "I thought women liked that rugged look..."

"This is better. It doesn't hurt my skin, for one thing."

He ran a knuckle along her cheek. "We gotta be careful
about that," he whispered. "Your skin is so soft..." He gave
her a short kiss. "Can I trust you now, Marty?"

"You can. You always could. I wasn't going to cheat on
you, Joe. There are two reasons I'd never do that—because
I know how it feels to be betrayed like that, and because I
know you'd never be able to forgive me. It would be the end
for you, and I might've been scared and lonely, but I wasn't
ready for us to be over..."

"I'm not going to go backward," he said, his voice a little hoarse. "I thought I lost you. I can't feel that way again,
Marty. You're everything to me. I can only move on if I'm
everything to you, too. I love you so much."

"Aw, Joe. It feels so good to hear that. Believe me, you're
everything."

"Show me," he said with a devilish smile.

She smiled back. "No. You show me, Joe."

He grinned. "Brace yourself..."

Julie was washing her face when Billy came up behind her,
slipped his arms around her waist and kissed the back of her
neck. "You did a very nice job on dinner tonight," he said.

"I didn't do much," she said. "I bought the meat, made the
cheesecake, brewed the coffee."

He started kissing down her back. "And you looked more
delicious than the food."

"Billy," she laughed. "Have you had too much to drink?"

"No. And I haven't had too much of you lately, either..."

"Can I dry my face?" she asked through laughter.

"I don't care. Do whatever you want…and do it fast…"

She grabbed the face towel, dried off and turned in his arms to meet his demanding kiss, his hands running up and down her back. When their lips parted, she said, "You smell like cigars."

He went after her neck. "It's that manly, musky, sexy smell. Give it a second—it'll turn you into a wild woman…"

"Do you think we could move out of the bathroom?"

"If you want…"

"I want," she said, pulling his hand, flipping off the light and heading to the bed. Before she could get there she found herself literally thrown on the bed with her husband on top of her. "For Pete's sake," she muttered. "I had a feeling you were in the mood, but you act like you haven't had sex in a year."

"I feel like I haven't. I'm getting so much sleep these days, I'm sure I'll be better than ever. Try me."

"I don't need you to be any better. But it might help if you were a little slower…"

"Okay," he said, tugging at her nightgown. "Let's get you naked and then I'll slow down. I promise."

She let him pull her gown over her head and fling it away. And then it began, the kissing and caressing, the sweet yet powerful physical love that had kept them so perfectly intimate since they were very young. I will still want him like this when I'm ninety, Julie thought, as his hands on her body brought all the familiar and delicious sensations that would culminate in a fiery satisfaction, leaving them soft and perfect in each other's arms. Then he would stay with her a while, holding her, whispering to her, praising her beauty and warmth, telling her how much he adored her.

"Hang on a second, baby…let me get the condoms…"

"I threw them out," she whispered.

He was jolted upright. He flipped on the bedside lamp. "You *what?*"

"I want one last shot at one last baby…"

"Oh, God," he said, rolling away from her. "I'm in hell— that's what this is. What are you talking about?"

She rolled onto her side and looked down into his eyes. "Before the last of those little sperms leave the last of our babies behind, I want to see if there's just one more in there."

He was quiet for a long moment, looking up at her, no longer as powerful as a steamroller. "You're totally out of your mind, right?"

"No. This is the first time I've felt like I'm sane. It's the first time we haven't been in desperate financial trouble. I'd give it a little more time, but there isn't more time…"

"Jules, you'll just be upset again…"

She shook her head. "I'm grieving that baby we lost. I feel so much regret, and it broke your heart even though it shouldn't have happened in the first place. I know we can't get it back, I understand that. And I also know this might not work. You probably only have five or six more chances before that vasectomy has your sperm count down to zero." She shrugged. "If we get a baby out of it, I'd love that. If we don't, it won't change how much we love each other."

"Julie, you're nuts. What if some disaster hits and we're strapped again—"

"I have it all worked out. I even called John, talked to him about it."

"You asked *John* if we could have another baby?"

"Well, not exactly. But I did tell him we'd lost a baby recently, that you'd had a vasectomy and there was still time to squeak one more baby out if we were quick, and that I wanted to try very badly. He said what I knew he'd say—he understood the feeling. He and his wife have four and they'd have four more if they could. So we talked about the money a little bit. I knew we were on the same page about that. Our medical is good, and for at least a few years another one isn't likely to make a significant financial impact. If it was the first baby, it could really trip us up budget-wise. That's one thing about a big family—you already have most of what you need. Billy, I even do my own diapers—disposables for Grandma and outings only. Our kids go from the breast to the table—we don't even buy fancy baby food. I know how to boil down carrots and mash peas."

"You've lost your mind."

"You don't want to? Wouldn't you like to see what I'm like when I'm actually all excited about a baby?"

"I have," he said. "You're always excited eventually, even when you know it's a bad idea..."

"I wish I'd tried everything to keep that baby instead of taking the chance I took. Billy, I was just so scared. I'm so sorry..."

He ran his fingers through her hair. "Baby, I'm not mad at you. You did the best you could with what you had on your plate. Nobody could take better care of our kids than you, even when the circumstances were impossible. I promise, I'm not upset with you."

"Okay, then we'll give it one last shot—"

"No," he said. "I'm not touching you till I have a chance to think about this in the clear light of day. Damn, you spoiled a potentially *great* roll in the hay! I think I really had my game on!"

"All right," she said somewhat morosely. "Really, I didn't think it was a bad idea at all. If I hadn't been so overwrought, we might be pregnant right now, anyway." She gave him a kiss. "And you love me pregnant."

"I love you not out of your mind and totally pissed off, too."

"Well, I thought I'd give it a try…"

"Why didn't you talk this over with me when you had your clothes on?" he asked a bit testily.

"I meant to. We were kind of busy…"

"Well, this is a shock. I have to think it over. I'm not sure it's a good idea."

"But if we hadn't lost that baby, you'd be happy."

"It's a weakness," he said with a shrug. "There's something about us, even broke and scared, giving life to that thing we have together…" He rubbed the back of her neck. "Jules, I don't think anyone else in the world has what we have. I have never, for one minute of one day, wondered about how much we love each other. I'd take that over a million bucks any day. When Joe told me Marty had moved out of their bedroom, I felt my gut just cinch in a knot. If that happened to us, I'd die inside."

"We won't let that happen to us. I don't know why we were this lucky—it's not as if either of us was old enough to know anything…"

"Well, we're this lucky. I don't know if we should tempt fate. We could get another wild lunatic like Clint."

"Or a nutcase like Clint in a girl suit…"

"Julie, Julie—what's the matter with you? Right now all I want in the world is to just love the hell out of you and you're talking babies… Why are you so crazy?"

She shrugged. "I never had that with you," she said. "I never actually had a chance to make a baby on purpose. I'm hopeless—I love kids. I love growing huge, having them, nursing them, playing with them, cleaning their awful rooms. I thought I was supposed to be sick of it pretty soon, start wanting to go back to school or something. But I'd rather have another baby than a boat or pool table. I admit, I hate being terrified the bank will take the house or PG&E will turn off the lights, but I never minded being careful, frugal. I'm kind of proud of how far I can stretch a dollar."

"You've been wanting a new couch real bad," he reminded her.

"I know. I'd like a new couch, but you only have five or six more ejaculations with viable sperm before it's over. And I can't save you until after we get a new couch… I like being a wife and mother. I think I'm pretty good at it."

"You're excellent at it…"

"It's not that it's enough for me. I'm not accepting it as my lot in life, it's everything. Ten years with you, and it's still everything."

"You think our love life could be any better if we were trying to make a baby?" he asked her.

"Nah," she said, shaking her head. "If it gets any better, it might kill me." She smiled at him. "I didn't throw them out," she said. "They're right in the drawer. You need to finish what you started. If you change your mind later, we still have a couple of outside chances at sneaking in one more…"

His eyes got big for a second. He rolled over and checked the drawer. He pulled one out and put it on the bedside table. "You didn't stick pins in these, did you?"

"No," she laughed.

"Because my brakes are not what they used to be."

"I know. That's one of my favorite parts…"

He rolled her gently onto her back, found her lips, let his hands enjoy their magic and, in no time at all, the steamroller mentality was back. For Billy, there was nothing in the world like the way Julie responded to him. Always. Even if she didn't want to. He worshiped her; she idolized him. There was nothing in his life closer to perfection than this love affair—it was steamy and virtuous, wild and pure. There had never been anyone else for him, for her. How many people had something like that? Every time they made love, it was like a primal force that bonded them even more closely. He felt a little more alive each time he could bring her pleasure, each time she gave herself completely to his pleasure. Married love like ours, he often thought, is as close to heaven as a man can get.

Ready, he reached for the little foil package. "You tired of holding back, baby?" he whispered. "You ready for the payoff?"

"Please," she whispered, her hands running over his chest, her lips on his neck.

He started to tear the package open, then froze for a second. He stared down into her smoldering eyes, gave her a light kiss and tossed the package away. He entered her sweetly, au naturel. "This may not work, you know…"

"It's never been up to us before, Billy," she whispered. "It won't be up to us this time, either."

13

It hadn't been very long since Cassie had realized she was in love with Walt, but it felt like forever. They were so comfortable together, so compatible. It was as if she'd known him since she was a girl. She kept asking herself if she'd ever felt this way before—this sure of her own feelings and his. She had a problem with rushing into things, but she hadn't done that this time. She'd kept Walt waiting a long time.

This was so different than any relationship she'd ever had. This time, rather than hoping to develop trust and confidence, it began with both already firmly in place. Instead of starting out with lust and infatuation, those things had followed a special bond, a deep friendship. And, oh, did the lust ever follow! Walt was a wonderful, tender yet powerful lover. When she was in his arms, no doubt in the world could disturb her. Never before had she felt so cherished, so secure.

There was talk of a gathering of his family soon, so she could meet all of them—Thanksgiving at the latest. In the meantime, they'd been out to dinner with Judy and Dick once more and had a Sunday brunch with Walt's older brother, his wife and three kids. Getting four boys and their families plus Mom and Dad all in one place at one time seemed to be something of a challenge with their schedules, but so far Cassie was very comfortable with everyone she'd met.

She'd finally been to his house. Small but very nice, just like he'd said. It was an older home—it had about fifty years on it—but it was reconditioned just beautifully with fresh paint, shiny hardwood floors and new appliances and countertops. And it was so tidy—that had shocked her.

"I admit, I went to a little trouble for the first showing," he said.

"It's almost brand-new inside," she said, looking around.

"I had some pretty good training at fixing up an old house," he said. "It might be in my blood."

So she and Steve had spent a couple of nights because, no matter what their work schedules, they couldn't stand to be apart. But typically they were at Cassie's house. She was the one with an early schedule in the E.R. most days. She'd get up at five-thirty and by the time she was dressed and ready to leave for work, Walt would be rising, heading for the coffeepot first, then into the shower. When they both had a day off, those bike rides didn't start so early.

On a not-very-typical day for them, Walt was the one up early. Cassie had a day off but Walt was needed at work first thing in the morning. He told her it could be a long day for him—it seemed there were quite a few things he had to finish up. But he promised he'd be caught up quickly so he could enjoy the weekend with her.

So Cassie thought she'd do a little shopping. The holidays were approaching and she always liked to buy a little at a time—it was the way she watched her spending carefully.

She spent the morning at Target and got Julie's kids taken care of. By about eleven, she was out of ideas. She'd like to get Walt something really special, but what do you buy a guy as simple and unpretentious as Walt? She had an impulsive idea; she could swing by the Roseville store and see if he was there. She hadn't done that in quite a while and that's where he spent the majority of his time. If she could coax him away for a quick cup of coffee or even lunch, maybe she could eke out of him what would make him happy.

Now that she'd taken the plunge into a relationship with him, she was learning that the bike dealership demanded a lot; this was a man who put in long hours. Seldom did a weekend go by that he didn't at least stop by to see if he was needed. That was good; he never seemed worn out and he clearly loved it. Plus, he liked to spend his money so he had to be about the business of making it! Walt was not afraid of hard work. And being a hard-working girl herself, that impressed Cassie. He was a rare bird.

When Cassie was on her way to his store, she wondered if he'd told anyone at work about her, about them. It was possible some of his coworkers knew and she was glad she wore her most expensive jeans, heeled boots, turtleneck sweater and dark wool jacket. Her hair was shiny and straight down her back, just the way he liked it. Walt loved scrunching her hair up in his big hands.

She hadn't been by there in a long time, but she recognized the same salesman on the showroom floor from months before. "Hi," she said. "Do you know if Walt Arneson is here today?"

"He sure is, I saw him," the guy said. "Let me ask about him."

He went to a phone on the sales counter, called someone and went back to her. "Someone's coming out to talk to you."

"Oh. Great," she said.

A woman in her fifties or so came out onto the floor. The salesman indicated Cassie and the woman approached her. "Hello," she said. "How can I help you?"

"I was looking for Walt Arneson," she said. "He's not expecting me. I thought I'd surprise him. Is that okay?"

"I'll have to know your name," she said, somewhat frostily.

Cassie immediately thought, Uh-oh. I'm going to get him in trouble. "Cassie Rasmussen," she said. "Really, I don't want to interrupt his schedule... I just thought if he could see me for a minute..."

"I'll check. Stay right here."

The woman whirled away and was gone. Cassie approached the salesman again and asked, "Excuse me. Who was that woman?"

"That would be Clarice, Walt's gatekeeper. Secretary." He smiled.

"He has a *secretary?*" she asked, totally shocked.

"Oh, yeah, and look out. She is a lioness. I don't think Walt loves it, but it works, you know? Everyone wants to talk to Walt personally. And he wants to talk to everyone personally, even if he doesn't have the time."

She remembered about the cell phone number he didn't give out too much. People liked to get his expertise over the phone, save themselves a trip into the shop. "Is that so?" she said.

"You looking for a bike? I'd be glad to help."

"No, thanks. I was just looking for Walt. But I didn't call ahead, so if he's tied up, I guess I'll have to... I could just leave," she said reluctantly.

"Wanna sit on a couple of new models while you wait?" he asked, grinning.

"Yeah, why not?"

So the salesman propped her up on several bikes in the showroom, showed her a very entertaining Harley Davidson video, gave her some statistics and when he started talking about their financing programs she looked at her watch and saw that forty-five minutes had lapsed.

"Thanks, but if I need any advice about Harley financing, I'll just ask Walt. I guess he can't break away. I'll let you get back to—"

"Cassie!" she heard Walt say. He came around the counter and approached her and she nearly fainted. It was Walt all right—ponytail, long sideburns, moustache and all, but he was also wearing a starched long-sleeved shirt and a tie with his pleated slacks and dress boots. He walked right up to her, put his hands on her shoulders and leaned down to kiss her briefly on the lips. "Is anything wrong, honey?"

"No. I thought I'd surprise you and take you out to coffee or even lunch, but…" She lifted the tie off his chest. "You weren't wearing this when you left this morning."

"I swung by the house and changed. I had to be a little more formal today."

"I think I caught you in the middle of things. This is odd…"

He looked a bit uncomfortable. He fidgeted, then took her elbow and said, "Come with me, honey. Come on," he said.

He pulled her through the break in the counter, back into an area that seemed to be made up of small offices. He stopped in front of Clarice. She scowled up at him unhappily. "Clarice," he said, "this is Cassie, my girlfriend. She never waits, all right? Never. Got that?"

"Got it," Clarice said. "You have board members in the—"

"Get them lunch. Order in and tell them I'll be right back. Come here, honey," he said, pulling her into another office. It was small but classy, lots of models, pictures of Harleys, trophies and awards decorated the shelves and walls. The desk was huge, cluttered with paperwork, stacks of files, and there was a window into a boardroom, a long table around which mostly middle-aged and older men sat, all wearing ties.

"What's up, Cassie?" he asked.

"What's up?" she repeated, looking through the window. "I should ask you that."

"Board meeting. I'm sorry, I had no idea you'd be stopping by today. I'm locked into this—it's important."

"Walt," she said, confused, "why in the world…"

"Honey, I didn't mean to tell you this way, but here it is—this is my store. It's my company. We're going to buy a store in Reno. They're board members and financiers. Bankers. It's going to be a long day. I'm sorry. I don't think I can get away."

She swallowed. "Your…*company?*"

"Yeah. Well, I have investors."

She looked through the glass again and saw Walt's father, Dick. Dick smiled and waved at her. She waved back weakly.

"He didn't buy it for me," Walt said quickly. "It was like I said—I went to work for a store, did what I could do, but then the owners wanted to sell. So I rounded up some investors, was in hock for a little while, got myself out of debt and bought another store and… Just like my dad did with the grocery stores—I had good training. I work on bikes, Cassie. I sell 'em, I take care of customers, I do a little of everything."

Cassie caught her breath. "You own this store?"

"Well, it's a franchise. There are four stores. Reno would be the fifth. But, yeah, I own 'em. And they own me."

"Do you have a title? What's your title?"

"Titles," he said. "They don't really mean any—"

"What?" she insisted.

"Chairman of the Board of Riders, Inc., CEO and President. It's a Harley franchise, a Riders, Inc., chain. It's a nice little business."

"Walt, it doesn't sound *little.*"

"It's doing great," he admitted.

"Why didn't you *tell* me?" she demanded. "You were talking about how you'd work as hard as you had to and... Why didn't you *tell* me?"

"Cassie, I kept telling you I had plenty of money. I'm sorry, honey. It was weird. Right away you started talking about how I was just a mechanic. Just a bike mechanic who shouldn't be spending his money. Honey, if we were going to fall in love, I wanted you to fall for Walt the bike mechanic, not Walt the..."

"The *what?*"

"The guy who owned a company. Now come on, nothing's different except you don't have to worry so much about me spending money on you. That's all that's different."

"But you misled me," she said quietly, disbelievingly, shaking her head.

"No, I really didn't. I'm still this," he said, his hands on his chest. "I like to work on bikes, take long rides, visit with the customers. I have a ponytail, a naked lady on my arm and I dress funny. That's the guy I am, Cassie, and even if I had ten stores, I'm still going to be this guy. I don't care about the other stuff. I care about the store. The people—the ones who come here to shop or for maintenance, and the ones who work for me. I like motorcycles. I don't want to shave or cut my hair. I thought it was worth the gamble." He eyes sparkled. "Was it worth the gamble?"

"Walt, you should have told me."

"At first, I just didn't want to make myself... I don't know... more acceptable. More presentable. I wanted you to go for me the way I am. Then I decided I'd save the details for when we were sure of each other, had talked about the future a little. I'm sorry, maybe that wasn't a good idea, but you held me off a long time. I never—"

"Was your family in on it? Did everyone know I thought

you were a dirt-poor motorcycle wrench and plot with you to keep the truth from me?"

"No," he insisted. "No, I never said anything about anything. This—it's just between you and me. Ironing out the details."

"What if it had come up? What if your dad asked you about the company when I was around?"

"Well, he did, a couple of times, but I don't think you even noticed. So did my brother, when we were with them. If it had come up sooner, if you had questions, I wouldn't have lied about it. But you had this idea about me..."

"Yeah," she said in a breath. "You must have thought it was pretty funny—me going on about how we might have to tighten up, about how I could work more overtime if I needed to..."

"No, honey, that wasn't funny, it was sweet. I wasn't making fun of you."

"There were a dozen times you could've stopped me and said, 'Don't worry about the big check, Cassie—I'm loaded.' How about that first ride—the seven-hundred-dollar jacket?" She shook her head and tears came into her eyes. "You have no idea how much I worried I was going to sweat in it or get makeup on it." She swallowed convulsively. "You could've said right then that it was *your* jacket. That the whole thing is *yours*."

"Cassie, listen, I thought when I laid it out for you, it would be good news."

"Walt, tell me the truth now—are you a millionaire?"

He shrugged. "Maybe on paper..."

"Just on paper?"

"Okay, probably. I'm not strapped for cash, all right? I'm pretty much set."

"Were you afraid if I found out you're rich, I'd fall in love with your money? Is that it? And then you'd never be sure…"

"Aw, Cassie, no," he said, reaching for her.

And what if I had? she asked herself. She skittered out of his reach. "What a hoot," she said, her voice shaky. "I trusted you a lot quicker than you trusted me."

"That's not—"

"Yeah, it's true. For months I've been worrying about how you're getting by, whether taking me out so much was going to put a strain on your paycheck, since you wouldn't even split the cost of a meal. A while back I even thought about not seeing you anymore if you were going to spend so much of your hard-earned money on things that… Things that didn't matter that much. Like wine that cost a hundred dollars." She shook her head. "Do you know how many hours I have to work for something like that?" she asked, a tear spilling down her cheek.

"This is all wrong," he said. "This wasn't supposed to happen like this. I knew you worried about things like that, but then I thought you'd be relieved to know that I'm not…"

"Not what, Walt? Not honest?"

"Honey… Cassie, I never meant for this to hurt you. I wanted it to make you feel better about things. It made me feel so proud that you couldn't stop from loving me even when you thought I didn't have a pot to piss in. It wasn't to keep you from falling in love with the money—I don't care about that. It was more about not changing who I am to try to fit some idea of what you'd find most acceptable. It's the same as not shaving so your friends would like me better."

"Sure," she said quietly. "Listen, you're tied up. Go back to your meeting. We'll connect later, okay?" She smiled tremulously. "I should've called ahead. I just didn't realize…who you were."

"Cassie, come on. It wasn't a game. It just wasn't the most

important part about us. Don't hold this against me. I didn't want to sidetrack you with...stuff. What we have—"

"I'm going to go, Walt. I might need to think about this a little bit. I'll talk to you later. Get back to your...board."

She turned away from him and made fast tracks past Clarice, past the salesman and to her car, where she put her hands over her eyes and cried. It was only seconds before her cell phone rang. She plucked it out of her purse and there he was, on the caller ID. Well, she just couldn't deal with him now— she had to think. She turned off the phone.

Cassie drove to the river where she liked to walk Steve. She parked and cried. He knew, she thought. The whole time he knew I was trying not to get involved with him, that he just wasn't the kind of guy I saw myself with. It wasn't as though he had to guess—eventually she *told* him! And the truth really stung. If she'd found out five months ago he was a millionaire, it might've changed her whole perspective. There's a great deal of difference between an eccentric and a loser. She'd had trouble seeing he was neither; it had taken her months! For a girl who'd been searching for that forever man, that perfect partner, he might have been too much to resist if she'd known the truth about him. Of course it didn't hurt that he was also wonderful, but wonderful or not, she'd been held back by a tattoo and a ponytail for a real long time.

Julie had said so. *What if he shaved, cut his hair and had a stethoscope hanging around his neck? Would you worry about us meeting him then?* Of course she wouldn't! This biker dude's presentation was weird and extreme, at least in the circles she moved in. She remembered her absolute surprise to find he was delightful and that almost everyone seemed to like him.

She wasn't sure what was harder—the thought that he'd found her resistance funny, knowing he could snag her quickly with the bottom line. Or was it the fact that poor, simple, penny-pinching Cassie worried about his spending on her, giving her things she'd never be able to afford to give herself? Or maybe it amused him just observing her—the way she slowly had to come to terms with her feelings, lowering her standards to accept an undereducated, low-paid bike mechanic.

She felt humiliated. And then something occurred to her as she drove home. Of course, the message light was flashing wildly; he was going to try to make this little mistake of not revealing himself sooner just go away. She ignored it, not listening to the messages. Instead, she got on the computer, researching Richard Arneson. And, oh, my Lord—of course it wasn't just Walt who'd made good. It was first his father. The Arnesons were wealthy; they gave money to more charities than she knew existed.

He knew—they probably all knew—in the back of her mind she was thinking he wasn't good enough for her when it was she—the poor girl who'd been on her own since the age of fourteen—who probably wasn't good enough for him.

The phone rang and she looked at the caller ID before picking up. It was Jules. She answered tearfully.

"Thank God—I've been looking for you! You haven't answered any phones!"

"I had a little…problem…"

"Well, your problem can wait. We're at Beth's. She collapsed at work. I brought her home and Marty came over. She's bad, Cassie. I don't know what's wrong."

She sniffed back tears. "I'm on my way."

Cassie tapped quietly at Beth's front door and Julie let her in, a finger to her lips. "She's sleeping. On the couch."

"What happened?" Cassie said, coming inside.

"I'm not sure," Julie said. "She collapsed at the clinic and didn't come to right away, but she wouldn't be admitted. She called me to come and pick her up. Cassie, she couldn't walk to the car! I had to take her in a wheelchair. I called Jerod. He's on his way over from the Bay Area. He's called twice from the car to see if she's all right."

"Let me see her," Cassie said, shedding her jacket and handing it to Julie. She went immediately to the small living room where Beth lay pale and still on the sofa. She knelt beside her, touched her brow, took her pulse, which was weak and kind of thready.

Beth turned her head, looked at Cassie and said, "I'm just weak from chemo," she said. "I just need to rest. Nothing to get excited about."

"You shouldn't be this weak," Cassie said.

"I just wanted some attention," Beth said with a small smile.

"Oh, you'll get plenty—Julie called Jerod and he's on his way."

"Oh, God, she shouldn't have done that. He has patients. He's two hours away."

"Be still—you know he'd expect to be called. Do you have any pain? Anywhere?"

"No. I'm just bone tired, that's all. And light-headed. The fatigue can be unbelievable."

"Your breathing is okay?"

"It's not an embolism," Beth said. "Just fatigue and weakness."

"Close your eyes. Rest. We'll be right in the kitchen."

Cassie rose and herded Marty and Julie out of the room. "Let's let her sleep. How long before Jerod gets here?"

Julie looked at her watch. "Within a half hour, I would think."

"Come on. We'll leave her alone and I'll check on her every five minutes."

They went to the adjacent kitchen where Marty had brewed

a pot of coffee. She got herself a refill and went to the table where Julie sat behind her own cup. "When did this happen?" Cassie asked, going to the cupboard for a cup.

"A couple of hours ago, I guess. She's not...you know..."

"What?" Cassie asked.

"She's not..." Julie mouthed the word *dying.*

"Dying?" Cassie whispered. "Oh, God, no! I mean, she's gotten real thin and her pulse is kind of weak, but she's been sleeping." Cassie joined them at the table. "Jerod will know what to do. I bet he puts her right in the hospital..."

"Where *were* you?" Julie whispered furiously. "I couldn't find you! I was scared to death. I didn't know what to do with her!"

"Sorry," she said. "I turned off my phone. Walt's been calling and calling."

"Why didn't you answer? Are you fighting or something?"

"No. Yes. I don't know..." She put her forehead in her hand. "It's a mess. I found out he's been lying to me. I was pretty upset, till you trumped him with Beth."

"Lying to you?" Marty whispered, scooting forward a little. "About what?"

"He's not a bike mechanic... He let me think that. For months! The whole time he was trying to win me over, just ever so patiently, giving me all the time in the world to fall for a complete fraud."

"Oh, God," Marty said, sitting back. "He's a Hells Angel!"

"Shh," Cassie shushed. "He's not a Hells Angel! He's a millionaire."

Complete silence answered her. Finally Julie said, "Well. Bummer."

"Wait a minute—he's a millionaire? Pretending to be a *biker?*"

"No, he's a biker. Sort of. I mean, he doesn't just work at

the bike shop. He owns it. He owns four of them and is in the middle of buying a fifth one. He let me think he was this dirt-poor grease monkey. He teased me about being afraid of how my friends would take to someone like him—he looks like such a hood."

Again, there was silence. "Um, Cass, you're not happy to find out he's not just a biker? What's up with that?"

"Don't you get it? He was holding out on me, probably to be sure I wouldn't fall for the money, the title..."

"What title?"

"Chairman of the Board. CEO. President. All of them, I guess."

"Well, I mean, that's very nice," Julie said, "but isn't it a small company? Are you sure he's a millionaire?"

"Oh, yeah, I asked. He admitted it. I don't know how big his company is, but I went home and researched his family. His parents—they're richer than God, invested in everything. Arneson Limited. Arneson family holdings. Arneson this, Arneson that. And here I was, afraid of sweating in the leather jacket he let me use on rides. He can probably afford to wipe his butt with leather jackets. He must have been laughing behind his fist the whole time."

"But he finally told you the truth?"

"No, I *caught* him! I went by the store to entice him out to lunch. I was going to get out of him what he'd like for Christmas." She laughed a little and her eyes welled up with tears. "I thought I'd go crazy, spend a hundred dollars on him. Maybe two hundred. I found him in a shirt and tie, in the middle of a board meeting. A shirt and tie? Jesus."

"What did he say?"

She sighed and a big tear rolled out. "He said that he thought I'd take it as good news."

"Why can't something like that ever happen to me?" Julie asked wearily. "I'd be a much better sport about it."

"Don't you get it?" Cassie said. "I've been holding back for months! I liked him right off, but I didn't want to get hooked up with some loser biker who'd never make anything of himself! The whole time I was thinking he wasn't quite good enough for me, he was making sure I was good enough for him!"

There was sound from the living room and all three women jumped up and hurried there. Beth had propped herself up on the couch pillows a little bit and was laughing softly, weakly. "You're better than vitamin B-12. Bring that gossip in here."

"You should be resting," Cassie said, sitting on the end of the sofa.

"Through this?" she said, amused. "He's a millionaire? Did I hear that right?"

"Man, do you have good ears. We were whispering."

"I have cancer, I'm not deaf. Besides, I'm more likely to strain to hear whispering."

Cassie sighed. "How's your stomach? Any nausea?"

"Not anymore. I'm past that and on to fatigue. I'm sorry for all the trouble."

"You're less trouble than some people," Cassie said. "I'm getting you a glass of orange juice." When she came back from the kitchen with a full glass in her hand, Julie was helping Beth sit up a little more.

Beth took a sip and said, "Really, you're the only person I know who'd be upset to find out her boyfriend is stinking rich. Don't you ever get tired of being so screwed up?"

"I was just thinking, I could probably learn to live with that," Marty said. "Is he tidy? Clean?"

"Very," Cassie said. "He looks like he should be a wreck, but he's not. He even gets manicures to keep his nails and hands nice after working on bikes. Apparently he really does work on bikes. But he lied to me."

"God, a chairman of the board who actually works on the bikes. I like him better all the time," Marty said.

"But I feel like a fool," Cassie said. "It's humiliating."

"Now why would you feel that way? It's not your fault he didn't tell you!"

"Because. He was right. I had to be strung along like that. I'm always looking for the wrong things in men—that's why I never find the real good ones. I look at the car and not the driver, which is how I find these jerks who look like they have potential, but they're worthless. I think he knew that about me. I think I *told* him that about me! So, to be sure I was seeing the man without seeing the fat wallet, he just let me believe he was a big nobody." She sniffed and wiped at her nose. "He's not a loser, though, and I don't mean the money. I mean, as a man, he's an exceptional man."

"Well, there's the real bottom line," Julie said.

"Lucky you," Beth said. "No more jerks and losers. If you can just find a way to suffer under the strain of having money for a change, you should be able to soldier on."

The doorbell rang and Julie jumped up. Jarod hurried into the room carrying his medical bag, closely followed by a uniformed messenger. He knelt beside Beth, kissed her forehead and opened his bag, pulling out a stethoscope. "Miss me?" he asked.

"I'm sorry about this," she said. "It was an overreaction. It's completely unnecessary."

"I doubt that," he said, listening to her heart. He sat her up and listened to her back. "Deep breath. Nice. Once more." Then he let her lie back down. "I'm going to get some blood work. I'm having it delivered to the lab by messenger with a stat order."

"I don't think I have any to spare," she said. "This is probably just normal. Though I don't remember fatigue and weakness this intense the last time."

"The treatment this time is more aggressive," he said, getting out his blood-draw supplies. He slipped a full tube into an envelope, handed it to the messenger, then pulled out an IV setup.

"Oh, you're going way overboard..."

"Are you milking this cow?" he asked. "I thought I was the doctor and you were the patient." He got the IV started. "You should be in the hospital..."

"I doubt it," she said.

"It would have saved me a messenger and I could get the results faster. It would have been more convenient. I see you gathered the troops..."

"I was just looking for a ride..."

"That so?" he asked. "You're done working now, until you complete your treatment and get a little stronger. I'll stay with you tonight, then I'll take you back to San Francisco. I'm turning you over to my partner—I'm sure you'll like him fine. I doubt he'll change anything. You'll stay with me where I can keep an eye on you."

"My parents will have a fit about that."

"Right. But you didn't want them trying to take care of you, anyway—they just get anxious and create more havoc than help. They're well-suited for having a fit. Besides, it's time I met them, don't you think?"

"I don't want you to take care of me," she said. "It'll ruin our relationship."

"You being so far away from me while you're going through this is more likely to ruin our relationship. Don't argue—I'm good at this. I'm going to get you through this so we can have a life."

She put a hand against his cheek and said, "How did I find you?"

He smiled and put his hand over hers. "The hard way."

Walt pulled up to Billy and Julie's in his truck. His shirt-sleeves were rolled up, collar open and the tie lay on the front seat. Billy was in the driveway, looking under the hood of one of the cars when he saw Walt walk toward him.

"Got a problem there, Bill?"

"Yeah. I hope it's the battery, but it won't jump. Could be many things."

"Want me to have a look?"

"Ah, you seem to be a little dressed up there, Walt."

"Nah. Here, let me. I was hoping to find Cassie here, but I don't see her car..."

"They're all over at Beth's. She passed out at work and Julie went to pick her up, take her home."

"Oh, man," he said. "She all right?"

"Yeah. Julie called. She said Jerod came right away, did some blood work, checked her over, started an IV. She's coming around. Jerod says it's side effects from the chemo and he's bringing her home with him, where he can take care of her. The girls are probably just getting in the way by now."

"Damn," Walt said. "Cassie's having a real bad day." He bent to look through Billy's toolbox, then went to the back of his truck and got his own. He opened it up on the driveway, selected a wrench and got back under the hood.

"I'm glad you stopped by. I was gonna try to find you at work. I have to tell you something."

"What's that?" Walt asked from under the hood.

"Me and Joe—we went to see Ken Baxter, captain over at that northwest firehouse. I told him." Walt lifted his head and glared at Billy through narrowed eyes. "I thought he should know one of his boys used his name to pick up a girl, then attacked her. I gave him the details. He was pretty pissed."

Walt stared him down for a long moment, then got back under the hood.

"Then we ran into Perkins on the way out. I asked him if he remembered Cassie, and he played dumb. Couldn't place her, he said. So I said, 'You know, front seat of your car, rescued by a big biker, broken window, et cetera.' He didn't respond at all, but he got it. And I told him she'd been one of my best friends for about fifteen years and he should know we're all watching him real close. No one knows what kind of creep he is, but I bet he doesn't use his captain's name to pick up girls anymore."

Walt dug around a little bit more under the hood, then said, "Try to start the engine, would you?"

"Sure." Billy got in his car, but it wouldn't turn over. He got back out.

Walt put the hood down and picked up a rag to wipe his hands on. "You tell him about me?"

"I didn't name you, if you're worried about that..."

"Why would I worry? He should come looking for me. That would be fun."

Billy laughed. "I told him we'd gotten real cozy with the biker who broke his window. He went a little pale. The important thing is, it won't come back on Cassie, not with a witness, with a bunch of F.D. knowing what he did. He wouldn't dare."

"The police also know. I gave them all the information. Did I mention my brother is a cop?"

"Jeez, Walt, you're just full of surprises," Billy said.

"Yeah, you don't know the half of it. So my brother, he said they were looking into this guy. If anyone else had reported him or someone who fits his description for something like that, it should have turned up by now. I told my brother if they ever need witnesses, I'd be there for him, and I was pretty sure Cassie would be, too. I guess it doesn't hurt that people know about him. He'll either straighten up or get caught. Either way, he's not getting away with it." He handed Billy the rag. "It's the starter. I'll get a new one, bring it out tomorrow or the next day. I get parts practically free. You need a car?"

"No, we're okay with the other one. Gee, that's awful nice of you, Walt. I hate to take advantage of you."

"You're not. I like this stuff. Glad to help. I have to find Cassie." He started to walk away. Then he turned back. "Listen, I got in a little trouble with Cassie and I don't want to be in the same place with you. What I told you—I work on bikes and do a lot of other things at the stores—that's true. But one of the other roles I play is owner. I'm the owner."

"Of the bike store?" Billy asked. "You own a Harley franchise?"

"Five of them," he said. "Almost. Number five won't close for two months."

"Well, holy shit, Walt! Didn't you think that was important?"

"To tell the truth, I didn't," he said. "It has a funny effect on some people. It had a real strange effect on Cassie, as a matter of fact. She wants to kill me right now. She thinks I was tricking her. I wasn't. I wasn't real smart about it, though. I guess I should've told her a lot sooner than I did." He put his hands in his pockets. "Do I need to apologize to you, too?"

"Hell, no," Billy laughed. "Good for you, man. Does that mean I have the manager putting in a starter for me?"

"No," he said. "The chairman. President. I have eight managers, three directors and two hundred employees, give or take."

Billy grinned and shook his head. "Unreal. Um, Walt? You got a little grease on your good shirt there."

Walt looked down. "It's okay. I have another one."

★ ★ ★

While Marty and Julie went home to their families, Cassie stayed at Beth's for a long time. She and Jerod put together a light supper and visited while Beth slept. It was the first time they'd ever had a long conversation, just the two of them, and he convinced her that no matter how it appeared at the moment, barring unforeseeable complications, Beth was going to pull through this with an excellent prognosis. Cassie knew what those complications were—embolisms, allergic reactions, aplastic anemia—all unusual, all best watched for in the hands of a physician.

The lab called Jerod's cell phone and gave him the results of Beth's blood workup. She was severely anemic—a combination of the chemotherapy's power to destroy healthy blood cells and her loss of appetite. He was going to take care of that right away, but it explained Beth's intense fatigue.

They talked a little while about Walt's surprise, as well. Jerod didn't show as much humor about it as the girls had, but neither was he shocked. "I wondered if there was a little more to him than met the eye. Very sharp fellow."

"I can't get over feeling he set me up, tricked me."

"You think that?" Jerod asked. "Maybe it's no more fun being judged as a financial success than it is to be judged as an ordinary biker with few prospects."

"He shouldn't have kept it from me, though."

"Perhaps not," Jerod said. "But try to keep this in perspective, Cassie."

"You mean, remember that he didn't conceal a prison record, but rather a huge success as a businessman?"

"No, that's not what I meant at all. Neither one of you is sick. Please, if you care about each other, give yourselves a break. It could be so much worse."

"God," Cassie said. "For a smart woman, I have been really stupid lately…"

Jerod put a gentle hand against her cheek. "Cassie, Cassie, you're just trying to figure out who you love and why. It's okay to be a little confused. But please, now that you've had a chance to see it all, weigh it all, remember your perspective. The plus side of all this is heavy."

"Yeah," she said in a whisper.

When Cassie pulled up to her small house, it was all dark. She should've left a light on for Steve. Then she saw someone lurking around her front door and her heart almost stopped. She quickly locked her car doors as the shadowy figure stood. She let out a sigh of relief as she recognized Walt, slowly rising from the front step. Parked not very far away from him, partially concealed by a tree and some shrubs, she saw his bike.

She got out of the car, but stayed right by it. "What are you doing here?"

"You won't call me back," he said. He lifted his hands; he was bearing gifts again. "I had to at least see you, Cassie. I wanted to say I'm sorry again."

"How long have you been here? Waiting?"

"I don't know." He shrugged. "Since five or so. What time is it?"

"You've been sitting there for hours?"

"I guess. My butt's asleep."

"What have you got there?"

"Flowers and wine. Grocery-store flowers, jug wine. No cork. I'm not a fancy guy, but I like you to have the best. You and my folks. You know."

She laughed a little bit. "Grocery-store flowers?"

"They look pretty shitty to me, but if that's what you

ROBYN CARR

want… I thought maybe we could put 'em in water, have a couple glasses of this bad wine and talk things over."

"Walt, you don't drink wine when you're on your bike."

"I could, if I…stayed awhile."

She slammed the car door closed and walked toward him.

"If you give me another chance, I promise not to keep anything from you again," he said.

"Would you dress the naked lady?"

"For you, I would. If I dress her, she'll be wearing a nurse's uniform." He grinned largely. "And I could get *Property of Cassie* tattooed on my biceps."

He made her laugh. He always made her laugh. "I was a little upset," she said.

"I know. And you were right to be—I shouldn't have done that. I never mentioned this, but women kept trying to fix me up. My mom, women in the office—they probably all think I'm hopeless. I hated it—it never worked. It was kind of fun getting to know you on my own, having you think I was, you know, just a simple guy who worked hard and would probably never amount to that much. And you went for me, anyway. It was wrong, but it was cool. Made me feel special. But I shouldn't have…"

"I was embarrassed," she said. "I thought I was seeing you for exactly what you were, and it turned out I wasn't seeing you at all. You must be brilliant, to turn a job at a bike shop into four stores. But I didn't even see that."

"Five," he said. "I got the store in Reno."

"Congratulations."

"I'm not brilliant, Cassie. I'm smart enough, but I have smarter people all around me and the smartest thing about me is I *know* they're smart, and I *listen*. Cassie, honey, I hated having you mad at me."

"I was just being stubborn," she said. "I think I might be

over it now." She looked at the flowers. "Yeah, I'll get over it. I can get used to better flowers, too."

"Yeah? Wait till you taste the wine. Cassie, I want to marry you. Get married, have kids, get a playmate for Steve. I want it all with you. You over being mad enough to do that? Marry me?"

"When?" she asked.

"As soon as we can. Maybe when Beth's better. We can't get it done without your girls. Your girls are as important to you as my family is to me."

"You're thinking of Beth at a time like this?" she asked.

"Sorry," he said. "Yeah, I was thinking about her. We're so lucky, Cass—our worst problems aren't that bad. Jerod says she's gonna be just fine and I believe him, but it's gonna take a while for her to get on her feet. That's okay, isn't it? I mean, it's not like we're saving ourselves for marriage…"

"Walt," she said, shaking her head at him and laughing. "That's wonderful, that you considered her. My girls, they are my family."

"So will you do it? Marry me? Have a dozen kids?"

"I'll marry you," she said. "Because I adore you. And I'll start with one and see where we end up, but I don't think I have time to squeak in a dozen. Thank God."

He pulled her close, still holding the cheap flowers and bad wine. "I love you so much," he said. "I never thought I'd get to feel like this."

"I was afraid I'd never get to, either," she said. "And to think, I could've missed you."

"It would've happened somehow," he said. "The important thing to me is you never tried to change me. God, do you have any idea how beautiful that is?"

She smiled up into his gorgeous blue eyes and said, "But if I marry you, if I have children with you, I am completely and entirely in charge of when the little ones get around a motorcycle. *Completely* in charge. You have to agree to that."

"Aw, Cassie. I wouldn't take any chances like—"

"How much do you want to marry me? Because I'm an E.R. nurse, I'm going to stay one, and that's a deal breaker."

"Are you going to be ridiculous about it?" he asked. "Because I own a bike company."

"Possibly. How bad do you want to marry me and have children with me?"

He didn't have to think long. "I guess if you have 'em, you can pull rank on certain things. After going through labor and everything," he said in something of a pout. "You know, my mother already likes you, but I have a feeling she's going to really love you pretty soon."

"Yeah, she told me. She fought that bike stuff, but she lost. Walt, I'm not going to lose. I'm the last word on that. You'll wait for me to approve. Yes?"

"Yes," he said slowly. "Anything else?"

She grinned at him, tightened her arms around him. "That's pretty much everything. You don't even have to dress the naked lady. I think she's growing on me." She got on her toes to kiss him. "Really, you're just right."

★ ★ ★ ★ ★

Turn the page for a sneak peek at
The Family Gathering
An emotional tale of fresh starts and finding home at
Sullivan's Crossing
by #1 New York Times *bestselling author Robyn Carr.*
Available now from MIRA Books.

1

DAKOTA JONES PULLED RIGHT UP TO THE BARN
that was now a house, and parked beside his brother's truck.
He left his duffel in the Jeep SUV and went to the door. He
stood in indecision for a moment—they had a six-month-old
baby. He knocked rather than ring the bell, just in case the
child was sleeping. A few moments later, he knocked again.
And a third time. Finally the door opened.

"Dakota!" Cal said with a grin. "What are you doing here?"

"I came by way of Australia. It's a long story—"

"I can't wait to hear what that's about," Cal said. "Want to
come in or stand out there awhile longer?"

"I don't want to wake the baby," Dakota said.

"The baby is in Denver with Maggie. They'll be back tonight."

"That sounds like an interesting arrangement," Dakota said.

"Like a tug-of-war, my friend. Something to drink?" Cal
offered. "Food?"

"A cold beer would be nice." He looked around. The place

was beautiful, but that came as no surprise. Cal's house with his first wife had been a showplace. Given the way the Jones siblings had grown up, something like a good, solid house that a person was proud to come home to would fill a need that had been neglected when they were kids. Cal put a beer in Dakota's hand. "The place looks great," Dakota said.

But Cal didn't respond to that. Instead, he said, "What were you doing in Australia?"

"I'd never been there," he said. "I wanted to walkabout. That's when—"

Cal cut him off with a laugh. "I know what a walkabout is." He tilted his beer toward Dakota in a toast. "I've never seen you with that much hair. On your face and everything."

Dakota stroked his beard. "I could probably use a trim."

"Why don't you tell me what's going on before Maggie and Elizabeth get home."

"Well, in Australia I visited one of the Rangers I served with years ago and together we checked in on another one. Then, with some input from them, I hit out on the trail for about a month, seeing some of the country, camping, fishing, practicing the identification and avoidance of snakes and crocodiles—"

"I meant, the Army! You're out? I knew you weren't happy there anymore. You said we'd talk about it someday."

"I wasn't sure where I'd end up but I was sure I'd get out here for a visit. With you and Sierra here and a new baby—I wanted to at least drop by."

Cal sighed. "Dakota. The Army."

"Well, I'm a little surprised I was in as long as I was. I never intended to make it a career. I wanted their offer of free travel and education."

Cal just lifted one brow. *Free travel? To a variety of war zones?*

Dakota grinned. "I had a small disagreement with a colonel.

We didn't see things the same way. Apparently I was insubordinate. It was time to think about doing something new."

"Were you honorably discharged?" Cal asked, pushing him.

Dakota shook his head. "But I wasn't dishonorably discharged."

He was simply discharged, but that said something. You had to screw up pretty bad to not get an honorable discharge.

"What'd you do?" Cal asked.

"I disagreed with his forward action and told him it would get people killed. Rangers—it could get Rangers killed. I had ten or a hundred times the experience he had but he was in competition with me or something because he was hellbent to drive five of our best Rangers right into the known hotbed of ISIS training and it was going to get people dead. I think they plucked that idiot out of the motor pool and put him in charge of a unit. I overrode his orders and he threatened me with jail. I thought that it was probably time for a career change."

"They sent you home?" Cal asked. "You must have done something even worse than disagree for them to send you home!"

Dakota squirmed. "I was acting in the best interest of my men."

"What'd you do?" Dakota didn't answer. "You hit him or something?"

"No, my guys wouldn't let me do that," he said. Then he hung his head briefly. "I let the air out of the tires until I could get in touch with another colonel I know who could try to intercede with the orders that would put us directly in harm's way."

"Jeeps?" Cal asked.

"No. MRAPs."

"MRAPs?"

"Mine resistant assault protective vehicles. The big ones."

"Those big mammoth desert beasts with tires taller than I am?" Cal asked. "How the hell do you let the air out of those?"

"With a .45," he said softly. "Or M16."

"You *shot* out the tires? How is it you're not in jail?"

"I was. Good behavior," he said. "And it was determined the colonel was incompetent and had done even worse things before. Cal, he was crazy. Homicidal. He had no idea what he was doing. He wasn't a Ranger—he had very little combat experience. He was a joke. I wasn't going to let him get any more people killed."

They sat in heavy silence for a little while, each tilting their beer bottle a couple of times. Finally Dakota broke the silence.

"Listen, it happens in the military sometimes. They take a guy who just made rank and give him a unit to command and sometimes the fit is bad. A buddy of mine, a doctor, his boss had no experience in the medical corps. He was a pilot. And he was making decisions for a bunch of doctors and a hospital that were dangerous to the patients, but he wouldn't compromise, he wouldn't listen to reason, he wouldn't ask for advice. According to my friend, people were left untreated, in pain, mishandled. A whole fleet of doctors mutinied and the colonel retaliated. That kind of thing doesn't happen all that often—usually there's at least one clear head in the game…" He took a breath. "They got my guy from the knitting battalion, I think. Jesus, I've worked for a few dipshits, but this one was exceptional."

"But you got out. With three years to retirement."

"Yeah, I have plenty of time for my next career move," he said. Then he grinned. "I'm still a kid."

"So you went walkabout," Cal said with a laugh. "Proving you're just like the rest of us?"

"You did it after Lynne's death. And it worked. But why?

That's my question. Why do we wander? It was the wandering while we were growing up that I hated the most."

Dakota's parents thought of themselves as wanderers. Or
hippies. Or new age thinkers, whatever. What they really
were was a father who was schizophrenic, often delusional
and paranoid, and a mother who was his keeper and protec-
tor. They took their four children with them as they roamed
the country in a van and then later a school bus converted
into an RV. They made regular stops at their grandparents'
farm in Iowa and finally lived there full-time when Dakota
was twelve, Cal, the oldest, was sixteen and their two sisters,
Sedona and Sierra, were fourteen and ten.

Cal was still patient and understanding with their parents,
with the father who wouldn't consider medication that would
make him functional, or at least more functional. He was even
tender with them. Sedona acted responsibly toward them in
a kind but businesslike way, visiting regularly and making
sure they weren't in need or in trouble. Sierra, the baby of
the family, was mostly confused by how they chose to live.
But Dakota? He'd spent much of his childhood not going to
school, taking his lessons in a bus from his mother. The whole
family worked when there was work, mostly harvesting vegetables with other migrant workers. When they did settle in
Iowa on his grandparents' farm, he went to school full-time.
He'd taken a lot of bullying in junior high and high school
because his parents, Jed and Marissa, were so weird. Dakota
was ashamed of them. They made no sense to him. Dakota was
decisive and action-oriented and would have gotten old Jed on
meds or kicked him out, but instead his mother coddled him,
shielded him, let him have his way even though his way was
crazy. So Dakota had been a loner. He'd had very few friends.

Dakota left the second he could, right after high school

graduation when he was seventeen. He enlisted in the Army and had visited his parents about four times since. Each time he went back to that farm in Iowa they seemed more weird than the time before. He rarely called. They had apparently hardly noticed.

He also protected himself against anyone getting too close while he waited to see if he was going to become mentally ill, as well. At thirty-five, he was now pretty sure he was safe from that. And, after all this time, his independent and aloof behavior was accepted by his brother and sisters.

It was easy to remain unattached in the military. He had friends whose company he enjoyed but there were very few with whom he had really bonded and their bond was one of military brothers. He would join the guys for a few beers, as he was regularly included in social events—parties, outings to the lake, ski trips, whatever his group was doing—and he was called, *You know, Dakota, the bachelor.*

There were women, of course. Dakota loved women. He just wasn't the type to make long-term commitments to anyone, especially girlfriends. Even if he was with a certain woman for a while, he wasn't exactly coupled. Well, there was one, but it had been so brief, and had ended so tragically, it reminded him that it was better not to get too involved. He wasn't the marrying kind. He was better off on his own. He was never lonely, never bored. The way he played it he didn't have to explain where he came from, how he grew up, how bizarre his family was. In seventeen years in the Army he had never met a guy who grew up like him—essentially homeless, raised in a bus by a couple of wackos.

But recently, something had changed for him. It was slow. Subtle. Cal lost his wife and then, two years later, remarried. Maggie, a neurosurgeon of all things, was awesome. Now they had a baby, were a family. Cal had never shied from commitment, as if very confident he'd be a better family man than his father was. Their little sister had joined Cal in Timberlake and was also settling down. Sierra had hooked up with a firefighter, a fantastic guy. Connie, short for Conrad, was smart, physical, loyal, the kind of guy he admired. Dakota knew in five minutes that Connie had integrity. And watching the way Sierra was with him almost made Dakota long for something like that. Sedona had been married since right after college, had a couple of kids, was by all accounts living a normal life. So far none of them had decided to live in a bus like their parents had. Little by little it had begun to tease his mind that possibly he could have a normal adult life. Maybe he could actually have friends and family and not have to protect himself from being himself.

But he was damn sure taking it slow.

Cal called everyone. Sierra and Connie came straight over with their golden retriever, Molly. Maggie's father, Sully, came after he had closed up the general store at his campground, Sullivan's Crossing. Maggie arrived with the baby and walked into a party atmosphere.

Since Dakota's arrival was unannounced and Cal wasn't prepared, everyone brought something to the table. Sierra had a platter of chicken breasts swimming in barbecue sauce and a big seven-layer salad, Connie brought beer and some of the cold green tea Sierra favored. Sully brought some broccoli sealed in a foil with garlic, olive oil, onions, mushrooms and pepperoncinis. They put it on the grill with the chicken. Cal supplied baked potatoes.

"How long are you staying?" Sierra wanted to know.

"I don't know," Dakota said. "I've been using the last few months to explore."

"Unfortunately, ain't nothin' to explore around here," Sully said.

"Oh, Cody," Sierra said, using his nickname from when they were kids. "Don't listen to Sully! I think I got my brain back hiking around here. Cal did the CDT for a month."

Dakota raised his eyebrows. "Did I know that?" he asked.

"I can't remember. But yes, I took the Continental Divide Trail north from Sully's place. I walked and camped for about two and a half weeks, then turned around and came back."

"Because I was here," Maggie said with a smile and lift of her chin. "And he wanted me. Bad."

"I wish I could do that," Connie said. "Longest I've been out there is four days. Sierra, we gotta do that. Go out there for a couple of months."

"I don't know," she said. "I'm so addicted to daily showers..."

"I have to decide where I'm going to stop exploring," Dakota said.

"As in, settle down?" Cal asked.

"I don't know if that's possible," he said. "After the Army? I might not have the temperament for staying in one place."

"Are you going to hang around at least awhile?" Sierra asked hopefully.

"You bet," he said. "I'll be around awhile. Maybe I can help out."

"You can babysit," Cal said.

"Now, that's one thing I'm pretty sure I can't do," Dakota said. "I'm good with kids, but it's best if they're college graduates."

There was a round of moans and laughter.

By nine o'clock Sully had gone back to the Crossing, Maggie and Elizabeth had gone to bed and it was only Sierra, Connie, Cal and Dakota. The men were having one more beer. Sierra, in recovery, a year and a half sober, was drinking her green tea.

"I'll have to go to two meetings tomorrow after spending the night with you big drinkers," she said.

Cal laughed at her. "Three of us had eight beers in six hours. As celebrations go, it was pretty tame."

"If it bothers you…" Dakota began.

"It doesn't," she said. "But I'm going to feel a lot better than you tomorrow morning."

"Since you're going to feel so good tomorrow, want to take me out on the trail?" Dakota asked. Molly rose from her sleeping spot, shook herself awake and leaned against Dakota's thigh. Waiting. "Does this one go hiking?"

"Sometimes I take Molly and Beau, Sully's lab. But I can only stay out there a couple of hours at most if they're with me." She stood. "I'll come for you at 8:20. Come on, Connie. Time to put the baby to bed."

Dakota and Cal snapped to attention.

"Molly," she said. "I meant Molly."

"Shew," Dakota said. "If there was another one, I was going to run for my life!"

"There's just Elizabeth," Sierra said. "And they won't commit to whether they'll add to the family. And I'm definitely not in the game."

"Oh? And why is that?"

"Duh. Our crazy father and his genetic code, for one thing. Come on, Connie. It's past our bedtime."

Dakota looked at his watch. "This is a real lively crowd," he said, standing to say good-night. He kissed his sister's cheek. "See you in the morning. By the way, you're looking good."

"Thanks," she said, beaming. "So are you. A little shaggy, but good."

Dakota flashed her a grin. Behind his dark beard, it was dazzling.

Sierra combed her fingers along his cheeks, through his beard. "Little gray coming in here, Cody."

"I earned it," he said. He kissed her forehead. "See you in the morning."

In the seventeen years since Dakota left his family behind for the Army, the time he spent with them was infrequent and brief. Cal and Sedona tried to keep up with him. He visited them for important events—Cal's wedding to Lynne, then his wedding to Maggie. When Sedona's children were born, he checked in. He never stayed long. Sierra, who was so special to him, had been a wild card until she found sobriety. He had visited for a couple of days at a time, that's all. He didn't want to get too attached to them.

This time was different. The second, third and fourth days came and went. He hiked with Sierra, then Cal, then just the dogs. He dug out Sully's garden for spring planting. They repaired the grills and picnic tables and talked all the while. Sully was very cool for an old guy. He admitted he came home from Vietnam with some PTSD and asked how Dakota had fared in that regard. "Oh, I've got PTSD all right," Dakota said. "Probably more from my personal life than my military experience."

"Then aren't you one of the lucky ones," Sully said.

Dakota cleaned out the gutters around Sully's house and store and threw the balls for the dogs. Then he had to bathe the dogs because it had rained and they got into the freshly turned soil and compost in the garden. While hanging out at the Crossing he met Tom Canaday, the guy who helped Cal renovate the barn that was now his stunning house. Tom was Sully's good friend and part-time handyman, a single dad with two kids in college and two still in high school. When Tom told him all the jobs he'd had while raising his kids, Dakota was inspired.

Maybe it wasn't necessary for him to make big, permanent decisions about what to do for work or where to settle. Maybe he could coast for a little while. "Think a guy like me could work on a road crew?" he asked Tom. "Or haul trash?"

Tom laughed. "A vet who served? Who has ties to the town? Hell, Dakota, anyone would hire you. I'll give you a recommendation. You just have to decide what you want to do. I've been working for the county for almost twenty years."

"I should probably pick up trash," he said. "Penance for all my misdeeds."

"Misdeeds?" Tom asked with a laugh. "Cal said you were a decorated soldier."

"I just about undecorated myself before it was all over," he said. He scratched his beard. "I guess I should get a haircut. Do I need to lose the beard?"

Tom laughed. "This is Colorado, man. You look homegrown."

"Good. I've grown kind of attached." He grinned. "So to speak."

"I'll find out what they're hiring for and get you an application."

When he went home from Sully's after a productive day, he found Cal in his home office, just hanging up the phone.

"So, you're still here," Cal said. "It's been five days. I think that's a record."

"Am I getting underfoot?" Dakota asked.

"I've hardly noticed you," he said. "You feeling underfoot?"

Dakota shook his head, leaning against the door frame.

"Baby bothering you?" Cal asked.

"The baby is kind of awesome," Dakota said. "I'm not babysitting, however."

Cal laughed. "We managed before you arrived, we'll continue to manage."

"So, what if I hung around?" he asked.

"What if?" Cal returned.

"Would that be weird for you?"

"Nah. I actually like you. Sort of." Then he sobered. "You're welcome here, Dakota. And thanks for helping Sully. It's appreciated."

"Everyone was helping him get the grounds ready, but I think now it's going to rain. For days."

"That's what I hear," Cal said. "Every March the rain comes, every March Sully gets the campground ready for summer. Well, spring and summer. We all help out. It wasn't expected of you, so thanks. Now what?"

"Well," he said, scratching his chin. "I'm going to get a haircut, trim the beard a little, get a job, look for a place to live…"

"I'm not throwing you out," Cal said. "If you can live with Elizabeth, you can stay here. The rent's cheap."

"Elizabeth is a hoot," he said. "I thought I'd rent something because it's what I do. That doesn't mean I won't hang out with you sometimes."

"This sounds kind of long-term," Cal said.

"For me," Dakota clarified. "A few months, anyway. I like the Crossing, the trails, the lake, the people. Seems like a good place to collect my thoughts."

"We'd love it if you were close," Cal said. "Listen, you okay here by yourself for a few days? It's time for Maggie to go to Denver again. Three to four days a week she operates and sees patients. She has a babysitter there but I don't have any clients or court appearances so I'm going along this time. I won't be back unless someone calls and needs me."

Dakota laughed and ran a hand over his head. "All this flexibility is giving me a rash. I'm used to a strict routine."

"Fine," Cal said. "Have a strict routine, that won't bother anyone. But Maggie and I have Elizabeth and two careers. Not to mention Sully and a campground. Just let me know if you're going to be around for a meal, that's all I need from you. Well, that and if you're going to stumble in at 3:00 a.m. and make me get out the rifle because I think someone's breaking in. That would involve communication, Dakota. You haven't exactly excelled in that."

"So I've been told," he said. "You have my cell number, right?"

"You have enough money to rent your own place? Because I—"

"I got it," Dakota said. "And I'll be sure to call so you can throw another potato in the soup."

Cal was quiet for a moment. "It's been good. Having you around," he finally said.

"I'll do my best not to screw that up," Dakota said.

Cal, Maggie and Elizabeth left very early in the morning for Denver. If Dakota understood things correctly, Maggie would go straight to work, seeing patients all morning, then operating all afternoon, then repeating that cycle again and again. One week it would be three long days, the next week it would be four days. Once a month she would be on call to the emergency room, adding a fifth day to her cycle. And Cal, a criminal defense attorney, was seeing clients in his home office or other meeting places—the diner, the Crossing on Sully's porch, the bookstore—and for anything from wills to real estate deals. Once in a while he actually got someone out of jail. Dakota filed that information away in case he needed it.

That left Dakota on his own for a few days. And as Sully had predicted, it rained. And rained.

He dropped into a real estate office and picked up a flyer of local rental properties, then headed for a haircut. He looked up and down the street and found that the barbershop was closed so he dropped in to the beauty shop. Fancy Cuts. He stepped inside the door and spied six chairs and three clients with hair stylists. He flashed that million-watt smile of his and said, "I'm not looking for anything real fancy, but can you handle a head and a beard left unattended awhile?"

Less than a moment passed. A beautiful young woman took a step toward him. "I've got this," she said confidently to the other stylists, both older women. "Give me five minutes. Have a seat."

She went back to her client, an elderly woman whose hair seemed to be a mass of pink sausages. "You can't be done in five minutes," the client said a bit more loudly than necessary.

"Oh, yes, I will," said the beauty. "And you'll love it."

"Well, it better not be—"

The stylist applied a brush and went to town. She fluffed out the woman's hair, did a little backcombing and shaping, sprayed some spray.

Dakota picked up a magazine and idly paged through it. Good oral hygiene had never served him better. In five minutes he was in the chair with the beautiful Alyssa running a comb casually through his dark hair. "What are we doing with you today?"

Dakota was suddenly conscious of how long it had been since he'd had sex. "Nothing special," he said. *Up against the wall work for you?* "Just trim it up, and can you trim the beard? Not Hollywood, just not *Duck Dynasty*."

"I've got it," she said, showing him a brilliant smile of her own. "Let's start with a good shampoo. Right this way."

He didn't mention he'd already done that in his morning shower but instead let her lead him to the back. While she massaged his scalp and quizzed him, he just let his eyes close gently. He had a brother not so far from here, he said. He was just out of the Army and planned on exploring the country a little, starting here. He liked to fish and hike. He wasn't making any plans for a while. He was deliberately vague. This was a small town. He didn't want to do or say anything that might reflect badly on Cal or Sierra and all those attached. Until he got the lay of the land, he'd be a little mysterious.

But her fingers in his hair felt amazing. "You married, Alyssa?" he asked in a soft, smoky voice.

"Still waiting for the right guy, Dakota," she whispered back. "Do you have a lot of friends around here?" she asked, smothering his head with a towel and leading him back to her station.

"My brother's friends," he said with a shrug. "A few nice people."

"No girlfriend?"

He met her eyes in the mirror. "No girlfriend."

"I take that to mean there's no wife or fiancée, either?" she asked.

He shook his head, feeling like great sex could be minutes away. It was a feeling, not something he'd act on. This was Cal and Sierra's town. Hit-and-run wouldn't work. The repercussions could make life difficult for people he cared about and he wouldn't risk it. But this Alyssa, long-legged, beautiful, friendly, ready—this held great promise. He might have found himself a woman to pass the time with. It was worth considering. And it was worth slowing down and using caution.

"You know your way around a pair of scissors," he said, looking in the mirror. The haircut was excellent; the beard was looking good.

"You okay with the gray?" she asked. "Because if you're not..."

"I think it's fine," he said. "I earned every one."

"That's good, because I like it. It's very attractive."

"Are you buttering me up for a good tip?" he teased.

"You're kidding, right? Since you're new to the area, could you use someone to show you around?"

"That might come in handy," he said. "Right now I have somewhere I have to be. Maybe you'd trust me with your phone number?"

"Sure," she said. She waited for him to get out his phone, then rattled off the digits. "I'd be more than happy to. This is a great little town. Full of possibilities."

"I can see that," he said. "Well, Alyssa, thanks for a good job. I'm sure we'll see each other soon."

He paid in cash; the tip was excellent. He put on his jacket, turned the collar up and walked out into the rain. He went down the block and across the street to the diner. Sierra was working today. He'd have lunch and show her his flyer of rental properties.

Dakota took a booth at the diner and let Sierra wait on him. He ordered a bowl of soup, half a sandwich and a coffee. It wasn't long before Sierra slid into the booth with a slice of blueberry pie.

"Is that for me?" he asked.

She looked at it for a second. "Yes," she said. Then she went back behind the counter and got another slice of pie, making him laugh at her.

"You're so thoughtful," he said.

"I am," she said. "In the early summer we have rhubarb pie and rhubarb cobbler. I think this year I'm going to learn to bake."

"When are you going to learn to get married?" he asked. "Seems like six months ago Connie asked us all if we would give consent and I guess I thought..."

"Well, you old fogy, you." She grinned at him. "We keep

meaning to plan something. Hey, Cal's gone, right? Connie's off tonight. It's going to be cold and rainy. We're having a fire and soup. Wanna come over?"

"I don't know. Is there any nightlife around here?" he asked.

"Yeah—at our house. Fire and soup. Connie's cooking. It's amazing. Firemen are excellent cooks. Maybe if you're very good, we'll put on a movie. Or play a board game."

He gave her a steady look. "I don't think it's going to take me long to get really bored."

"You coming?"

"Sure," he said with a shrug.

The Family Gathering
by Robyn Carr.
Available now from MIRA Books.